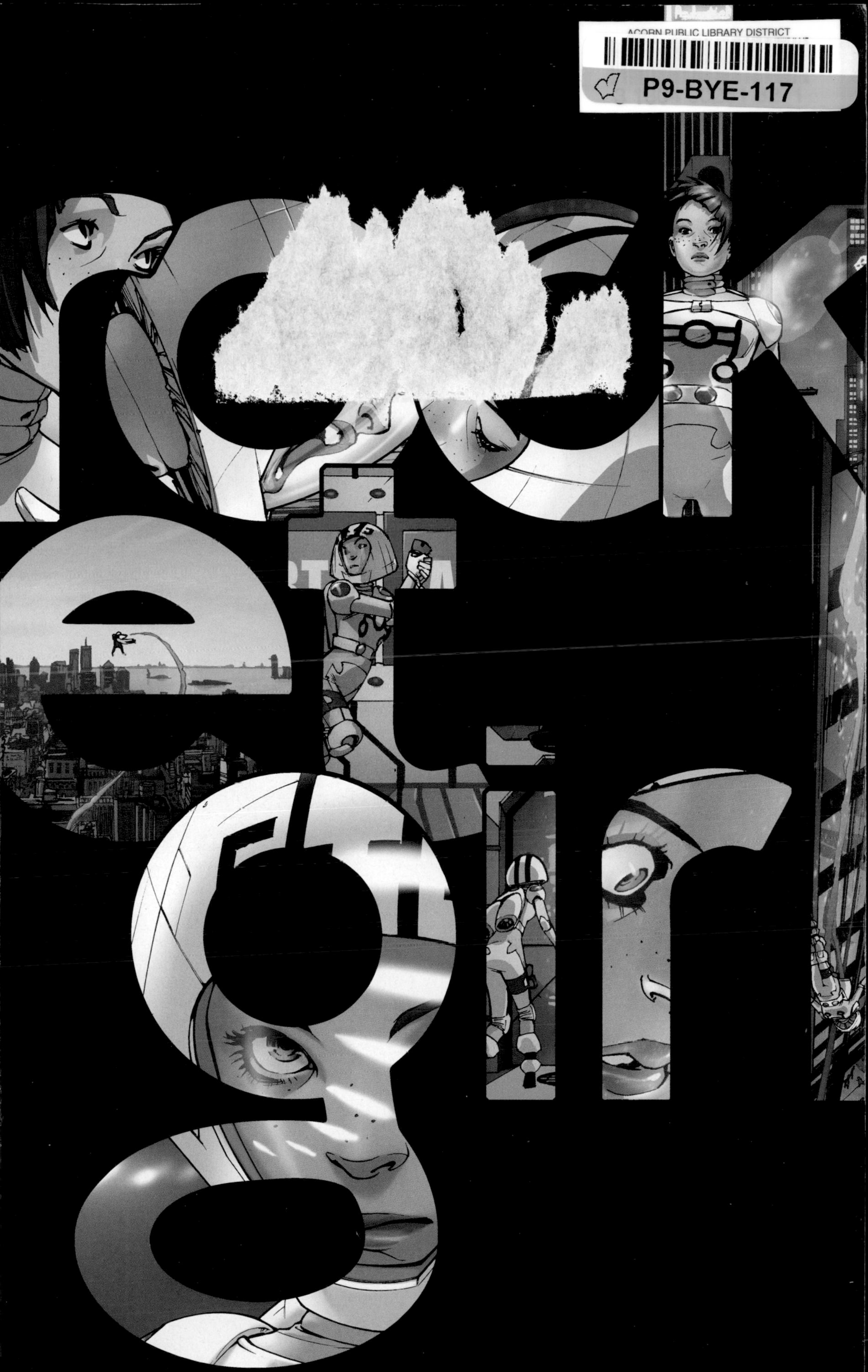

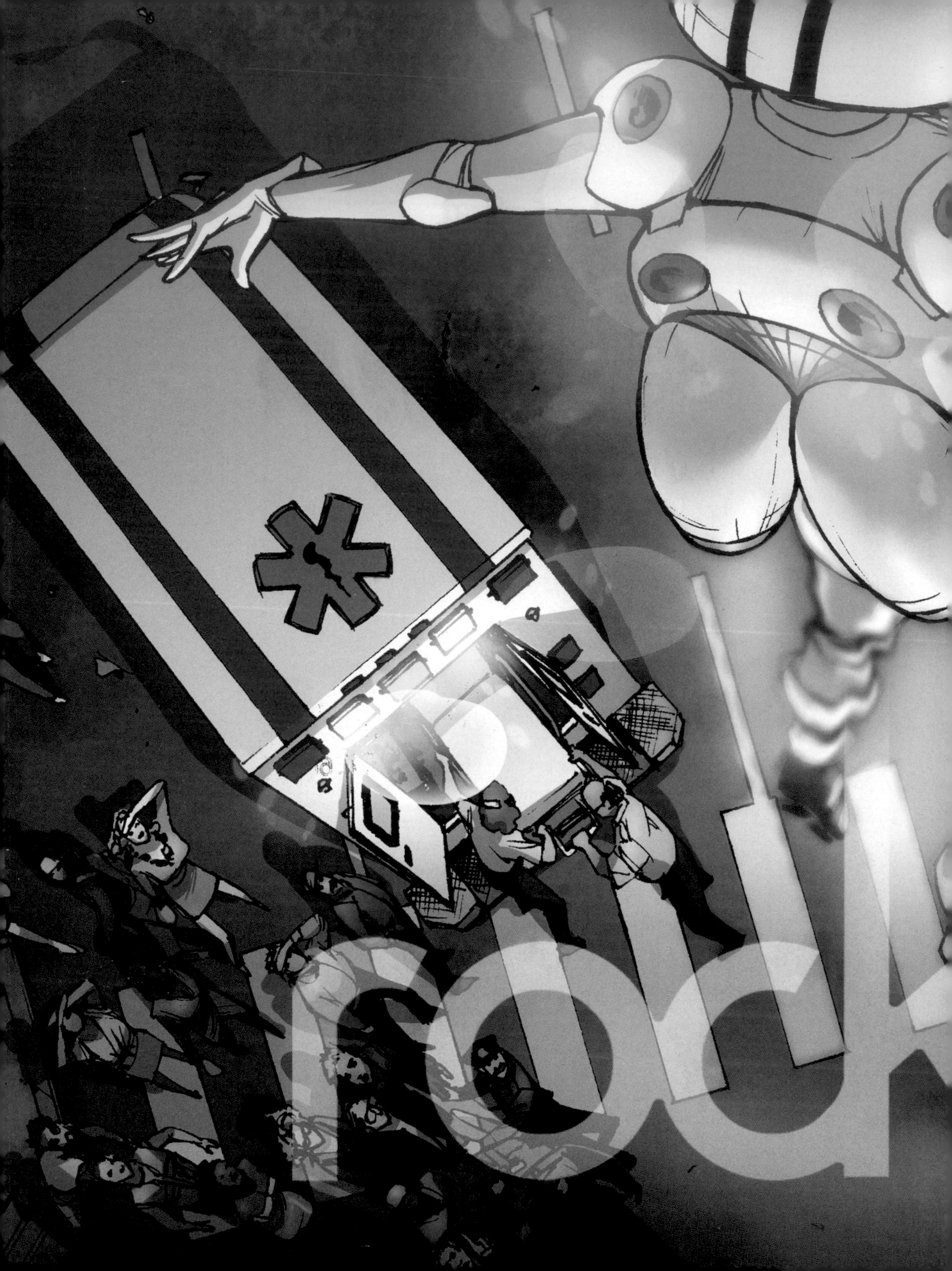

VOL:01

"times squared"

writer
brandon MONTCLARE

artist
amy REEDER

ACORN PUBLIC LIBRARY
15624 S. CENTRAL AVE.
OAK FOREST, IL

IMAGE COMICS, INC.
Robert Kirkman – Chief Operating Officer
Erik Larsen – Chief Financial Officer
Todd McFarlane – President
Marc Silvestri – Chief Executive Officer
Jim Valentino – Vice-President

Eric Stephenson – Publisher
Ron Richards – Director of Business Development
Jennifer de Guzman – Director of Trade Book Sales
Kat Salazar – Director of PR & Marketing
Corey Murphy – Director of Retail Sales
Jeremy Sullivan – Director of Digital Sales
Emilio Bautista – Sales Assistant
Branwyn Bigglestone – Senior Accounts Manager
Emily Miller – Accounts Manager
Jessica Ambriz – Administrative Assistant
Tyler Shainline – Events Coordinator
David Brothers – Content Manager
Jonathan Chan – Production Manager
Drew Gill – Art Director
Meredith Wallace – Print Manager
Monica Garcia – Senior Production Artist
Addison Duke – Production Artist
Tricia Ramos – Production Assistant
IMAGECOMICS.COM

Rocket Girl, Vol. 1: Times Squared. Second Printing. January 2015.
ISBN: 978-1-63215-055-4.
Published by Image Comics, Inc. Office of publication: 2001 Center
Street, 6th Floor, Berkeley, CA 94704. Copyright © 2014 Brandon
Montclare and Amy Reeder. All rights reserved. Originally published
in single magazine form as Rocket Girl #1-5. Rocket Girl™ (including
all prominent characters featured herein), its logo and all character
likenesses are trademarks of Brandon Montclare and Amy Reeder, unless
otherwise noted. Image Comics® and its logos are registered trademarks
of Image Comics, Inc. No part of this publication may be reproduced
or transmitted, in any form or by any means (except for short excerpts
for review purposes) without the express written permission of Image
Comics, Inc. All names, characters, events and locales in this publication
are entirely fictional. Any resemblance to actual persons (living or dead),
events or places, without satiric intent, is coincidental. PRINTED IN
USA. For information regarding the CPSIA on this printed material call:
203-595-3636 and provide reference # RICH - 599841. International
Rights / Foreign Licensing -- foreignlicensing@imagecomics.com

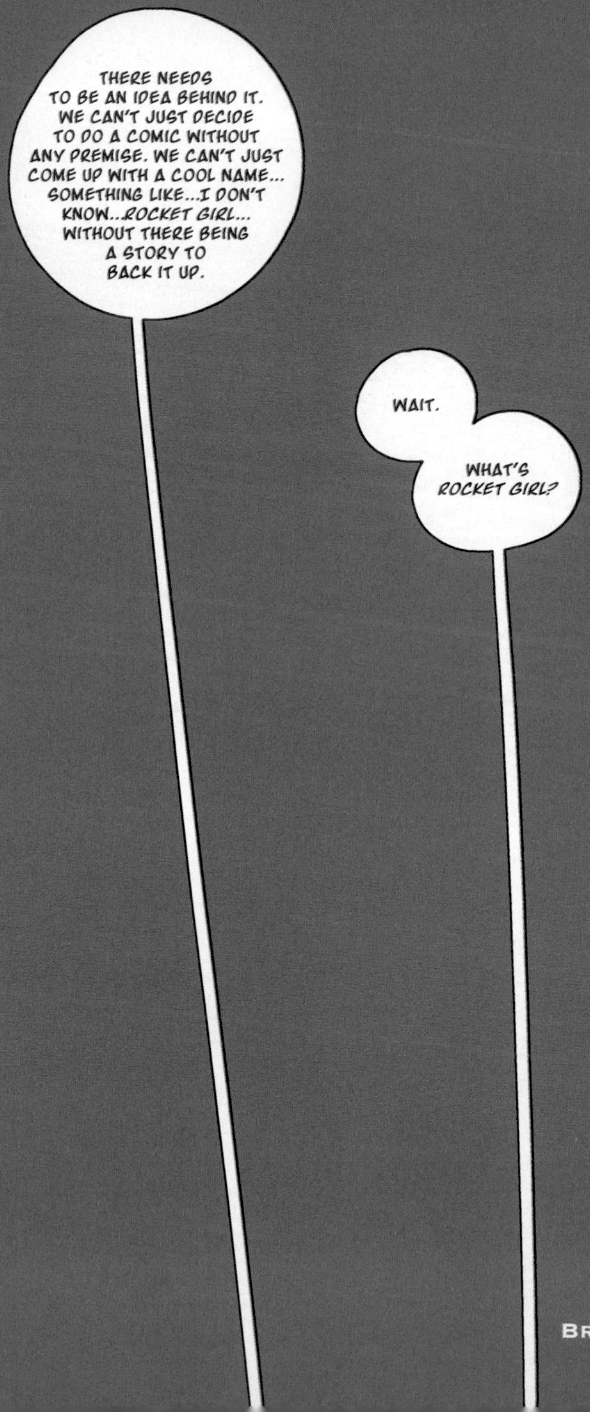
THERE NEEDS TO BE AN IDEA BEHIND IT. WE CAN'T JUST DECIDE TO DO A COMIC WITHOUT ANY PREMISE. WE CAN'T JUST COME UP WITH A COOL NAME... SOMETHING LIKE...I DON'T KNOW...*ROCKET GIRL*... WITHOUT THERE BEING A STORY TO BACK IT UP.
WAIT.
WHAT'S *ROCKET GIRL?*

Brandon & Amy, circa 2012.

Chapter 1_Times Squared >>

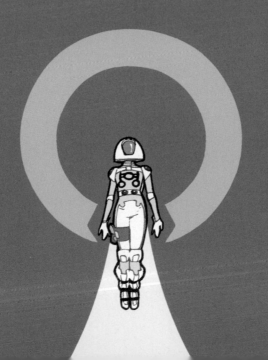

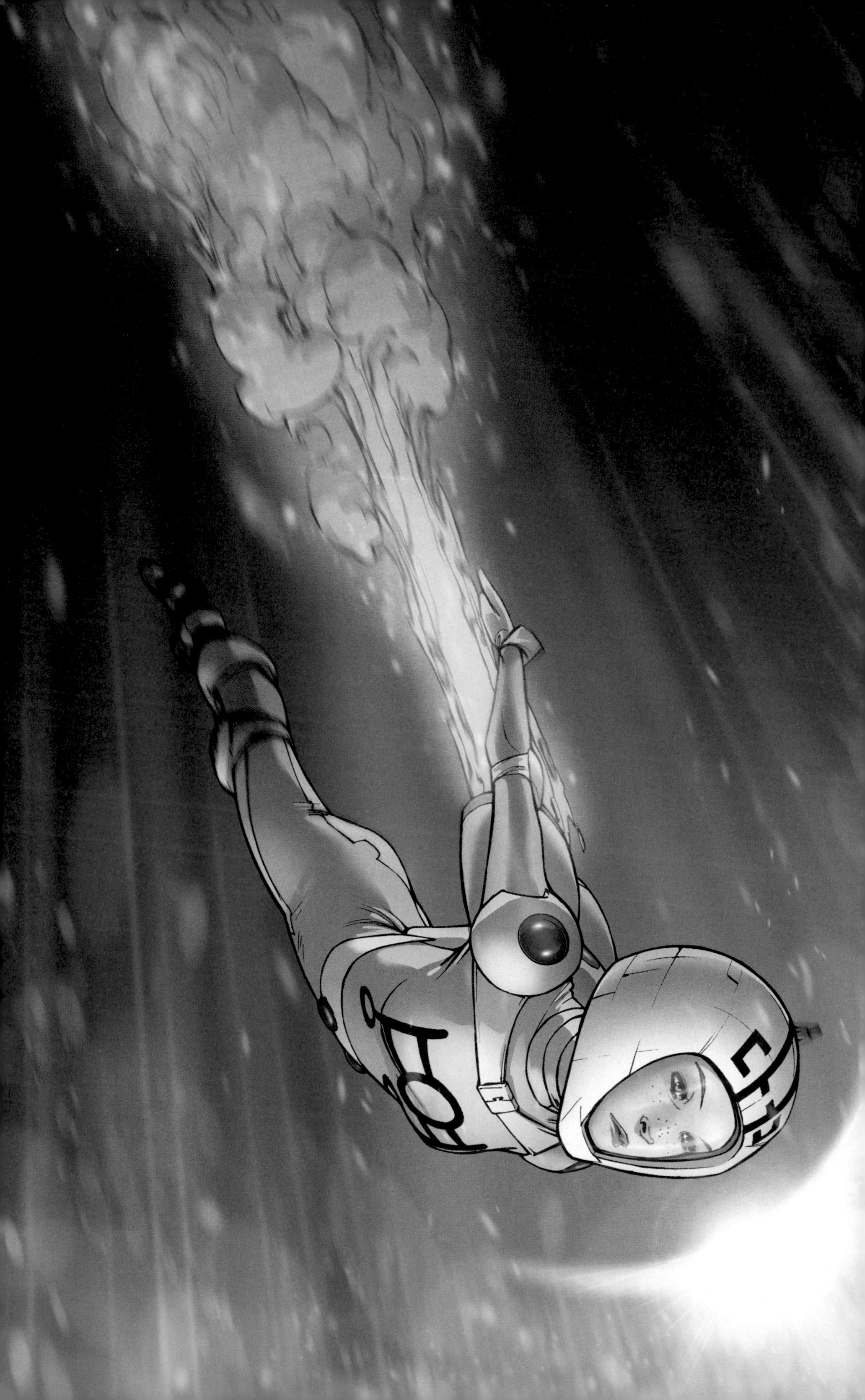

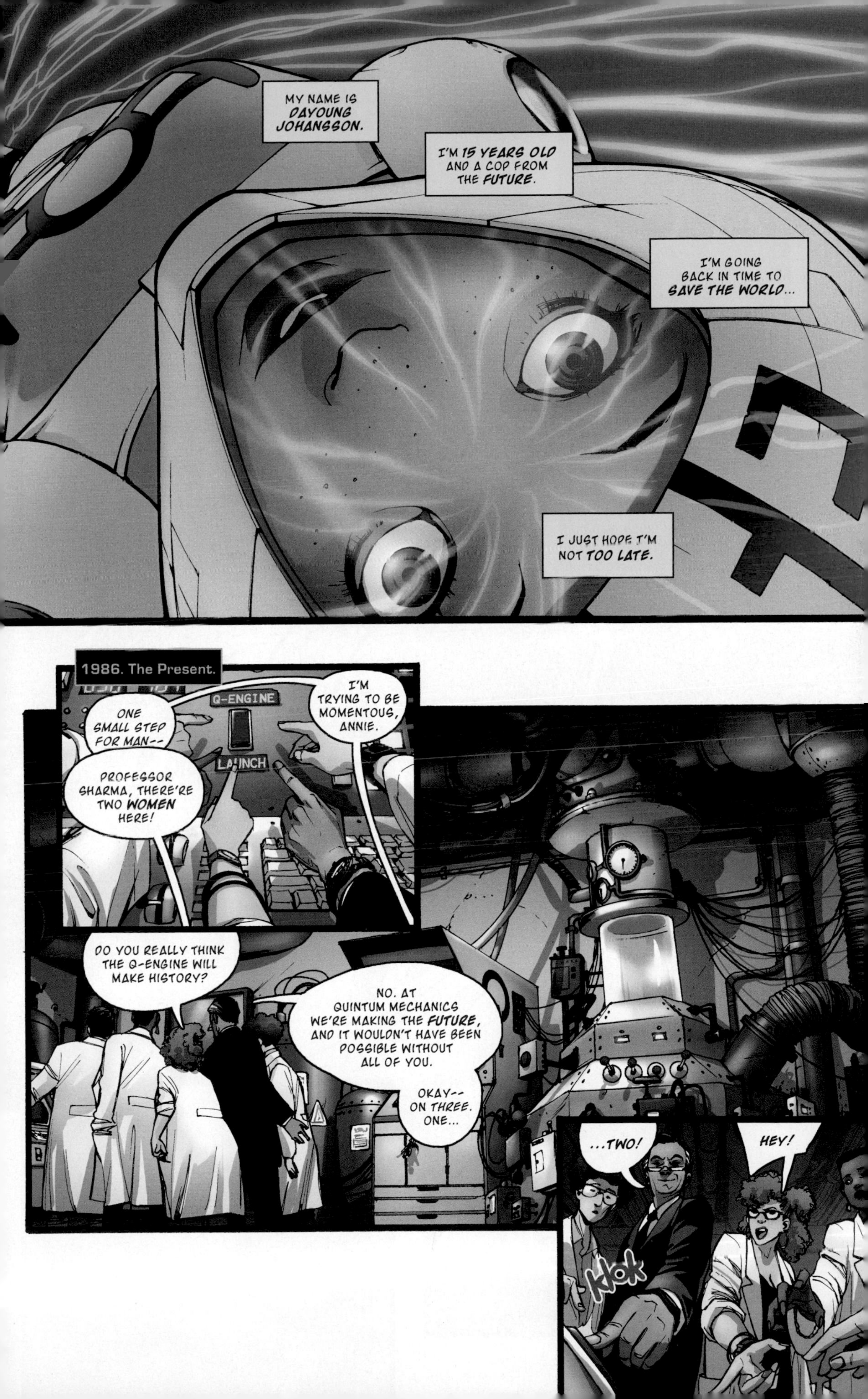

MY NAME IS DAYOUNG JOHANSSON.
I'M 15 YEARS OLD AND A COP FROM THE FUTURE.
I'M GOING BACK IN TIME TO SAVE THE WORLD...
I JUST HOPE I'M NOT TOO LATE.
1986. The Present.
Q-ENGINE
LAUNCH
ONE SMALL STEP FOR MAN--
I'M TRYING TO BE MOMENTOUS, ANNIE.
PROFESSOR SHARMA, THERE'RE TWO WOMEN HERE!
DO YOU REALLY THINK THE Q-ENGINE WILL MAKE HISTORY?
NO. AT QUINTUM MECHANICS WE'RE MAKING THE FUTURE, AND IT WOULDN'T HAVE BEEN POSSIBLE WITHOUT ALL OF YOU.
OKAY-- ON THREE. ONE...
...TWO!
HEY!
KLOK

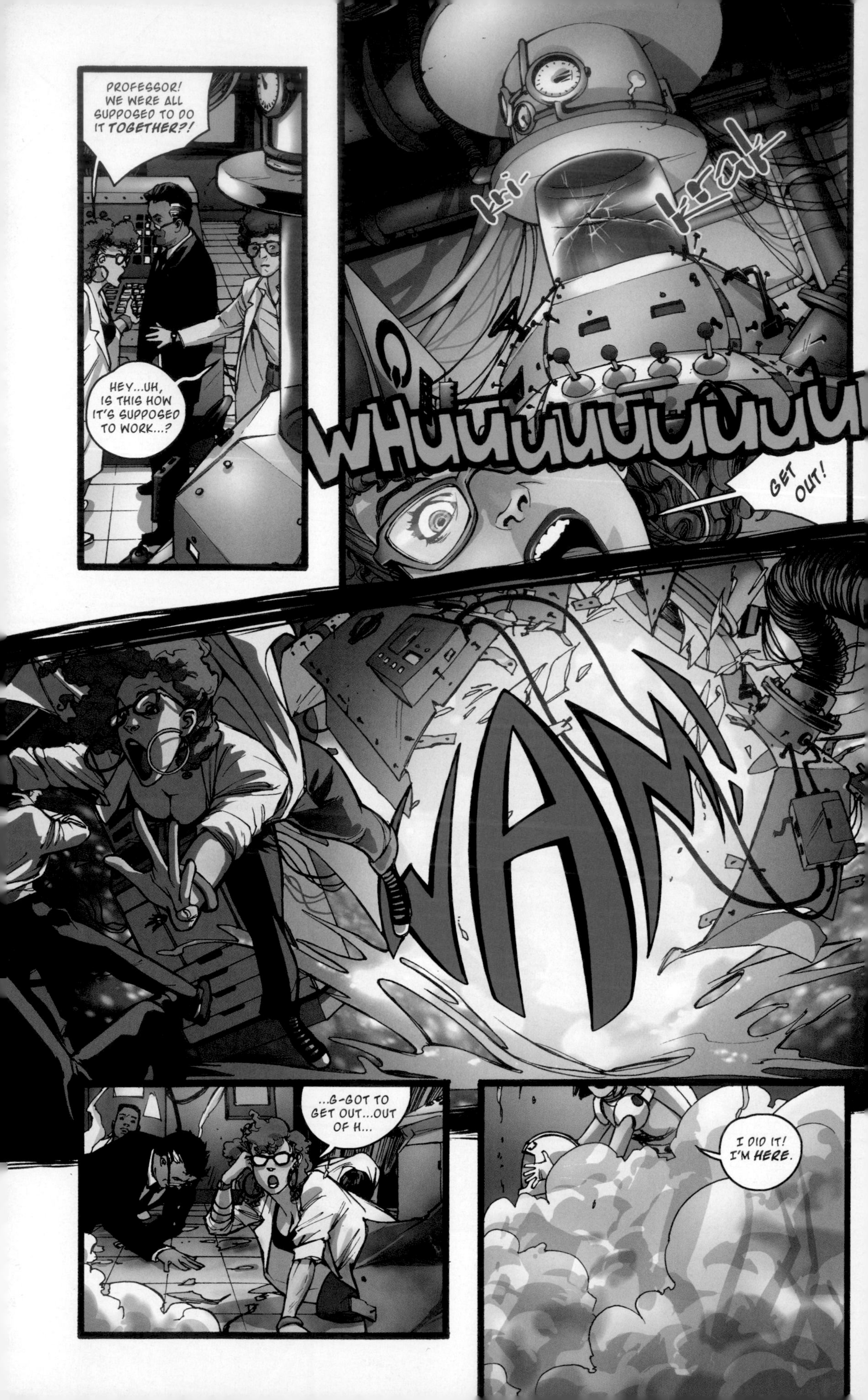
PROFESSOR! WE WERE ALL SUPPOSED TO DO IT TOGETHER?!
HEY...UH, IS THIS HOW IT'S SUPPOSED TO WORK...?
kri-
krak
WHUUUUUUUUUU
GET OUT!
WAM!
...G-GOT TO GET OUT...OUT OF H...
I DID IT! I'M HERE.

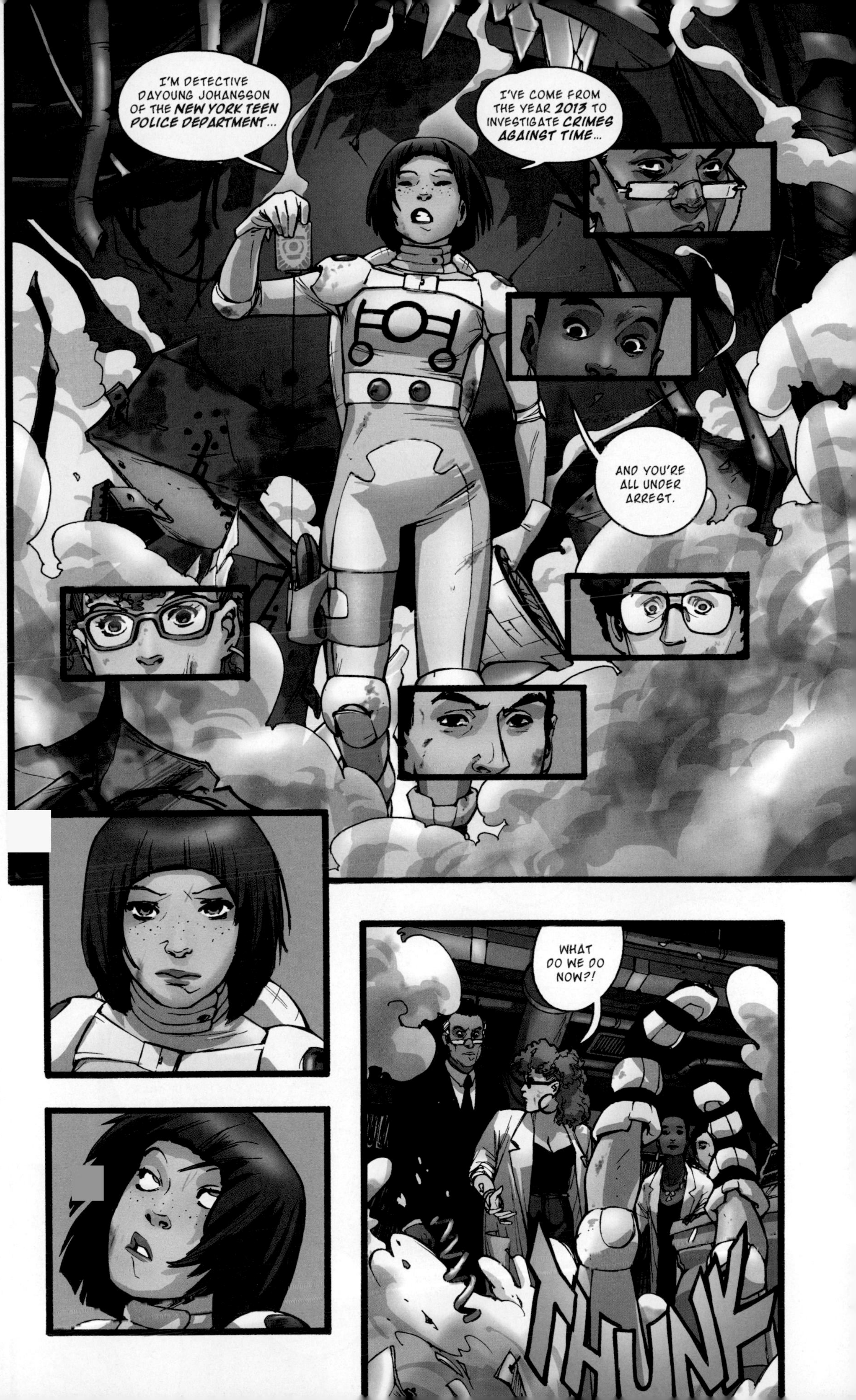
I'M DETECTIVE DAYOUNG JOHANSSON OF THE NEW YORK TEEN POLICE DEPARTMENT...
I'VE COME FROM THE YEAR 2013 TO INVESTIGATE CRIMES AGAINST TIME...
AND YOU'RE ALL UNDER ARREST.
WHAT DO WE DO NOW?!
THUNK

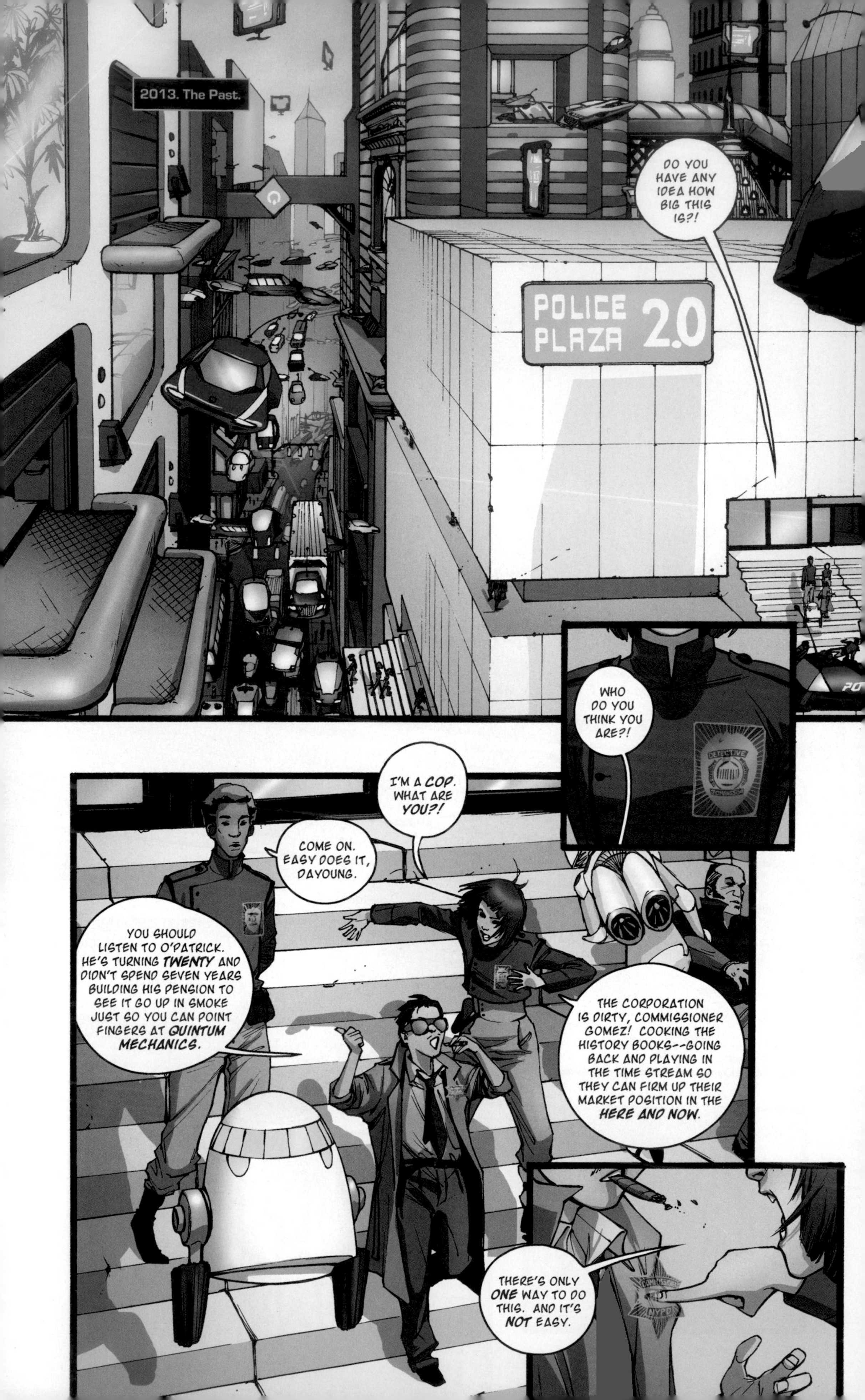
2013. The Past.
DO YOU HAVE ANY IDEA HOW BIG THIS IS?!
POLICE PLAZA 2.0
WHO DO YOU THINK YOU ARE?!
I'M A COP. WHAT ARE YOU?!
COME ON. EASY DOES IT, DAYOUNG.
YOU SHOULD LISTEN TO O'PATRICK. HE'S TURNING TWENTY AND DIDN'T SPEND SEVEN YEARS BUILDING HIS PENSION TO SEE IT GO UP IN SMOKE JUST SO YOU CAN POINT FINGERS AT QUINTUM MECHANICS.
THE CORPORATION IS DIRTY, COMMISSIONER GOMEZ! COOKING THE HISTORY BOOKS--GOING BACK AND PLAYING IN THE TIME STREAM SO THEY CAN FIRM UP THEIR MARKET POSITION IN THE HERE AND NOW.
THERE'S ONLY ONE WAY TO DO THIS. AND IT'S NOT EASY.

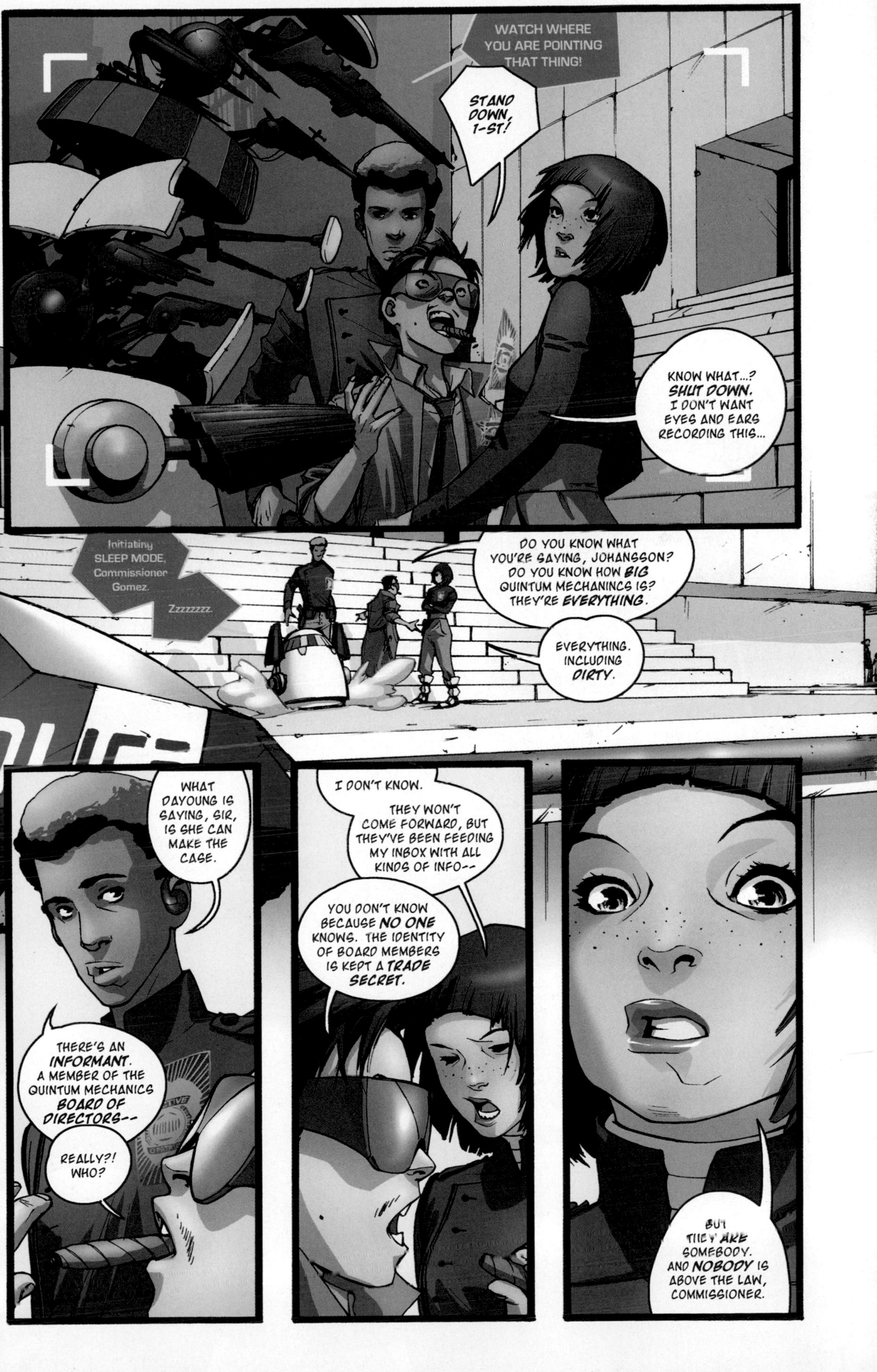
WATCH WHERE YOU ARE POINTING THAT THING!
STAND DOWN, 1-ST!
KNOW WHAT...? SHUT DOWN. I DON'T WANT EYES AND EARS RECORDING THIS...
Initiating SLEEP MODE, Commissioner Gomez.
Zzzzzzz.
DO YOU KNOW WHAT YOU'RE SAYING, JOHANSSON? DO YOU KNOW HOW BIG QUINTUM MECHANINCS IS? THEY'RE EVERYTHING.
EVERYTHING. INCLUDING DIRTY.
WHAT DAYOUNG IS SAYING, SIR, IS SHE CAN MAKE THE CASE.
THERE'S AN INFORMANT. A MEMBER OF THE QUINTUM MECHANICS BOARD OF DIRECTORS--
REALLY?! WHO?
I DON'T KNOW.
THEY WON'T COME FORWARD, BUT THEY'VE BEEN FEEDING MY INBOX WITH ALL KINDS OF INFO--
YOU DON'T KNOW BECAUSE NO ONE KNOWS. THE IDENTITY OF BOARD MEMBERS IS KEPT A TRADE SECRET.
BUT THEY ARE SOMEBODY. AND NOBODY IS ABOVE THE LAW, COMMISSIONER.

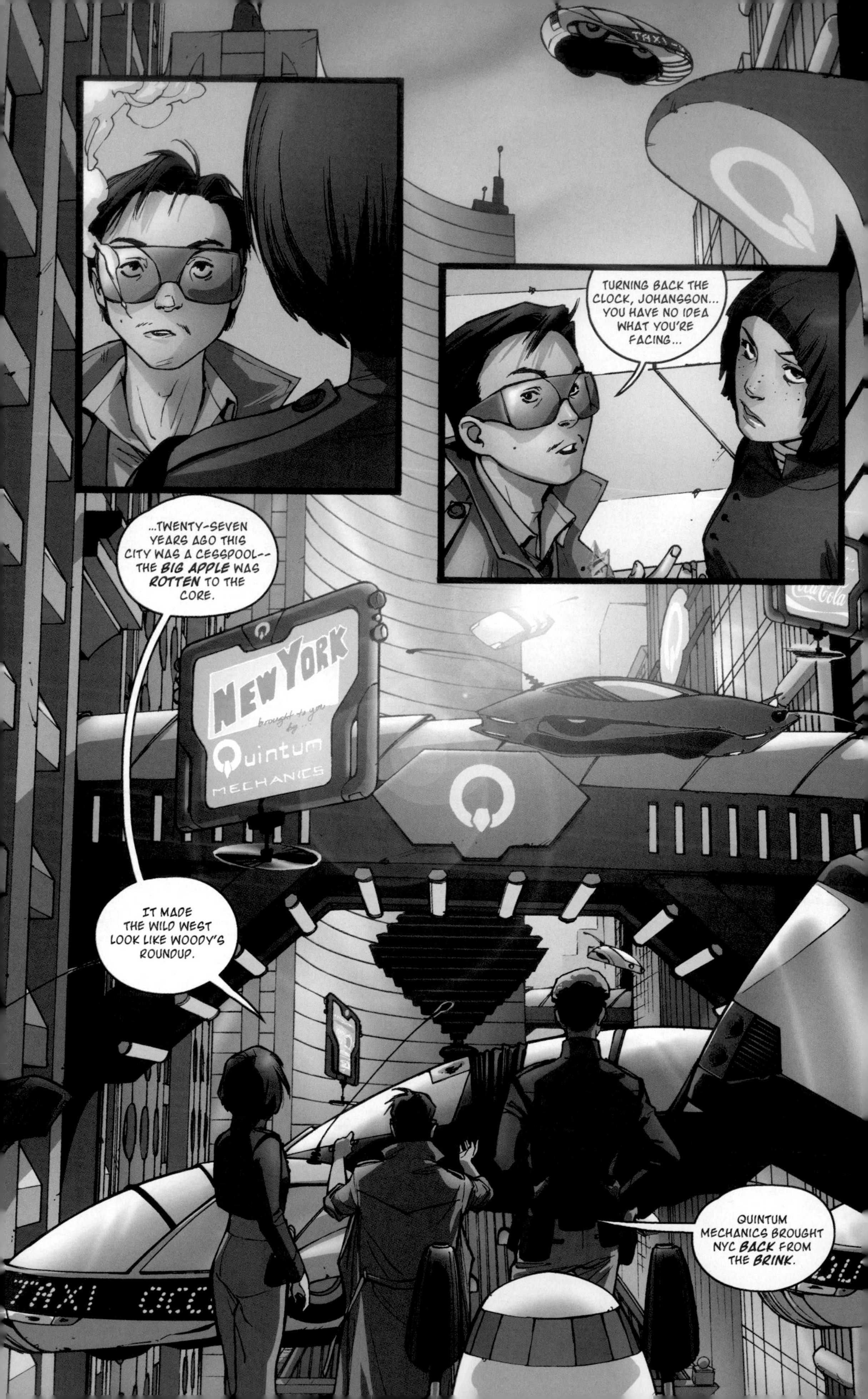
TAXI
TURNING BACK THE CLOCK, JOHANSSON... YOU HAVE NO IDEA WHAT YOU'RE FACING...
...TWENTY-SEVEN YEARS AGO THIS CITY WAS A CESSPOOL--THE **BIG APPLE** WAS **ROTTEN** TO THE CORE.
NEW YORK brought to you by... Quintum MECHANICS
Coca-Cola
IT MADE THE WILD WEST LOOK LIKE WOODY'S ROUNDUP.
QUINTUM MECHANICS BROUGHT NYC **BACK** FROM THE **BRINK**.
TAXI

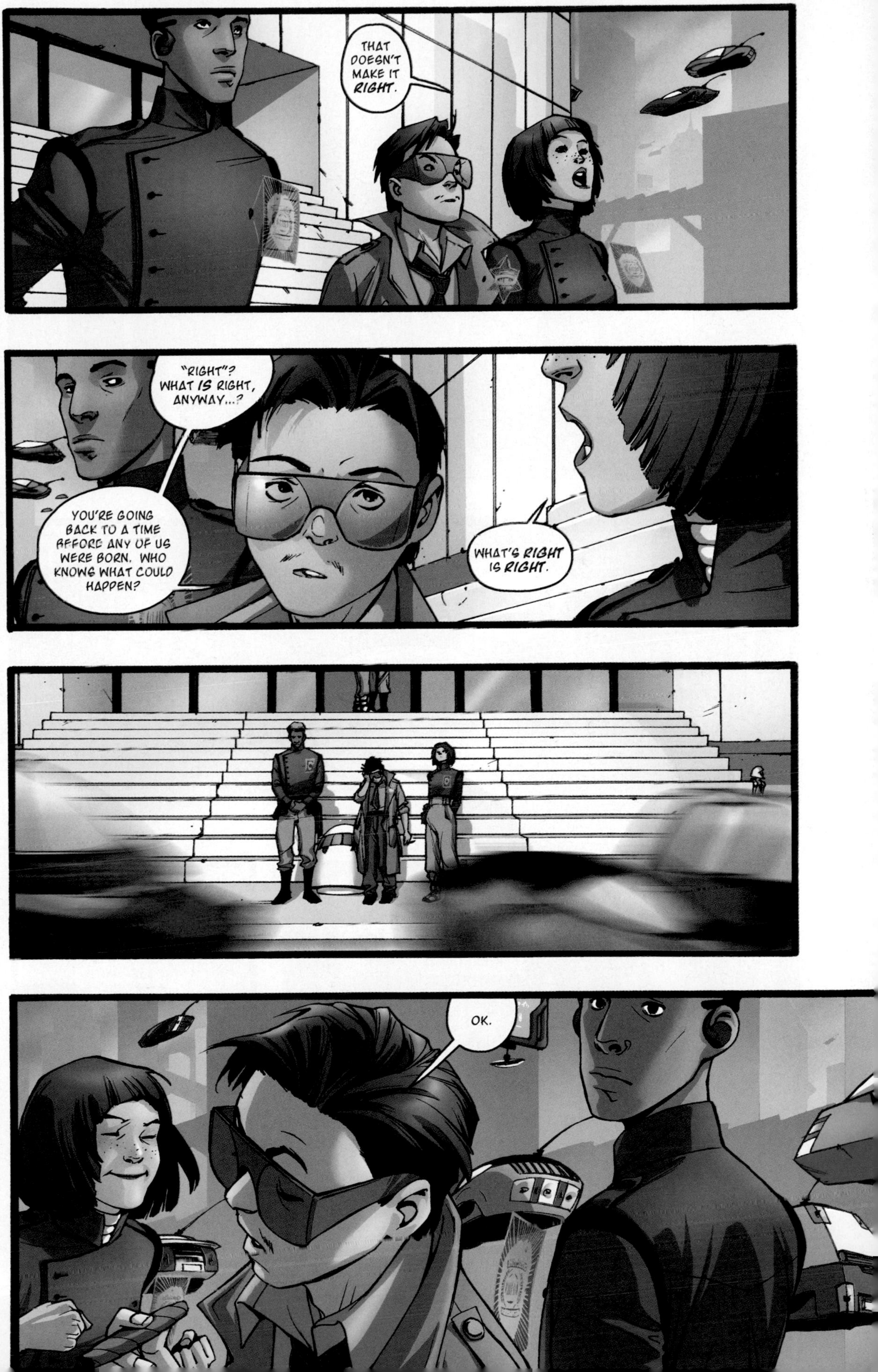
THAT DOESN'T MAKE IT RIGHT.
"RIGHT"? WHAT IS RIGHT, ANYWAY...?
YOU'RE GOING BACK TO A TIME BEFORE ANY OF US WERE BORN. WHO KNOWS WHAT COULD HAPPEN?
WHAT'S RIGHT IS RIGHT.
OK.

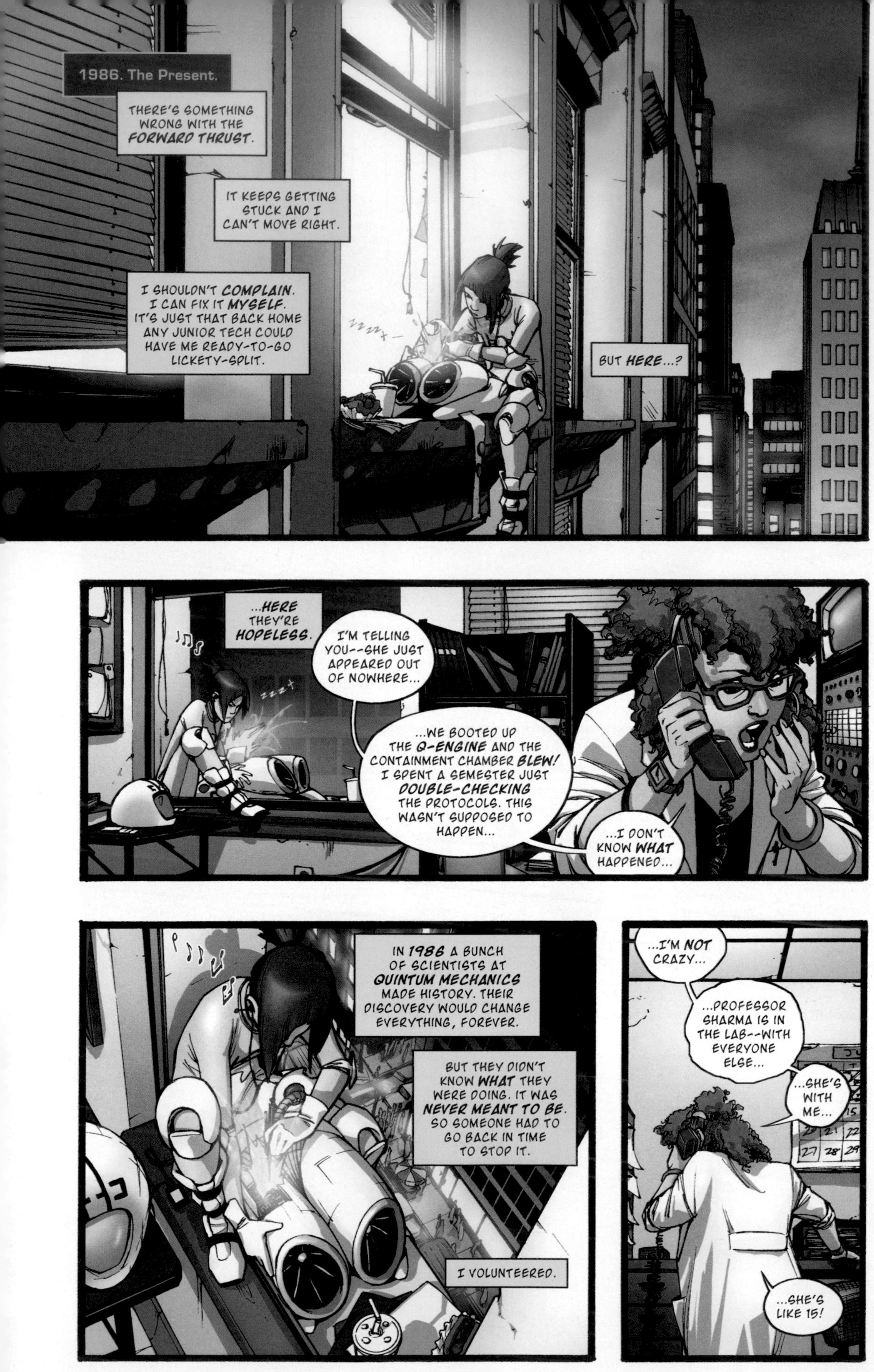
1986. The Present.
THERE'S SOMETHING WRONG WITH THE FORWARD THRUST.
IT KEEPS GETTING STUCK AND I CAN'T MOVE RIGHT.
I SHOULDN'T COMPLAIN. I CAN FIX IT MYSELF. IT'S JUST THAT BACK HOME ANY JUNIOR TECH COULD HAVE ME READY-TO-GO LICKETY-SPLIT.
BUT HERE...?
...HERE THEY'RE HOPELESS.
I'M TELLING YOU--SHE JUST APPEARED OUT OF NOWHERE...
...WE BOOTED UP THE Q-ENGINE AND THE CONTAINMENT CHAMBER BLEW! I SPENT A SEMESTER JUST DOUBLE-CHECKING THE PROTOCOLS. THIS WASN'T SUPPOSED TO HAPPEN...
...I DON'T KNOW WHAT HAPPENED...
IN 1986 A BUNCH OF SCIENTISTS AT QUINTUM MECHANICS MADE HISTORY. THEIR DISCOVERY WOULD CHANGE EVERYTHING, FOREVER.
BUT THEY DIDN'T KNOW WHAT THEY WERE DOING. IT WAS NEVER MEANT TO BE. SO SOMEONE HAD TO GO BACK IN TIME TO STOP IT.
I VOLUNTEERED.
...I'M NOT CRAZY...
...PROFESSOR SHARMA IS IN THE LAB--WITH EVERYONE ELSE...
...SHE'S WITH ME...
...SHE'S LIKE 15!

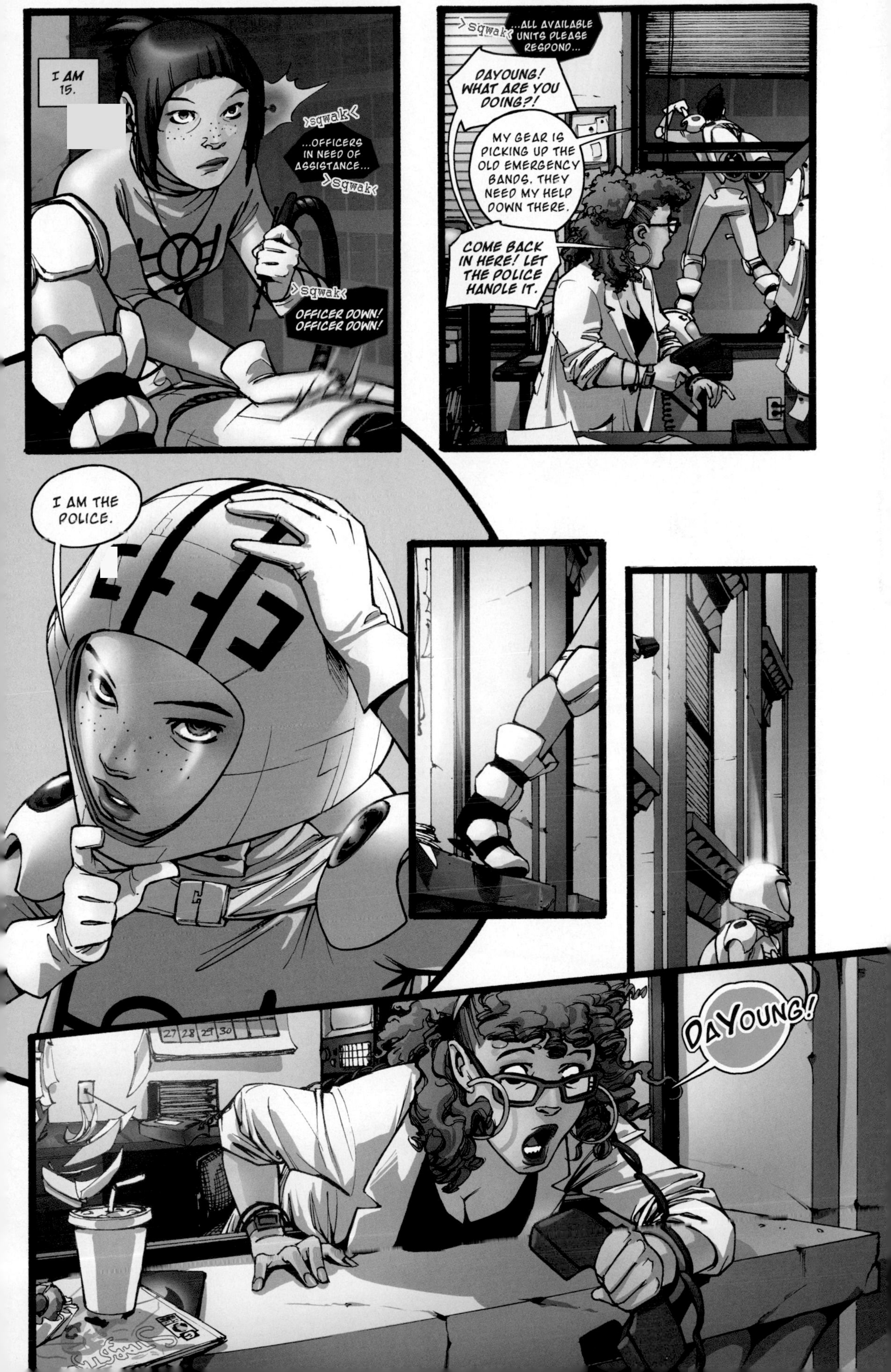

I AM 15.
>sqwak<
...OFFICERS IN NEED OF ASSISTANCE...
>sqwak<
>sqwak<
OFFICER DOWN! OFFICER DOWN!
>sqwak<
...ALL AVAILABLE UNITS PLEASE RESPOND...
DAYOUNG! WHAT ARE YOU DOING?!
MY GEAR IS PICKING UP THE OLD EMERGENCY BANDS. THEY NEED MY HELP DOWN THERE.
COME BACK IN HERE! LET THE POLICE HANDLE IT.
I AM THE POLICE.
DAYOUNG!

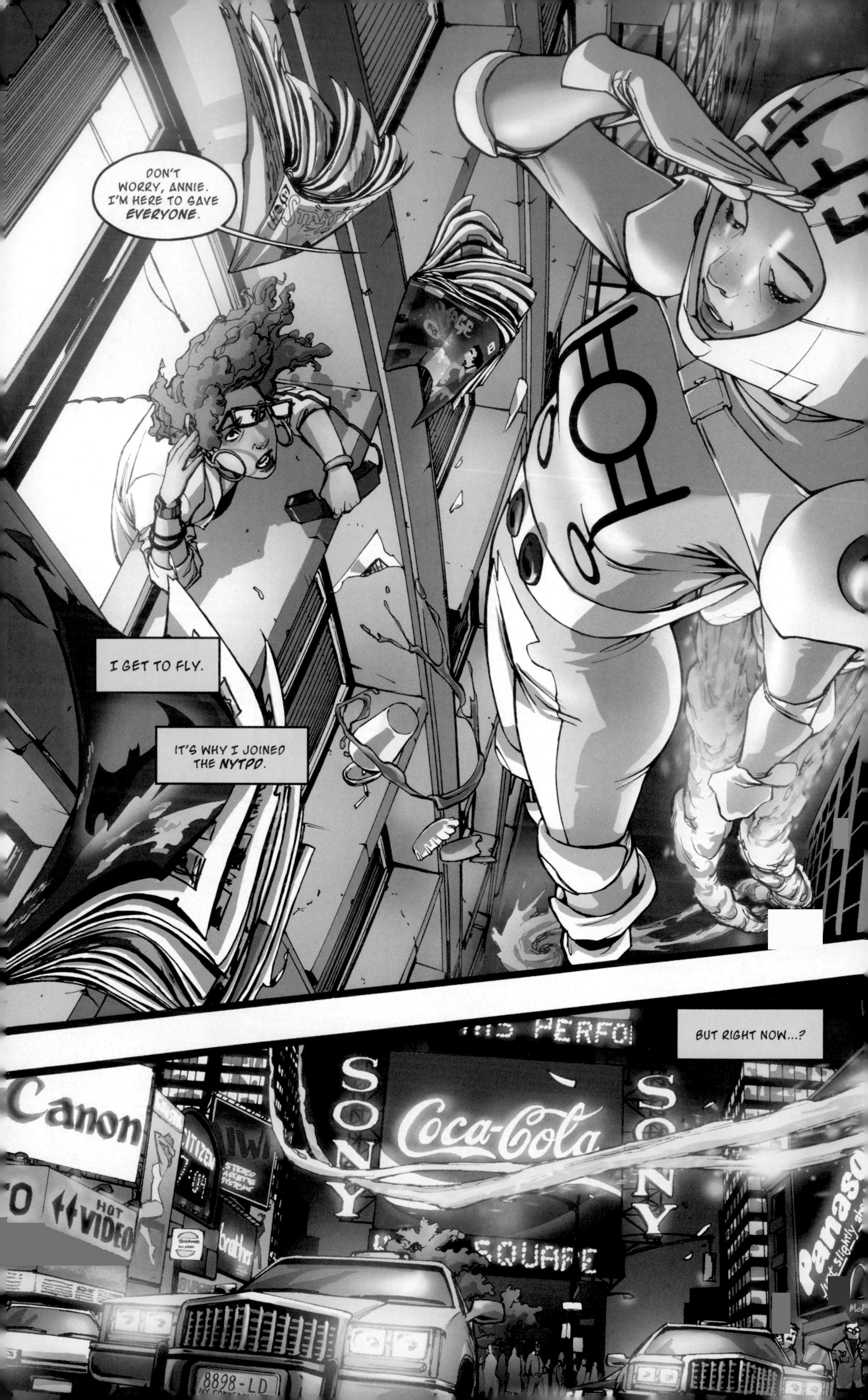

DON'T WORRY, ANNIE. I'M HERE TO SAVE EVERYONE.
I GET TO FLY.
IT'S WHY I JOINED THE NYTPD.
BUT RIGHT NOW...?
Canon
HOT VIDEO
CITIZEN
SONY
Coca-Cola
SONY
SQUARE
Panaso
8898-LD

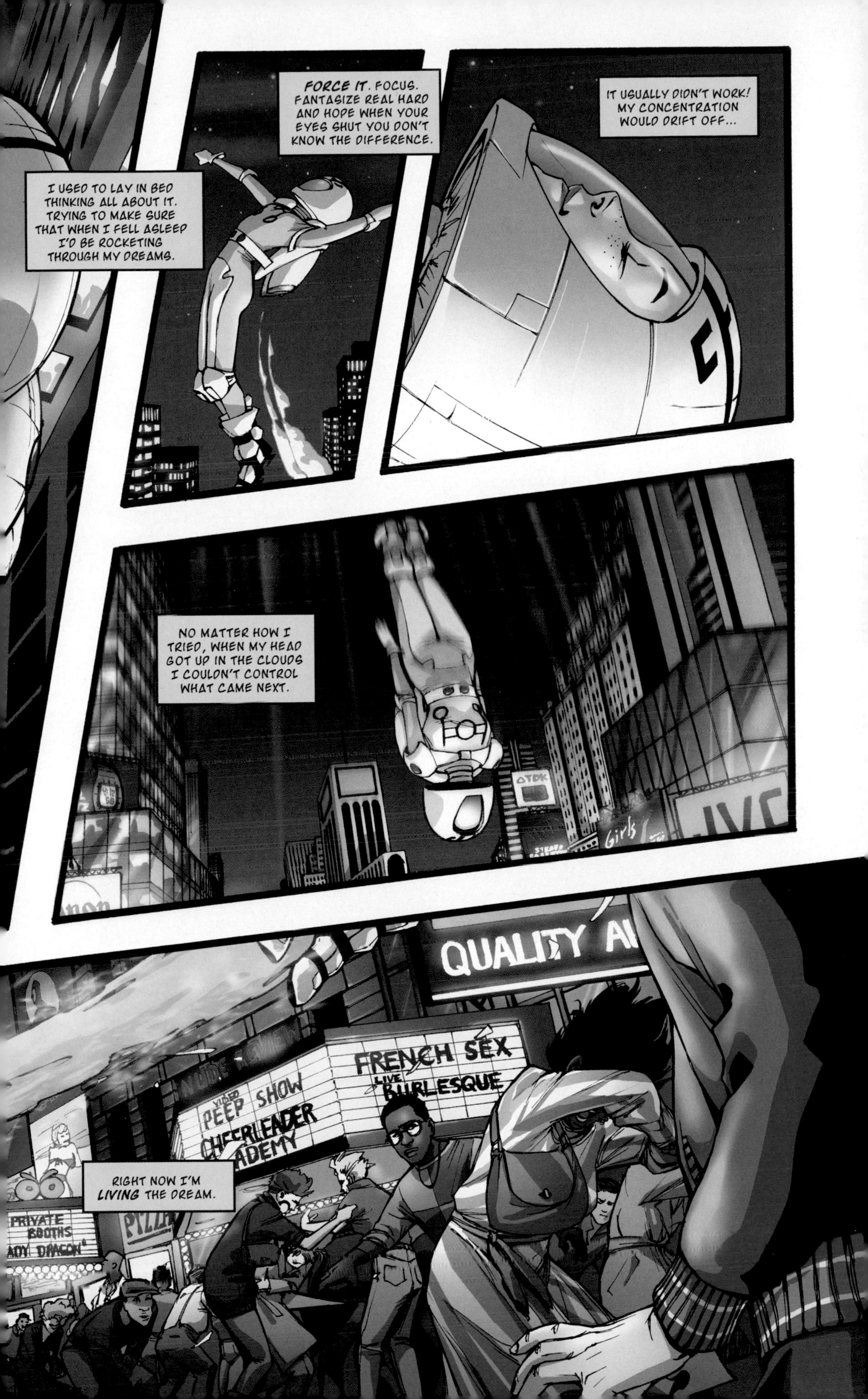
I USED TO LAY IN BED THINKING ALL ABOUT IT. TRYING TO MAKE SURE THAT WHEN I FELL ASLEEP I'D BE ROCKETING THROUGH MY DREAMS.
FORCE IT. FOCUS. FANTASIZE REAL HARD AND HOPE WHEN YOUR EYES SHUT YOU DON'T KNOW THE DIFFERENCE.
IT USUALLY DIDN'T WORK! MY CONCENTRATION WOULD DRIFT OFF...
NO MATTER HOW I TRIED, WHEN MY HEAD GOT UP IN THE CLOUDS I COULDN'T CONTROL WHAT CAME NEXT.
QUALITY A
FRENCH SEX
LIVE BURLESQUE
VIDEO PEEP SHOW
CHEERLEADER ACADEMY
RIGHT NOW I'M *LIVING* THE DREAM.
PRIVATE BOOTHS

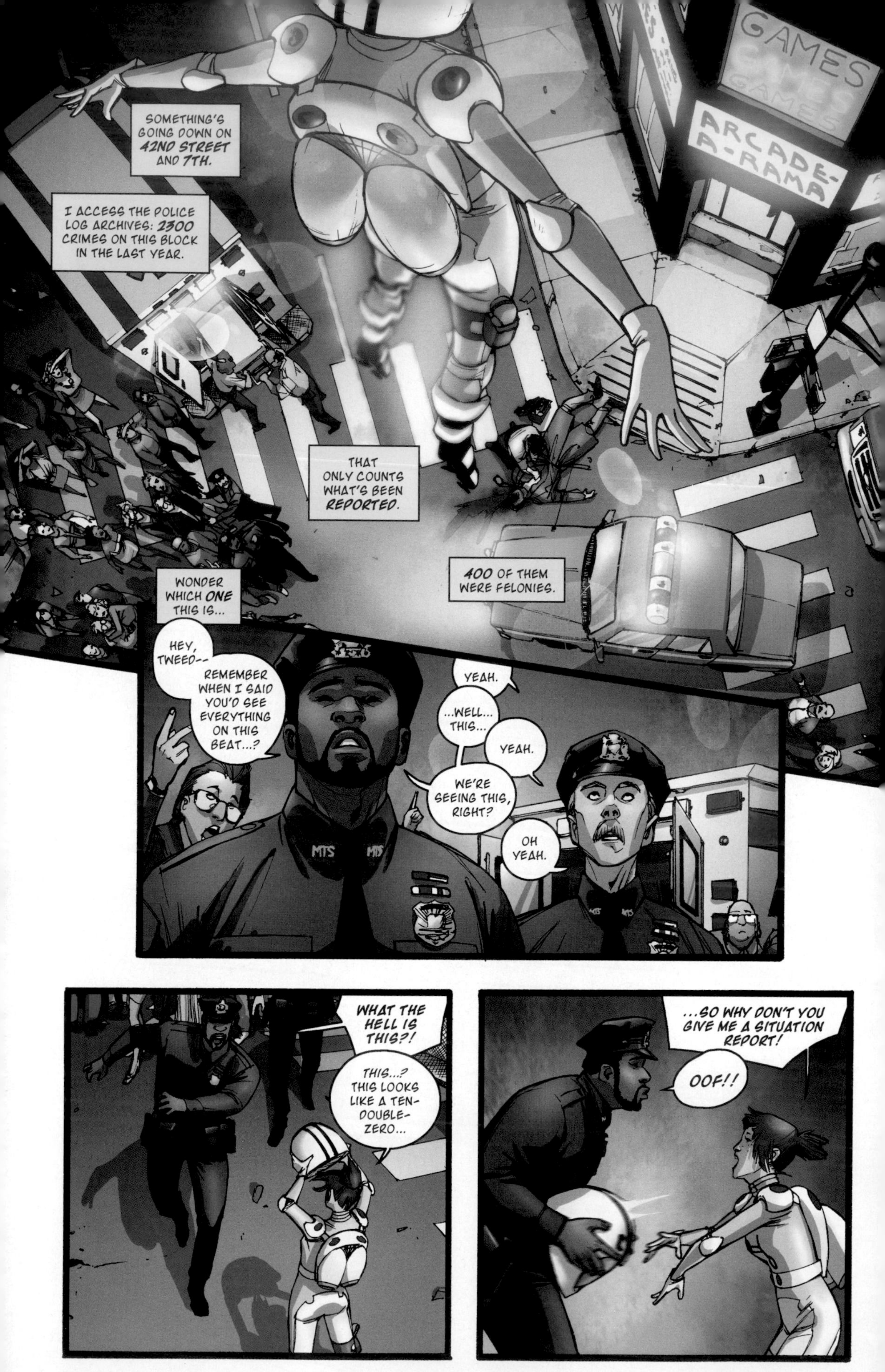

GAMES
ARCADE-A-RAMA
SOMETHING'S GOING DOWN ON 42ND STREET AND 7TH.
I ACCESS THE POLICE LOG ARCHIVES: 2300 CRIMES ON THIS BLOCK IN THE LAST YEAR.
THAT ONLY COUNTS WHAT'S BEEN REPORTED.
400 OF THEM WERE FELONIES.
WONDER WHICH ONE THIS IS...
HEY, TWEED--
REMEMBER WHEN I SAID YOU'D SEE EVERYTHING ON THIS BEAT...?
YEAH.
...WELL... THIS...
YEAH.
WE'RE SEEING THIS, RIGHT?
OH YEAH.
MTS
WHAT THE HELL IS THIS?!
THIS...? THIS LOOKS LIKE A TEN-DOUBLE-ZERO...
...SO WHY DON'T YOU GIVE ME A SITUATION REPORT!
OOF!!

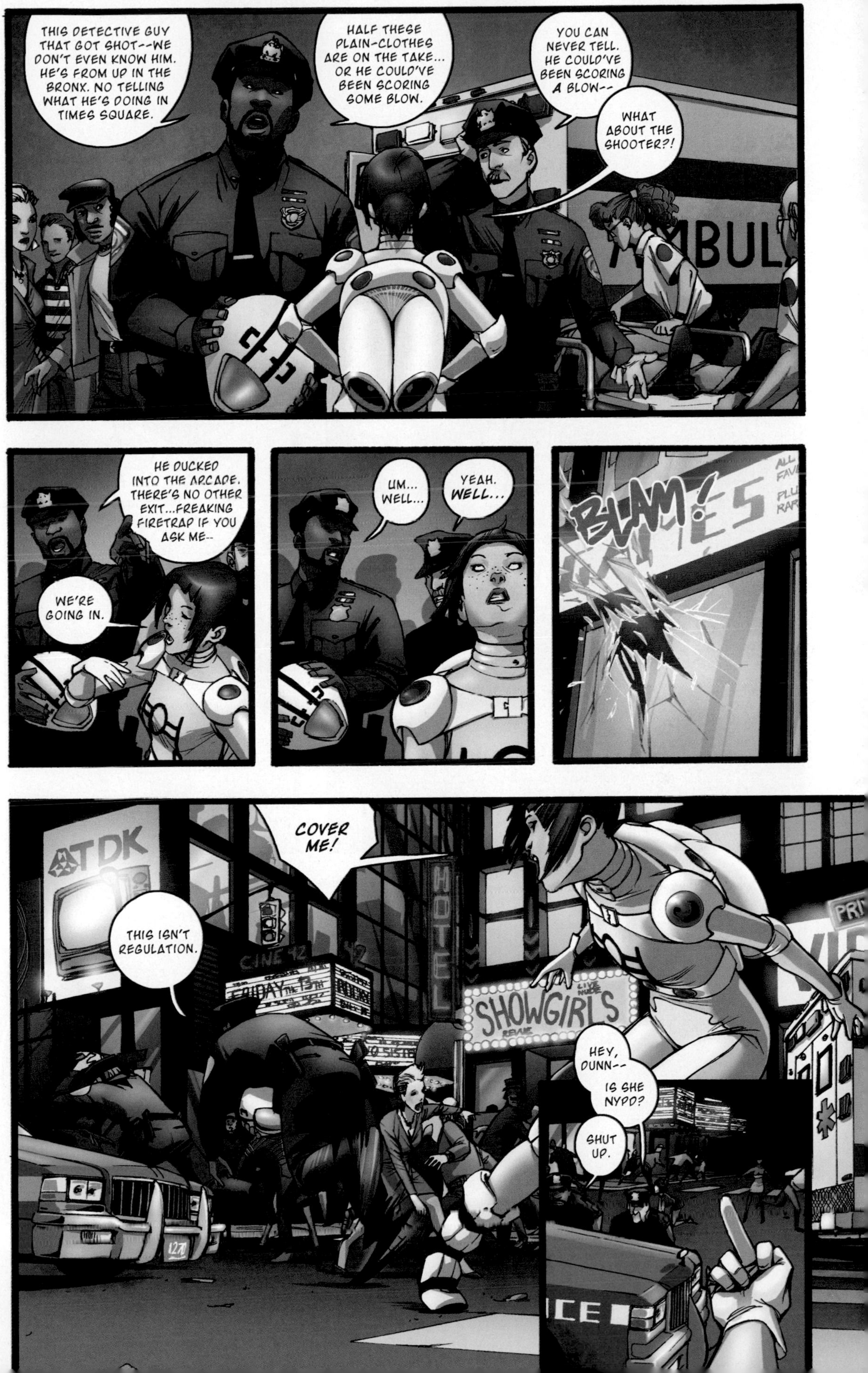

THIS DETECTIVE GUY THAT GOT SHOT--WE DON'T EVEN KNOW HIM. HE'S FROM UP IN THE BRONX. NO TELLING WHAT HE'S DOING IN TIMES SQUARE.
HALF THESE PLAIN-CLOTHES ARE ON THE TAKE... OR HE COULD'VE BEEN SCORING SOME BLOW.
YOU CAN NEVER TELL. HE COULD'VE BEEN SCORING A BLOW--
WHAT ABOUT THE SHOOTER?!
HE DUCKED INTO THE ARCADE. THERE'S NO OTHER EXIT...FREAKING FIRETRAP IF YOU ASK ME--
WE'RE GOING IN.
UM... WELL...
YEAH. **WELL...**
BLAM!
COVER ME!
THIS ISN'T REGULATION.
TDK
CINE 42
HOTEL
SHOWGIRLS
HEY, DUNN--
IS SHE NYPD?
SHUT UP.

shwp

HAVEN'T HAD TWO COPS ACT LIKE THAT *BEFORE.*

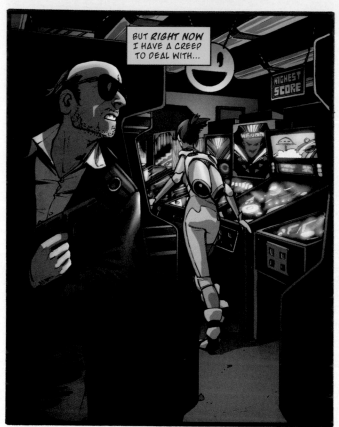

BUT *RIGHT NOW* I HAVE A CREEP TO DEAL WITH...

HIGHEST SCORE

THE COMMISSIONER WAS RIGHT. AND LESHAWN. THIS IS A DIFFERENT WORLD.

HERE I DON'T HAVE TWO PARTNERS LIKE THEM.

BEGIN

WHAT AM I GOING TO DO FOR BACK-UP...?

HEH.

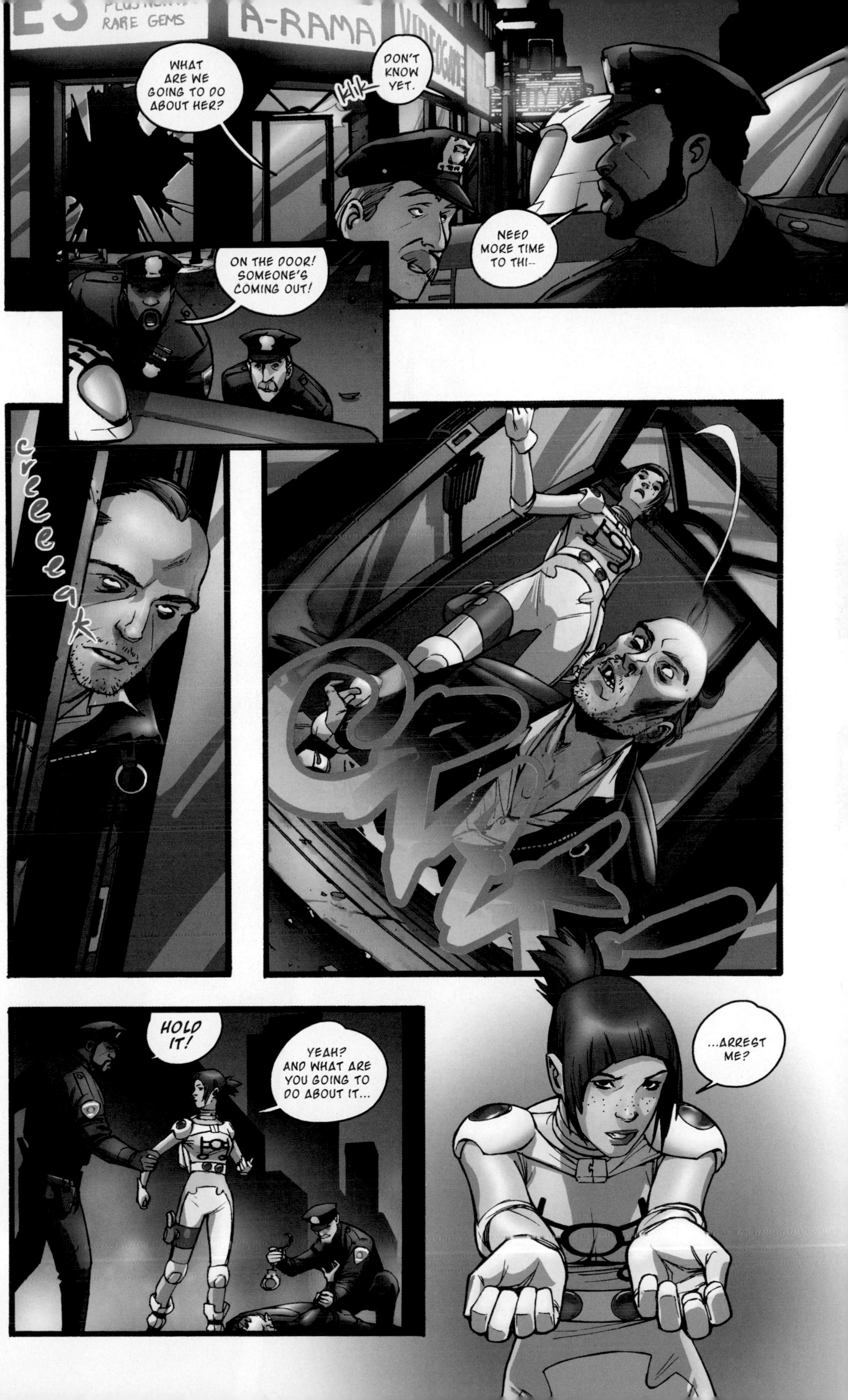
PLUS NON... RARE GEMS
A-RAMA
WHAT ARE WE GOING TO DO ABOUT HER?
KLIK
DON'T KNOW YET.
NEED MORE TIME TO THI--
ON THE DOOR! SOMEONE'S COMING OUT!
CREEEAK
HOLD IT!
YEAH? AND WHAT ARE YOU GOING TO DO ABOUT IT...
...ARREST ME?

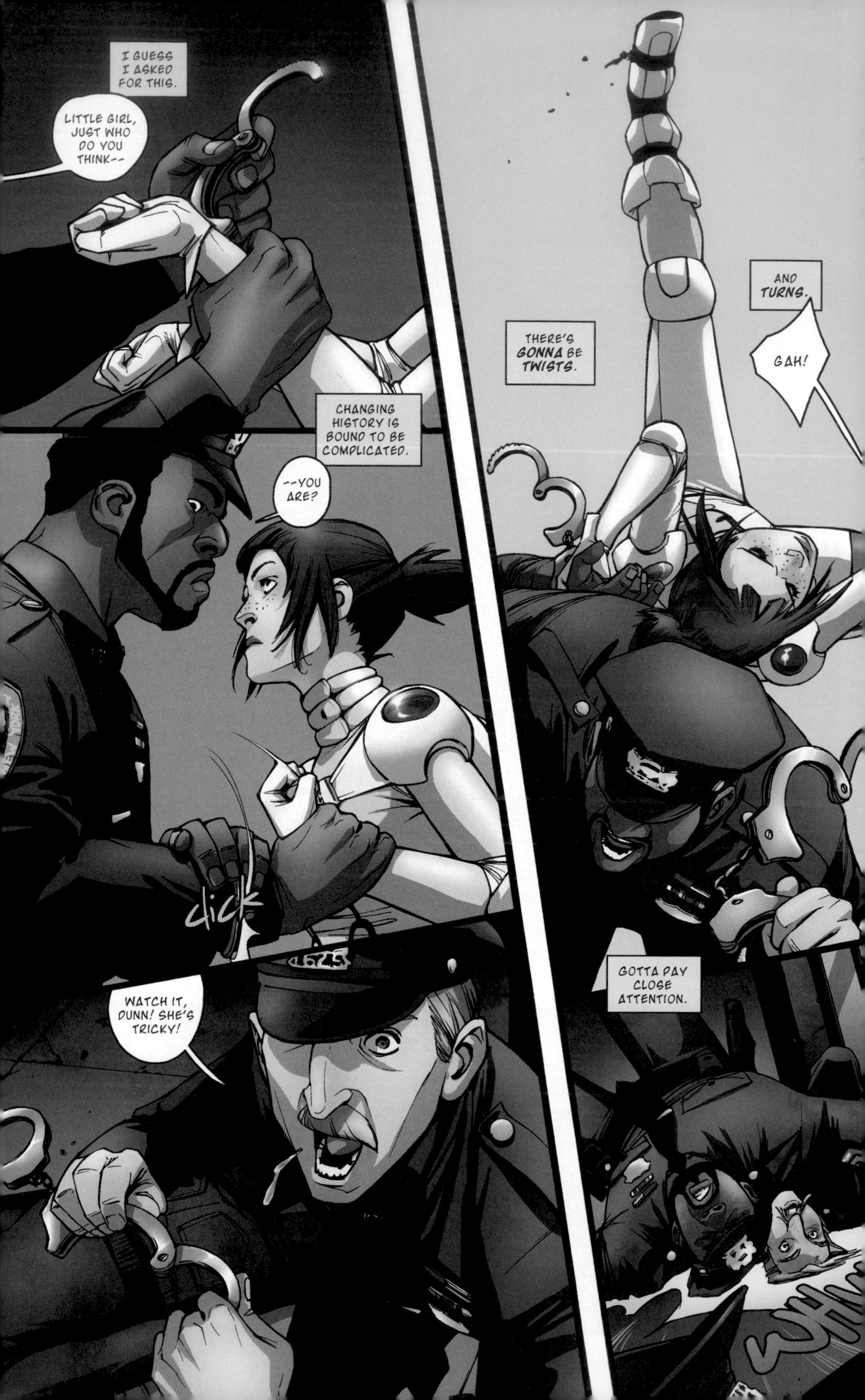
I GUESS I ASKED FOR THIS.
LITTLE GIRL, JUST WHO DO YOU THINK--
CHANGING HISTORY IS BOUND TO BE COMPLICATED.
--YOU ARE?
CLICK
WATCH IT, DUNN! SHE'S TRICKY!
THERE'S GONNA BE TWISTS.
AND TURNS.
GAH!
GOTTA PAY CLOSE ATTENTION.

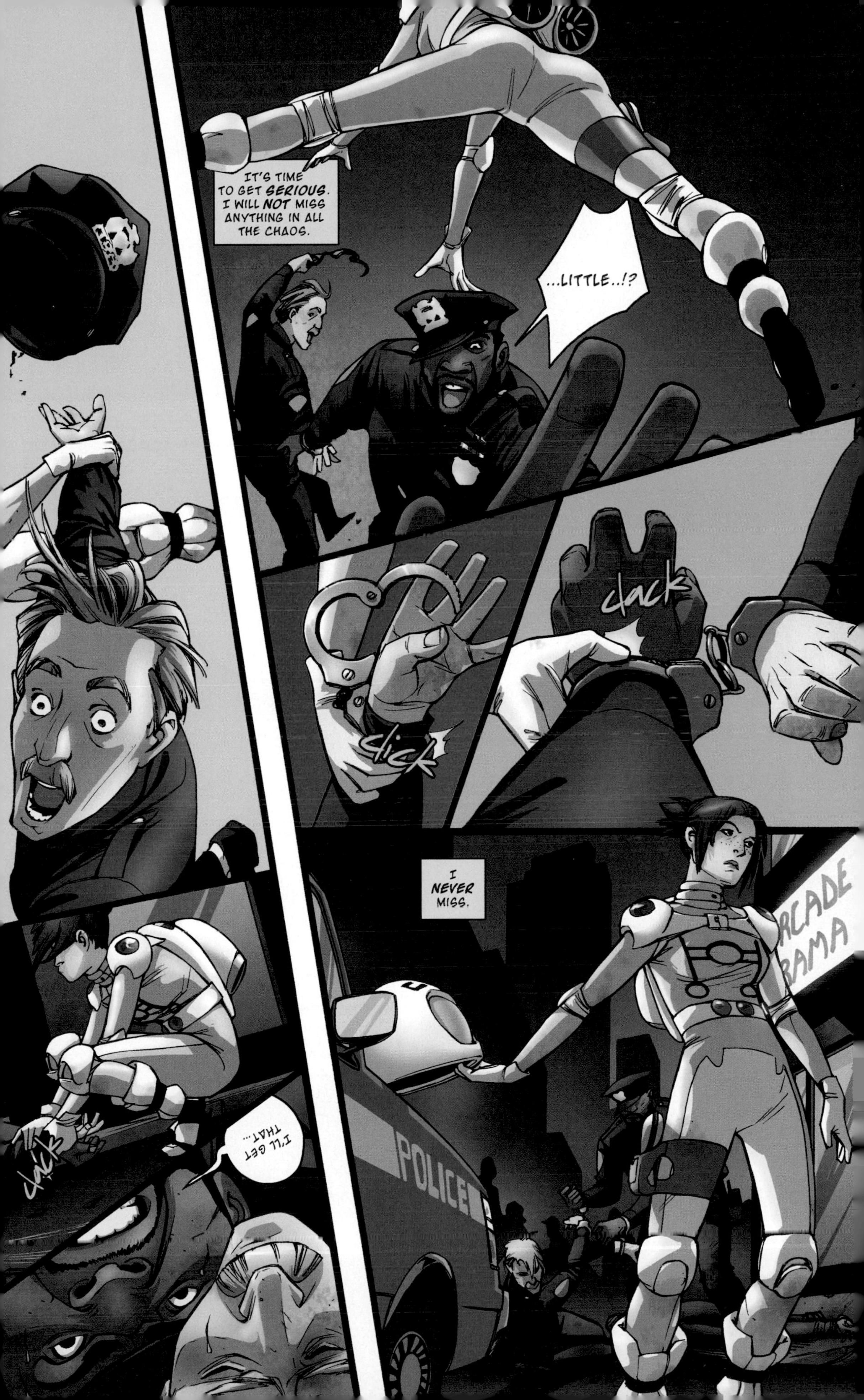

IT'S TIME TO GET SERIOUS. I WILL NOT MISS ANYTHING IN ALL THE CHAOS.
...LITTLE..!?
click
clack
I'LL GET THAT...
clack
I NEVER MISS.
RCADE
RAMA
POLICE

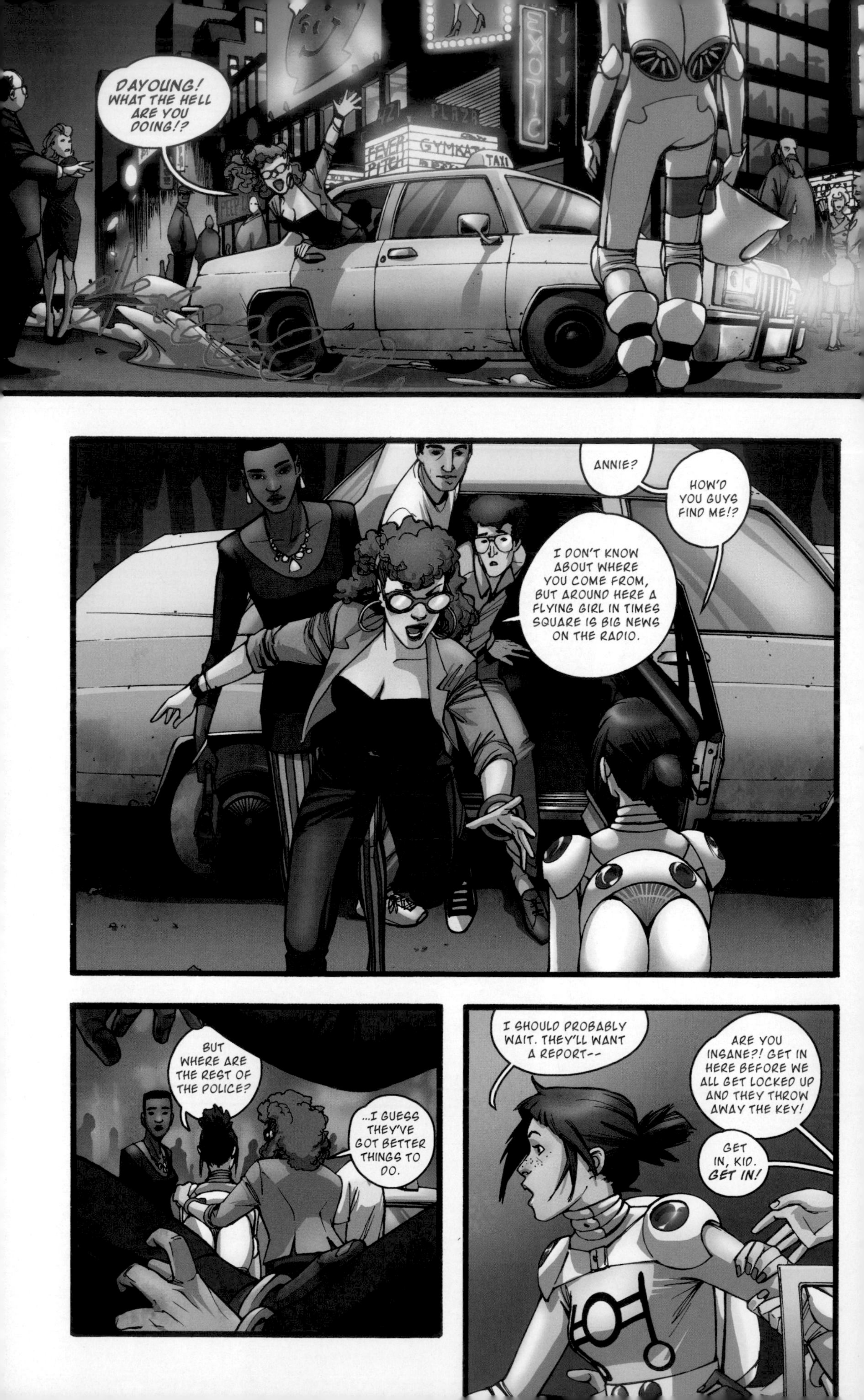
DAYOUNG! WHAT THE HELL ARE YOU DOING!?
EXOTIC
PLAZA
GYMKATA
FEVER PITCH
TAXI
ANNIE?
HOW'D YOU GUYS FIND ME!?
I DON'T KNOW ABOUT WHERE YOU COME FROM, BUT AROUND HERE A FLYING GIRL IN TIMES SQUARE IS BIG NEWS ON THE RADIO.
BUT WHERE ARE THE REST OF THE POLICE?
...I GUESS THEY'VE GOT BETTER THINGS TO DO.
I SHOULD PROBABLY WAIT. THEY'LL WANT A REPORT--
ARE YOU INSANE?! GET IN HERE BEFORE WE ALL GET LOCKED UP AND THEY THROW AWAY THE KEY!
GET IN, KID. GET IN!

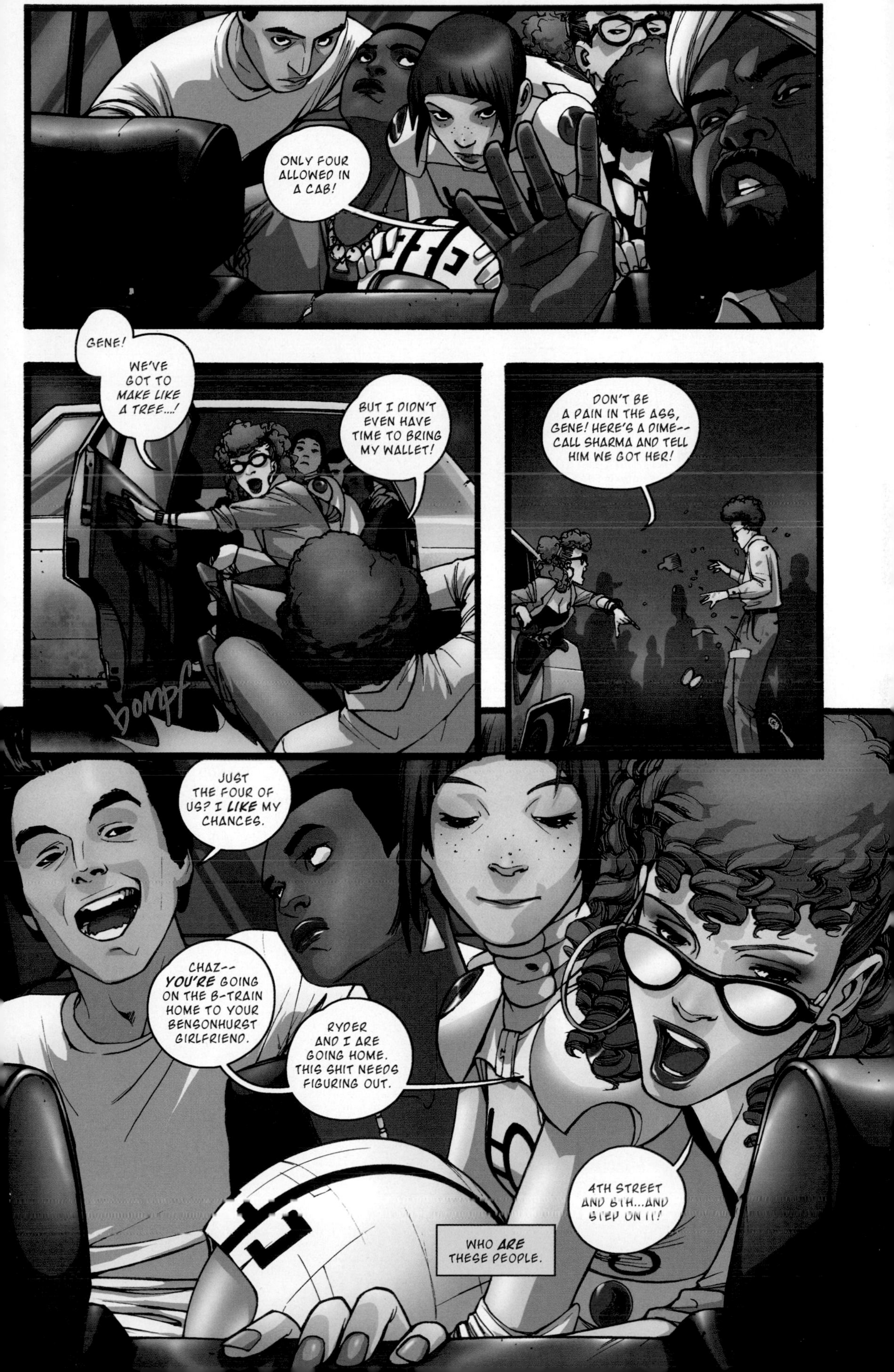

ONLY FOUR ALLOWED IN A CAB!
GENE!
WE'VE GOT TO MAKE LIKE A TREE...!
BUT I DIDN'T EVEN HAVE TIME TO BRING MY WALLET!
bompf
DON'T BE A PAIN IN THE ASS, GENE! HERE'S A DIME-- CALL SHARMA AND TELL HIM WE GOT HER!
JUST THE FOUR OF US? I *LIKE* MY CHANCES.
CHAZ-- ***YOU'RE*** GOING ON THE B-TRAIN HOME TO YOUR BENSONHURST GIRLFRIEND.
RYDER AND I ARE GOING HOME. THIS SHIT NEEDS FIGURING OUT.
4TH STREET AND 6TH...AND STEP ON IT!
WHO *ARE* THESE PEOPLE.

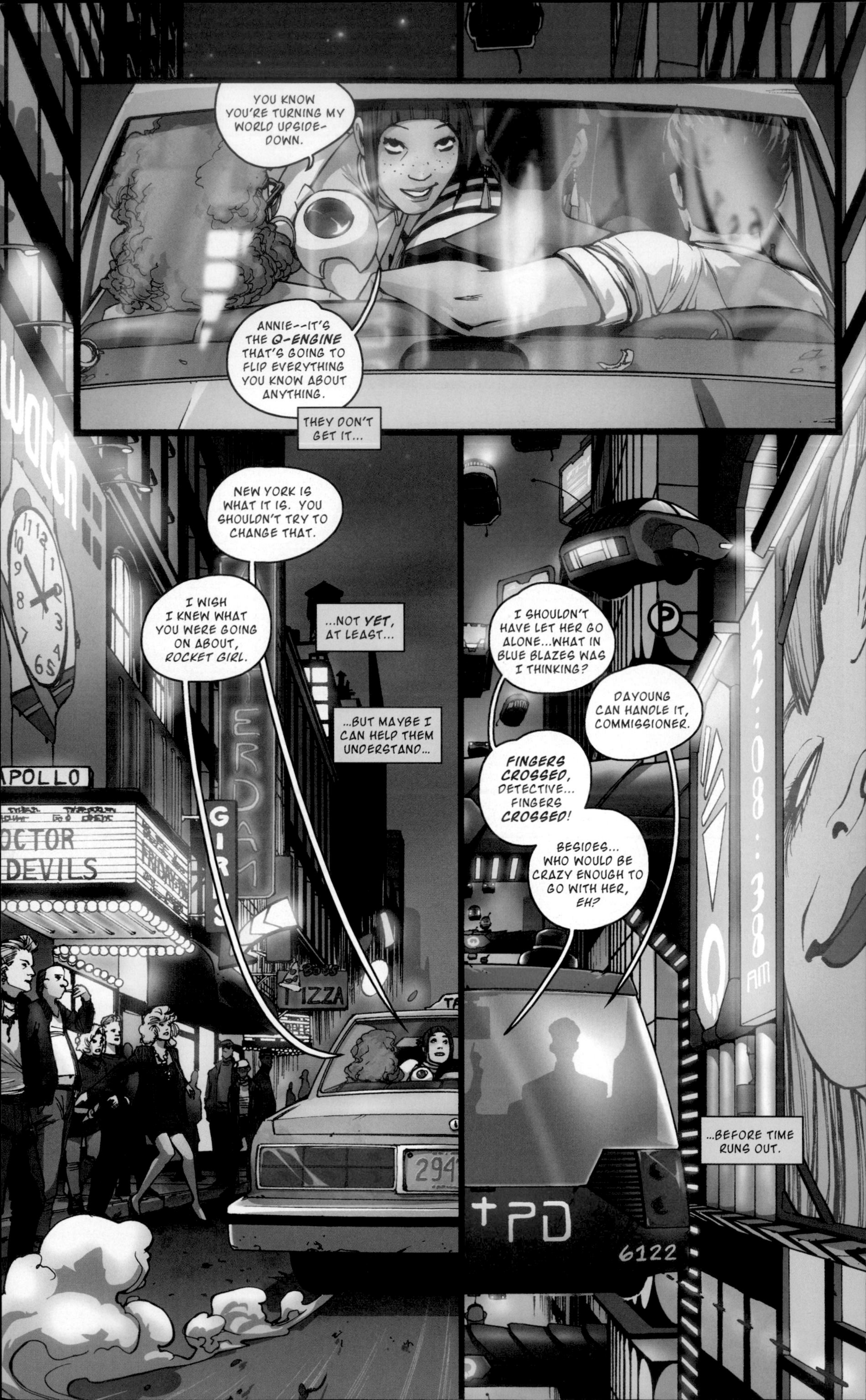
YOU KNOW YOU'RE TURNING MY WORLD UPSIDE-DOWN.
ANNIE--IT'S THE **Q-ENGINE** THAT'S GOING TO FLIP EVERYTHING YOU KNOW ABOUT ANYTHING.
THEY DON'T GET IT...
NEW YORK IS WHAT IT IS. YOU SHOULDN'T TRY TO CHANGE THAT.
I WISH I KNEW WHAT YOU WERE GOING ON ABOUT, ROCKET GIRL.
...NOT *YET*, AT LEAST...
...BUT MAYBE I CAN HELP THEM UNDERSTAND...
APOLLO
OCTOR DEVILS
PIZZA
I SHOULDN'T HAVE LET HER GO ALONE...WHAT IN BLUE BLAZES WAS I THINKING?
DAYOUNG CAN HANDLE IT, COMMISSIONER.
FINGERS CROSSED, DETECTIVE... FINGERS **CROSSED!**
BESIDES... WHO WOULD BE CRAZY ENOUGH TO GO WITH HER, EH?
12:08:38 AM
TPD
6122
...BEFORE TIME RUNS OUT.

Chapter 2_Objects in Motion Tend to Stay in Motion...>>

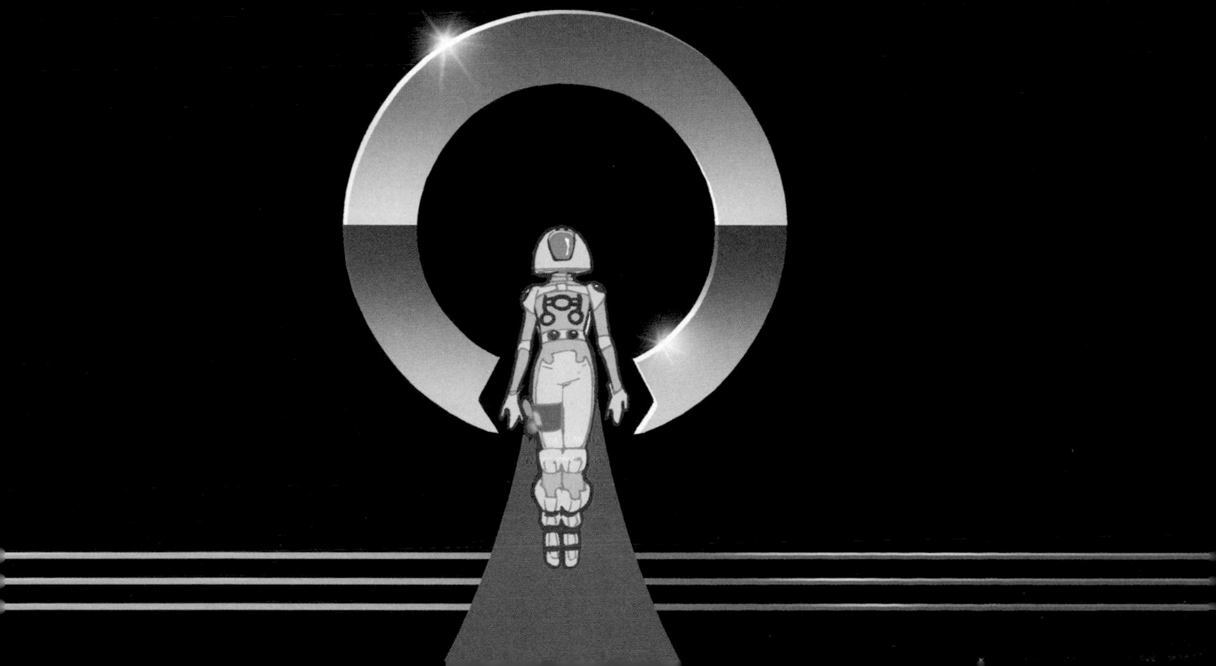

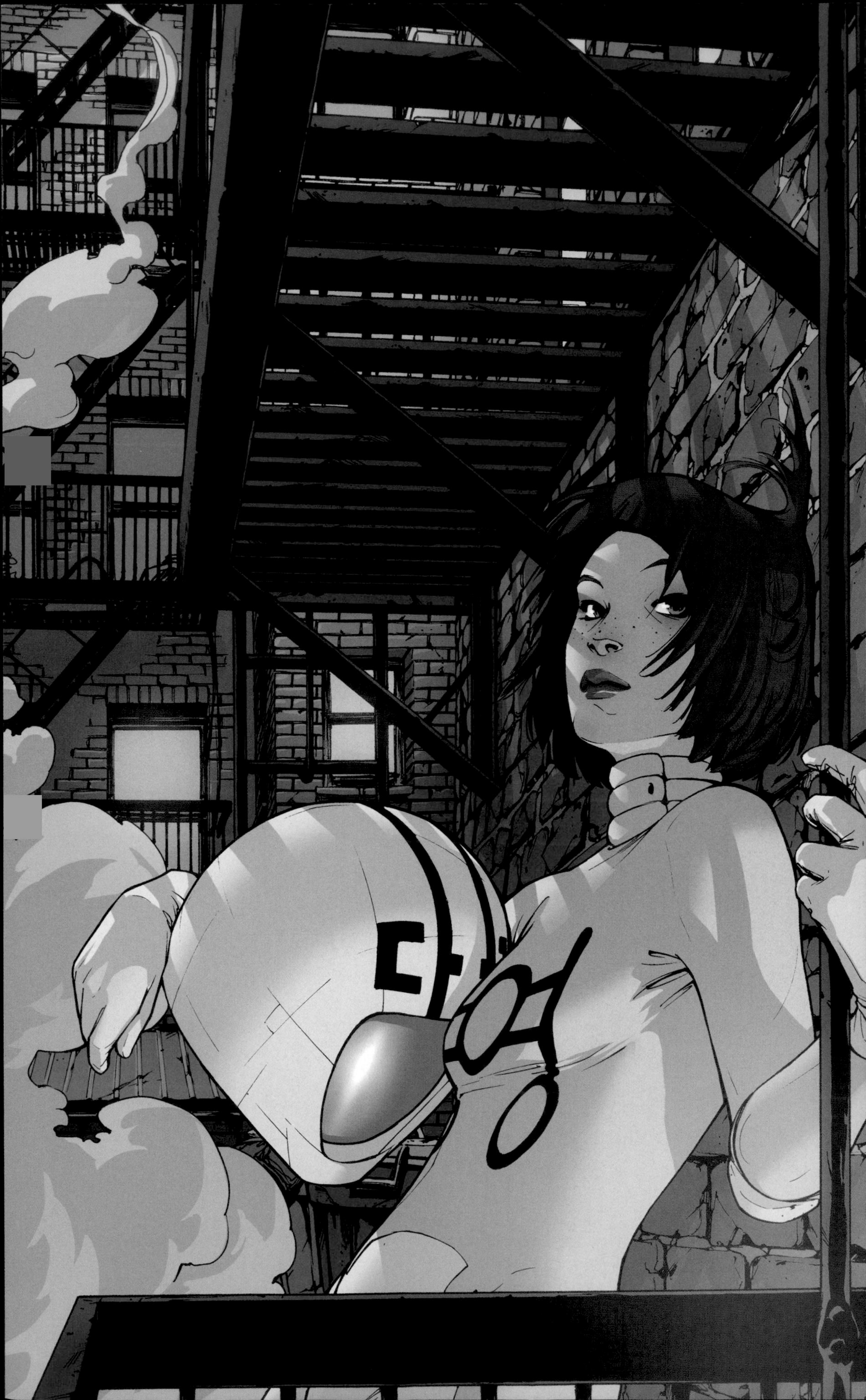

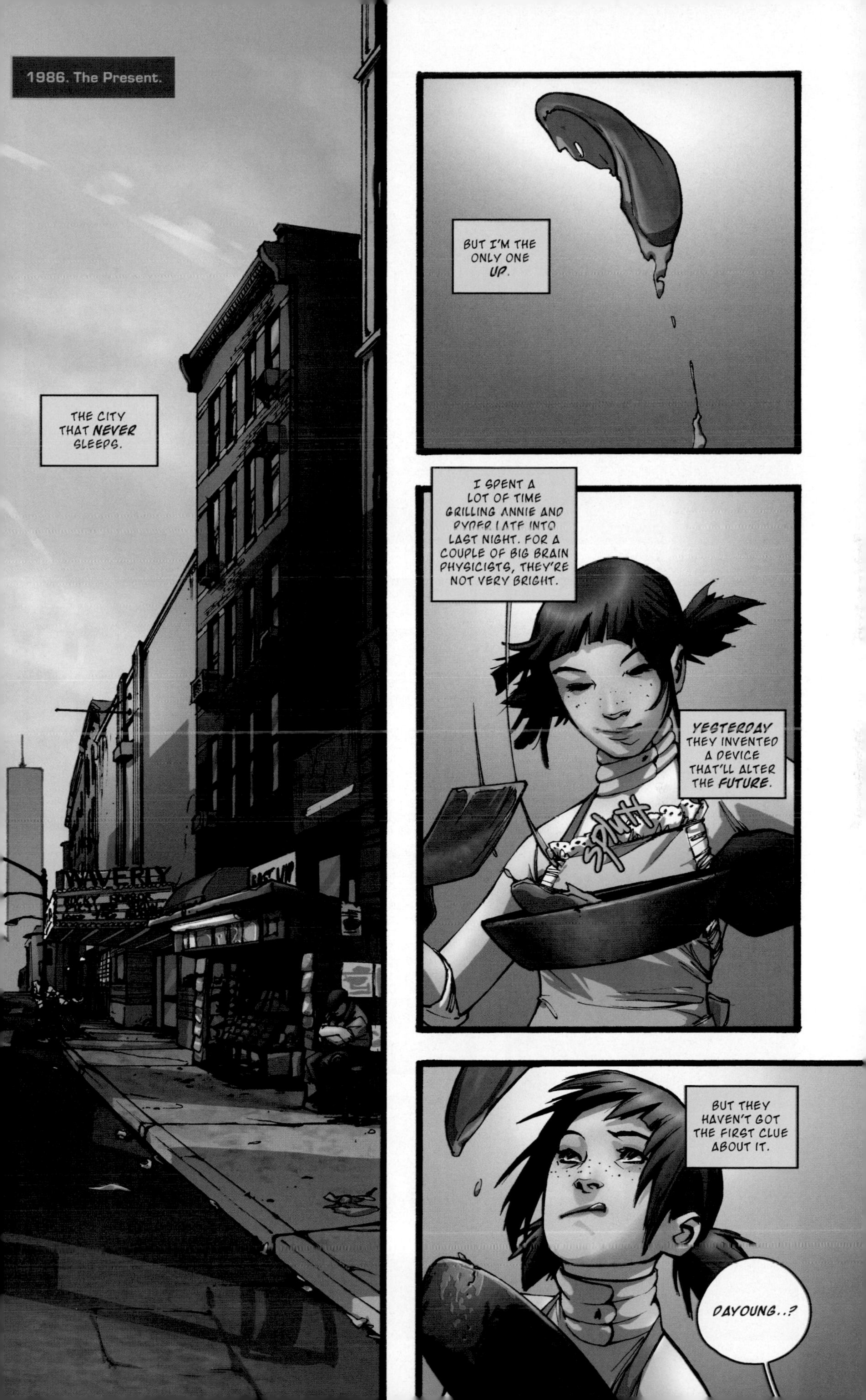

1986. The Present.
THE CITY THAT NEVER SLEEPS.
WAVERLY
BUT I'M THE ONLY ONE UP.
I SPENT A LOT OF TIME GRILLING ANNIE AND RYDER LATE INTO LAST NIGHT. FOR A COUPLE OF BIG BRAIN PHYSICISTS, THEY'RE NOT VERY BRIGHT.
YESTERDAY THEY INVENTED A DEVICE THAT'LL ALTER THE FUTURE.
BUT THEY HAVEN'T GOT THE FIRST CLUE ABOUT IT.
DAYOUNG..?

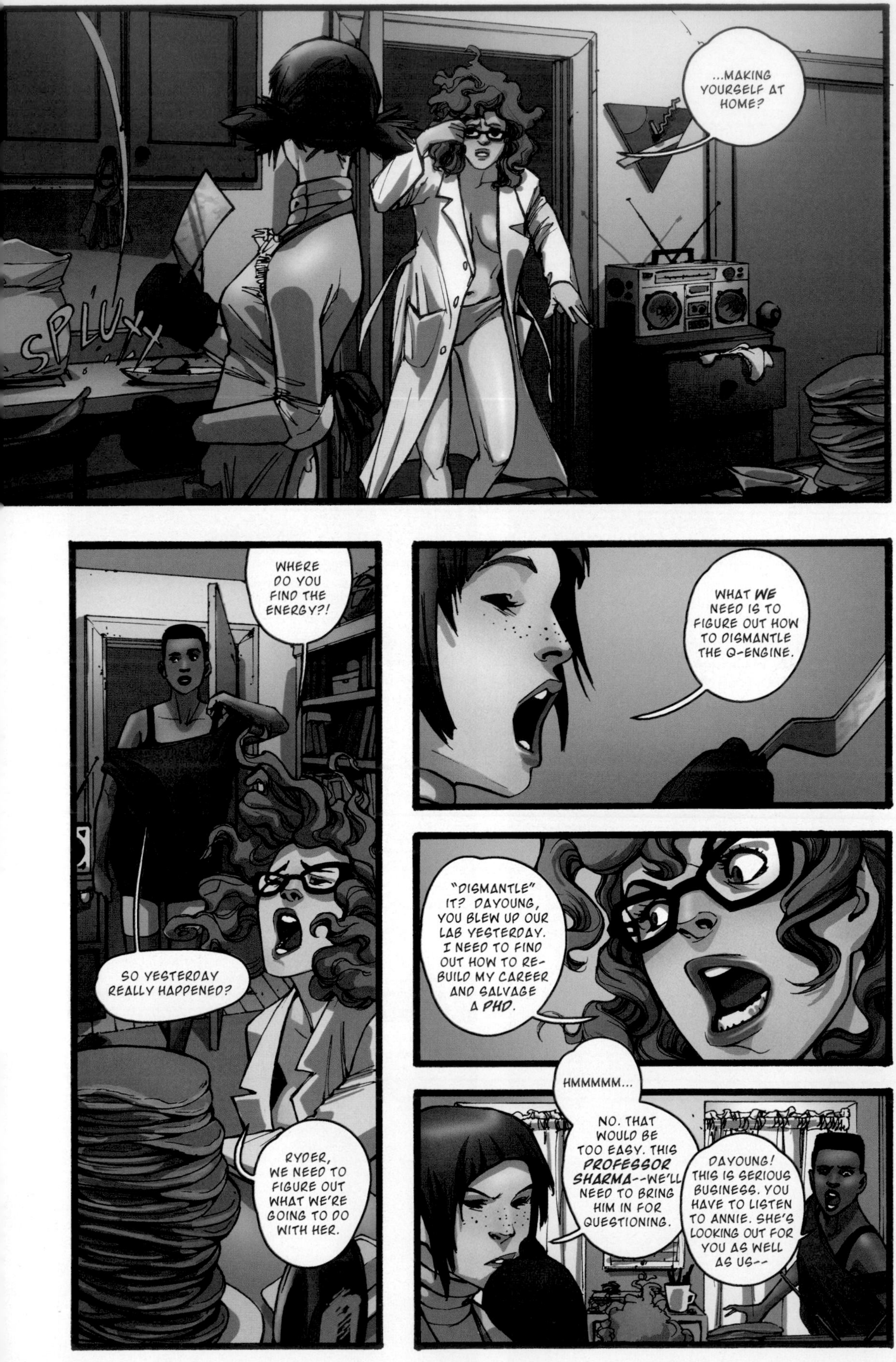
...MAKING YOURSELF AT HOME?
SPLUXX
WHERE DO YOU FIND THE ENERGY?!
SO YESTERDAY REALLY HAPPENED?
RYDER, WE NEED TO FIGURE OUT WHAT WE'RE GOING TO DO WITH HER.
WHAT WE NEED IS TO FIGURE OUT HOW TO DISMANTLE THE Q-ENGINE.
"DISMANTLE" IT? DAYOUNG, YOU BLEW UP OUR LAB YESTERDAY. I NEED TO FIND OUT HOW TO RE-BUILD MY CAREER AND SALVAGE A PHD.
HMMMMM...
NO. THAT WOULD BE TOO EASY. THIS PROFESSOR SHARMA--WE'LL NEED TO BRING HIM IN FOR QUESTIONING.
DAYOUNG! THIS IS SERIOUS BUSINESS. YOU HAVE TO LISTEN TO ANNIE. SHE'S LOOKING OUT FOR YOU AS WELL AS US--

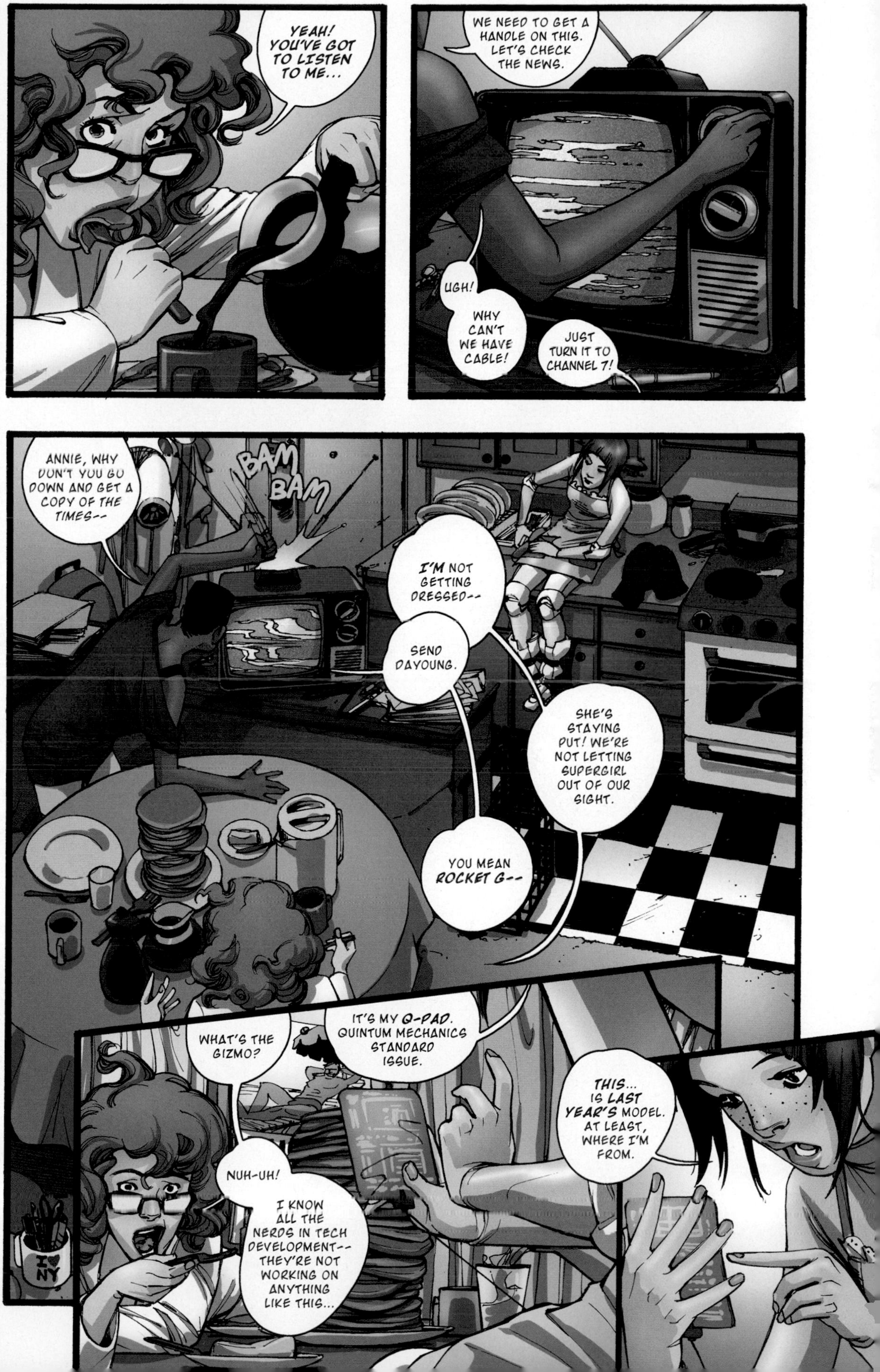

YEAH! YOU'VE GOT TO LISTEN TO ME...
WE NEED TO GET A HANDLE ON THIS. LET'S CHECK THE NEWS.
UGH!
WHY CAN'T WE HAVE CABLE!
JUST TURN IT TO CHANNEL 7!
ANNIE, WHY DON'T YOU GO DOWN AND GET A COPY OF THE TIMES--
BAM BAM
I'M NOT GETTING DRESSED--
SEND DAYOUNG.
SHE'S STAYING PUT! WE'RE NOT LETTING SUPERGIRL OUT OF OUR SIGHT.
YOU MEAN ROCKET G--
WHAT'S THE GIZMO?
IT'S MY Q-PAD. QUINTUM MECHANICS STANDARD ISSUE.
NUH-UH!
I KNOW ALL THE NERDS IN TECH DEVELOPMENT-- THEY'RE NOT WORKING ON ANYTHING LIKE THIS...
THIS... IS LAST YEAR'S MODEL. AT LEAST, WHERE I'M FROM.
I ♥ NY

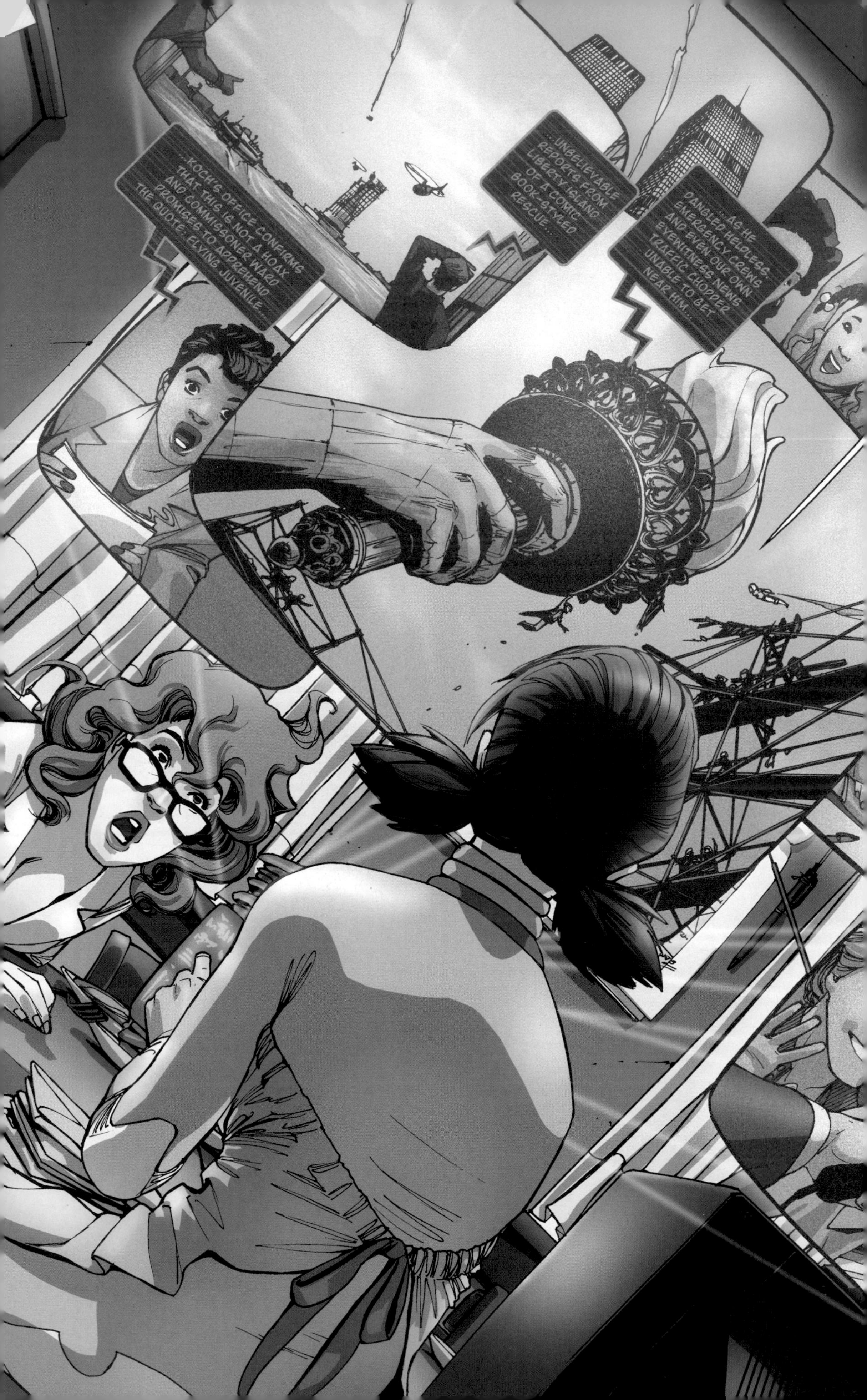
...UNBELIEVABLE REPORTS FROM LIBERTY ISLAND OF A COMIC BOOK-STYLED RESCUE...
...AS HE DANGLED HELPLESS, EMERGENCY CREWS AND EVEN OUR OWN EYEWITNESS NEWS TRAFFIC CHOPPER UNABLE TO GET NEAR HIM...
...KOCH'S OFFICE CONFIRMS THAT THIS IS NOT A HOAX AND COMMISSONER WARD PROMISES TO APPREHEND THE QUOTE, FLYING JUVENILE...

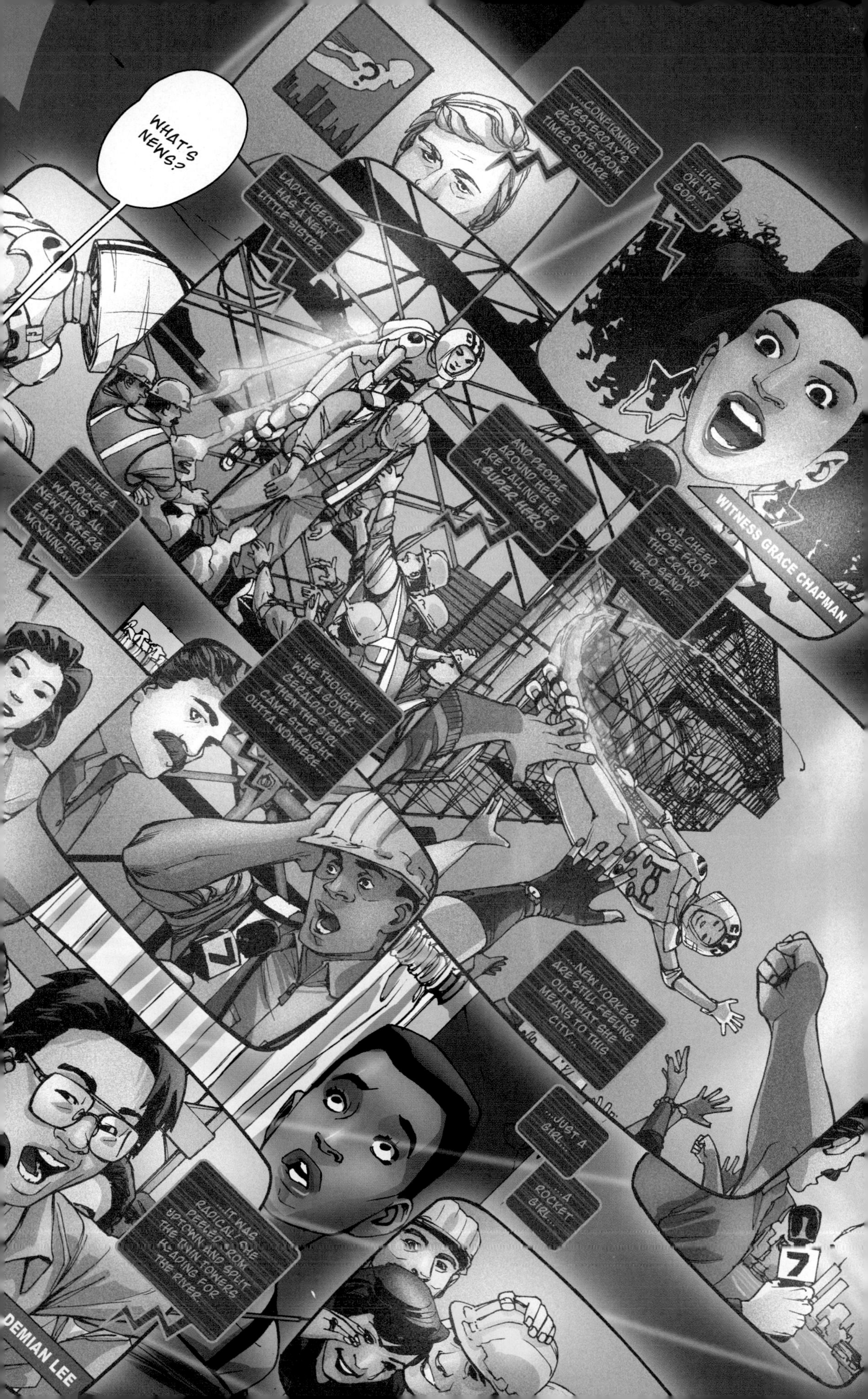

WHAT'S NEWS?
...CONFIRMING YESTERDAY'S REPORTS FROM TIMES SQUARE...
LADY LIBERTY HAS A NEW LITTLE SISTER.
...LIKE, OH MY GOD...
AND PEOPLE AROUND HERE ARE CALLING HER A SUPER HERO.
...LIKE A ROCKET WAKING ALL NEW YORKERS EARLY THIS MORNING...
...A CHEER ROSE FROM THE CROWD TO SEND HER OFF...
WITNESS GRACE CHAPMAN
...WE THOUGHT HE WAS A GONER, GERALDO! BUT THEN THE GIRL CAME STRAIGHT OUTTA NOWHERE...
...NEW YORKERS ARE STILL FEELING OUT WHAT SHE MEANS TO THIS CITY...
...JUST A GIRL...
...A ROCKET GIRL...
...IT WAS RADICAL! SHE PEELED FROM UPTOWN AND SPLIT THE TWIN TOWERS HEADING FOR THE RIVER.
DEMIAN LEE

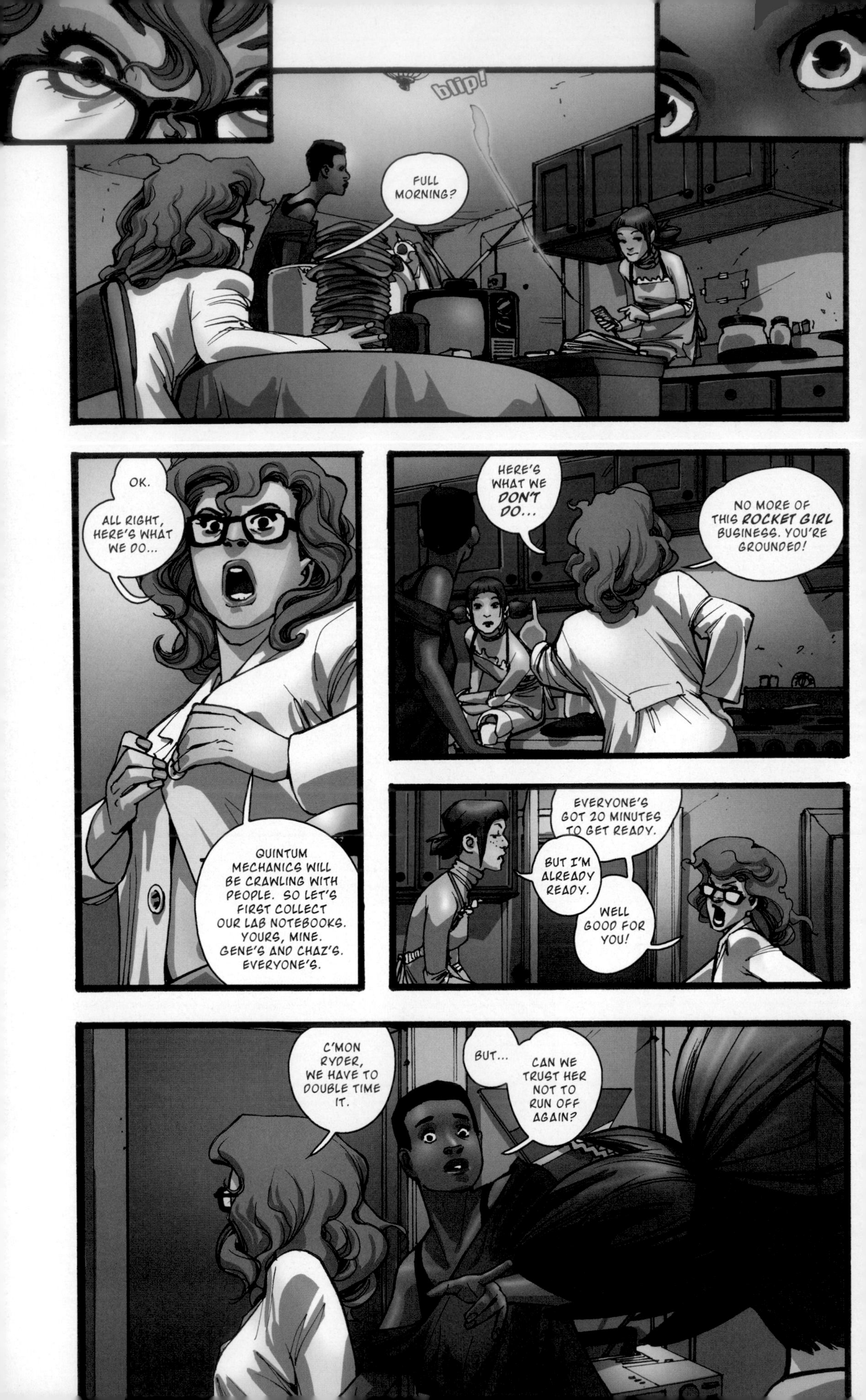
blip!
FULL MORNING?
OK.
ALL RIGHT, HERE'S WHAT WE DO...
QUINTUM MECHANICS WILL BE CRAWLING WITH PEOPLE. SO LET'S FIRST COLLECT OUR LAB NOTEBOOKS. YOURS, MINE. GENE'S AND CHAZ'S. EVERYONE'S.
HERE'S WHAT WE DON'T DO...
NO MORE OF THIS ROCKET GIRL BUSINESS. YOU'RE GROUNDED!
EVERYONE'S GOT 20 MINUTES TO GET READY.
BUT I'M ALREADY READY.
WELL GOOD FOR YOU!
C'MON RYDER, WE HAVE TO DOUBLE TIME IT.
BUT...
CAN WE TRUST HER NOT TO RUN OFF AGAIN?

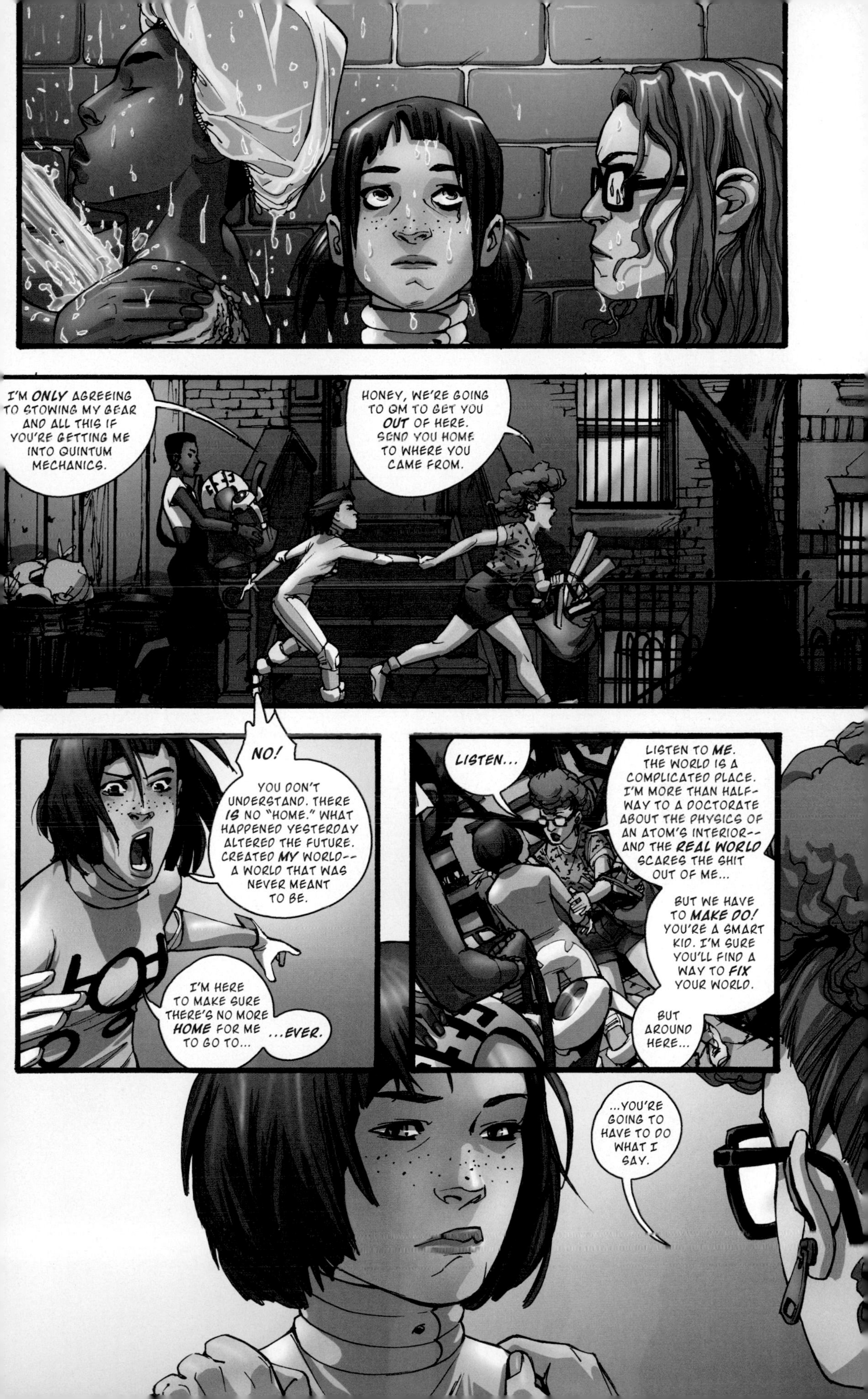

I'M ONLY AGREEING TO STOWING MY GEAR AND ALL THIS IF YOU'RE GETTING ME INTO QUINTUM MECHANICS.
HONEY, WE'RE GOING TO QM TO GET YOU OUT OF HERE. SEND YOU HOME TO WHERE YOU CAME FROM.
NO!
YOU DON'T UNDERSTAND. THERE IS NO "HOME." WHAT HAPPENED YESTERDAY ALTERED THE FUTURE. CREATED MY WORLD-- A WORLD THAT WAS NEVER MEANT TO BE.
I'M HERE TO MAKE SURE THERE'S NO MORE HOME FOR ME TO GO TO...
...EVER.
LISTEN...
LISTEN TO ME. THE WORLD IS A COMPLICATED PLACE. I'M MORE THAN HALF-WAY TO A DOCTORATE ABOUT THE PHYSICS OF AN ATOM'S INTERIOR-- AND THE REAL WORLD SCARES THE SHIT OUT OF ME...
BUT WE HAVE TO MAKE DO! YOU'RE A SMART KID. I'M SURE YOU'LL FIND A WAY TO FIX YOUR WORLD.
BUT AROUND HERE...
...YOU'RE GOING TO HAVE TO DO WHAT I SAY.

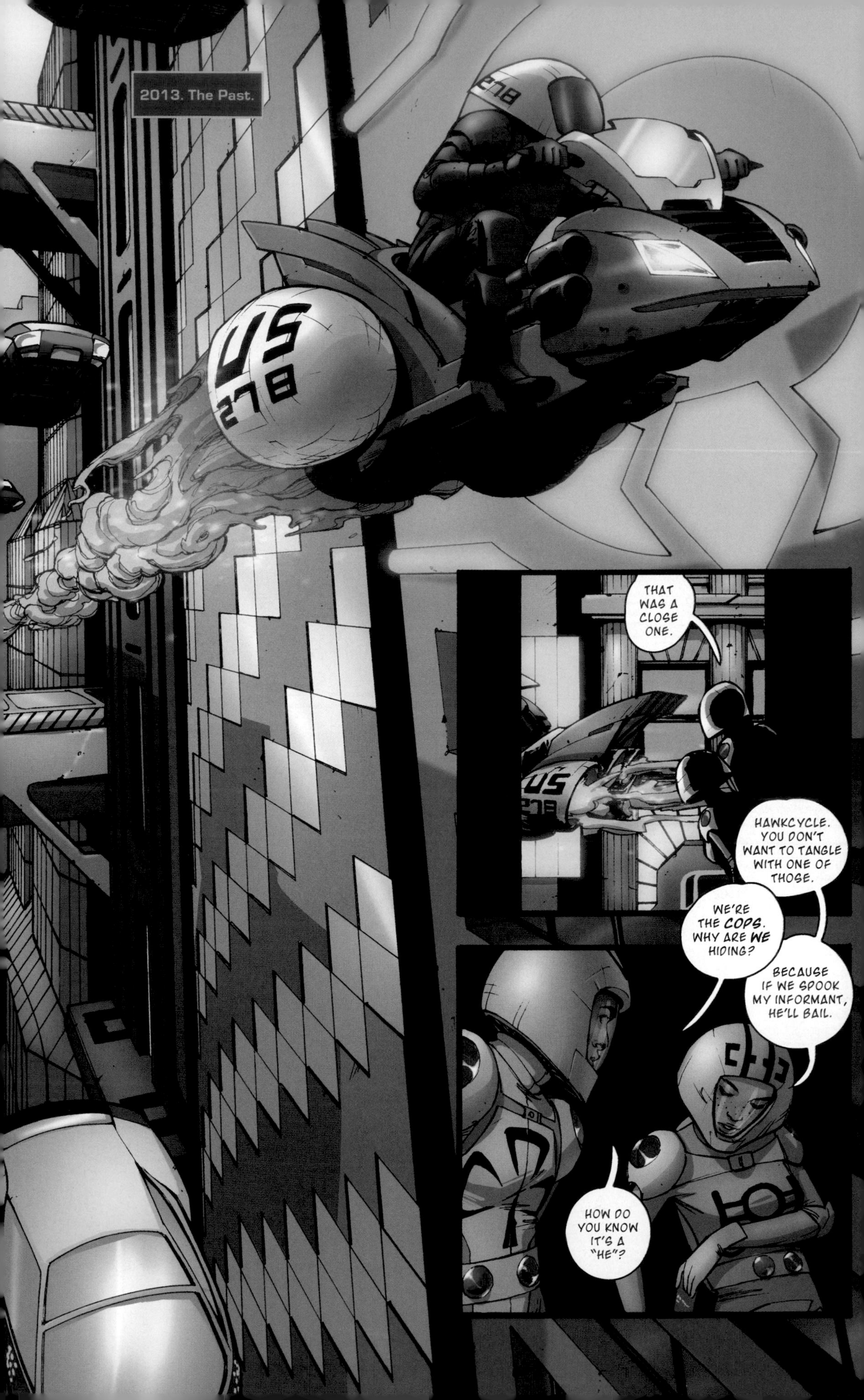
2013. The Past.
THAT WAS A CLOSE ONE.
HAWKCYCLE. YOU DON'T WANT TO TANGLE WITH ONE OF THOSE.
WE'RE THE COPS. WHY ARE WE HIDING?
BECAUSE IF WE SPOOK MY INFORMANT, HE'LL BAIL.
HOW DO YOU KNOW IT'S A "HE"?

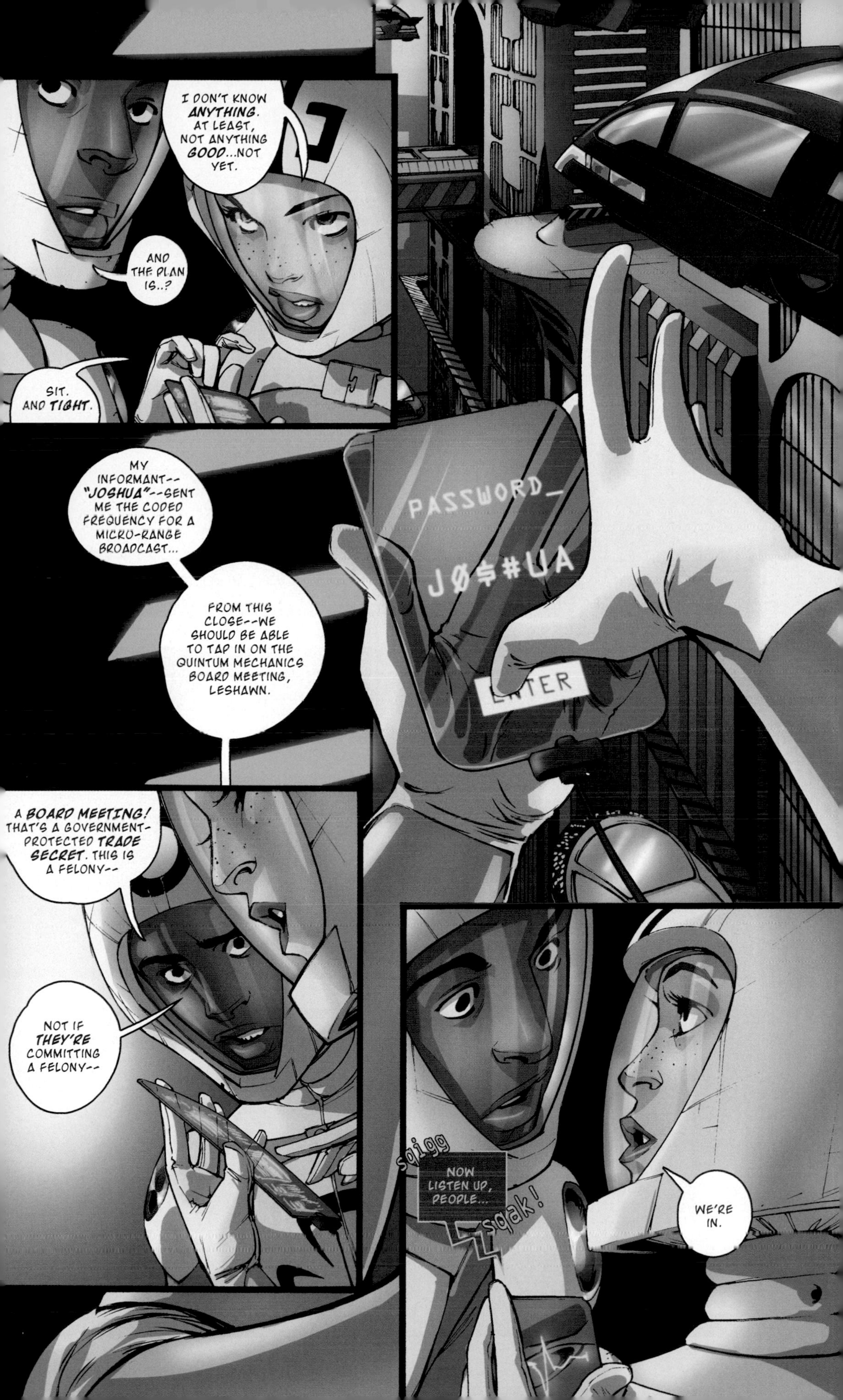
I DON'T KNOW ANYTHING. AT LEAST, NOT ANYTHING GOOD...NOT YET.
AND THE PLAN IS..?
SIT. AND TIGHT.
MY INFORMANT--"JOSHUA"--SENT ME THE CODED FREQUENCY FOR A MICRO-RANGE BROADCAST...
FROM THIS CLOSE--WE SHOULD BE ABLE TO TAP IN ON THE QUINTUM MECHANICS BOARD MEETING, LESHAWN.
PASSWORD_
J0$#UA
ENTER
A BOARD MEETING! THAT'S A GOVERNMENT-PROTECTED TRADE SECRET. THIS IS A FELONY--
NOT IF THEY'RE COMMITTING A FELONY--
sqigg
NOW LISTEN UP, PEOPLE...
sqak!
WE'RE IN.

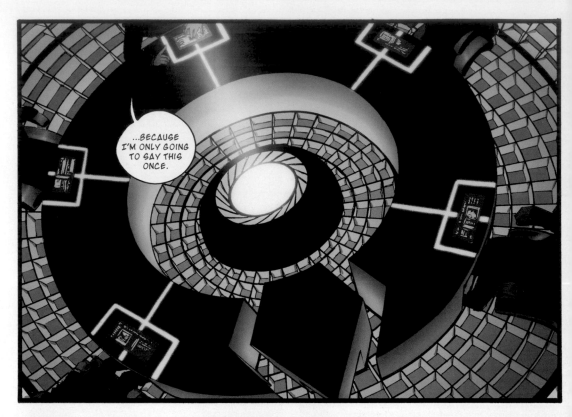

...BECAUSE I'M ONLY GOING TO SAY THIS ONCE.

WE DID IT.

IT TOOK US *TWENTY-SEVEN* YEARS, BUT THE CORPORATION HAS REVERSE-ENGINEERED THE Q-ENGINE.

IT'S ABOUT TIME--

YOU CAN SAY *THAT* AGAIN!

WE *THINK* IT WORKS...AS YOU KNOW, STARTING WITH A PARTIAL UNDERSTANDING OF THE MECHANICS SINCE 1986, WE'VE BUILT OUR ENTIRE COMPANY INVENTORY.

NOW WE'RE TALKING FULL INTEGRATION-- INCLUDING THE *TIME/SPACE* MANIPULATED DISPLACEMENT WE PREVIOUSLY THEORIZED.

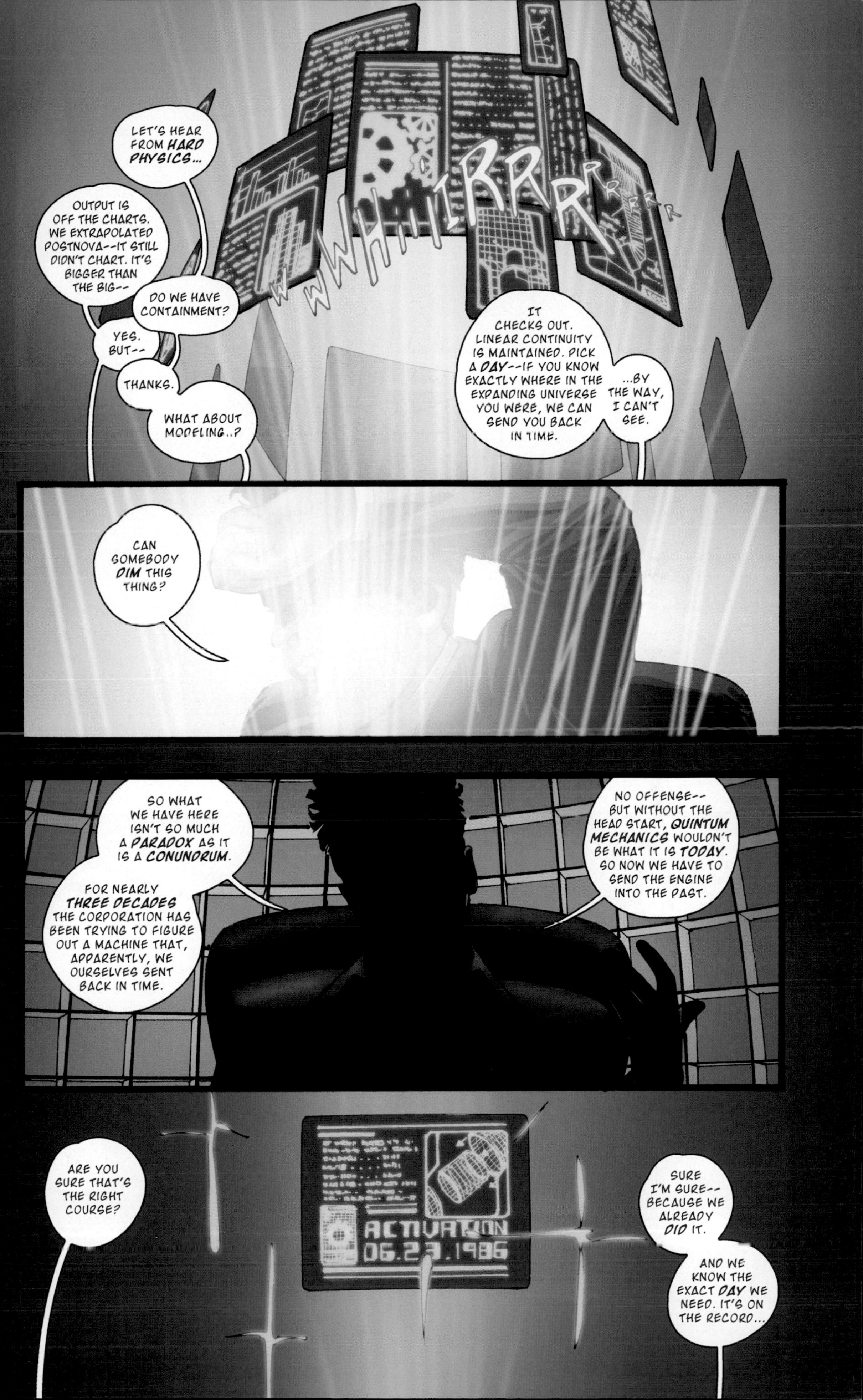
LET'S HEAR FROM HARD PHYSICS...
OUTPUT IS OFF THE CHARTS. WE EXTRAPOLATED POSTNOVA--IT STILL DIDN'T CHART. IT'S BIGGER THAN THE BIG--
DO WE HAVE CONTAINMENT?
YES. BUT--
THANKS.
WHAT ABOUT MODELING..?
WWWHIIIRRRrrrr
IT CHECKS OUT. LINEAR CONTINUITY IS MAINTAINED. PICK A DAY--IF YOU KNOW EXACTLY WHERE IN THE EXPANDING UNIVERSE YOU WERE, WE CAN SEND YOU BACK IN TIME.
...BY THE WAY, I CAN'T SEE.
CAN SOMEBODY DIM THIS THING?
SO WHAT WE HAVE HERE ISN'T SO MUCH A PARADOX AS IT IS A CONUNDRUM.
FOR NEARLY THREE DECADES THE CORPORATION HAS BEEN TRYING TO FIGURE OUT A MACHINE THAT, APPARENTLY, WE OURSELVES SENT BACK IN TIME.
NO OFFENSE--BUT WITHOUT THE HEAD START, QUINTUM MECHANICS WOULDN'T BE WHAT IT IS TODAY. SO NOW WE HAVE TO SEND THE ENGINE INTO THE PAST.
ARE YOU SURE THAT'S THE RIGHT COURSE?
ACTIVATION 06.23.1986
SURE I'M SURE--BECAUSE WE ALREADY DID IT.
AND WE KNOW THE EXACT DAY WE NEED. IT'S ON THE RECORD...

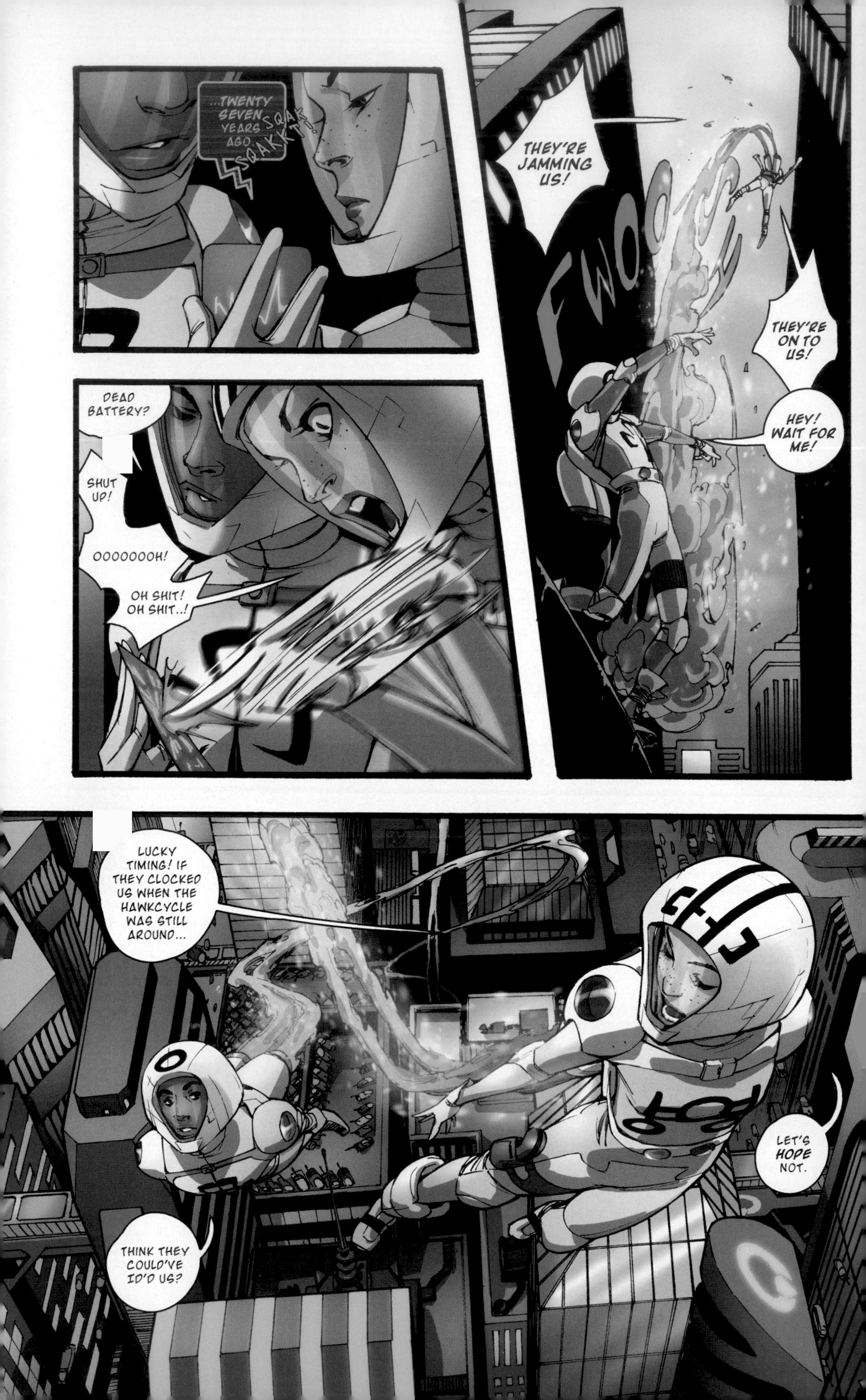
...TWENTY SEVEN YEARS AGO.
SQAK-
SQAKKT-
DEAD BATTERY?
SHUT UP!
OOOOOOOH!
OH SHIT! OH SHIT...!
THEY'RE JAMMING US!
FWOOSH
THEY'RE ON TO US!
HEY! WAIT FOR ME!
LUCKY TIMING! IF THEY CLOCKED US WHEN THE HAWKCYCLE WAS STILL AROUND...
LET'S HOPE NOT.
THINK THEY COULD'VE ID'D US?

POLICE PLAZA 2.0

WHAT ARE WE GOING TO DO?

"...WE"?

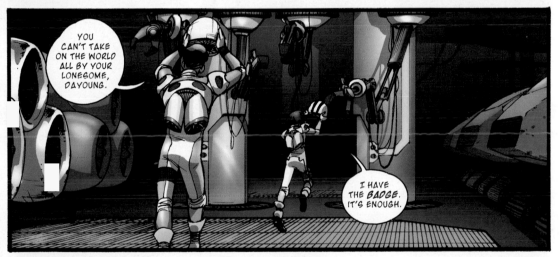

YOU CAN'T TAKE ON THE WORLD ALL BY YOUR LONESOME, DAYOUNG.

I HAVE THE *BADGE*. IT'S ENOUGH.

I HAVE COMMISSIONER GOMEZ'S GO-AHEAD. THERE'S NO ONE WHO CAN STOP ME FROM STOPPING THIS--

DAYOUNG... YOU'VE GOT TO *EASE UP*.

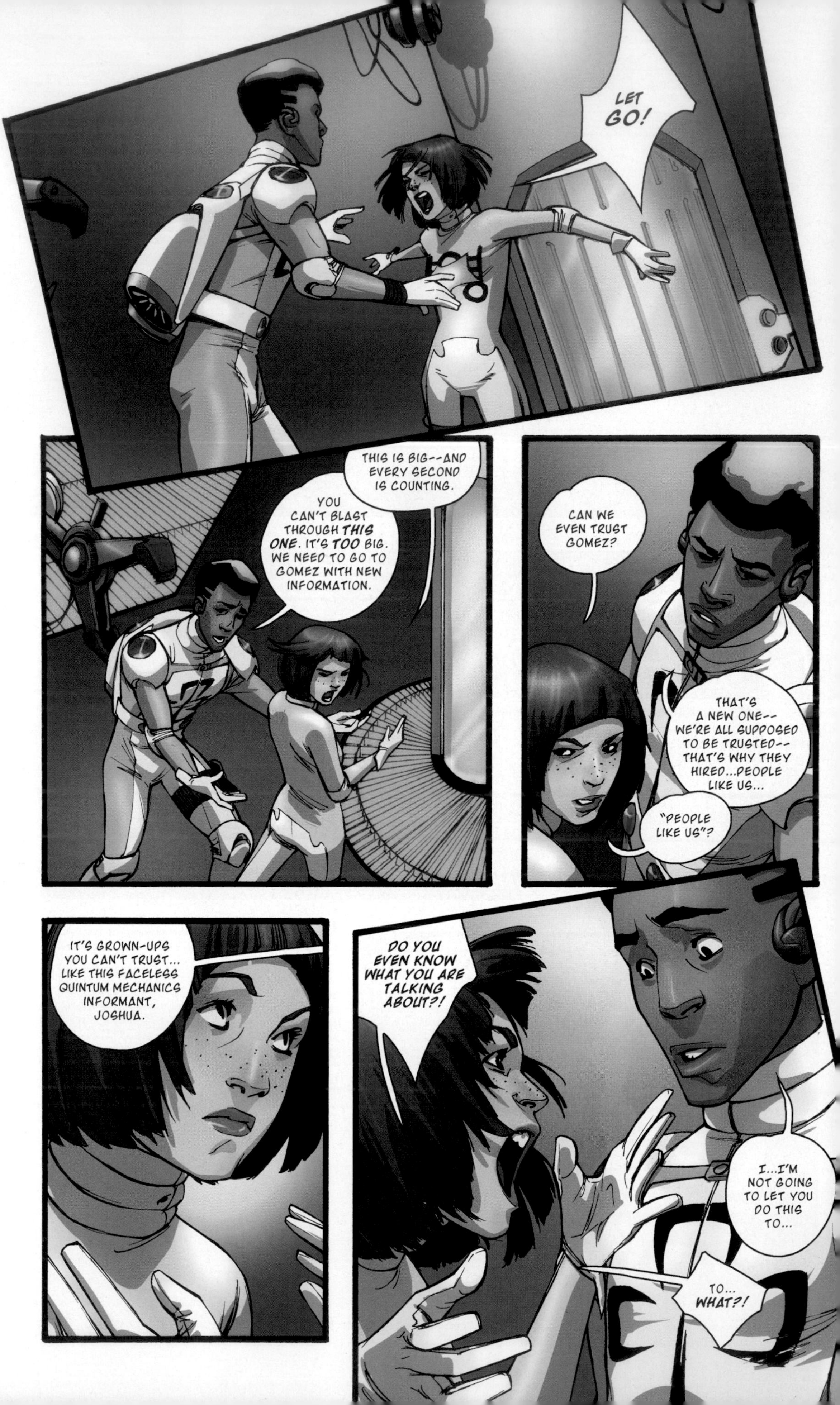
LET GO!
THIS IS BIG--AND EVERY SECOND IS COUNTING.
YOU CAN'T BLAST THROUGH THIS ONE. IT'S TOO BIG. WE NEED TO GO TO GOMEZ WITH NEW INFORMATION.
CAN WE EVEN TRUST GOMEZ?
THAT'S A NEW ONE--WE'RE ALL SUPPOSED TO BE TRUSTED--THAT'S WHY THEY HIRED...PEOPLE LIKE US...
"PEOPLE LIKE US"?
IT'S GROWN-UPS YOU CAN'T TRUST... LIKE THIS FACELESS QUINTUM MECHANICS INFORMANT, JOSHUA.
DO YOU EVEN KNOW WHAT YOU ARE TALKING ABOUT?!
I...I'M NOT GOING TO LET YOU DO THIS TO...
TO... WHAT?!

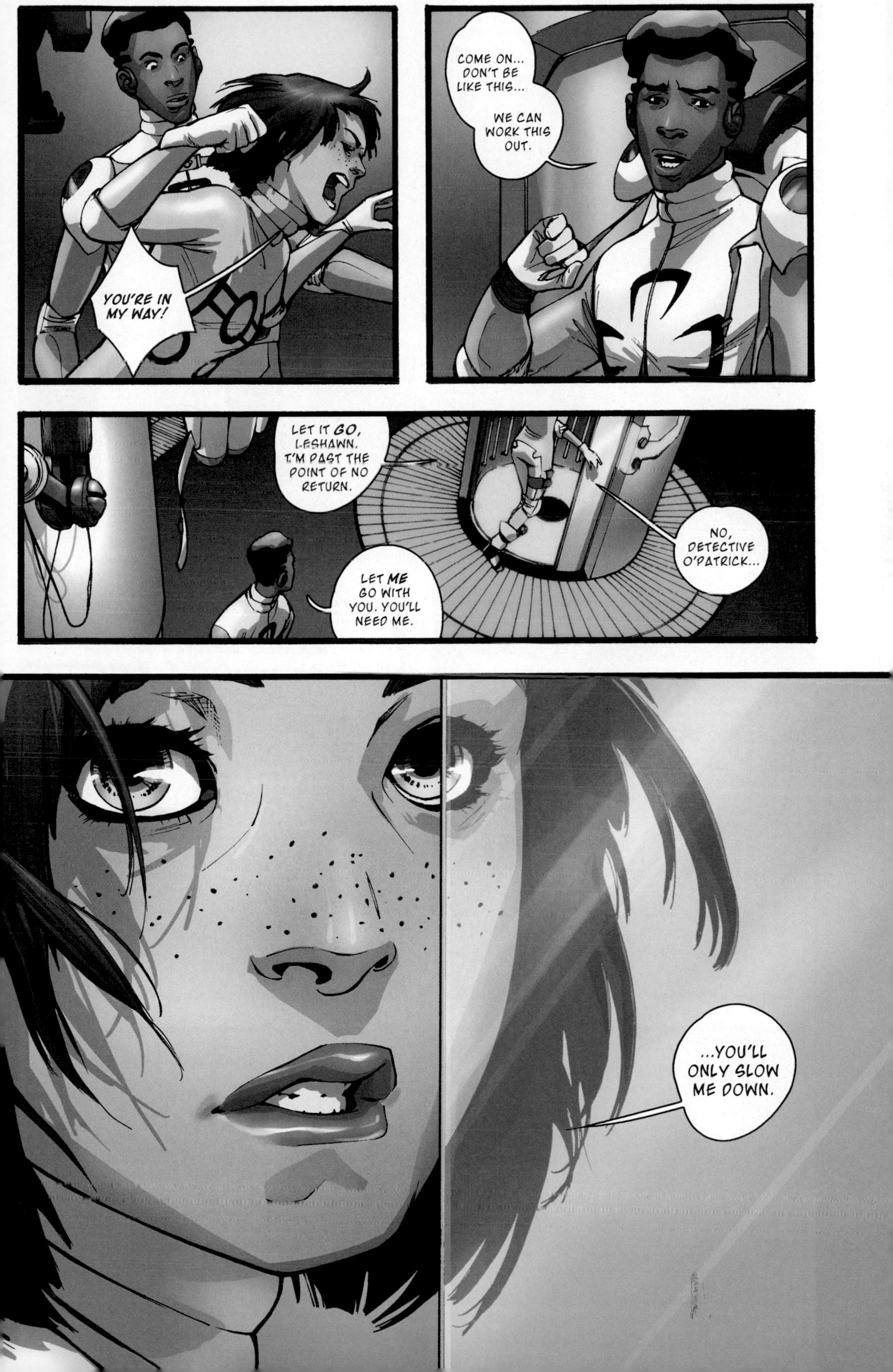
YOU'RE IN MY WAY!
COME ON... DON'T BE LIKE THIS...
WE CAN WORK THIS OUT.
LET IT GO, LESHAWN. I'M PAST THE POINT OF NO RETURN.
LET ME GO WITH YOU. YOU'LL NEED ME.
NO, DETECTIVE O'PATRICK...
...YOU'LL ONLY SLOW ME DOWN.

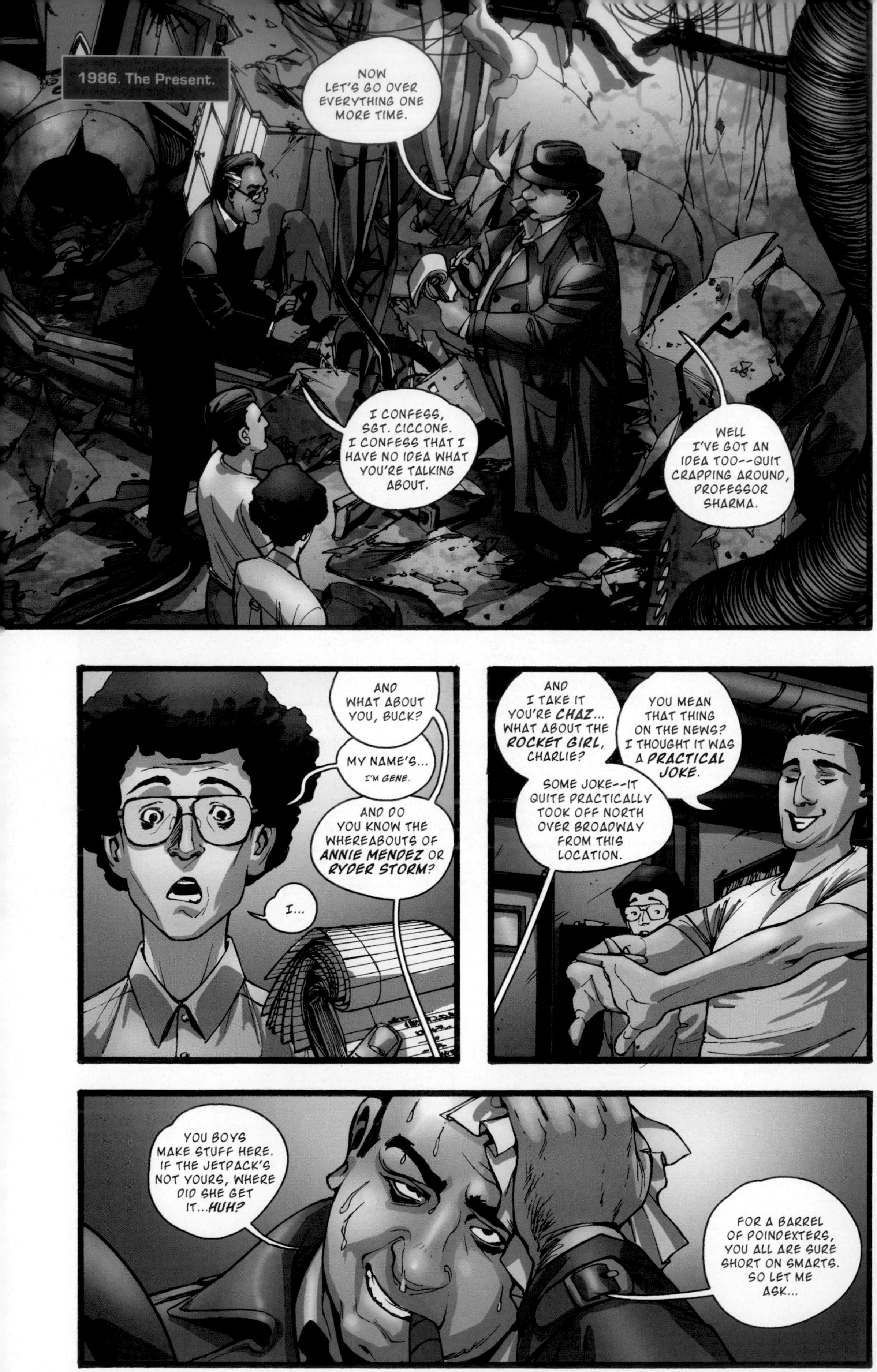
1986. The Present.
NOW LET'S GO OVER EVERYTHING ONE MORE TIME.
I CONFESS, SGT. CICCONE. I CONFESS THAT I HAVE NO IDEA WHAT YOU'RE TALKING ABOUT.
WELL I'VE GOT AN IDEA TOO--QUIT CRAPPING AROUND, PROFESSOR SHARMA.
AND WHAT ABOUT YOU, BUCK?
MY NAME'S... I'M GENE.
AND DO YOU KNOW THE WHEREABOUTS OF ANNIE MENDEZ OR RYDER STORM?
I...
AND I TAKE IT YOU'RE CHAZ... WHAT ABOUT THE ROCKET GIRL, CHARLIE?
YOU MEAN THAT THING ON THE NEWS? I THOUGHT IT WAS A PRACTICAL JOKE.
SOME JOKE--IT QUITE PRACTICALLY TOOK OFF NORTH OVER BROADWAY FROM THIS LOCATION.
YOU BOYS MAKE STUFF HERE. IF THE JETPACK'S NOT YOURS, WHERE DID SHE GET IT...HUH?
FOR A BARREL OF POINDEXTERS, YOU ALL ARE SURE SHORT ON SMARTS. SO LET ME ASK...

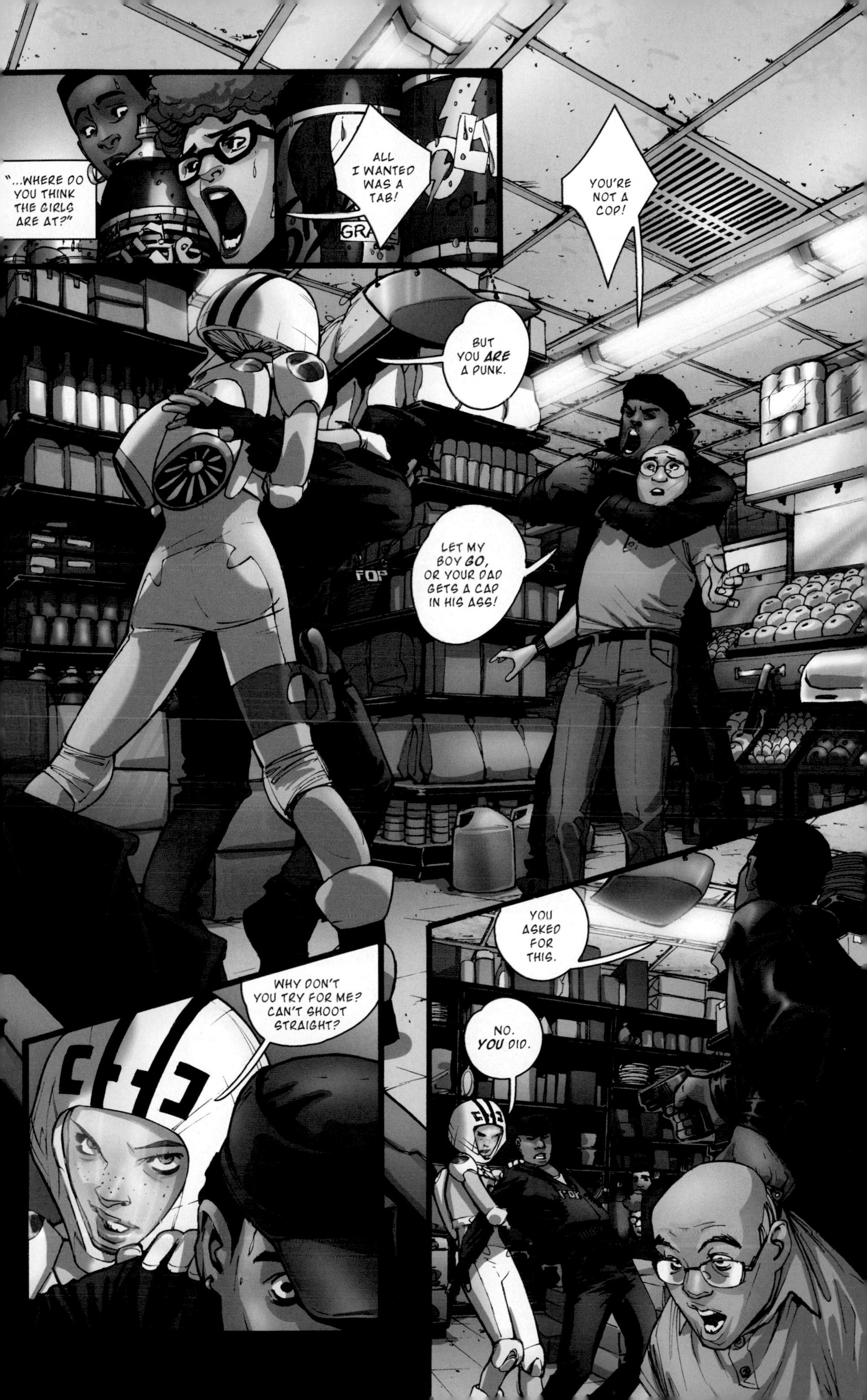
"...WHERE DO YOU THINK THE GIRLS ARE AT?"
ALL I WANTED WAS A TAB!
YOU'RE NOT A COP!
BUT YOU ARE A PUNK.
LET MY BOY GO, OR YOUR DAD GETS A CAP IN HIS ASS!
YOU ASKED FOR THIS.
WHY DON'T YOU TRY FOR ME? CAN'T SHOOT STRAIGHT?
NO. YOU DID.

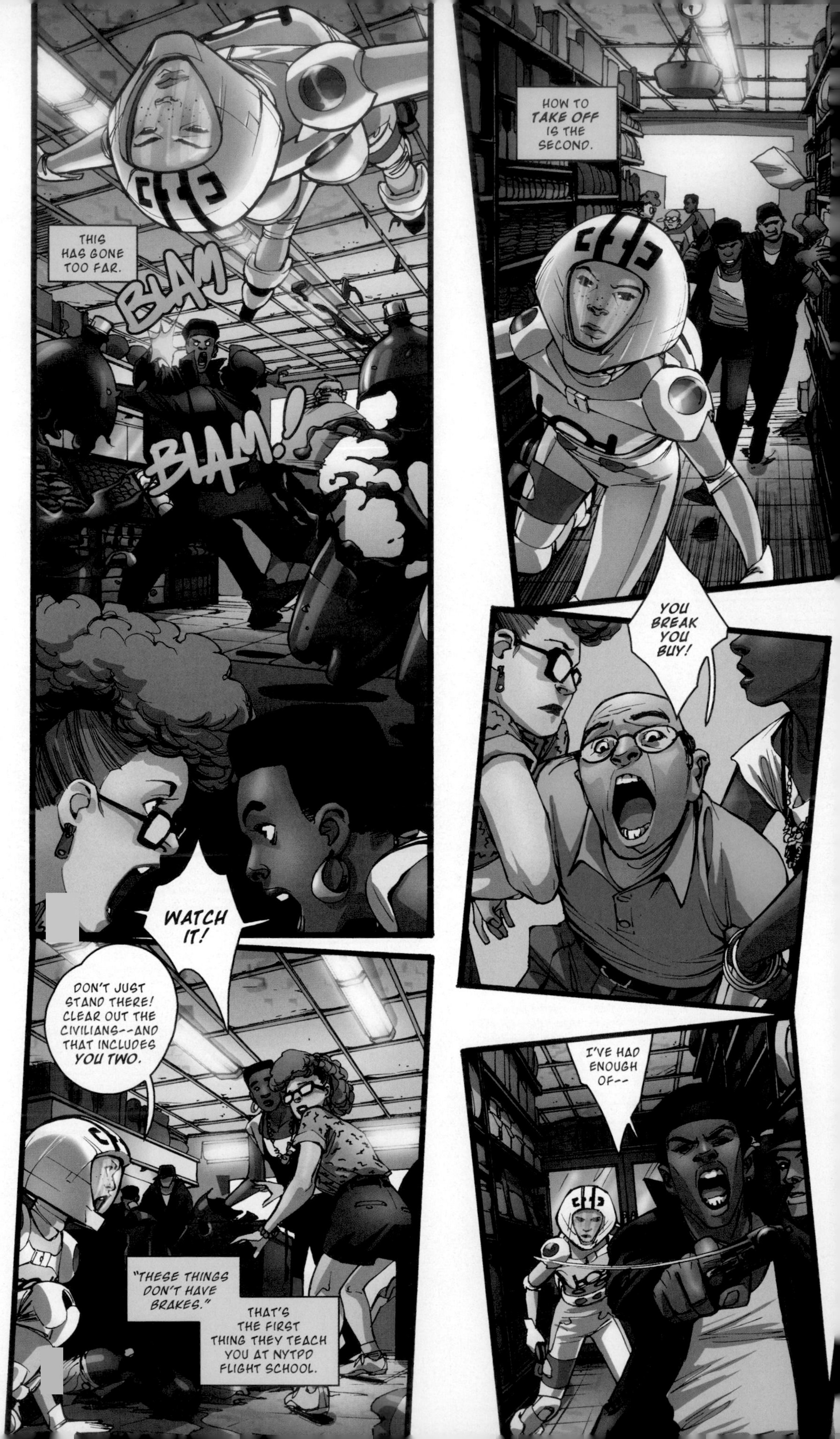
THIS HAS GONE TOO FAR.
BLAM
BLAM!!
WATCH IT!
DON'T JUST STAND THERE! CLEAR OUT THE CIVILIANS--AND THAT INCLUDES YOU TWO.
"THESE THINGS DON'T HAVE BRAKES."
THAT'S THE FIRST THING THEY TEACH YOU AT NYTPD FLIGHT SCHOOL.
HOW TO TAKE OFF IS THE SECOND.
YOU BREAK YOU BUY!
I'VE HAD ENOUGH OF--

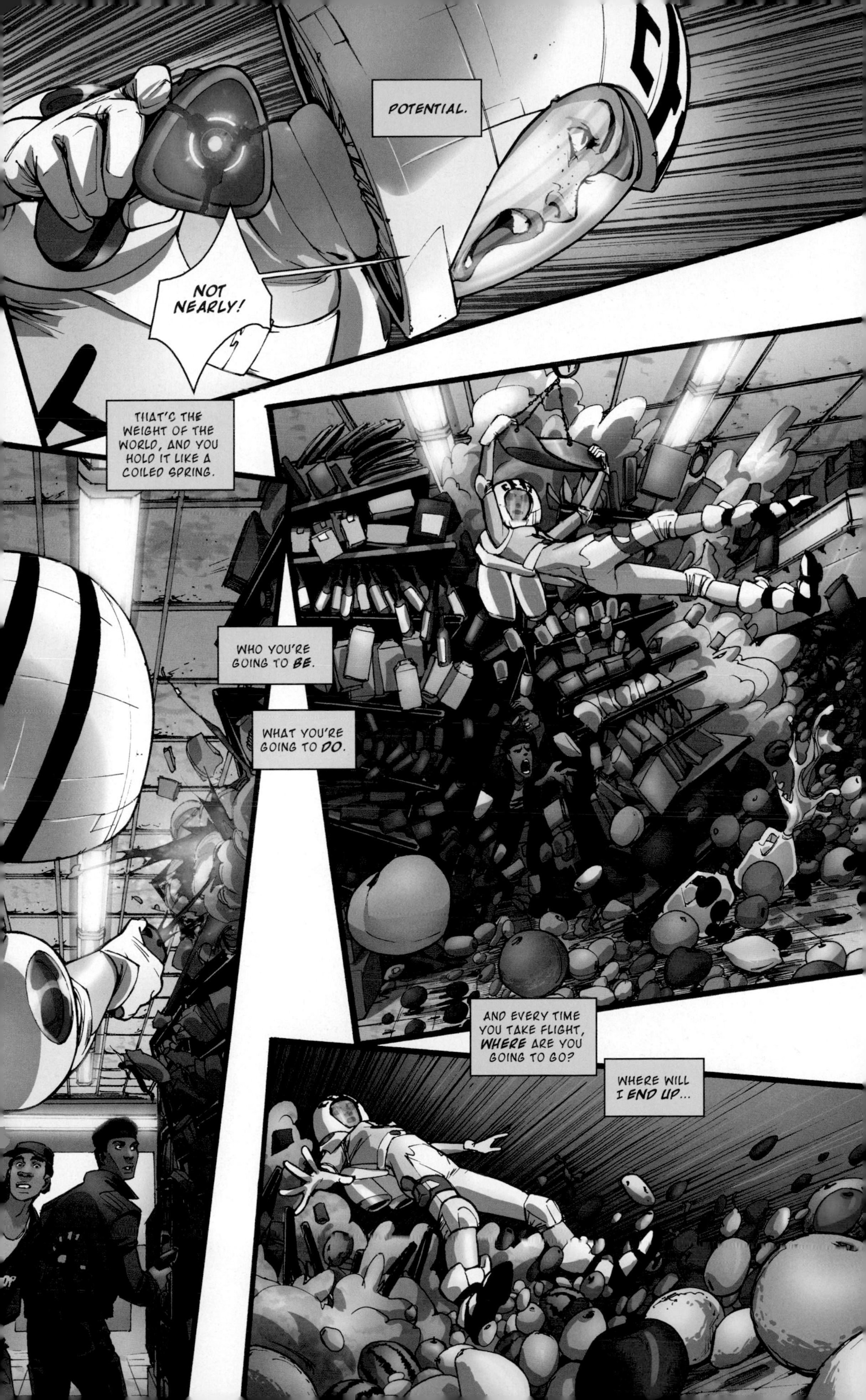
POTENTIAL.
NOT NEARLY!
THAT'S THE WEIGHT OF THE WORLD, AND YOU HOLD IT LIKE A COILED SPRING.
WHO YOU'RE GOING TO BE.
WHAT YOU'RE GOING TO DO.
AND EVERY TIME YOU TAKE FLIGHT, WHERE ARE YOU GOING TO GO?
WHERE WILL I END UP...

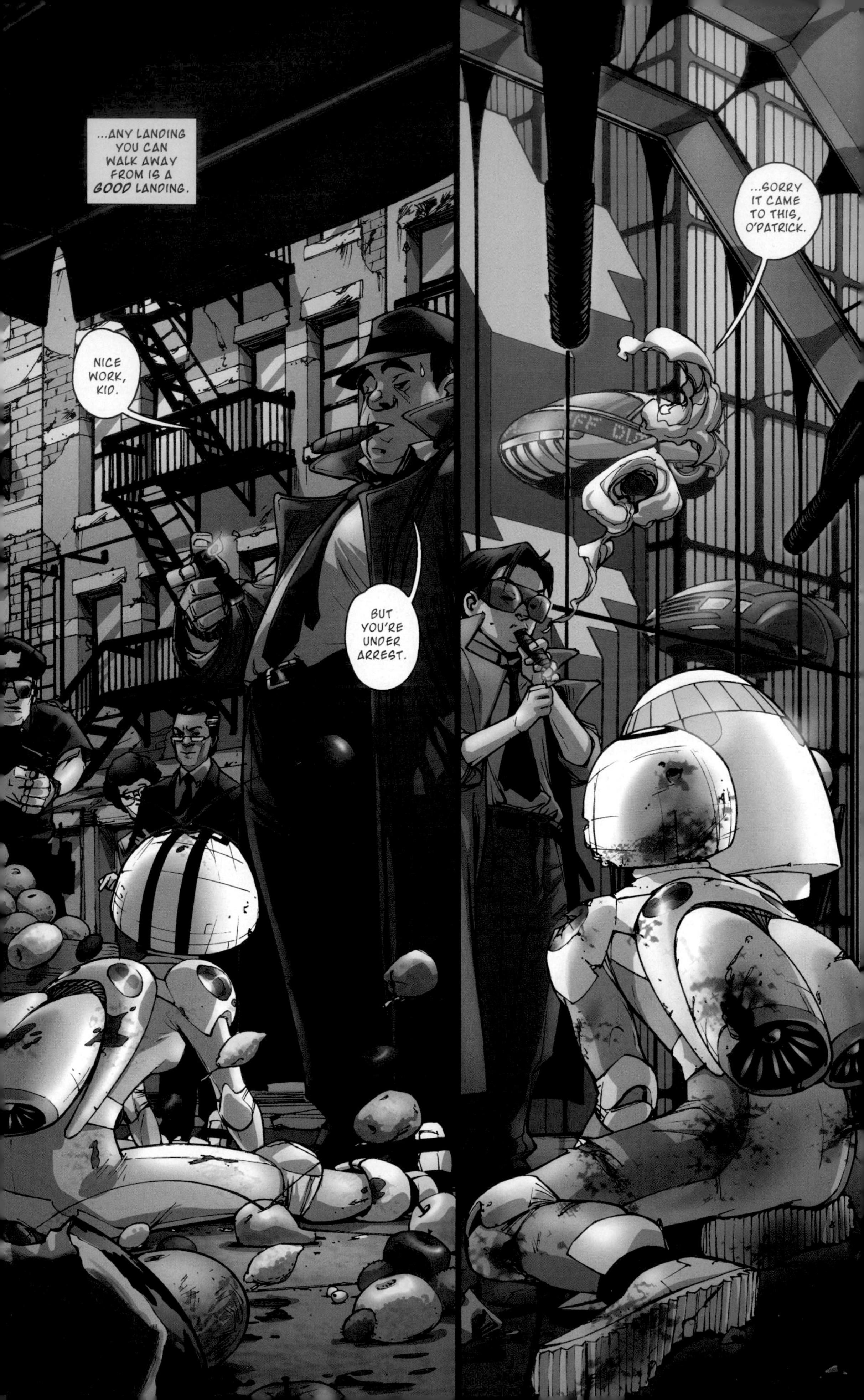
...ANY LANDING YOU CAN WALK AWAY FROM IS A GOOD LANDING.
NICE WORK, KID.
BUT YOU'RE UNDER ARREST.
...SORRY IT CAME TO THIS, O'PATRICK.

Chapter 3_Double Reagent >>

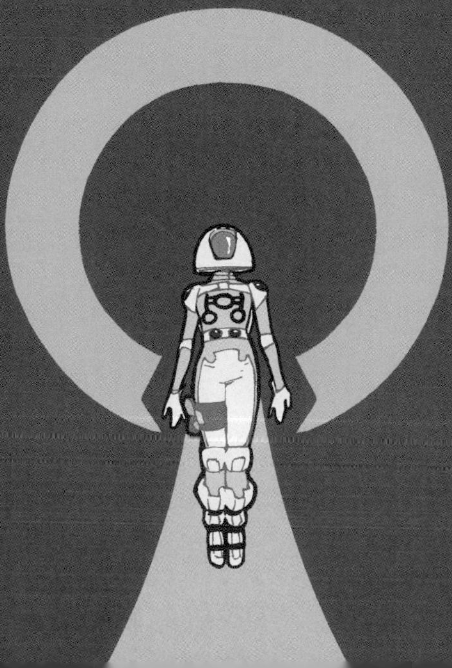

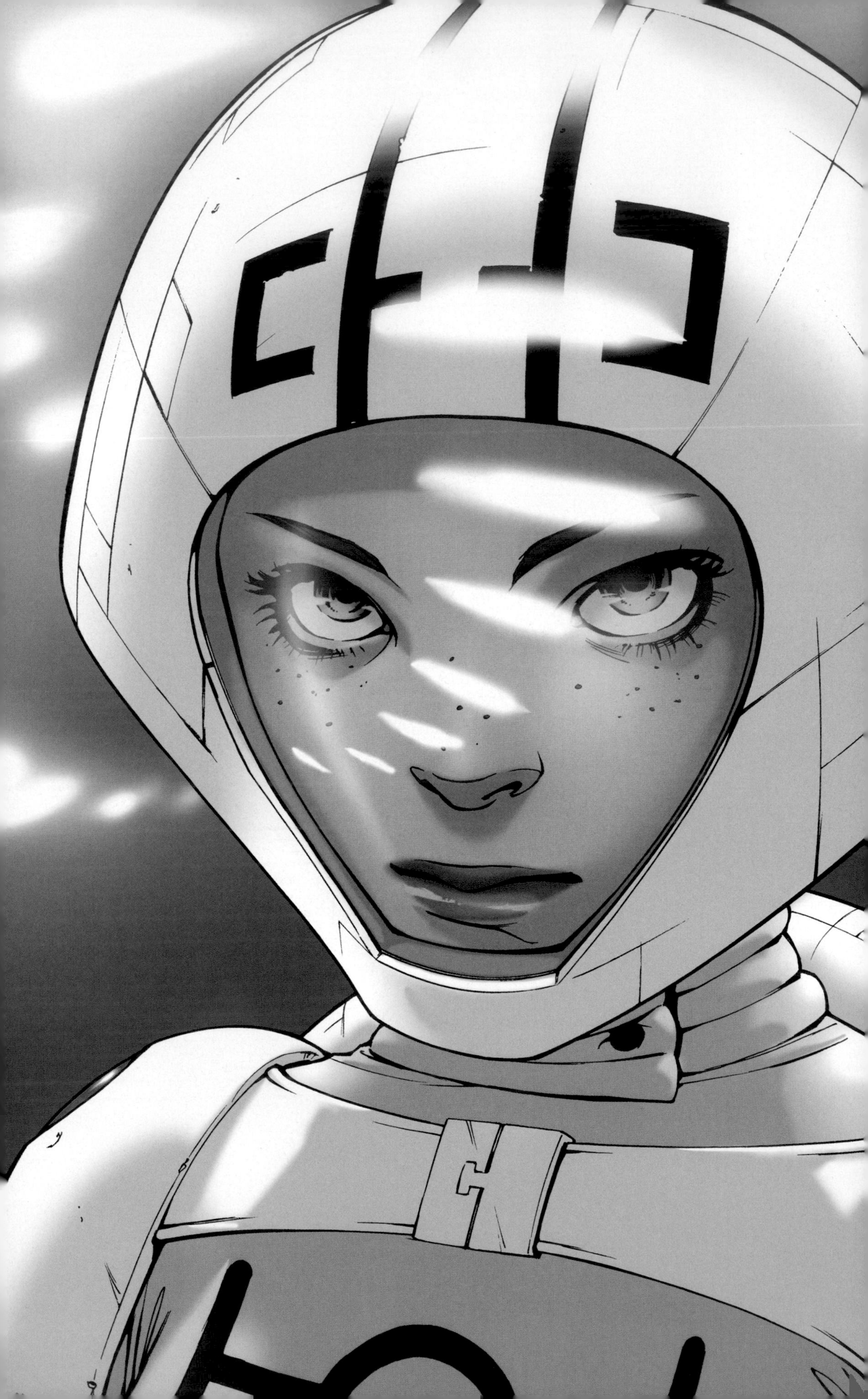

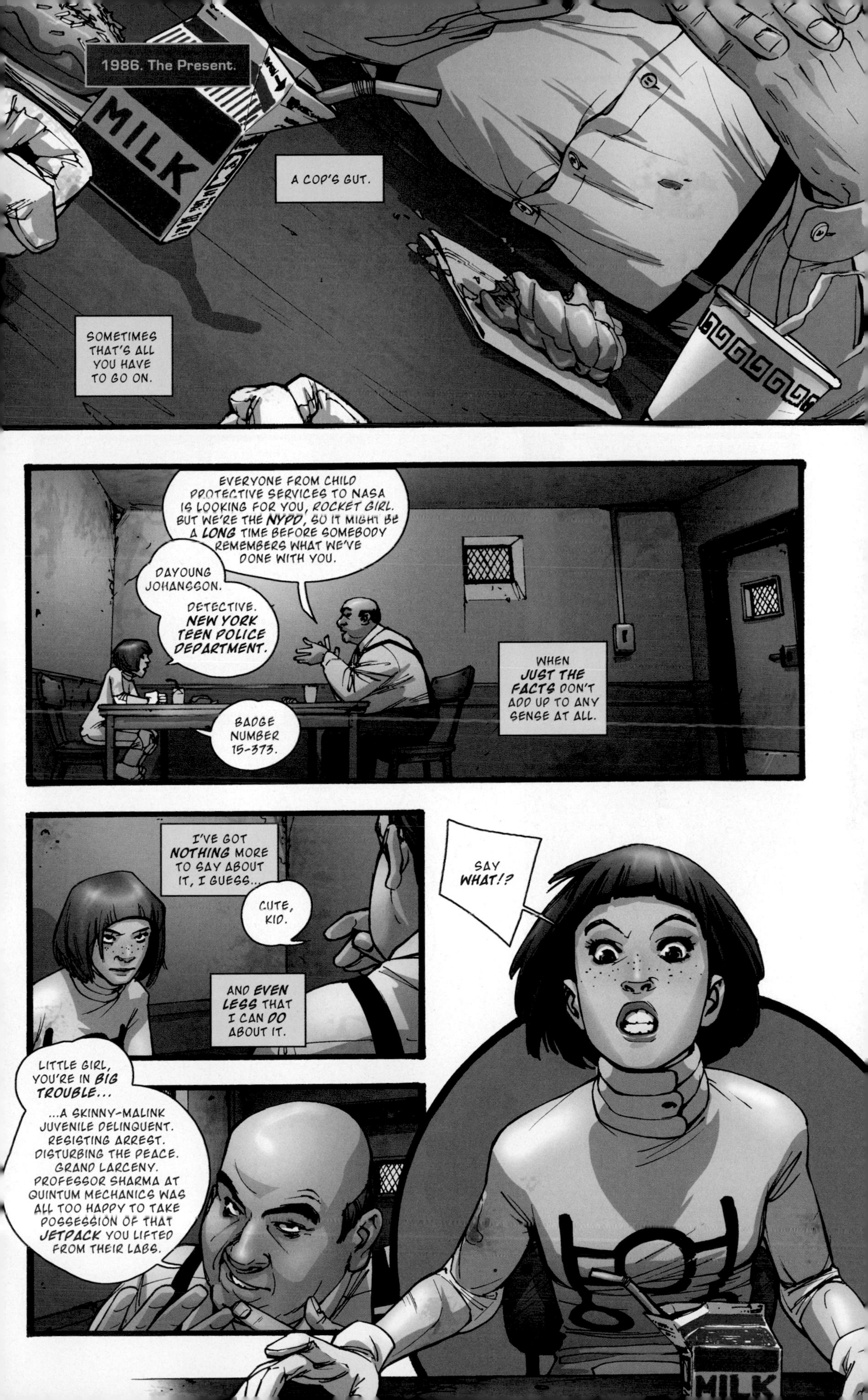

1986. The Present.
MILK
A COP'S GUT.
SOMETIMES THAT'S ALL YOU HAVE TO GO ON.
EVERYONE FROM CHILD PROTECTIVE SERVICES TO NASA IS LOOKING FOR YOU, ROCKET GIRL. BUT WE'RE THE NYPD, SO IT MIGHT BE A LONG TIME BEFORE SOMEBODY REMEMBERS WHAT WE'VE DONE WITH YOU.
DAYOUNG JOHANSSON.
DETECTIVE. NEW YORK TEEN POLICE DEPARTMENT.
BADGE NUMBER 15-373.
WHEN JUST THE FACTS DON'T ADD UP TO ANY SENSE AT ALL.
I'VE GOT NOTHING MORE TO SAY ABOUT IT, I GUESS...
CUTE, KID.
AND EVEN LESS THAT I CAN DO ABOUT IT.
LITTLE GIRL, YOU'RE IN BIG TROUBLE...
...A SKINNY-MALINK JUVENILE DELINQUENT. RESISTING ARREST. DISTURBING THE PEACE. GRAND LARCENY. PROFESSOR SHARMA AT QUINTUM MECHANICS WAS ALL TOO HAPPY TO TAKE POSSESSION OF THAT JETPACK YOU LIFTED FROM THEIR LABS.
SAY WHAT!?
MILK

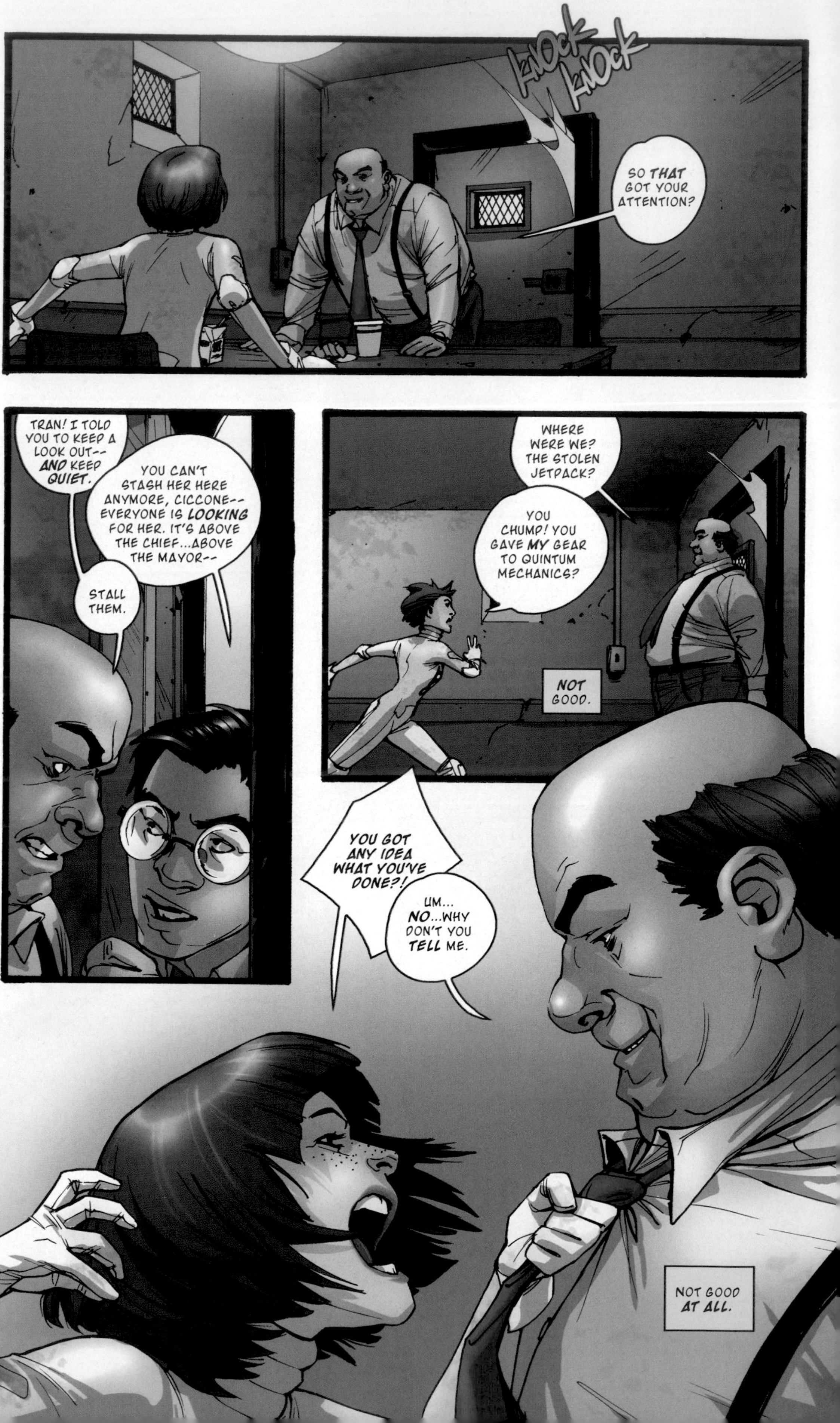
KNOCK KNOCK
SO THAT GOT YOUR ATTENTION?
TRAN! I TOLD YOU TO KEEP A LOOK OUT-- AND KEEP QUIET.
YOU CAN'T STASH HER HERE ANYMORE, CICCONE-- EVERYONE IS LOOKING FOR HER. IT'S ABOVE THE CHIEF...ABOVE THE MAYOR--
STALL THEM.
WHERE WERE WE? THE STOLEN JETPACK?
YOU CHUMP! YOU GAVE MY GEAR TO QUINTUM MECHANICS?
NOT GOOD.
YOU GOT ANY IDEA WHAT YOU'VE DONE?!
UM... NO...WHY DON'T YOU TELL ME.
NOT GOOD AT ALL.

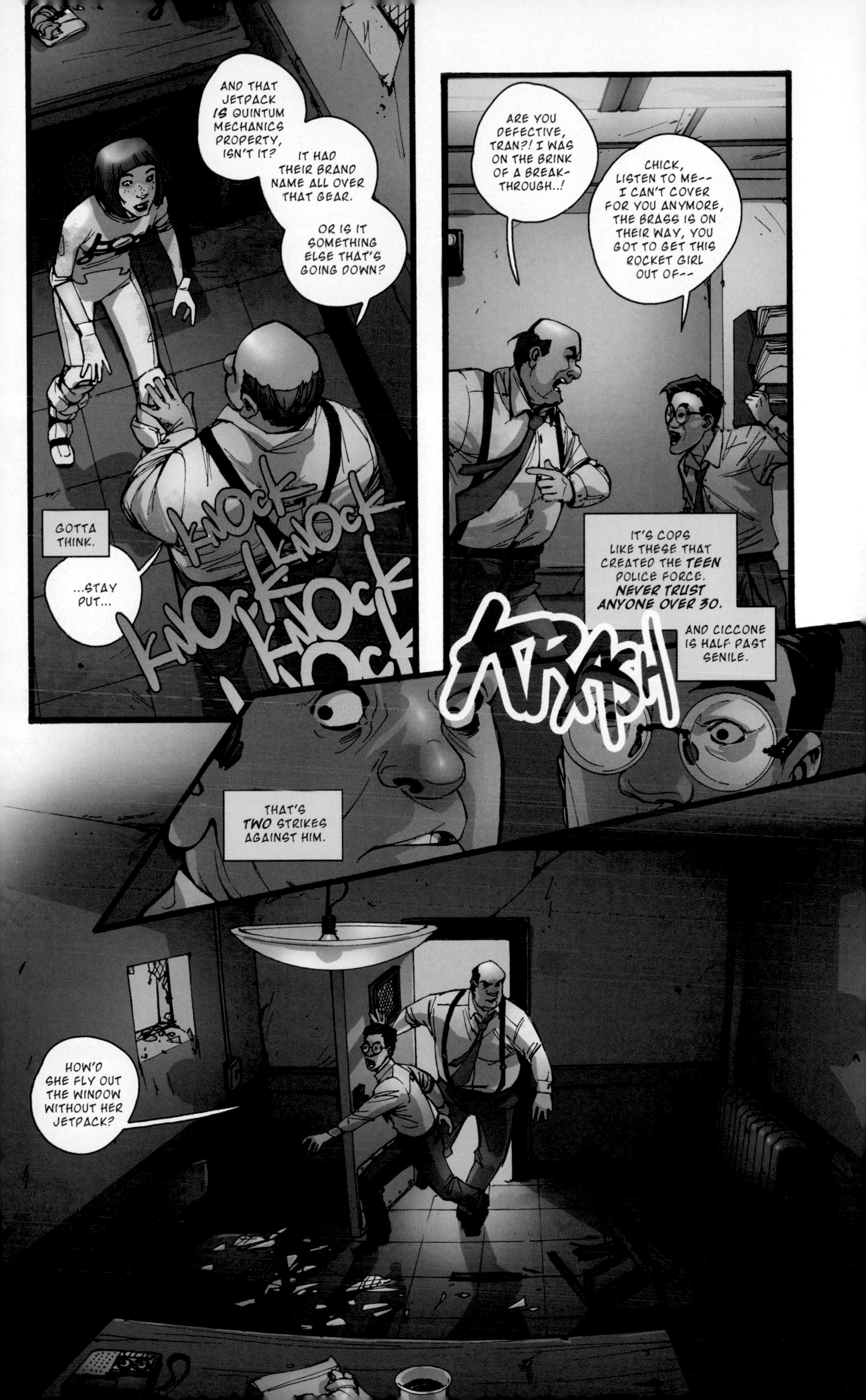
AND THAT JETPACK IS QUINTUM MECHANICS PROPERTY, ISN'T IT?
IT HAD THEIR BRAND NAME ALL OVER THAT GEAR.
OR IS IT SOMETHING ELSE THAT'S GOING DOWN?
GOTTA THINK.
...STAY PUT...
KNOCK KNOCK KNOCK KNOCK KNOCK
ARE YOU DEFECTIVE, TRAN?! I WAS ON THE BRINK OF A BREAK-THROUGH..!
CHICK, LISTEN TO ME-- I CAN'T COVER FOR YOU ANYMORE, THE BRASS IS ON THEIR WAY, YOU GOT TO GET THIS ROCKET GIRL OUT OF--
IT'S COPS LIKE THESE THAT CREATED THE TEEN POLICE FORCE. NEVER TRUST ANYONE OVER 30.
AND CICCONE IS HALF PAST SENILE.
KRASH
THAT'S TWO STRIKES AGAINST HIM.
HOW'D SHE FLY OUT THE WINDOW WITHOUT HER JETPACK?

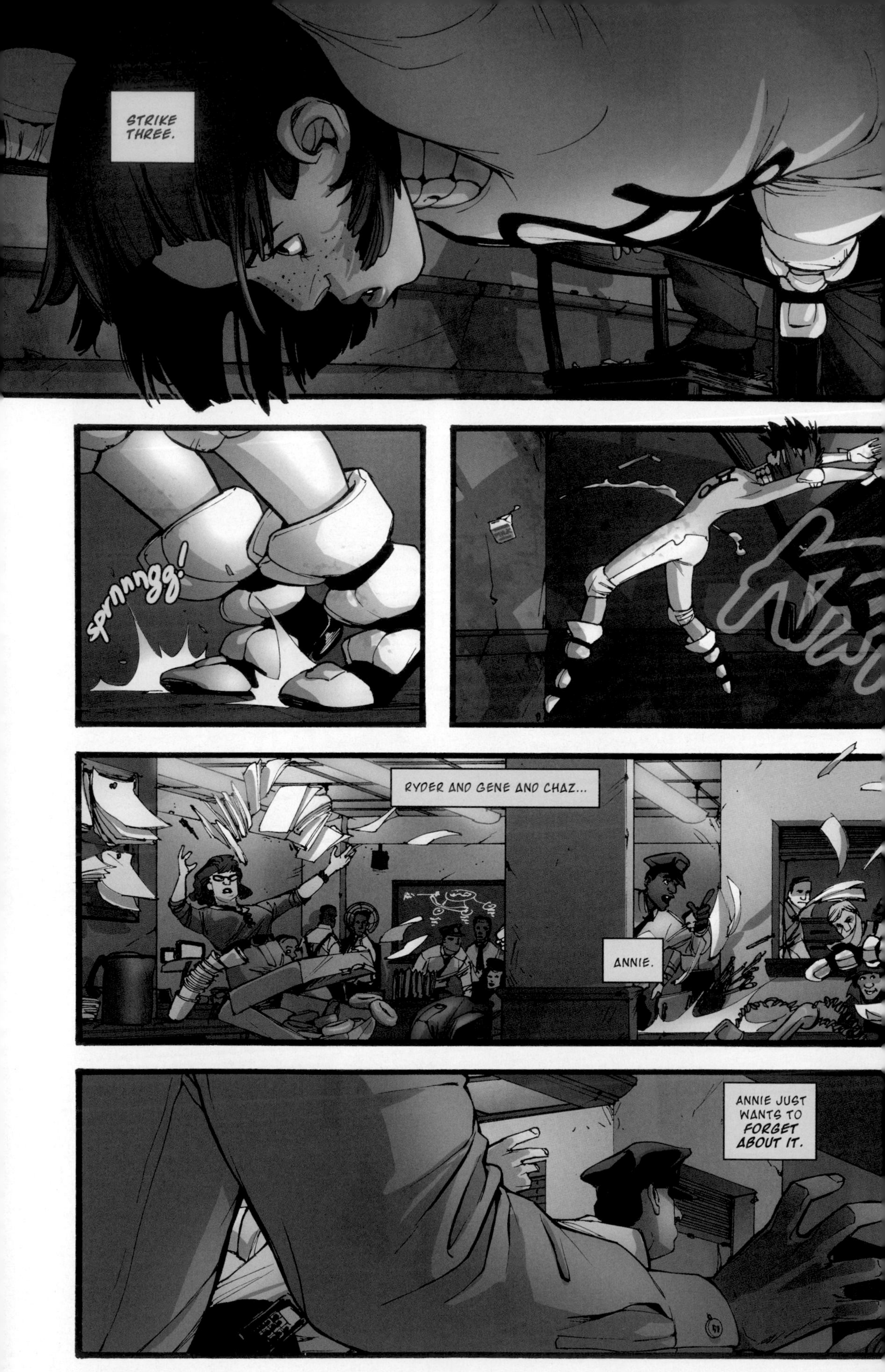

STRIKE THREE.
SPRNNNGG!
RYDER AND GENE AND CHAZ...
ANNIE.
ANNIE JUST WANTS TO FORGET ABOUT IT.

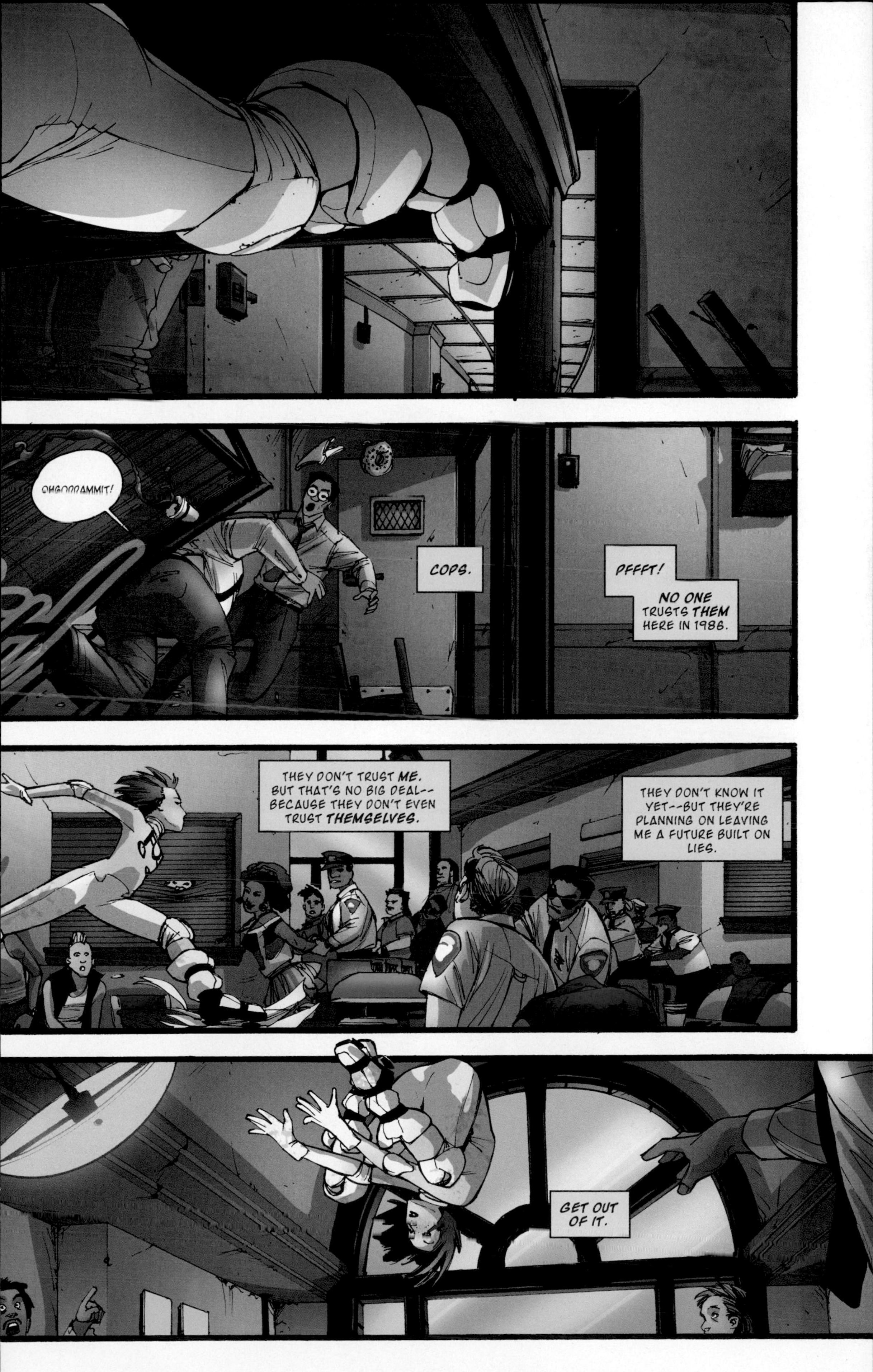
OHGODDAMMIT!
COPS.
PFFFT!
NO ONE TRUSTS THEM HERE IN 1986.
THEY DON'T TRUST ME. BUT THAT'S NO BIG DEAL--BECAUSE THEY DON'T EVEN TRUST THEMSELVES.
THEY DON'T KNOW IT YET--BUT THEY'RE PLANNING ON LEAVING ME A FUTURE BUILT ON LIES.
GET OUT OF IT.

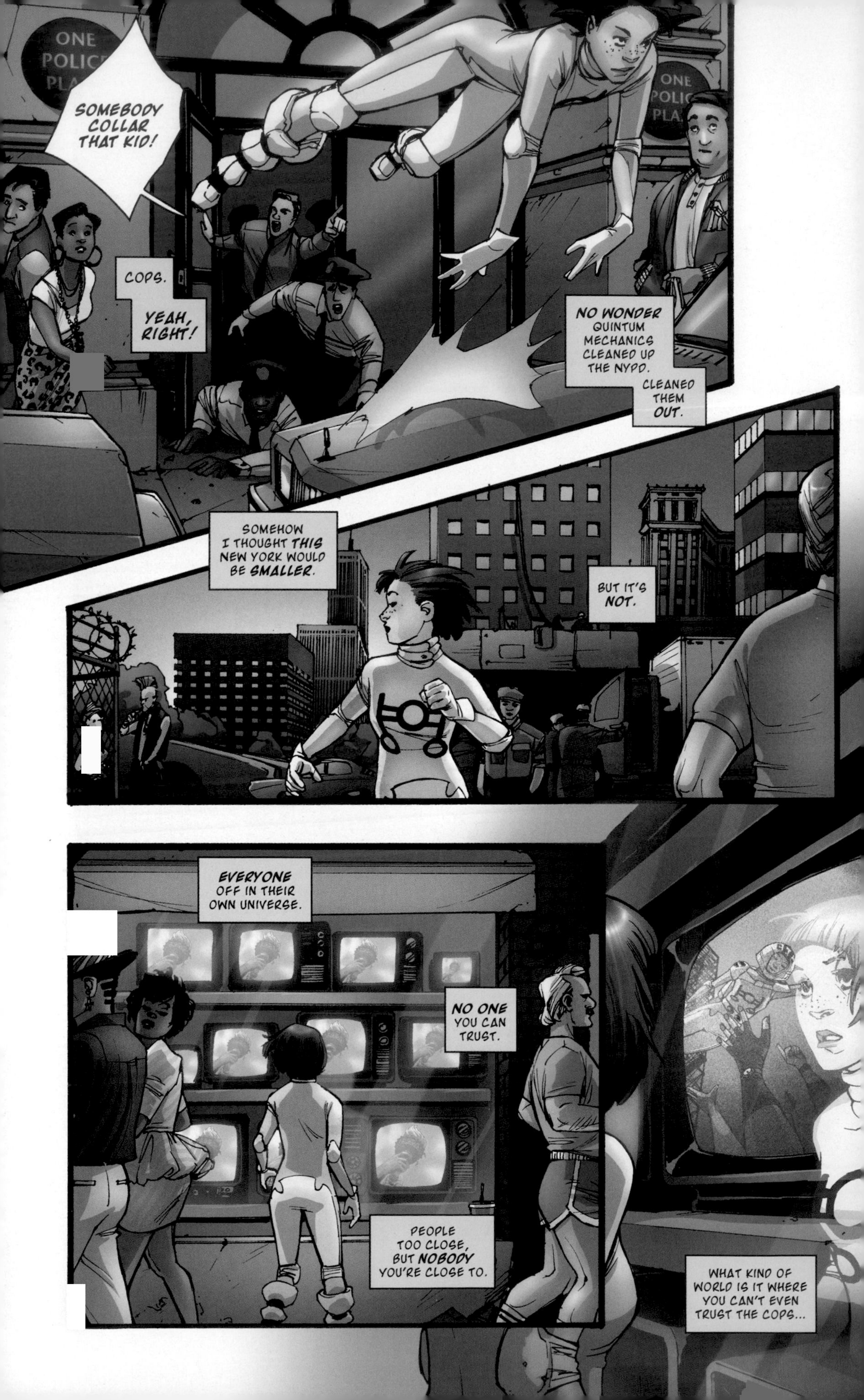
ONE POLICE PLAZA
SOMEBODY COLLAR THAT KID!
COPS.
YEAH, RIGHT!
NO WONDER QUINTUM MECHANICS CLEANED UP THE NYPD.
CLEANED THEM OUT.
SOMEHOW I THOUGHT THIS NEW YORK WOULD BE SMALLER.
BUT IT'S NOT.
EVERYONE OFF IN THEIR OWN UNIVERSE.
NO ONE YOU CAN TRUST.
PEOPLE TOO CLOSE, BUT NOBODY YOU'RE CLOSE TO.
WHAT KIND OF WORLD IS IT WHERE YOU CAN'T EVEN TRUST THE COPS...

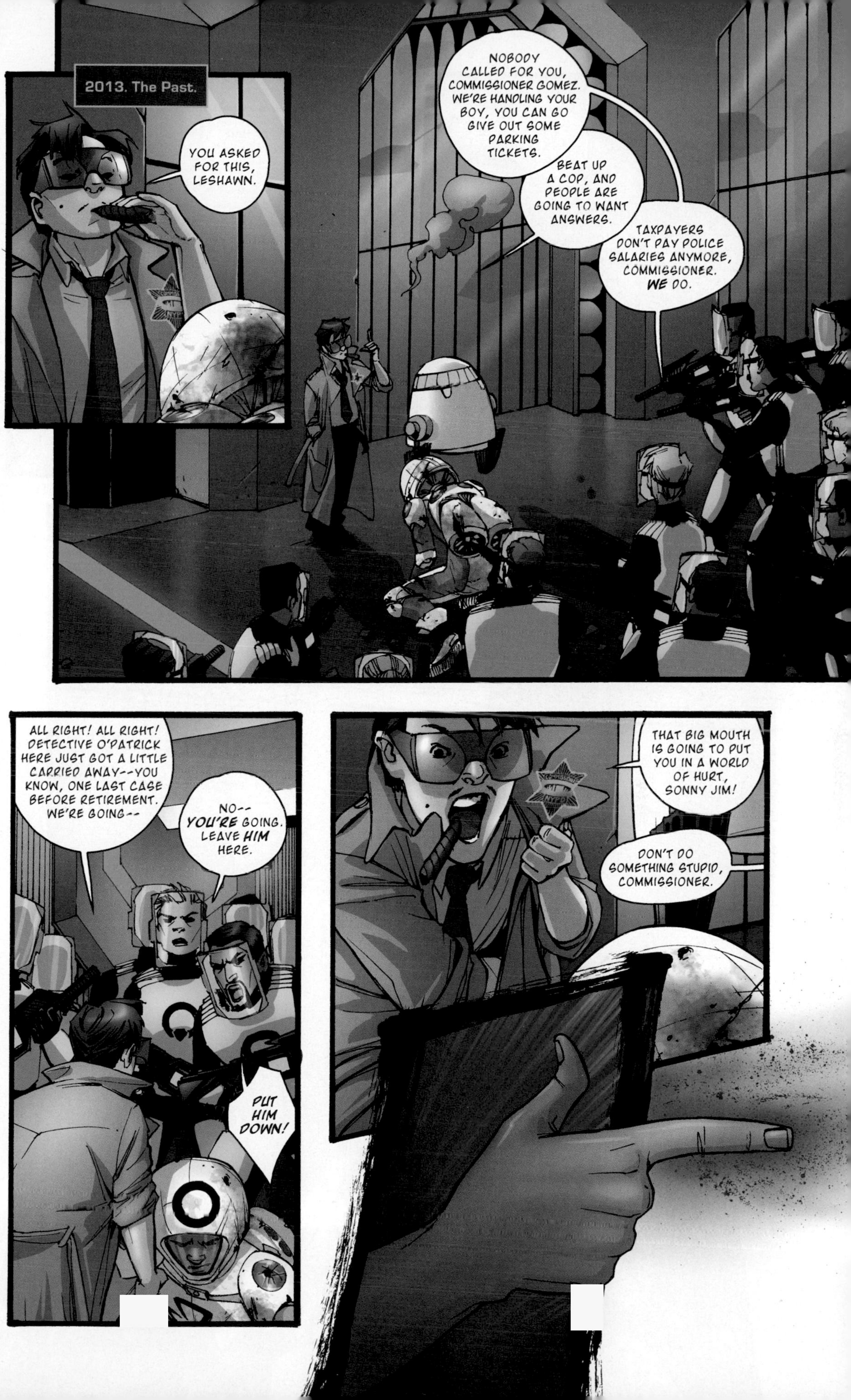
2013. The Past.
YOU ASKED FOR THIS, LESHAWN.
NOBODY CALLED FOR YOU, COMMISSIONER GOMEZ. WE'RE HANDLING YOUR BOY, YOU CAN GO GIVE OUT SOME PARKING TICKETS.
BEAT UP A COP, AND PEOPLE ARE GOING TO WANT ANSWERS.
TAXPAYERS DON'T PAY POLICE SALARIES ANYMORE, COMMISSIONER. WE DO.
ALL RIGHT! ALL RIGHT! DETECTIVE O'PATRICK HERE JUST GOT A LITTLE CARRIED AWAY--YOU KNOW, ONE LAST CASE BEFORE RETIREMENT. WE'RE GOING--
NO-- YOU'RE GOING. LEAVE HIM HERE.
PUT HIM DOWN!
THAT BIG MOUTH IS GOING TO PUT YOU IN A WORLD OF HURT, SONNY JIM!
DON'T DO SOMETHING STUPID, COMMISSIONER.

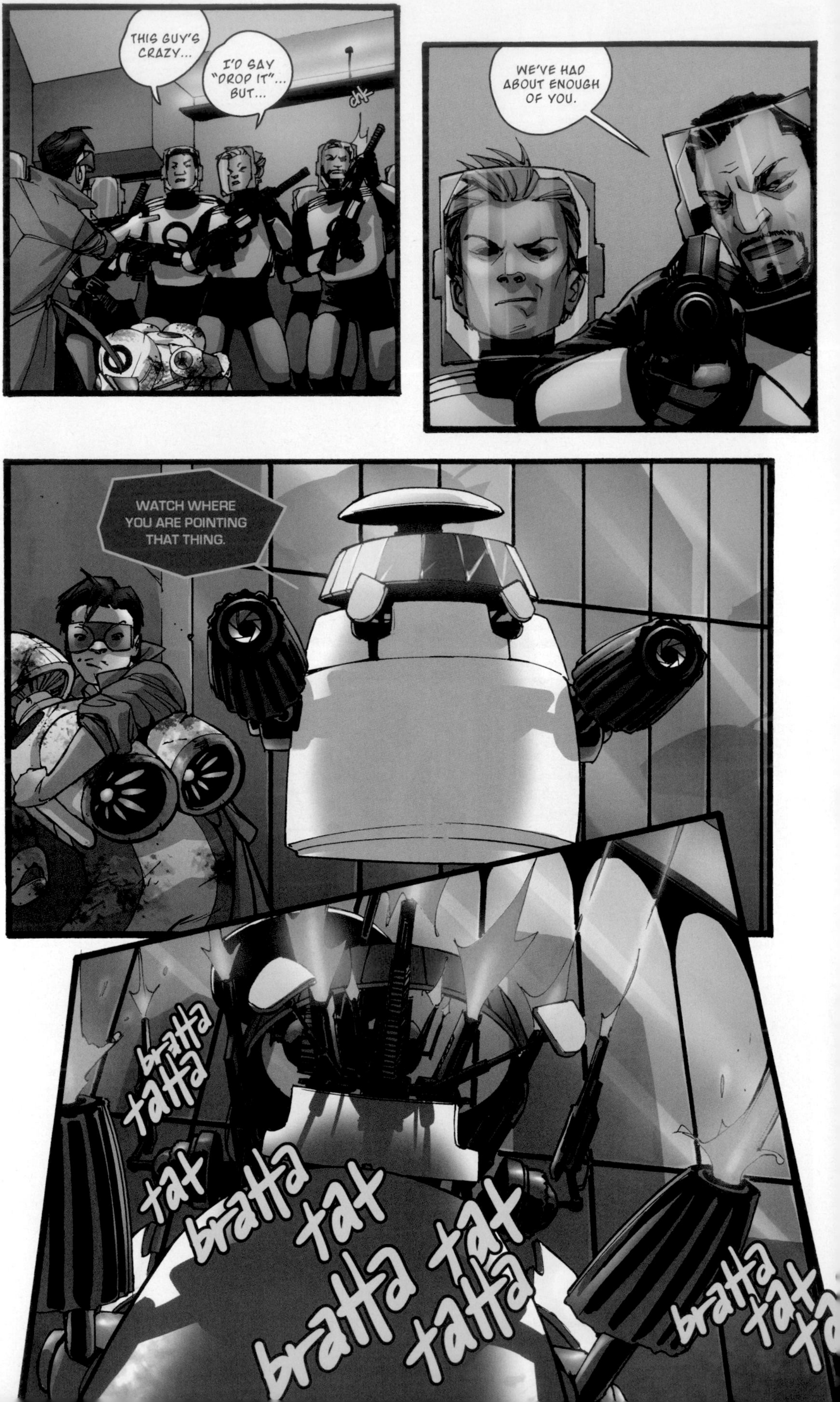
THIS GUY'S CRAZY...
I'D SAY "DROP IT"... BUT...
chk
WE'VE HAD ABOUT ENOUGH OF YOU.
WATCH WHERE YOU ARE POINTING THAT THING.
bratta tatta
tat
bratta tat
bratta tat tatta
bratta tat tatta

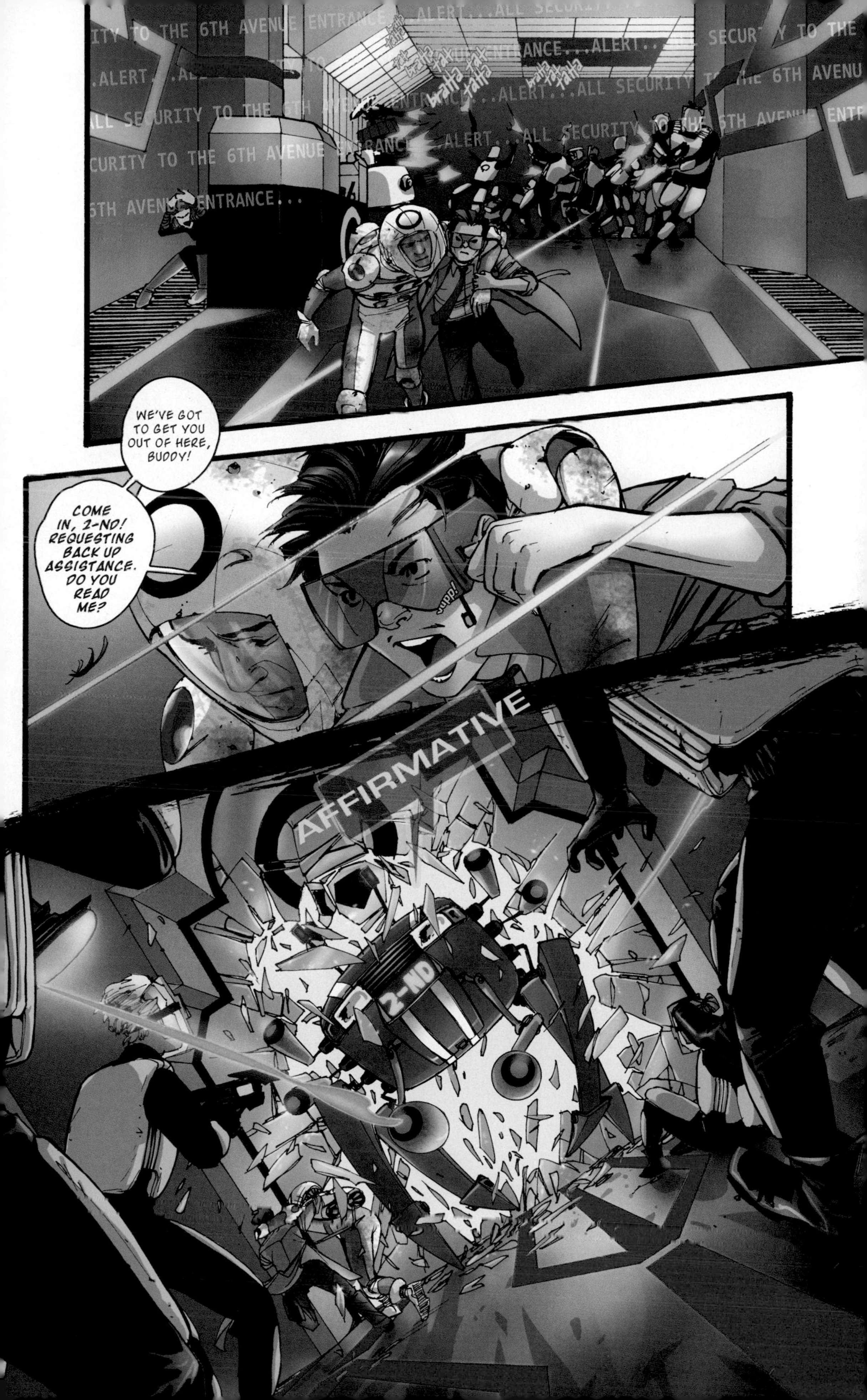
ALL SECURITY TO THE 6TH AVENUE ENTRANCE...ALERT...ALL SECURITY TO THE 6TH AVENUE ENTRANCE...
bratta tak tatta
WE'VE GOT TO GET YOU OUT OF HERE, BUDDY!
COME IN, 2-ND! REQUESTING BACK UP ASSISTANCE. DO YOU READ ME?
vupp!
AFFIRMATIVE
2-ND

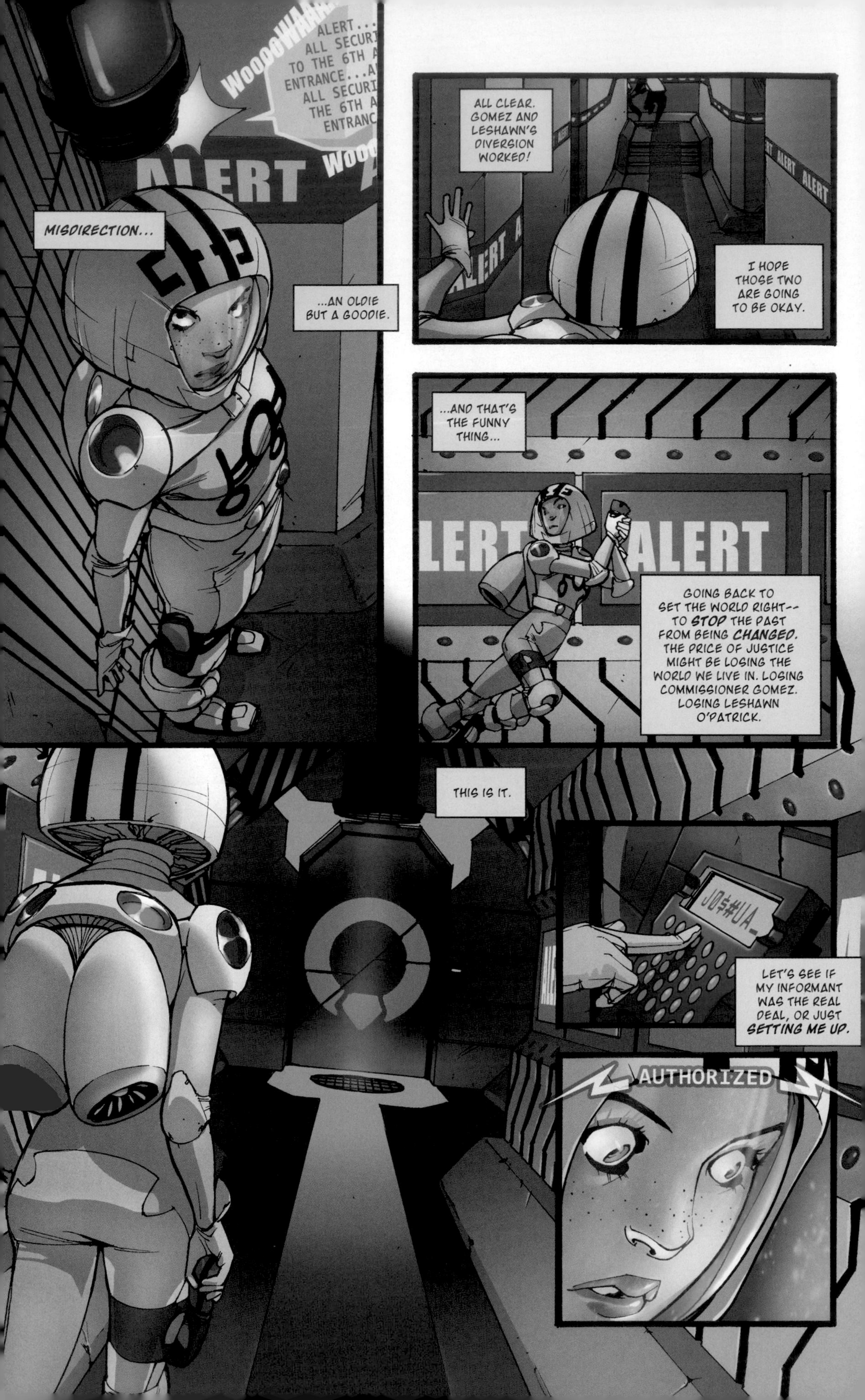
WOOOWHAAA
ALERT... ALL SECURI TO THE 6TH A ENTRANCE...A ALL SECURI THE 6TH A ENTRANC
WOOO
ALERT
MISDIRECTION...
...AN OLDIE BUT A GOODIE.
ALL CLEAR. GOMEZ AND LESHAWN'S DIVERSION WORKED!
I HOPE THOSE TWO ARE GOING TO BE OKAY.
...AND THAT'S THE FUNNY THING...
ALERT ALERT
GOING BACK TO SET THE WORLD RIGHT-- TO STOP THE PAST FROM BEING CHANGED. THE PRICE OF JUSTICE MIGHT BE LOSING THE WORLD WE LIVE IN. LOSING COMMISSIONER GOMEZ. LOSING LESHAWN O'PATRICK.
THIS IS IT.
JO$#UA_
LET'S SEE IF MY INFORMANT WAS THE REAL DEAL, OR JUST SETTING ME UP.
AUTHORIZED

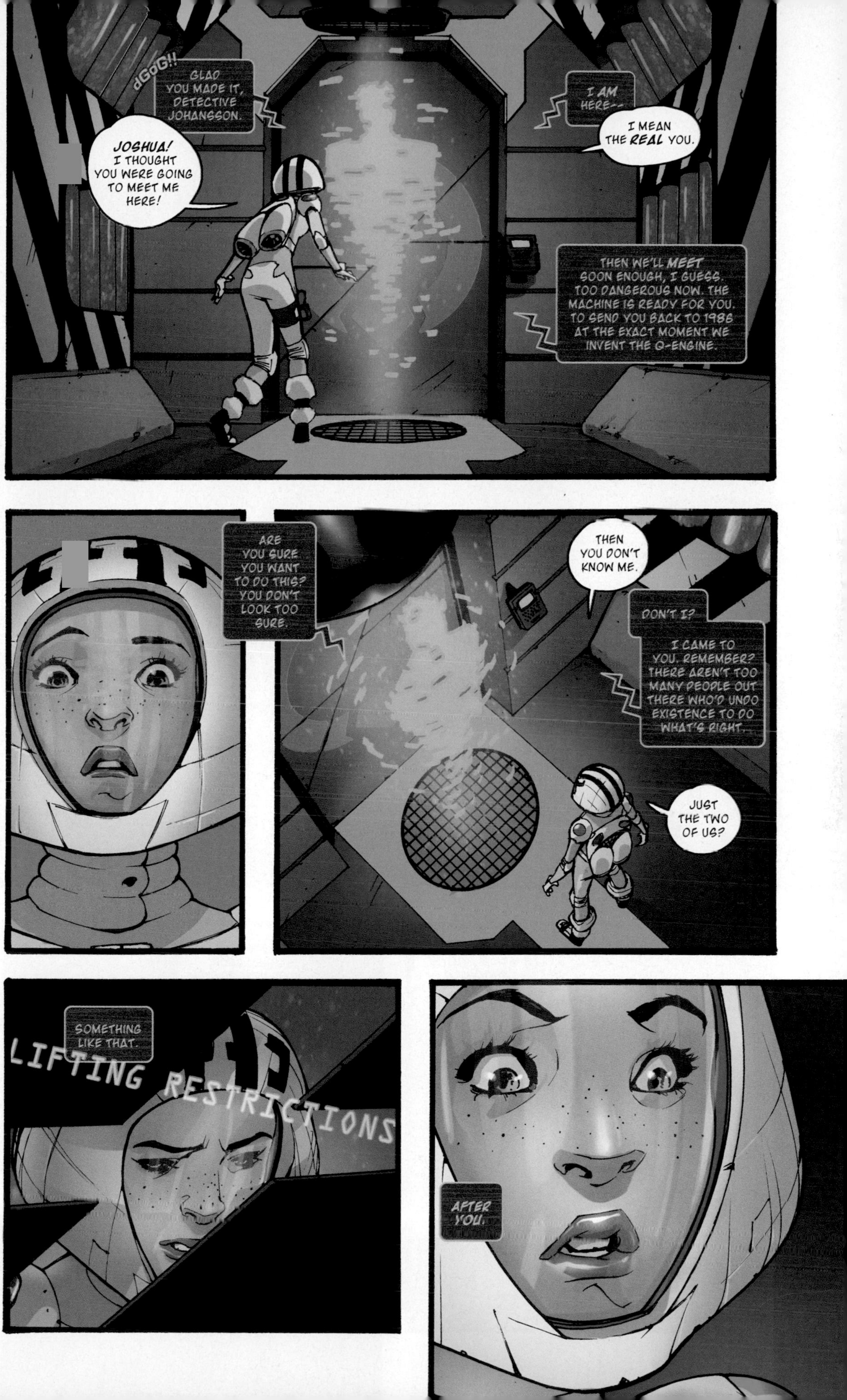
dGoG!!
GLAD YOU MADE IT, DETECTIVE JOHANSSON.
JOSHUA! I THOUGHT YOU WERE GOING TO MEET ME HERE!
I AM HERE--
I MEAN THE REAL YOU.
THEN WE'LL MEET SOON ENOUGH, I GUESS. TOO DANGEROUS NOW. THE MACHINE IS READY FOR YOU. TO SEND YOU BACK TO 1986 AT THE EXACT MOMENT WE INVENT THE Q-ENGINE.
ARE YOU SURE YOU WANT TO DO THIS? YOU DON'T LOOK TOO SURE.
THEN YOU DON'T KNOW ME.
DON'T I?
I CAME TO YOU, REMEMBER? THERE AREN'T TOO MANY PEOPLE OUT THERE WHO'D UNDO EXISTENCE TO DO WHAT'S RIGHT.
JUST THE TWO OF US?
SOMETHING LIKE THAT.
LIFTING RESTRICTIONS
AFTER YOU.

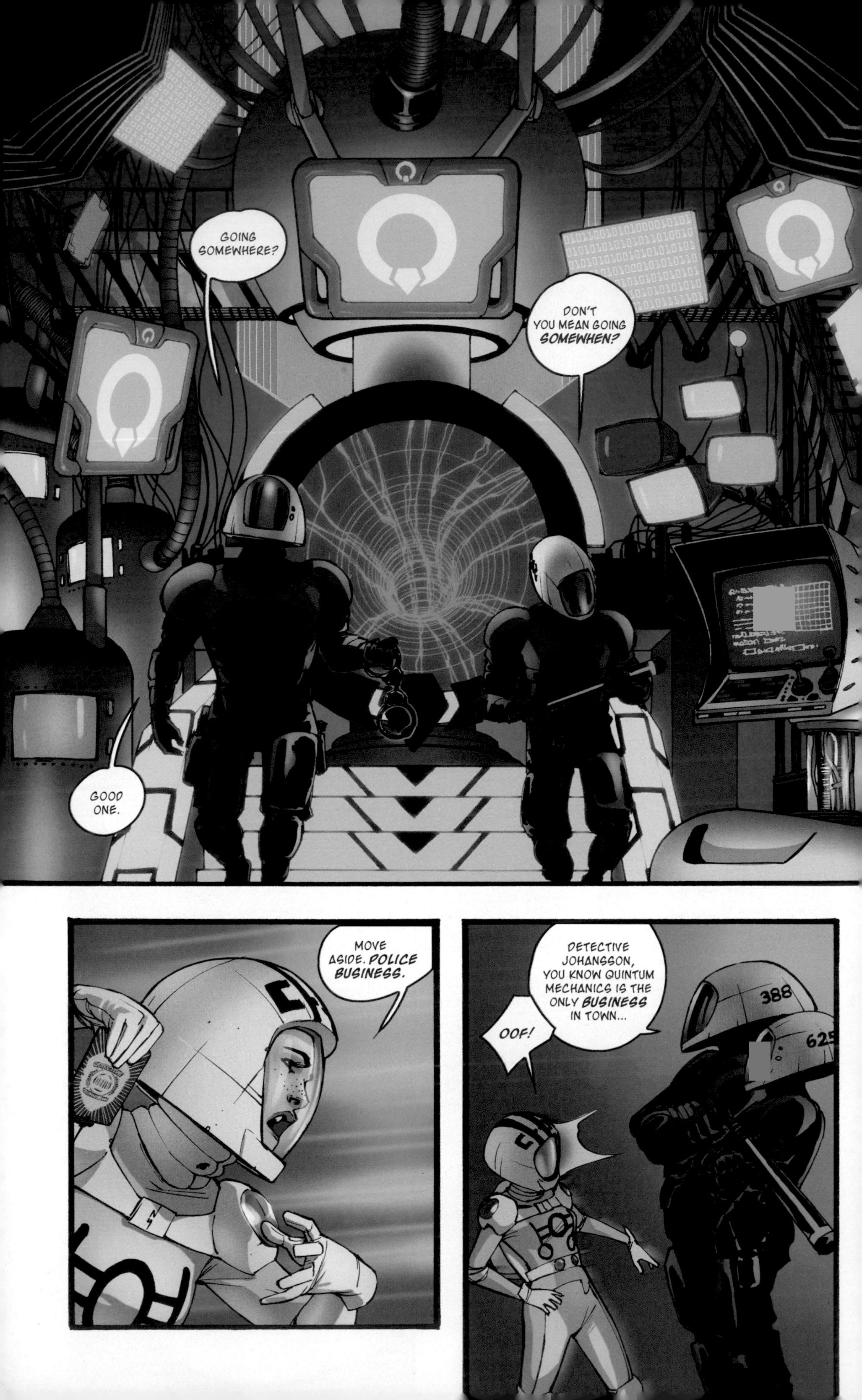
GOING SOMEWHERE?
DON'T YOU MEAN GOING SOMEWHEN?
GOOD ONE.
MOVE ASIDE. POLICE BUSINESS.
DETECTIVE JOHANSSON, YOU KNOW QUINTUM MECHANICS IS THE ONLY BUSINESS IN TOWN...
OOF!
388
625

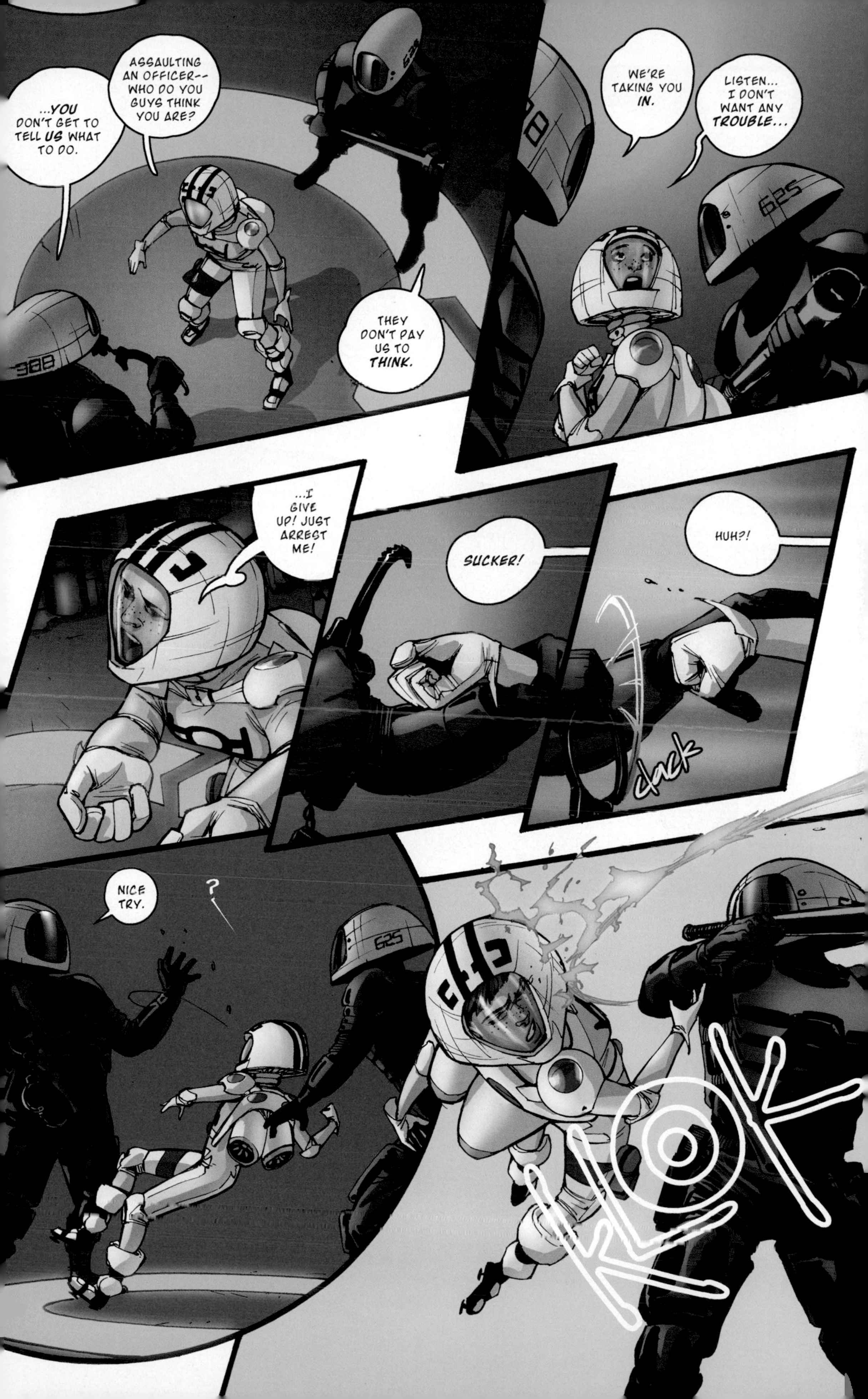

...YOU DON'T GET TO TELL US WHAT TO DO.
ASSAULTING AN OFFICER-- WHO DO YOU GUYS THINK YOU ARE?
THEY DON'T PAY US TO THINK.
WE'RE TAKING YOU IN.
LISTEN... I DON'T WANT ANY TROUBLE...
...I GIVE UP! JUST ARREST ME!
SUCKER!
HUH?!
clack
NICE TRY.
?
KLOK

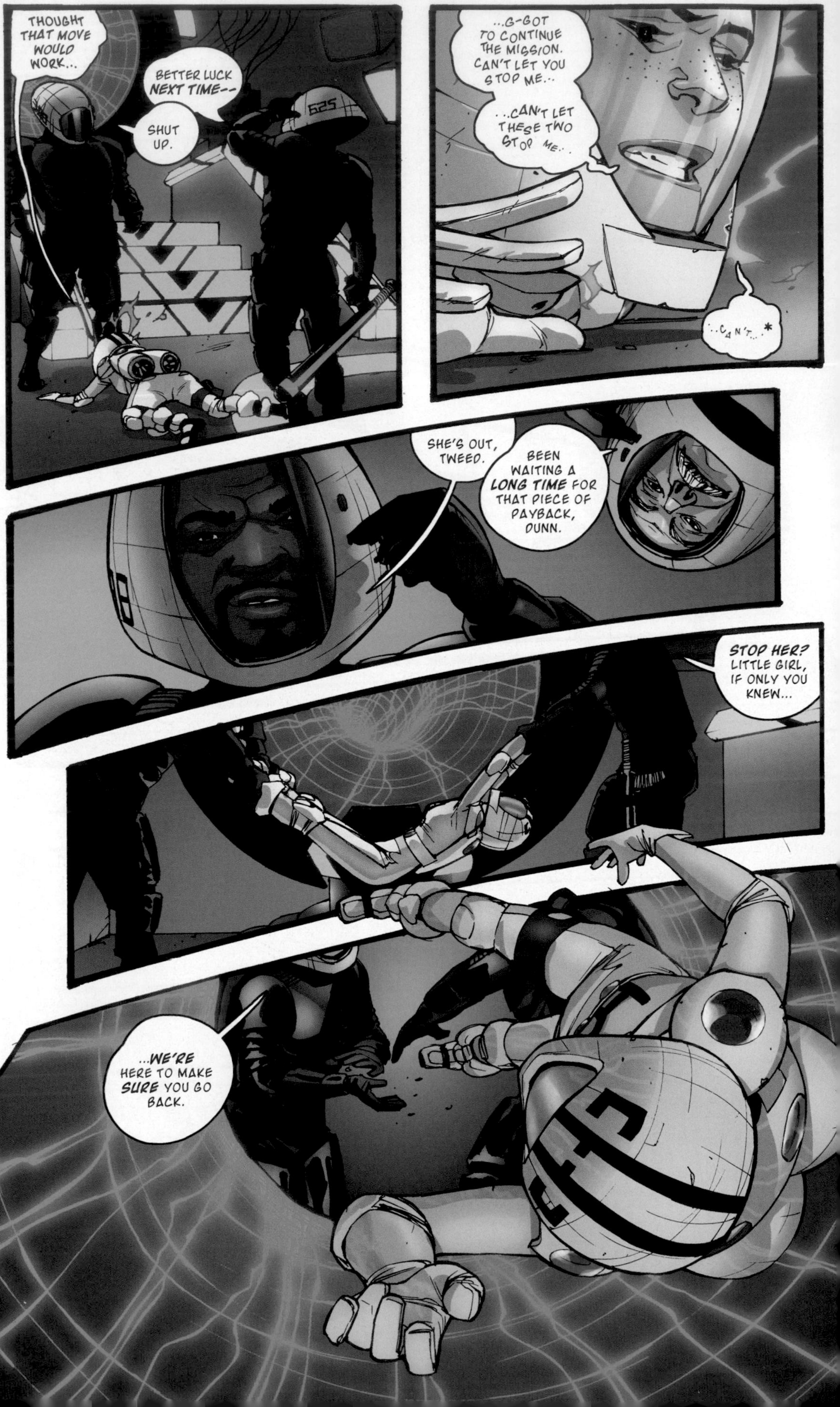
THOUGHT THAT MOVE WOULD WORK...
BETTER LUCK NEXT TIME--
SHUT UP.
...G-GOT TO CONTINUE THE MISSION. CAN'T LET YOU STOP ME...
...CAN'T LET THESE TWO STOP ME...
...CAN'T...*
SHE'S OUT, TWEED.
BEEN WAITING A LONG TIME FOR THAT PIECE OF PAYBACK, DUNN.
STOP HER? LITTLE GIRL, IF ONLY YOU KNEW...
...WE'RE HERE TO MAKE SURE YOU GO BACK.

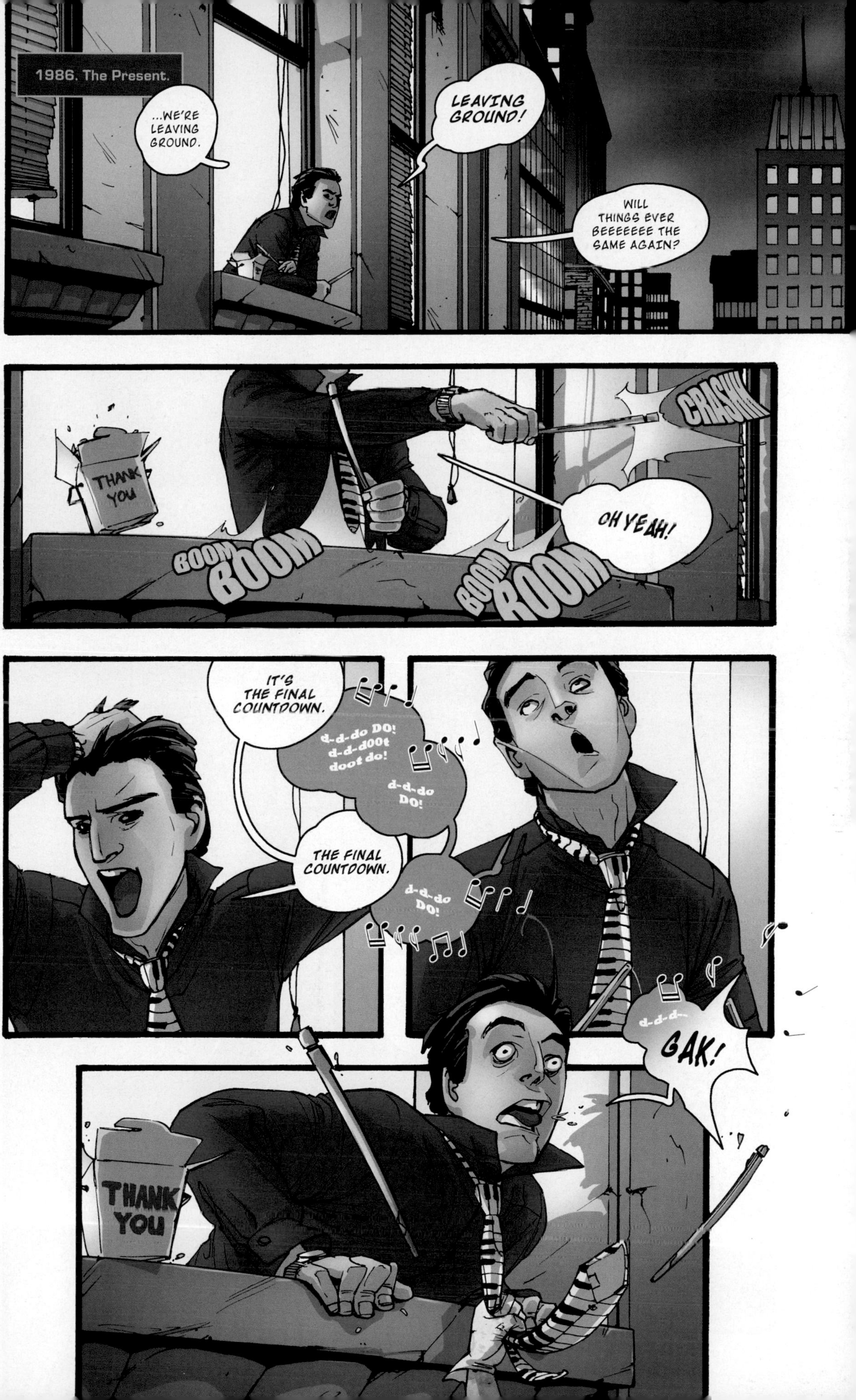
1986. The Present.
...WE'RE LEAVING GROUND.
LEAVING GROUND!
WILL THINGS EVER BEEEEEEE THE SAME AGAIN?
THANK YOU
CRASH!
OH YEAH!
BOOM BOOM
BOOM BOOM
IT'S THE FINAL COUNTDOWN.
d-d-do DO! d-d-doot doot do!
d-d-do DO!
THE FINAL COUNTDOWN.
d-d-do DO!
d-d-d--
GAK!
THANK YOU

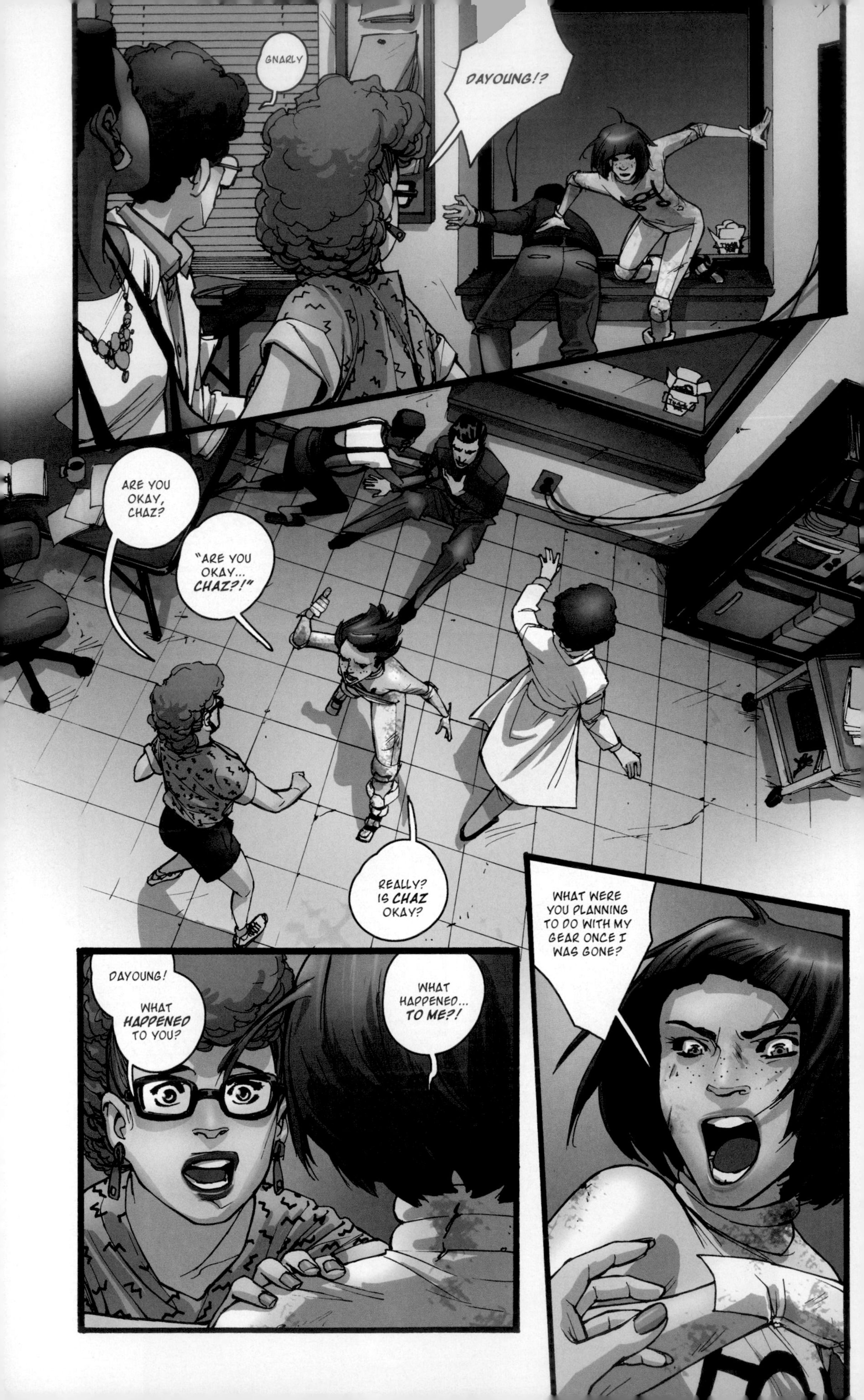
GNARLY
DAYOUNG!?
ARE YOU OKAY, CHAZ?
"ARE YOU OKAY... CHAZ?!"
REALLY? IS CHAZ OKAY?
DAYOUNG!
WHAT HAPPENED TO YOU?
WHAT HAPPENED... TO ME?!
WHAT WERE YOU PLANNING TO DO WITH MY GEAR ONCE I WAS GONE?

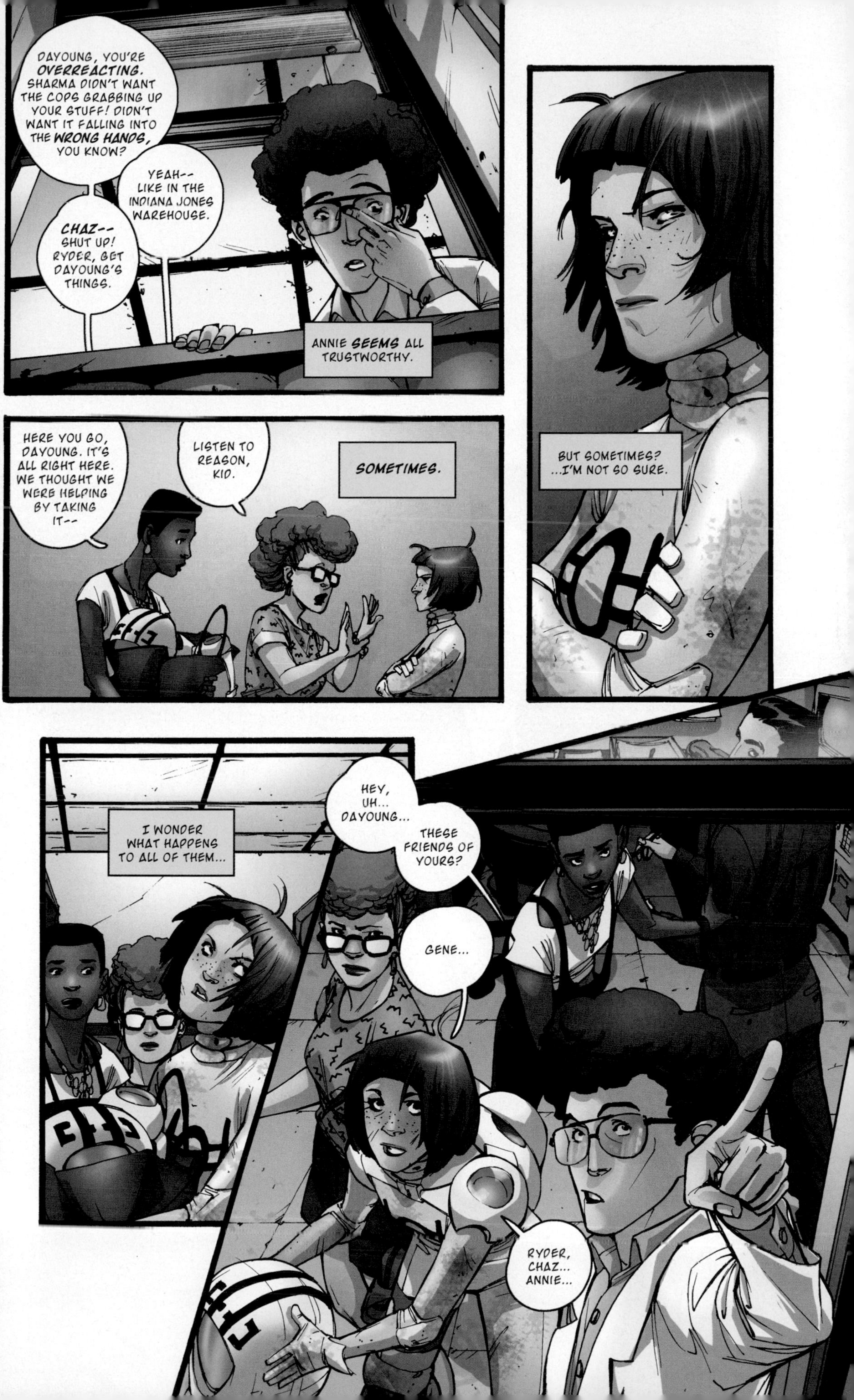
DAYOUNG, YOU'RE OVERREACTING. SHARMA DIDN'T WANT THE COPS GRABBING UP YOUR STUFF! DIDN'T WANT IT FALLING INTO THE WRONG HANDS, YOU KNOW?
YEAH-- LIKE IN THE INDIANA JONES WAREHOUSE.
CHAZ-- SHUT UP! RYDER, GET DAYOUNG'S THINGS.
ANNIE SEEMS ALL TRUSTWORTHY.
BUT SOMETIMES? ...I'M NOT SO SURE.
HERE YOU GO, DAYOUNG. IT'S ALL RIGHT HERE. WE THOUGHT WE WERE HELPING BY TAKING IT--
LISTEN TO REASON, KID.
SOMETIMES.
I WONDER WHAT HAPPENS TO ALL OF THEM...
HEY, UH... DAYOUNG...
THESE FRIENDS OF YOURS?
GENE...
RYDER, CHAZ... ANNIE...

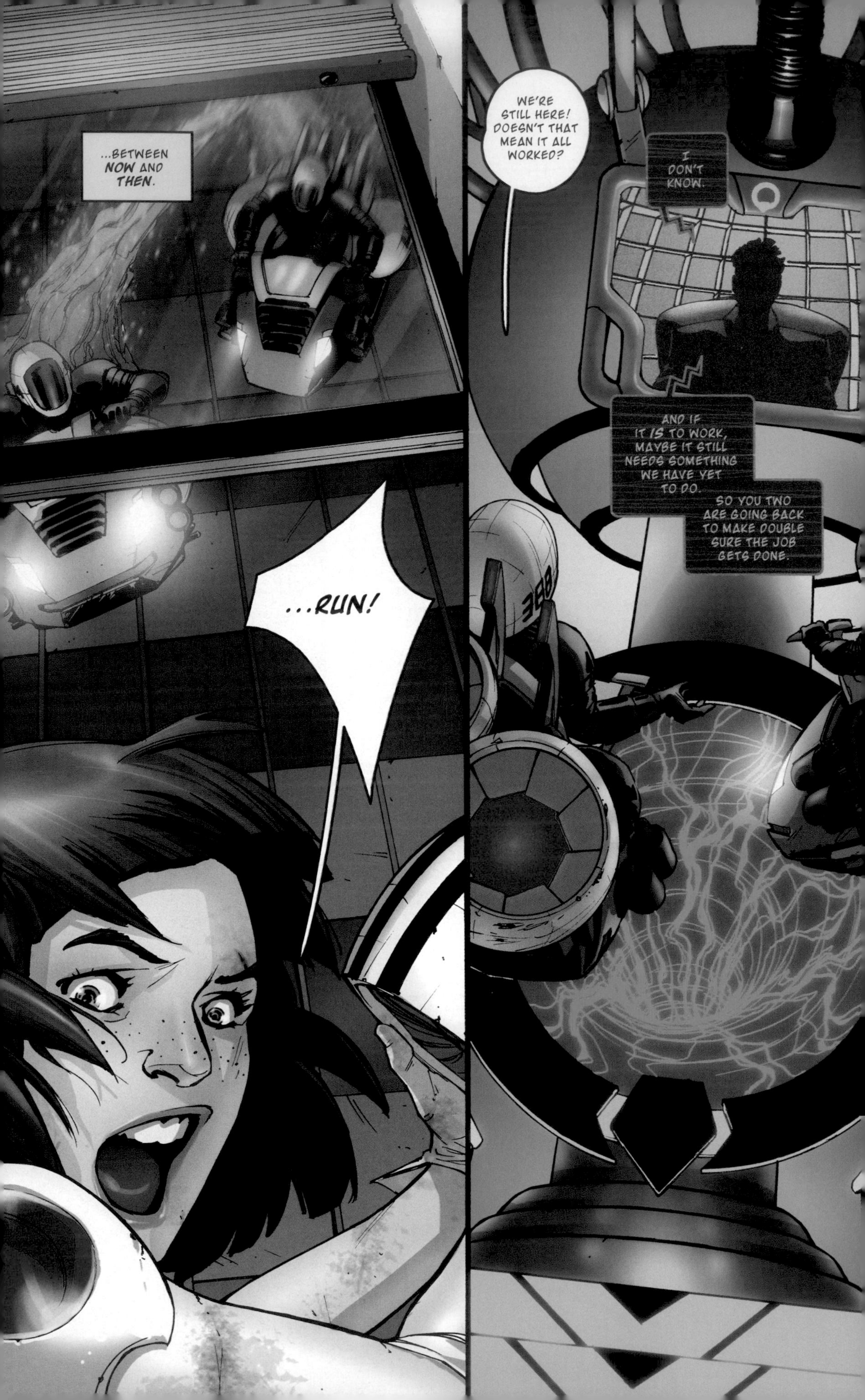
...BETWEEN NOW AND THEN.
...RUN!
WE'RE STILL HERE! DOESN'T THAT MEAN IT ALL WORKED?
I DON'T KNOW.
AND IF IT IS TO WORK, MAYBE IT STILL NEEDS SOMETHING WE HAVE YET TO DO.
SO YOU TWO ARE GOING BACK TO MAKE DOUBLE SURE THE JOB GETS DONE.

Chapter 4_Nowhere Fast >>

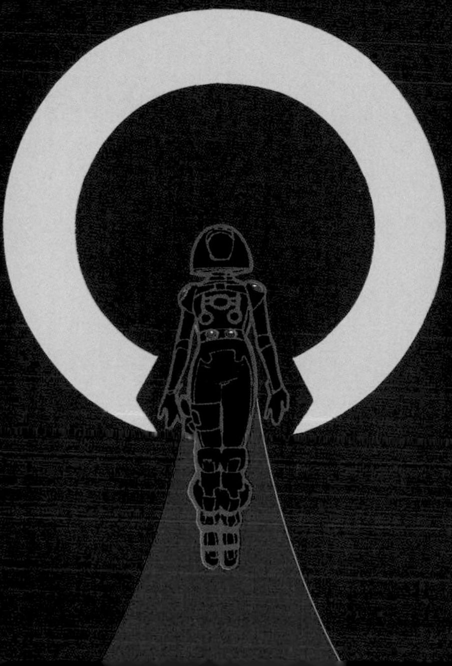

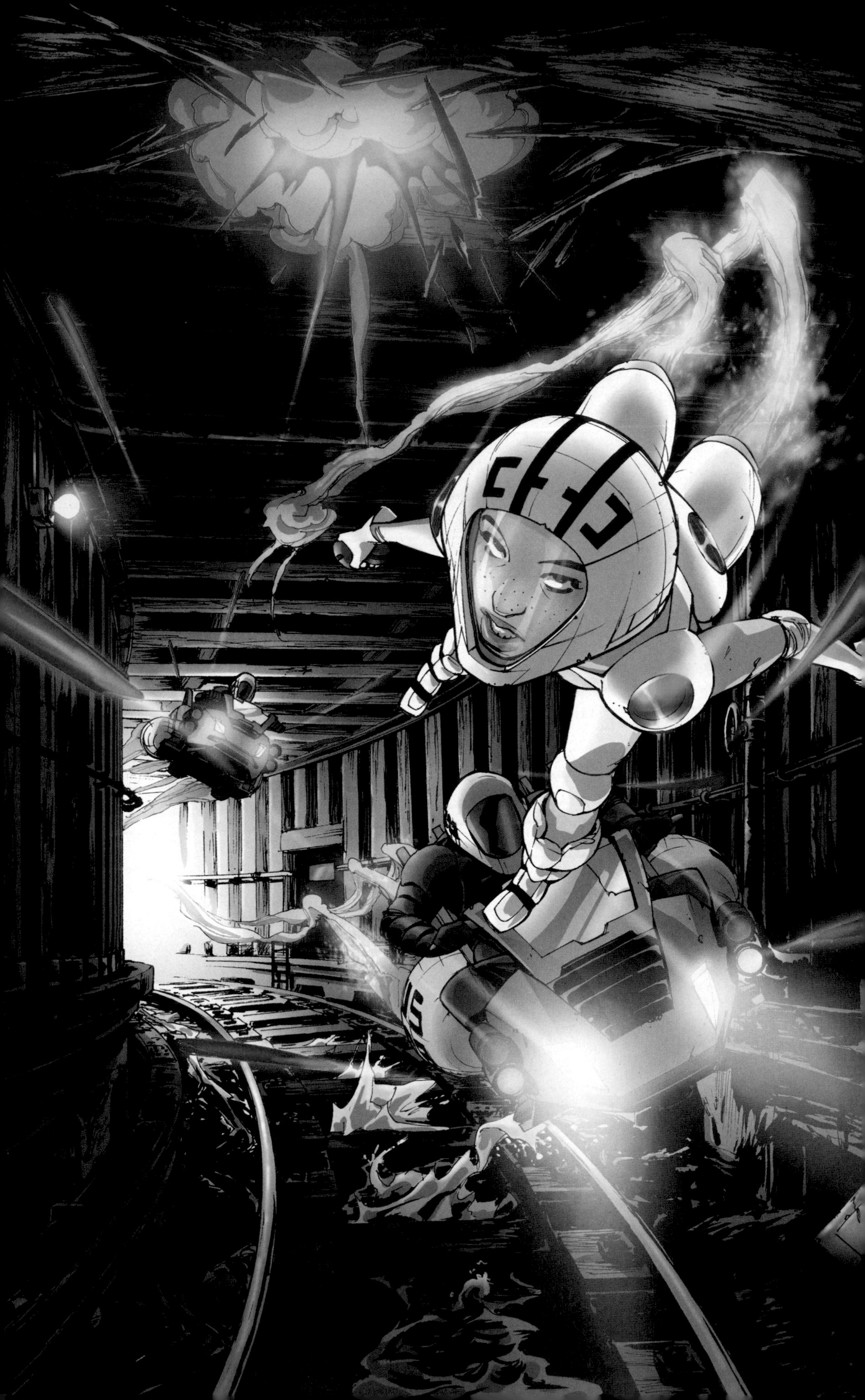

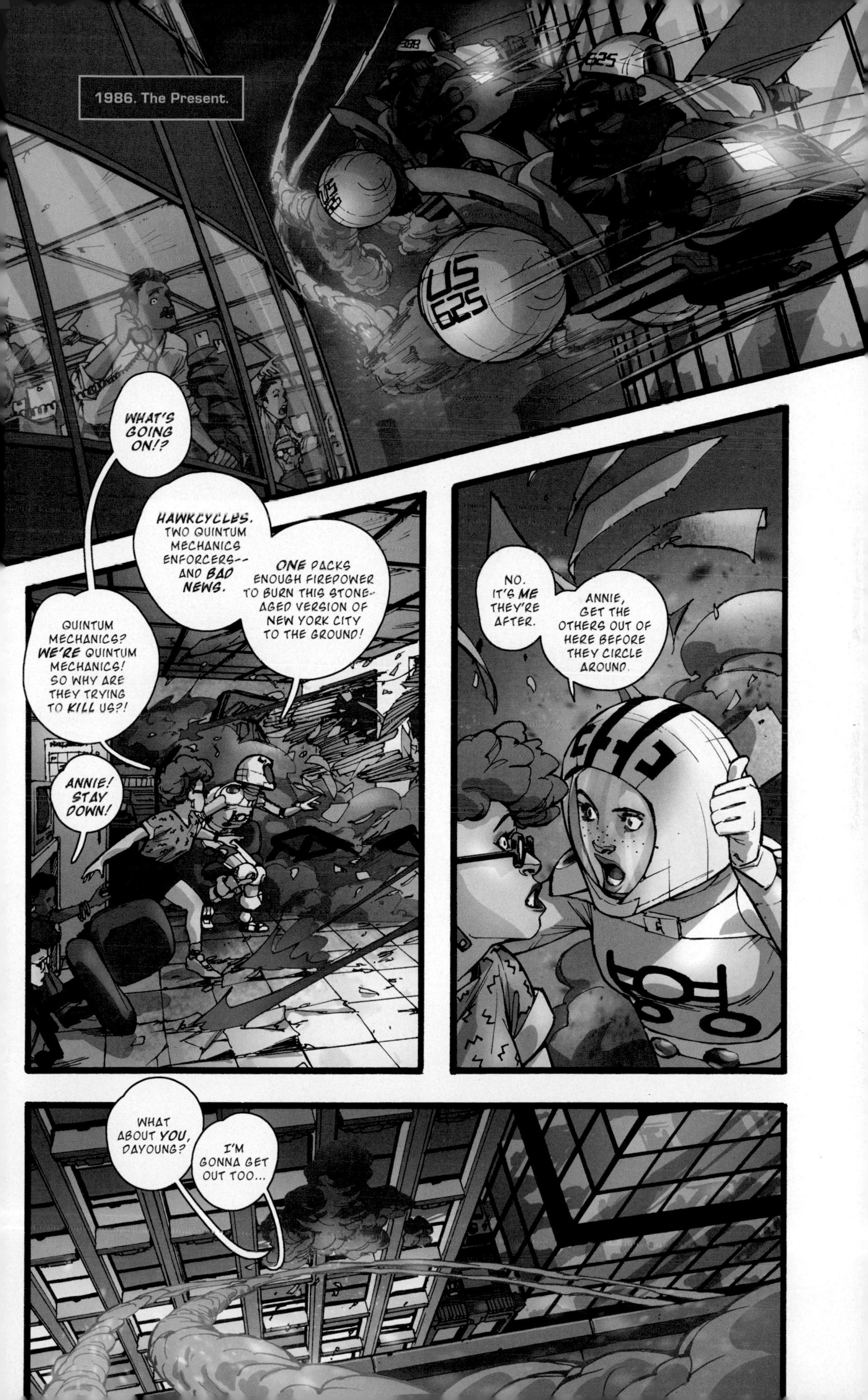
1986. The Present.
US 625
WHAT'S GOING ON!?
HAWKCYCLES. TWO QUINTUM MECHANICS ENFORCERS-- AND BAD NEWS.
ONE PACKS ENOUGH FIREPOWER TO BURN THIS STONE-AGED VERSION OF NEW YORK CITY TO THE GROUND!
QUINTUM MECHANICS? WE'RE QUINTUM MECHANICS! SO WHY ARE THEY TRYING TO KILL US?!
ANNIE! STAY DOWN!
NO. IT'S ME THEY'RE AFTER.
ANNIE, GET THE OTHERS OUT OF HERE BEFORE THEY CIRCLE AROUND.
WHAT ABOUT YOU, DAYOUNG?
I'M GONNA GET OUT TOO...

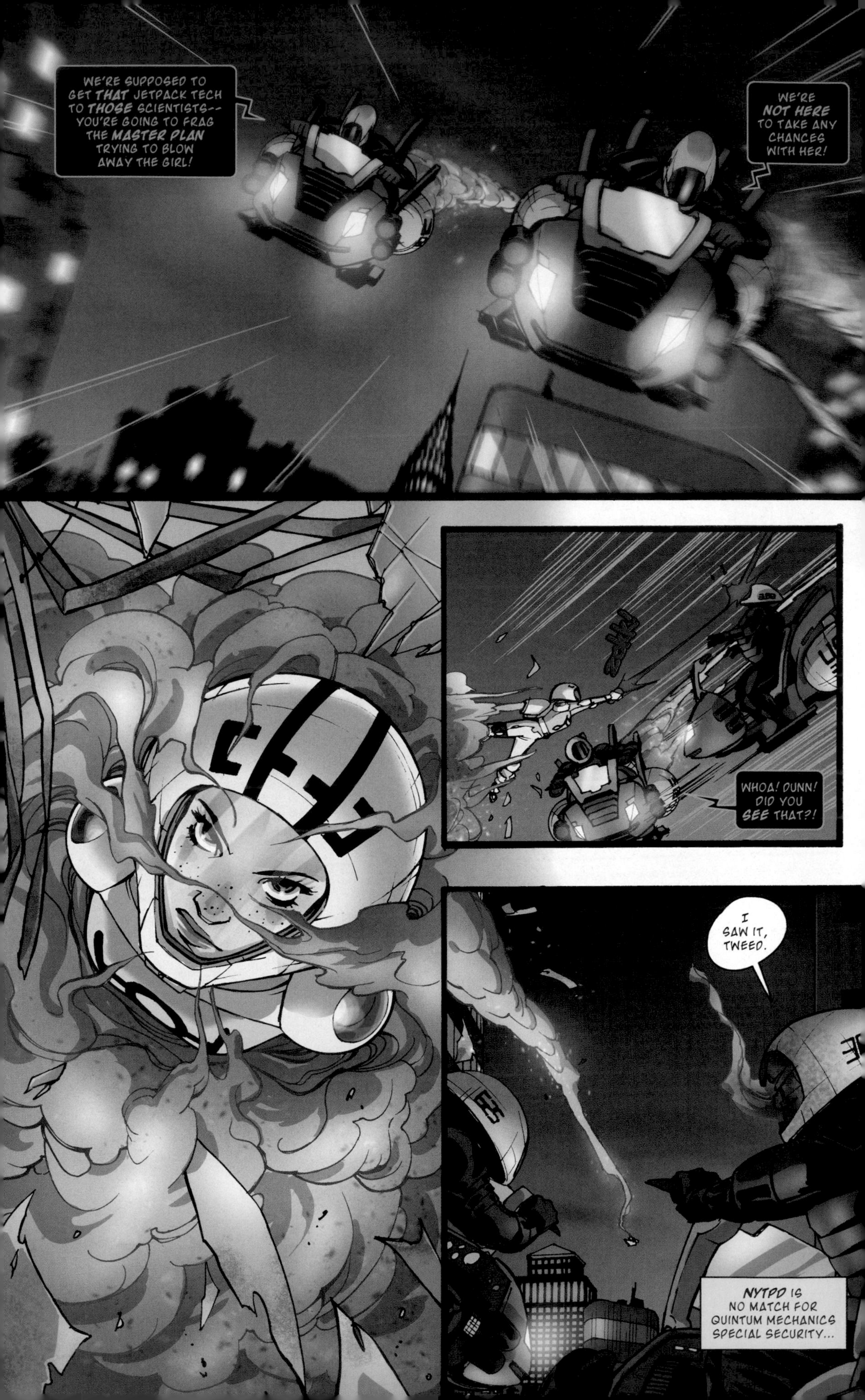
WE'RE SUPPOSED TO GET THAT JETPACK TECH TO THOSE SCIENTISTS-- YOU'RE GOING TO FRAG THE MASTER PLAN TRYING TO BLOW AWAY THE GIRL!
WE'RE NOT HERE TO TAKE ANY CHANCES WITH HER!
WHOA! DUNN! DID YOU SEE THAT?!
I SAW IT, TWEED.
NYTPD IS NO MATCH FOR QUINTUM MECHANICS SPECIAL SECURITY...

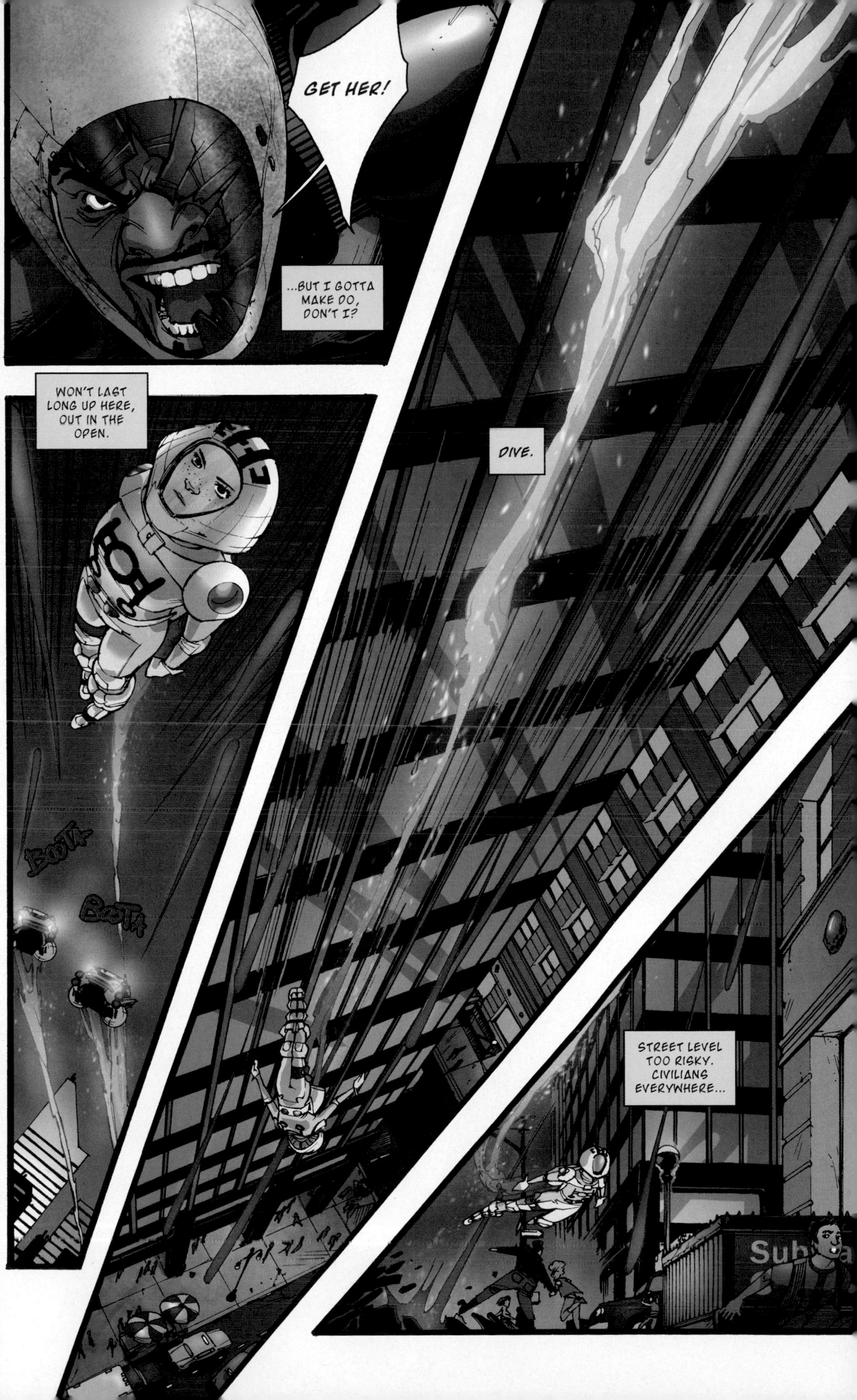
GET HER!
...BUT I GOTTA MAKE DO, DON'T I?
WON'T LAST LONG UP HERE, OUT IN THE OPEN.
BOOTA
BOOTA
DIVE.
STREET LEVEL TOO RISKY. CIVILIANS EVERYWHERE...

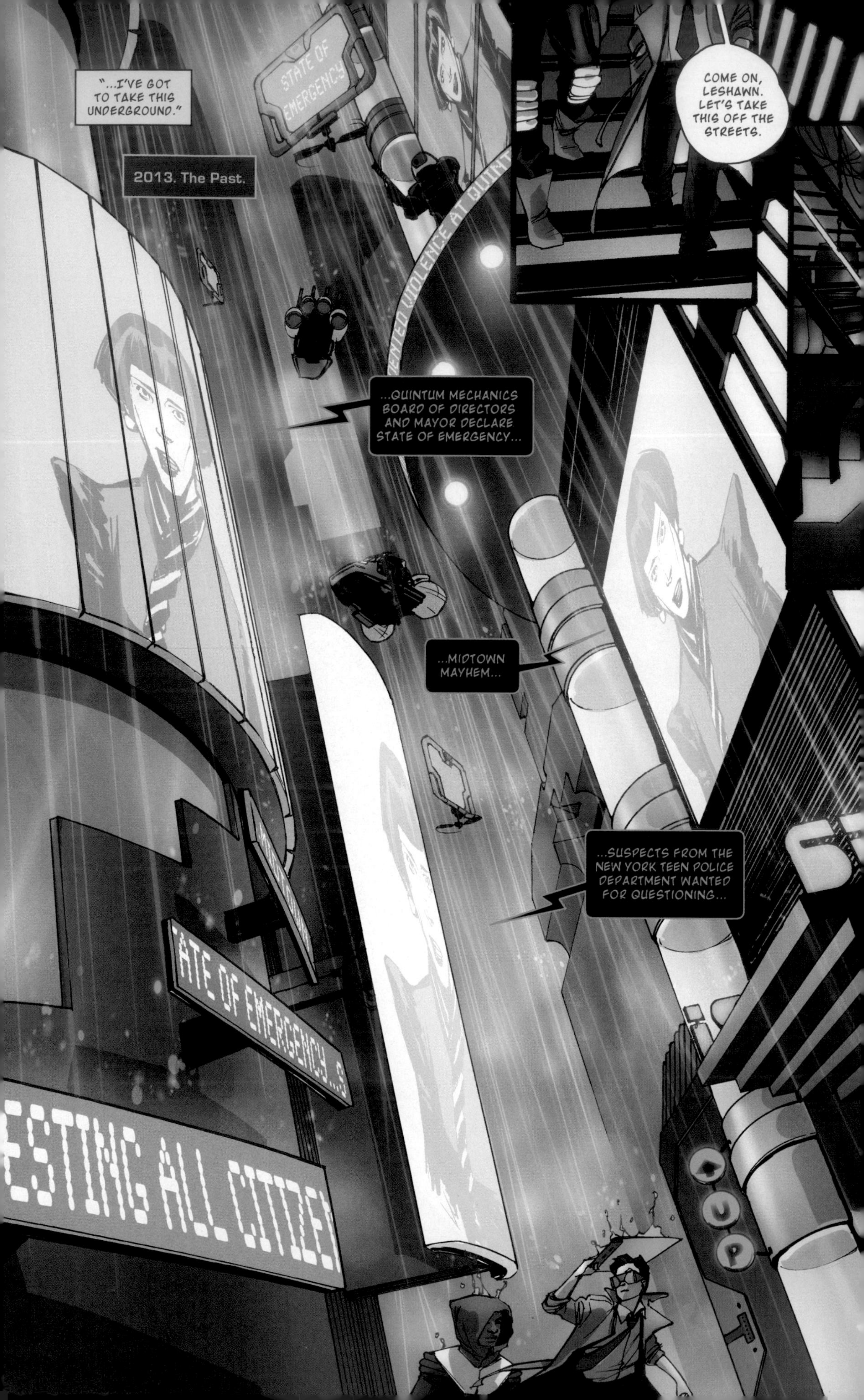
"...I'VE GOT TO TAKE THIS UNDERGROUND."
2013. The Past.
STATE OF EMERGENCY
COME ON, LESHAWN. LET'S TAKE THIS OFF THE STREETS.
...QUINTUM MECHANICS BOARD OF DIRECTORS AND MAYOR DECLARE STATE OF EMERGENCY...
...MIDTOWN MAYHEM...
...SUSPECTS FROM THE NEW YORK TEEN POLICE DEPARTMENT WANTED FOR QUESTIONING...
TATE OF EMERGENCY...
ESTING ALL CITIZE
UP

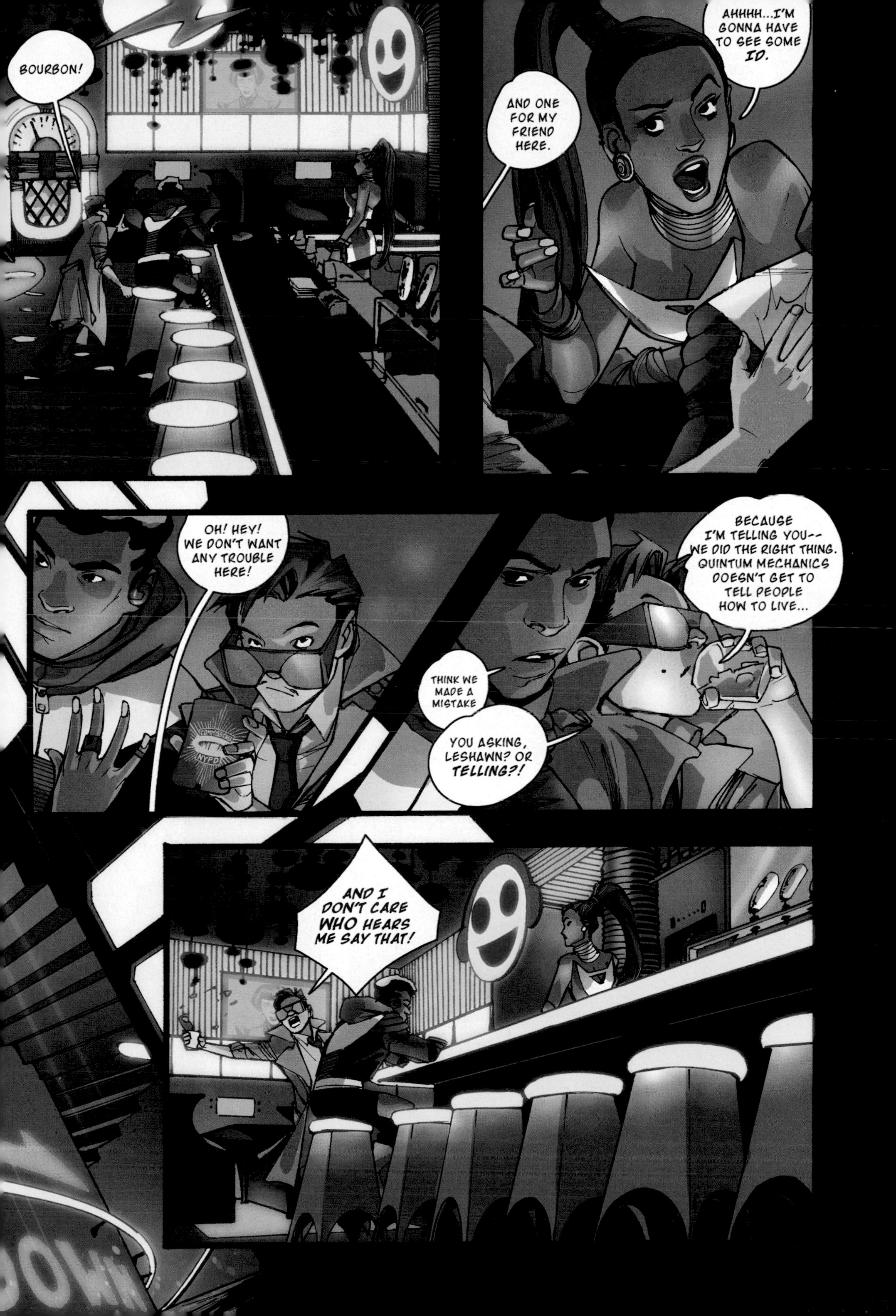
BOURBON!
AND ONE FOR MY FRIEND HERE.
AHHHH...I'M GONNA HAVE TO SEE SOME ID.
OH! HEY! WE DON'T WANT ANY TROUBLE HERE!
BECAUSE I'M TELLING YOU-- WE DID THE RIGHT THING. QUINTUM MECHANICS DOESN'T GET TO TELL PEOPLE HOW TO LIVE...
THINK WE MADE A MISTAKE
YOU ASKING, LESHAWN? OR TELLING?!
AND I DON'T CARE WHO HEARS ME SAY THAT!

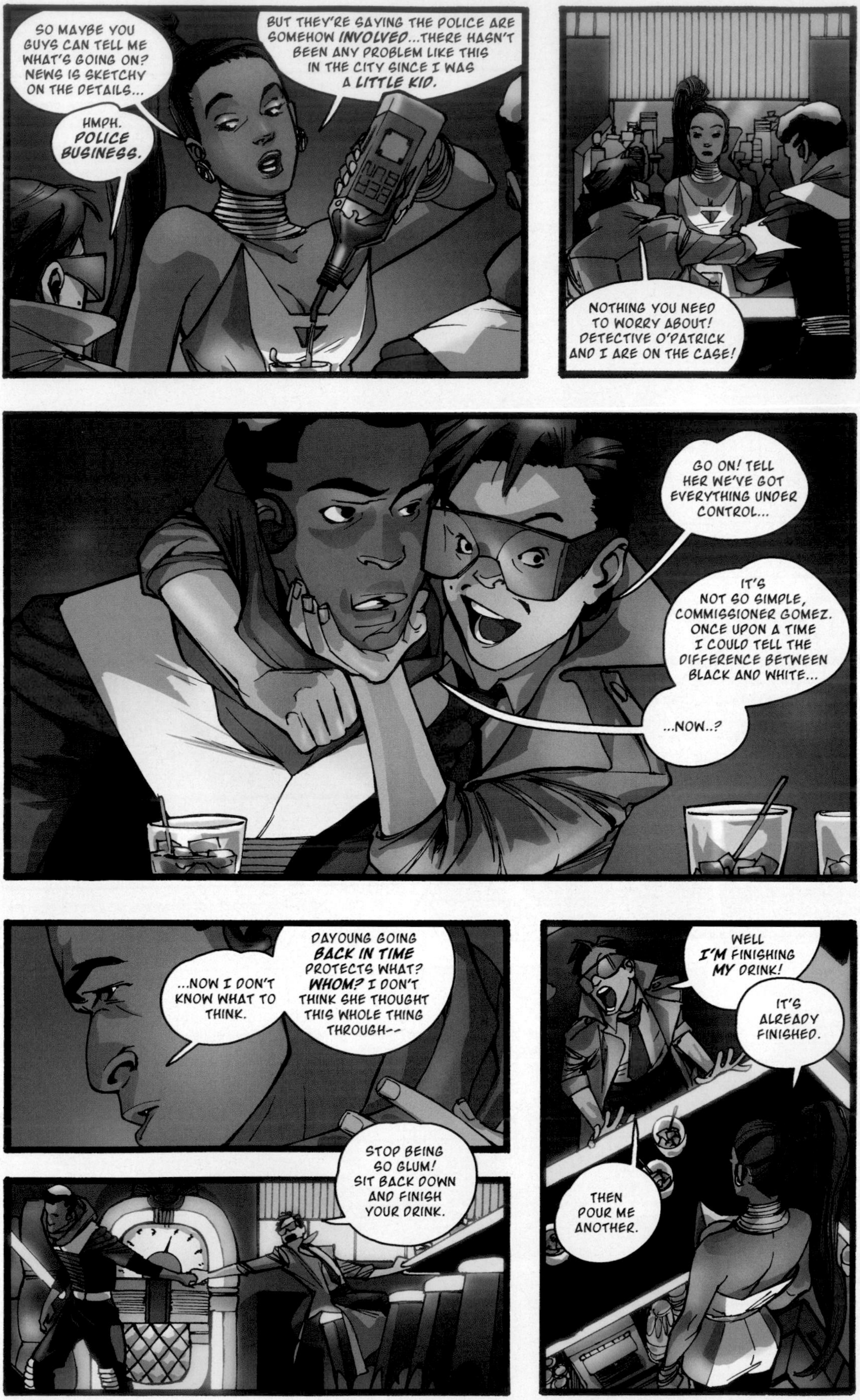
SO MAYBE YOU GUYS CAN TELL ME WHAT'S GOING ON? NEWS IS SKETCHY ON THE DETAILS...
BUT THEY'RE SAYING THE POLICE ARE SOMEHOW INVOLVED...THERE HASN'T BEEN ANY PROBLEM LIKE THIS IN THE CITY SINCE I WAS A LITTLE KID.
HMPH. POLICE BUSINESS.
NOTHING YOU NEED TO WORRY ABOUT! DETECTIVE O'PATRICK AND I ARE ON THE CASE!
GO ON! TELL HER WE'VE GOT EVERYTHING UNDER CONTROL...
IT'S NOT SO SIMPLE, COMMISSIONER GOMEZ. ONCE UPON A TIME I COULD TELL THE DIFFERENCE BETWEEN BLACK AND WHITE...
...NOW..?
...NOW I DON'T KNOW WHAT TO THINK.
DAYOUNG GOING BACK IN TIME PROTECTS WHAT? WHOM? I DON'T THINK SHE THOUGHT THIS WHOLE THING THROUGH--
STOP BEING SO GLUM! SIT BACK DOWN AND FINISH YOUR DRINK.
WELL I'M FINISHING MY DRINK!
IT'S ALREADY FINISHED.
THEN POUR ME ANOTHER.

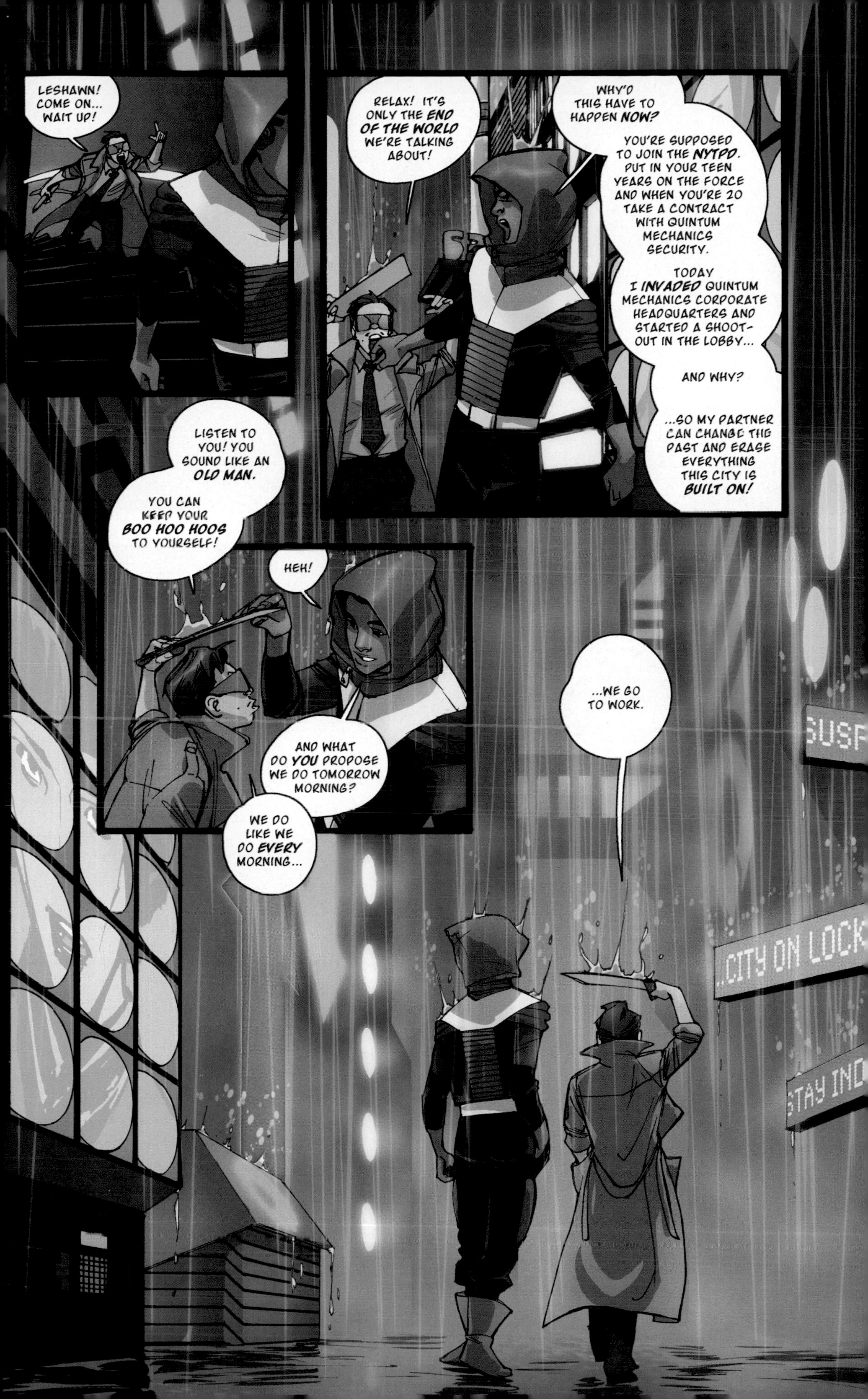
LESHAWN! COME ON... WAIT UP!
RELAX! IT'S ONLY THE END OF THE WORLD WE'RE TALKING ABOUT!
WHY'D THIS HAVE TO HAPPEN NOW?
YOU'RE SUPPOSED TO JOIN THE NYPD. PUT IN YOUR TEEN YEARS ON THE FORCE AND WHEN YOU'RE 20 TAKE A CONTRACT WITH QUINTUM MECHANICS SECURITY.
TODAY I INVADED QUINTUM MECHANICS CORPORATE HEADQUARTERS AND STARTED A SHOOT-OUT IN THE LOBBY...
AND WHY?
...SO MY PARTNER CAN CHANGE THE PAST AND ERASE EVERYTHING THIS CITY IS BUILT ON!
LISTEN TO YOU! YOU SOUND LIKE AN OLD MAN.
YOU CAN KEEP YOUR BOO HOO HOOS TO YOURSELF!
HEH!
AND WHAT DO YOU PROPOSE WE DO TOMORROW MORNING?
WE DO LIKE WE DO EVERY MORNING...
...WE GO TO WORK.
SUSP
...CITY ON LOCK
STAY IND

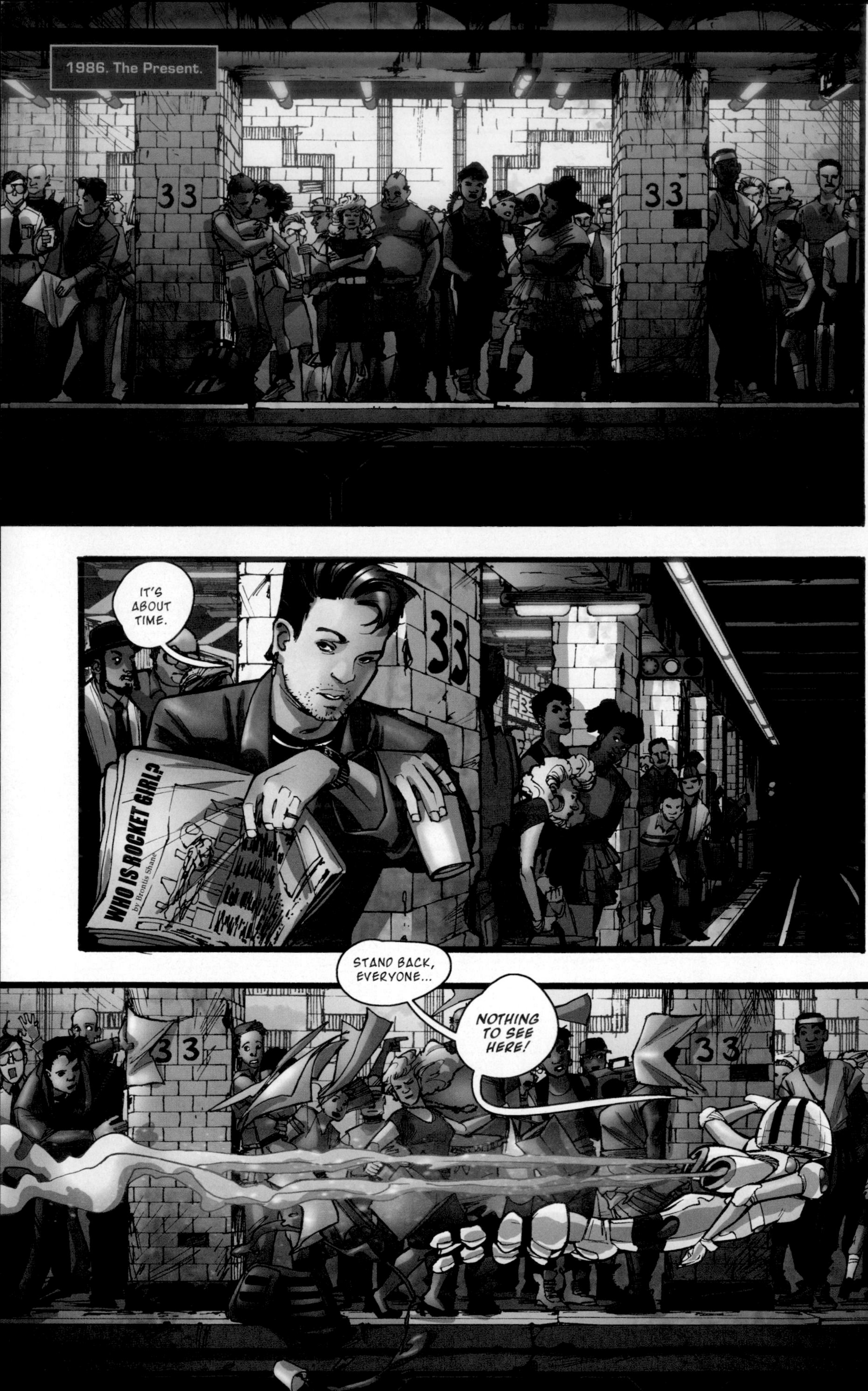
1986. The Present.
33
33
IT'S ABOUT TIME.
WHO IS ROCKET GIRL?
by Brontis Shane
33
STAND BACK, EVERYONE...
NOTHING TO SEE HERE!
33
33

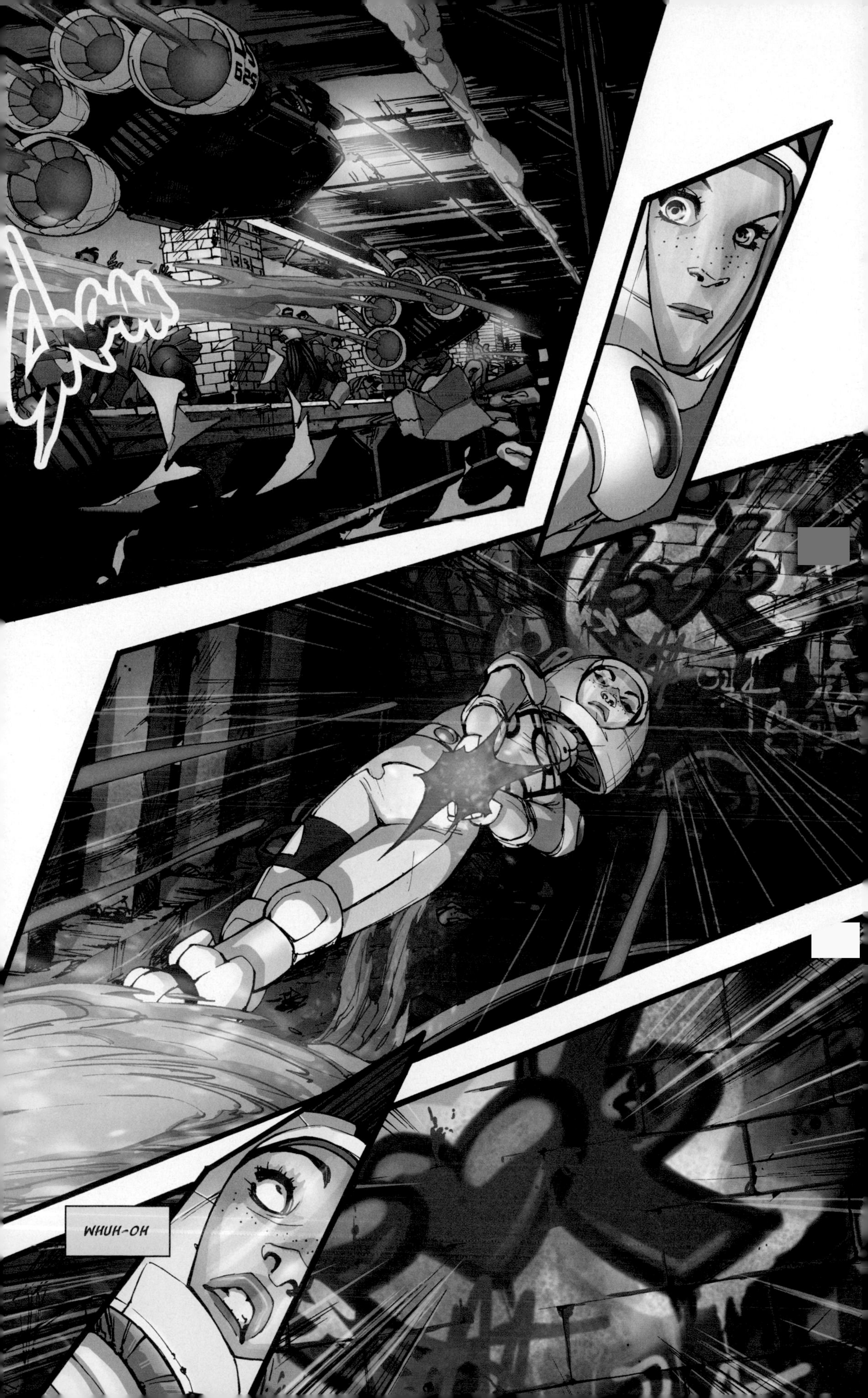
WHUH-OH

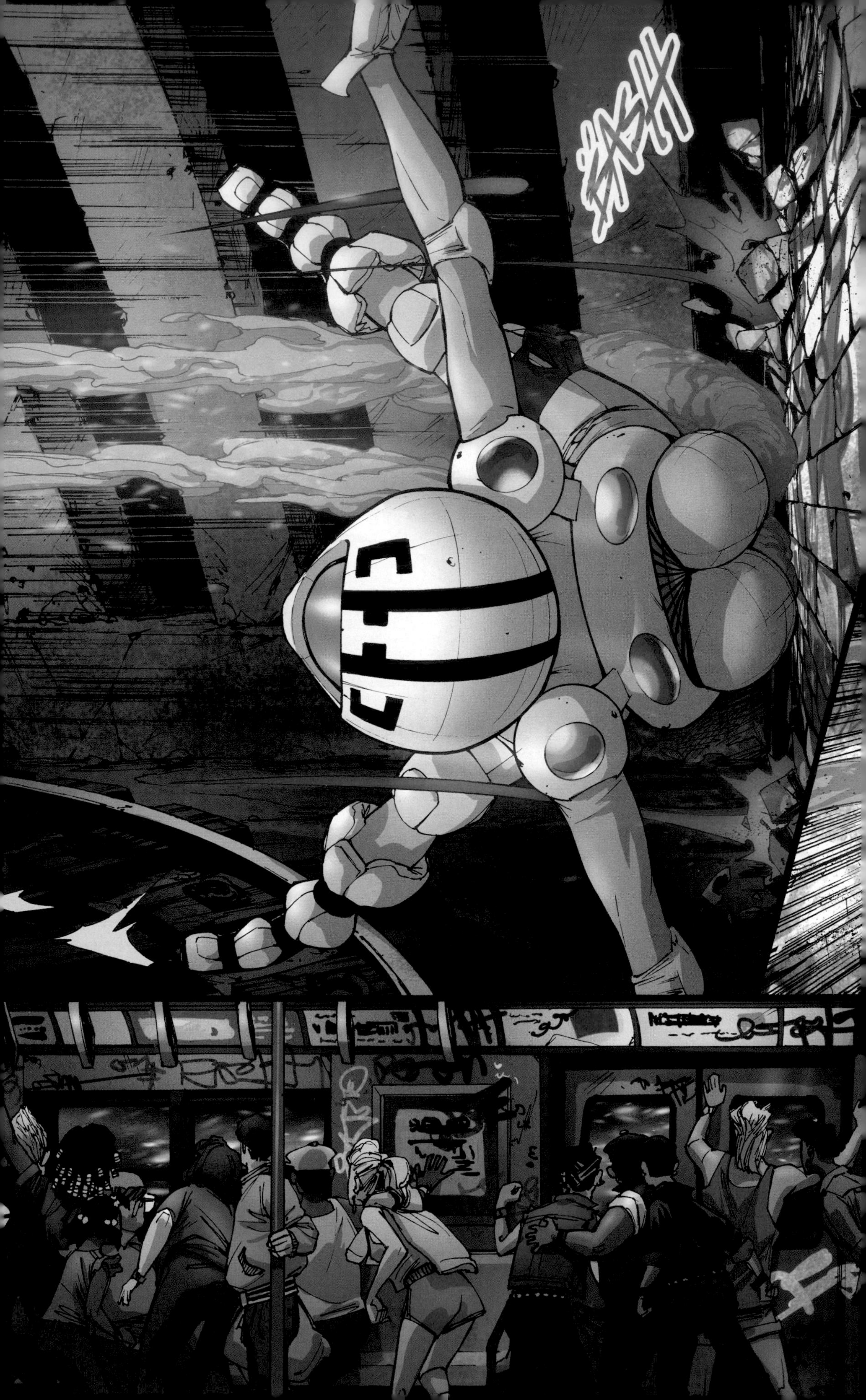

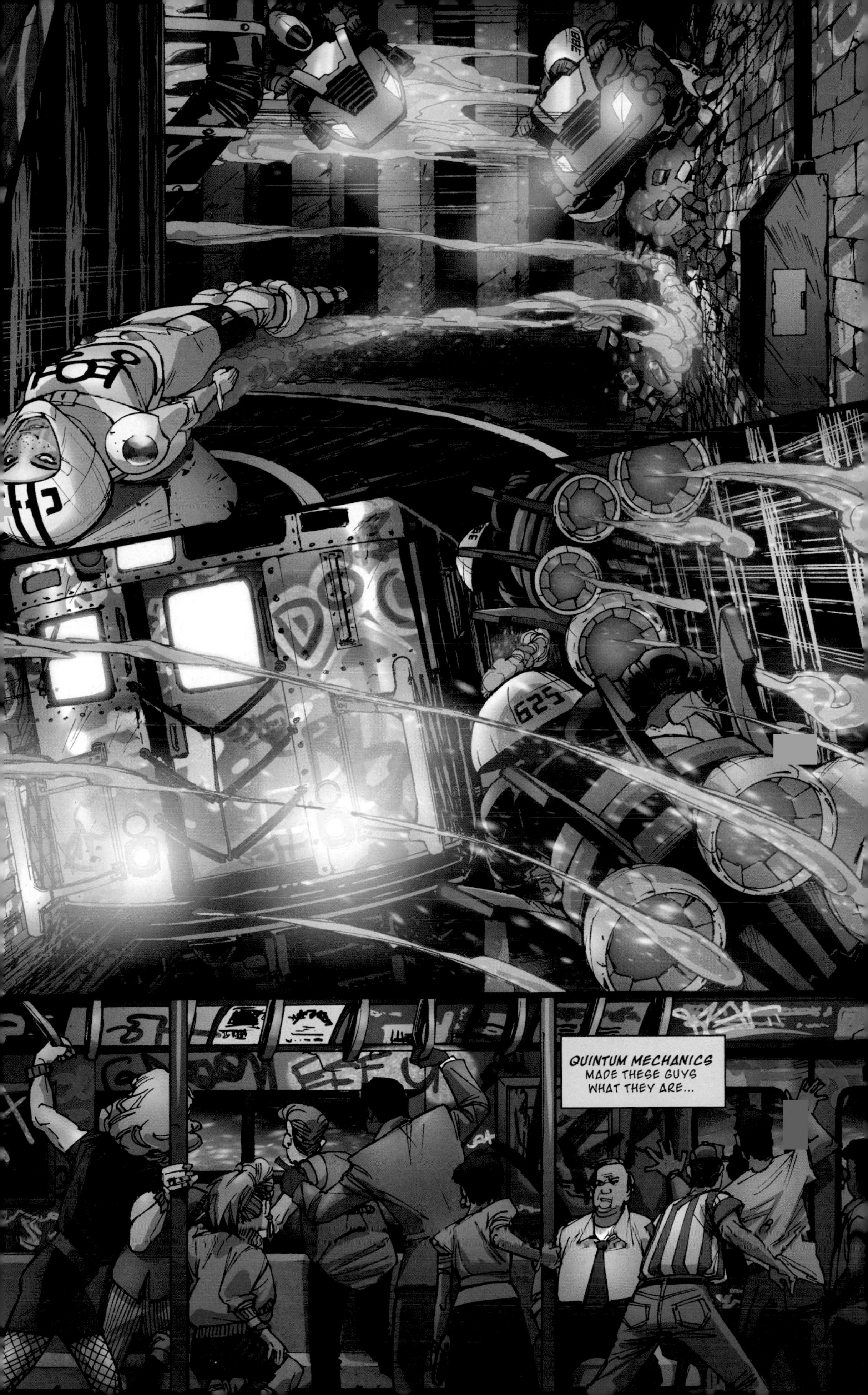
625
QUINTUM MECHANICS
MADE THESE GUYS
WHAT THEY ARE...

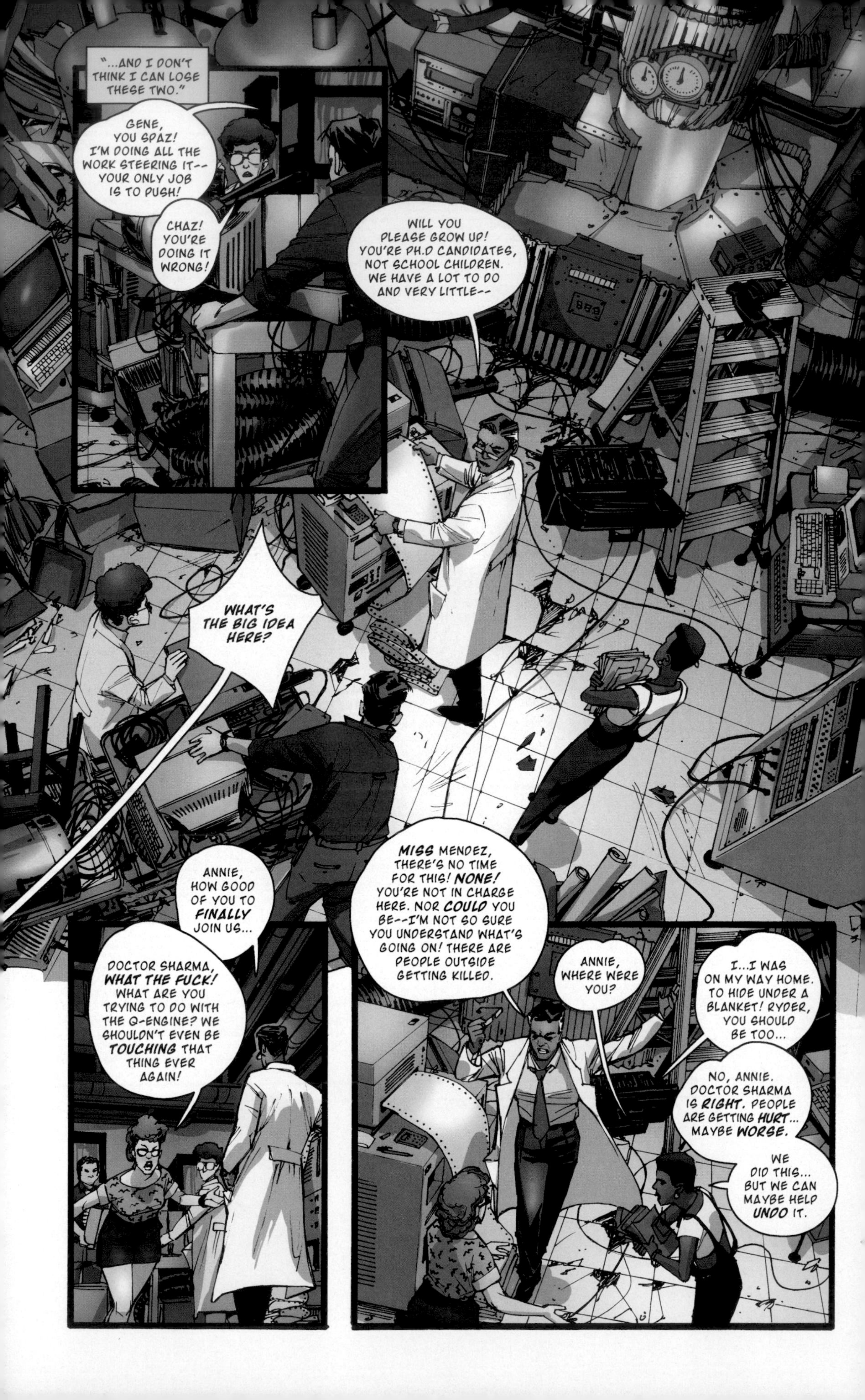
"...AND I DON'T THINK I CAN LOSE THESE TWO."
GENE, YOU SPAZ! I'M DOING ALL THE WORK STEERING IT-- YOUR ONLY JOB IS TO PUSH!
CHAZ! YOU'RE DOING IT WRONG!
WILL YOU PLEASE GROW UP! YOU'RE PH.D CANDIDATES, NOT SCHOOL CHILDREN. WE HAVE A LOT TO DO AND VERY LITTLE--
WHAT'S THE BIG IDEA HERE?
ANNIE, HOW GOOD OF YOU TO FINALLY JOIN US...
DOCTOR SHARMA, WHAT THE FUCK! WHAT ARE YOU TRYING TO DO WITH THE Q-ENGINE? WE SHOULDN'T EVEN BE TOUCHING THAT THING EVER AGAIN!
MISS MENDEZ, THERE'S NO TIME FOR THIS! NONE! YOU'RE NOT IN CHARGE HERE. NOR COULD YOU BE--I'M NOT SO SURE YOU UNDERSTAND WHAT'S GOING ON! THERE ARE PEOPLE OUTSIDE GETTING KILLED.
ANNIE, WHERE WERE YOU?
I...I WAS ON MY WAY HOME. TO HIDE UNDER A BLANKET! RYDER, YOU SHOULD BE TOO...
NO, ANNIE. DOCTOR SHARMA IS RIGHT. PEOPLE ARE GETTING HURT... MAYBE WORSE.
WE DID THIS... BUT WE CAN MAYBE HELP UNDO IT.

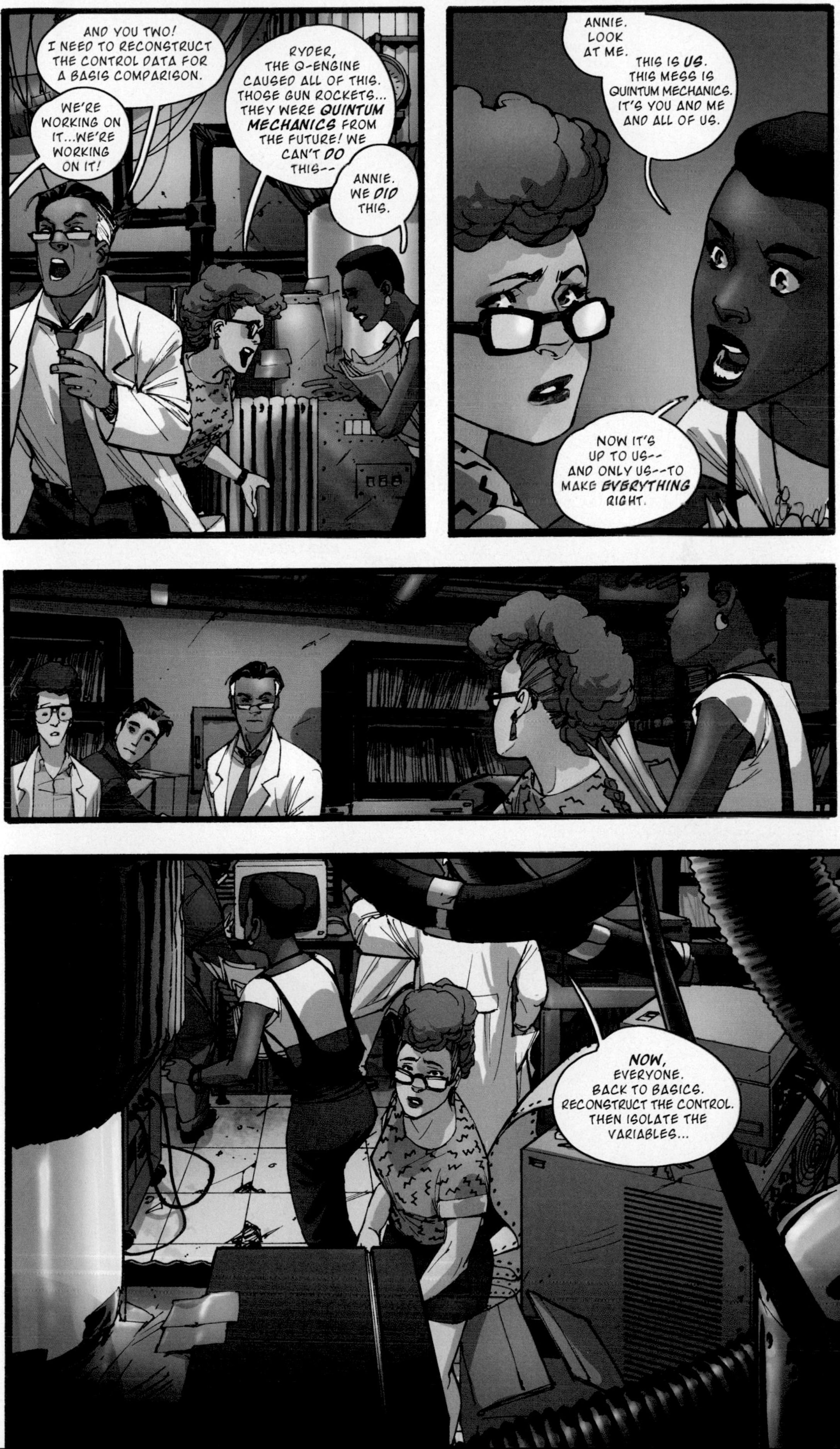
AND YOU TWO! I NEED TO RECONSTRUCT THE CONTROL DATA FOR A BASIS COMPARISON.
WE'RE WORKING ON IT...WE'RE WORKING ON IT!
RYDER, THE Q-ENGINE CAUSED ALL OF THIS. THOSE GUN ROCKETS... THEY WERE QUINTUM MECHANICS FROM THE FUTURE! WE CAN'T DO THIS--
ANNIE. WE DID THIS.
ANNIE. LOOK AT ME.
THIS IS US. THIS MESS IS QUINTUM MECHANICS. IT'S YOU AND ME AND ALL OF US.
NOW IT'S UP TO US-- AND ONLY US--TO MAKE EVERYTHING RIGHT.
NOW, EVERYONE. BACK TO BASICS. RECONSTRUCT THE CONTROL. THEN ISOLATE THE VARIABLES...

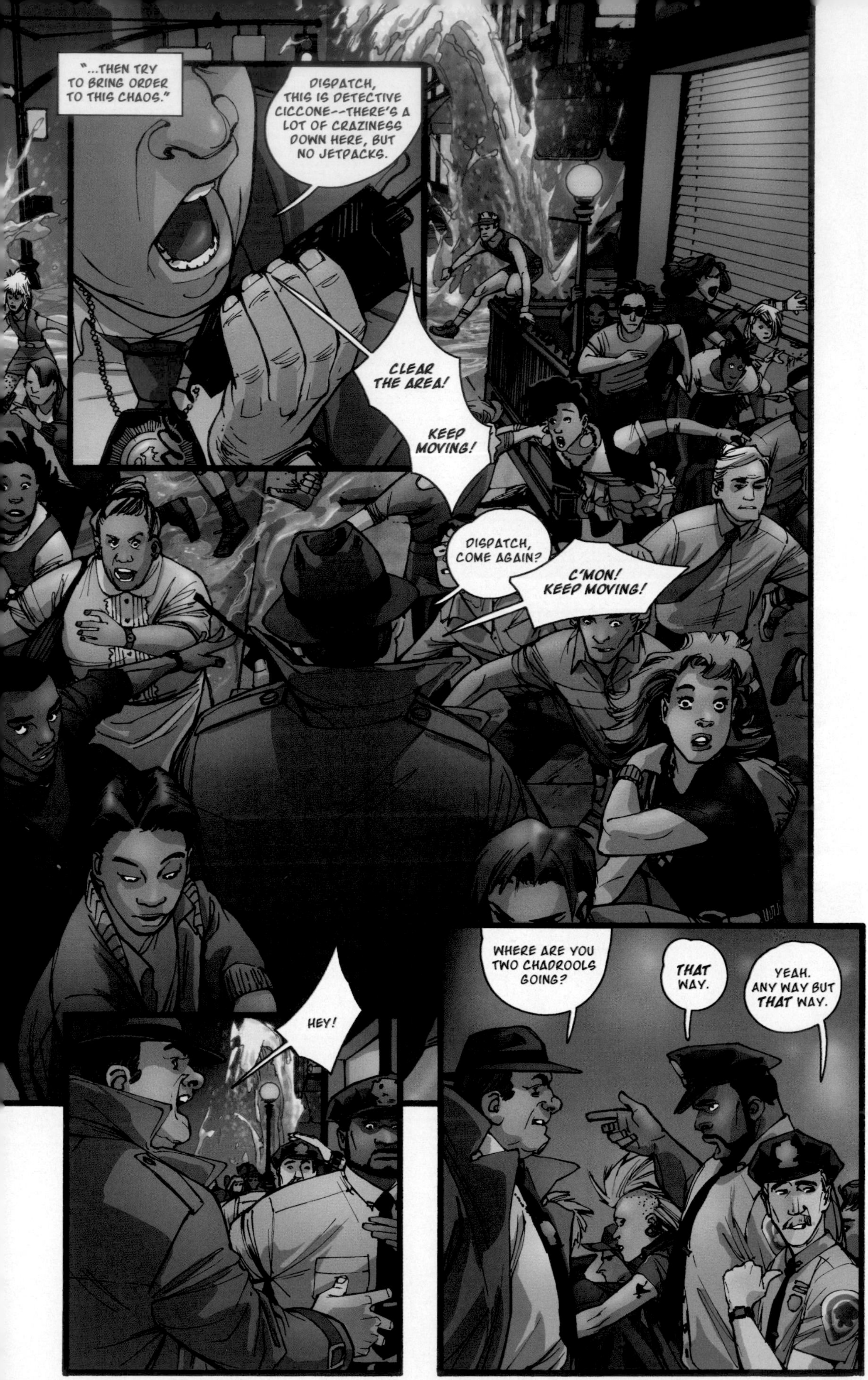
"...THEN TRY TO BRING ORDER TO THIS CHAOS."
DISPATCH, THIS IS DETECTIVE CICCONE--THERE'S A LOT OF CRAZINESS DOWN HERE, BUT NO JETPACKS.
CLEAR THE AREA!
KEEP MOVING!
DISPATCH, COME AGAIN?
C'MON! KEEP MOVING!
HEY!
WHERE ARE YOU TWO CHADROOLS GOING?
THAT WAY.
YEAH. ANY WAY BUT THAT WAY.

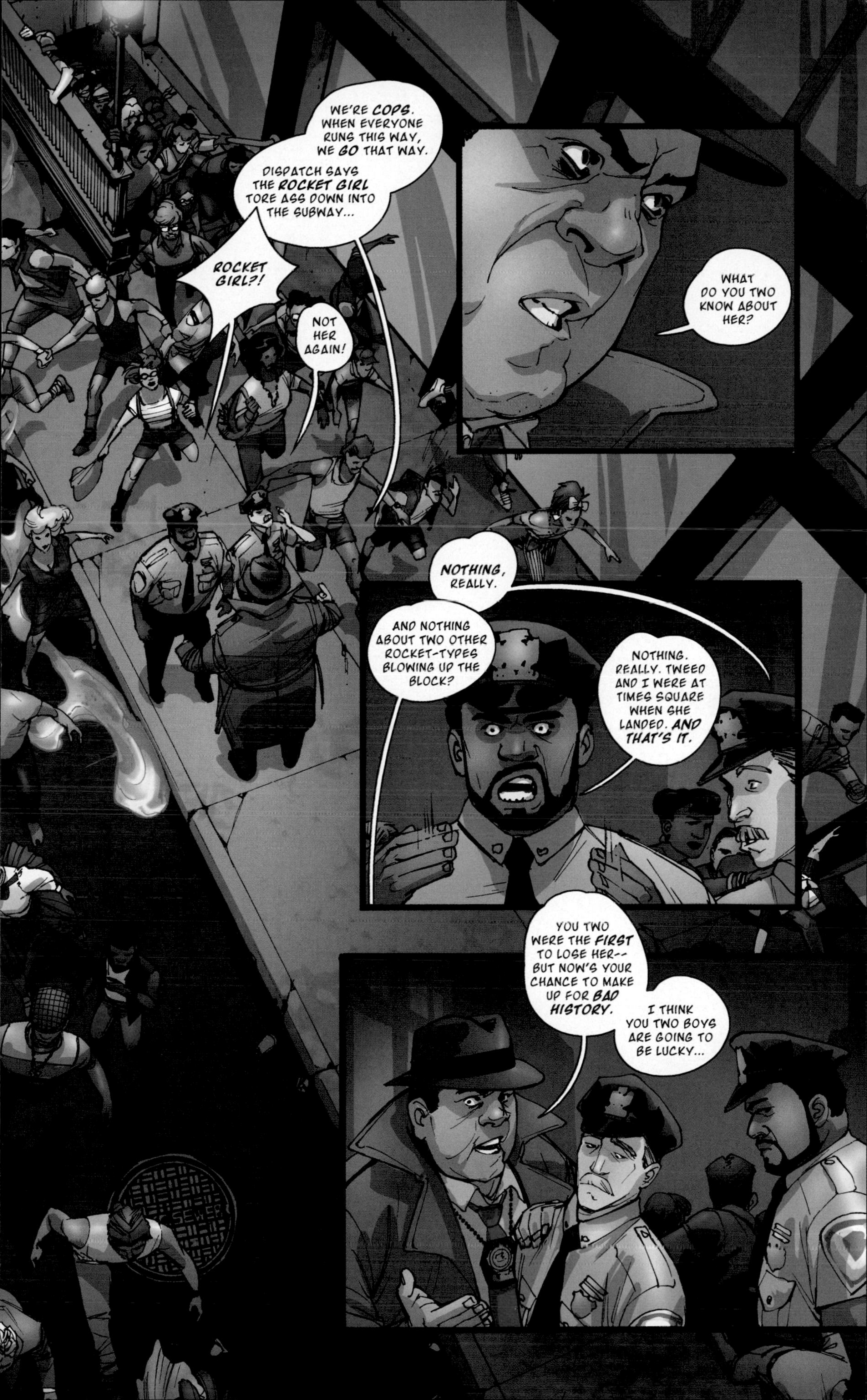

WE'RE COPS. WHEN EVERYONE RUNS THIS WAY, WE GO THAT WAY.
DISPATCH SAYS THE ROCKET GIRL TORE ASS DOWN INTO THE SUBWAY...
ROCKET GIRL?!
NOT HER AGAIN!
WHAT DO YOU TWO KNOW ABOUT HER?
NOTHING, REALLY.
AND NOTHING ABOUT TWO OTHER ROCKET-TYPES BLOWING UP THE BLOCK?
NOTHING. REALLY. TWEED AND I WERE AT TIMES SQUARE WHEN SHE LANDED. AND THAT'S IT.
YOU TWO WERE THE FIRST TO LOSE HER-- BUT NOW'S YOUR CHANCE TO MAKE UP FOR BAD HISTORY.
I THINK YOU TWO BOYS ARE GOING TO BE LUCKY...
SEWER

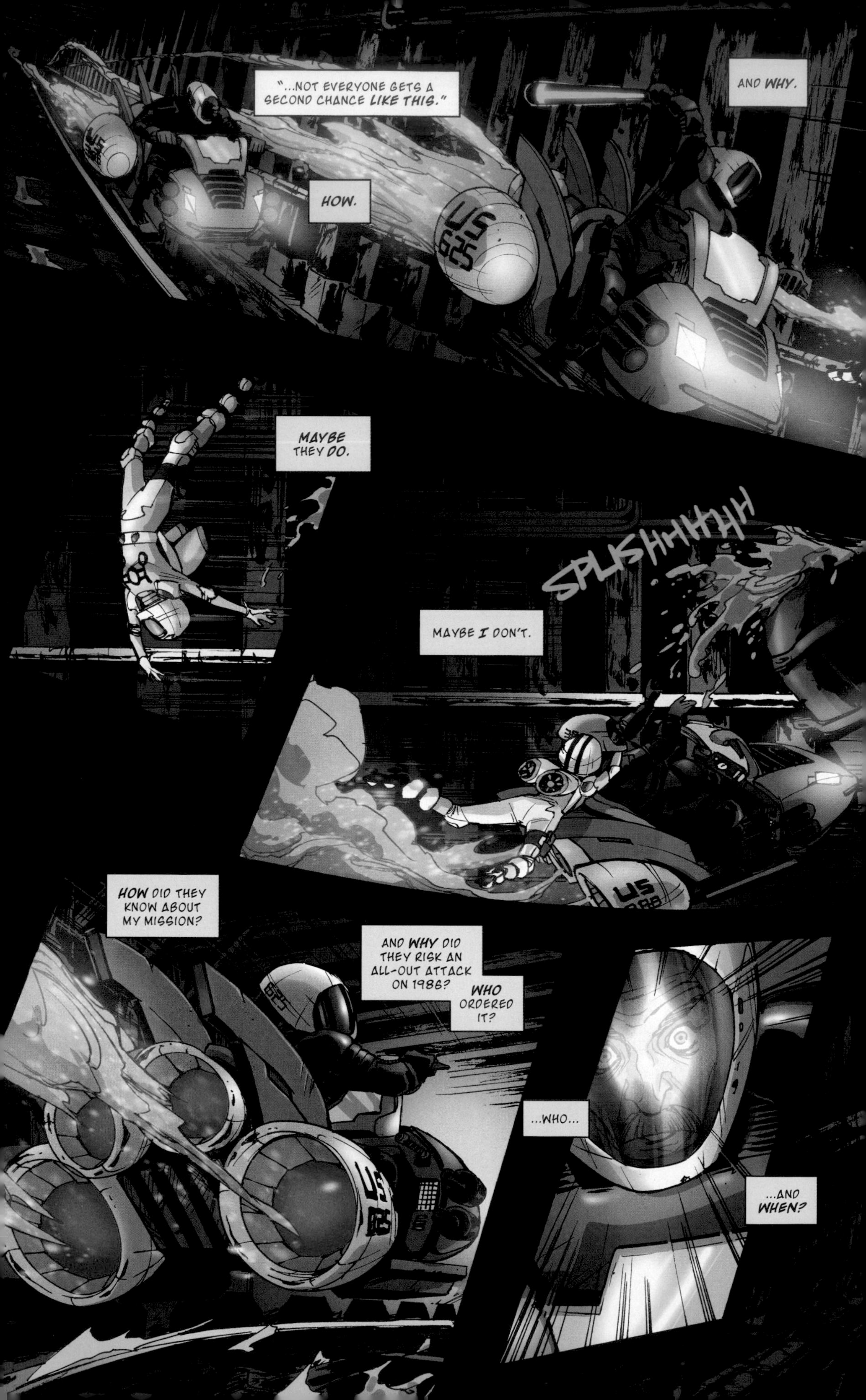
"...NOT EVERYONE GETS A SECOND CHANCE LIKE THIS."
HOW.
AND WHY.
MAYBE THEY DO.
SPLISHHHHHH
MAYBE I DON'T.
HOW DID THEY KNOW ABOUT MY MISSION?
AND WHY DID THEY RISK AN ALL-OUT ATTACK ON 1986?
WHO ORDERED IT?
...WHO...
...AND WHEN?

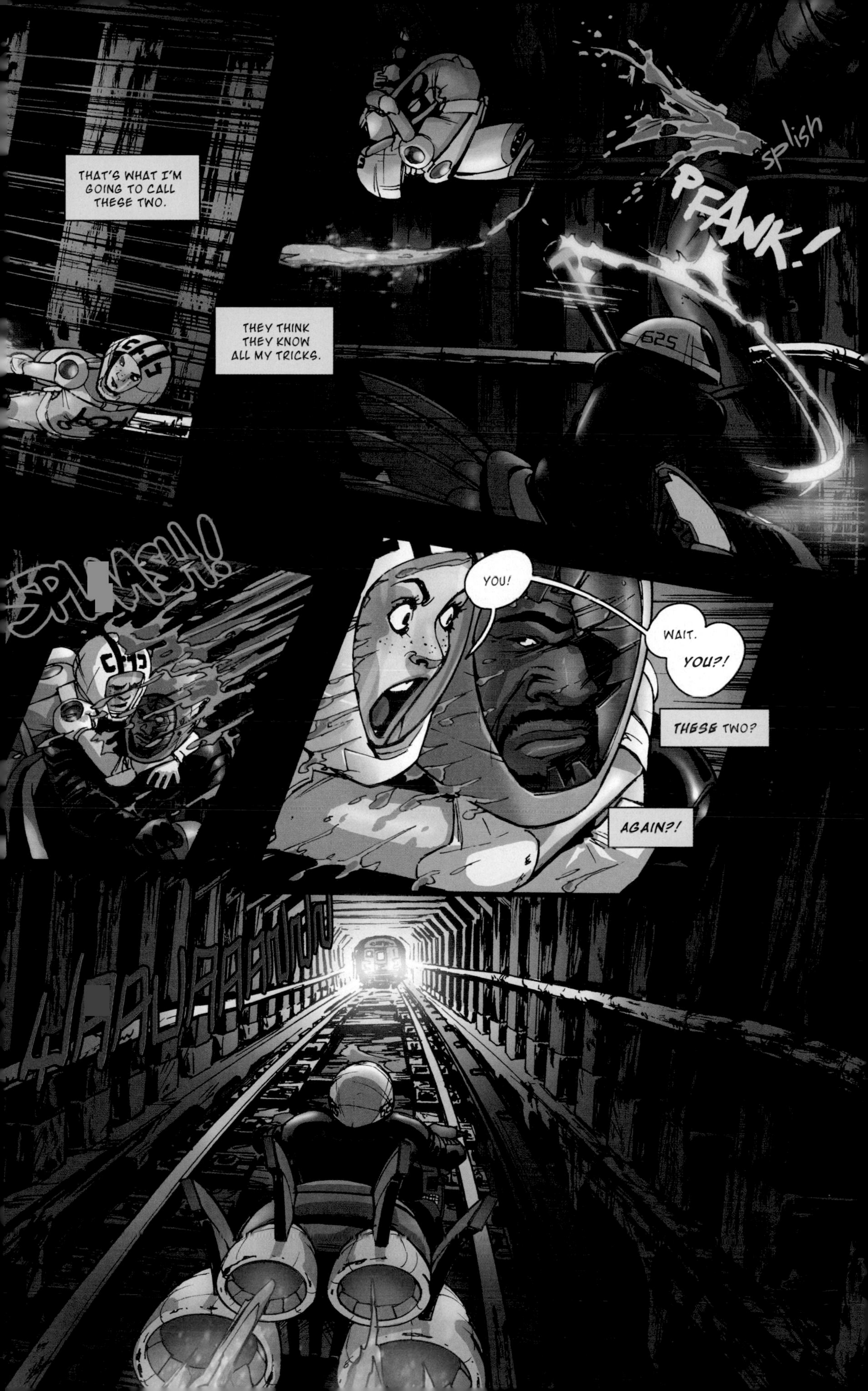

THAT'S WHAT I'M GOING TO CALL THESE TWO.
THEY THINK THEY KNOW ALL MY TRICKS.
splish
PFANK!
YOU!
WAIT. YOU?!
THESE TWO?
AGAIN?!

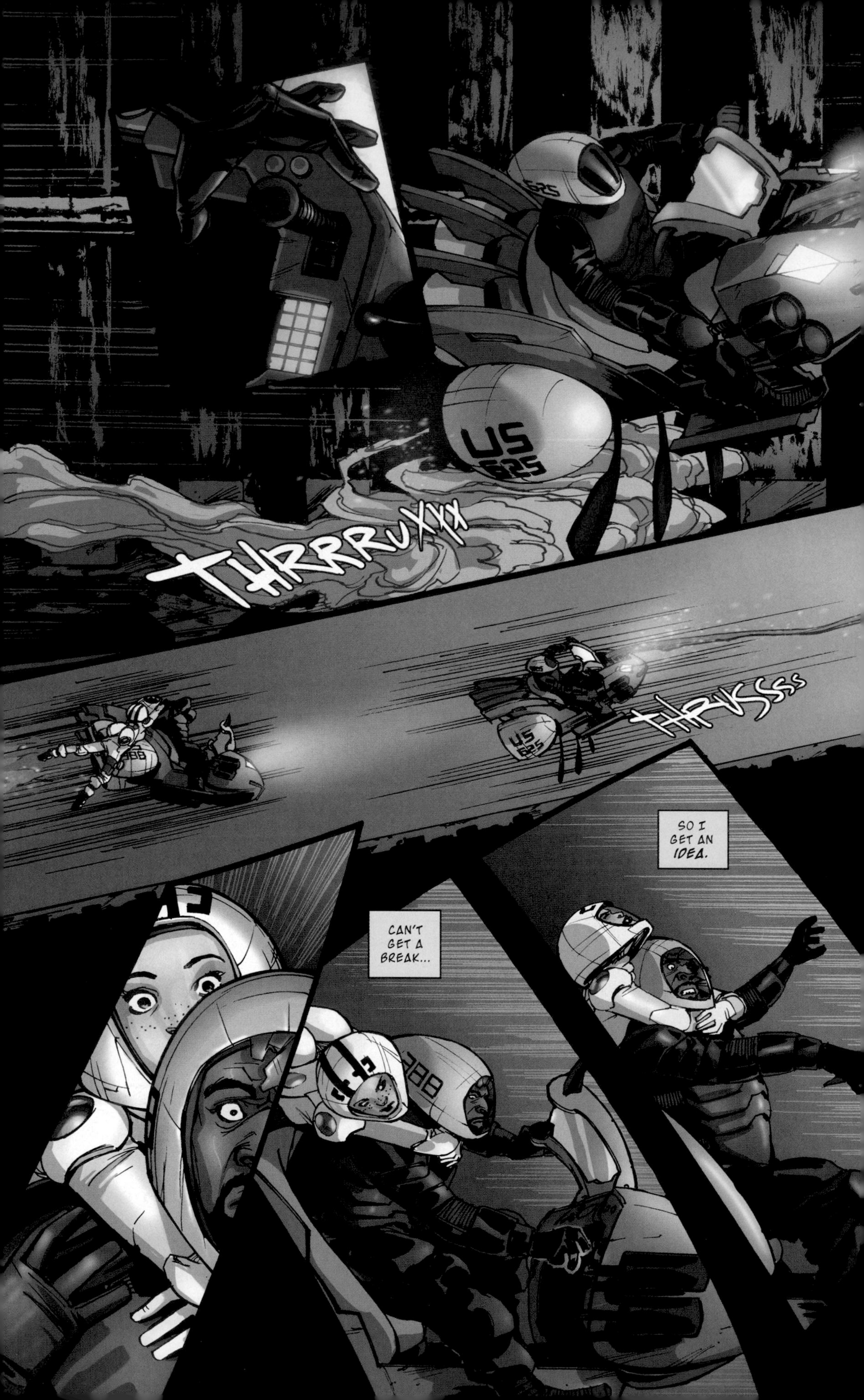
US 625
THRRRUXXX
US 625
THRUSSSS
SO I GET AN IDEA.
CAN'T GET A BREAK...

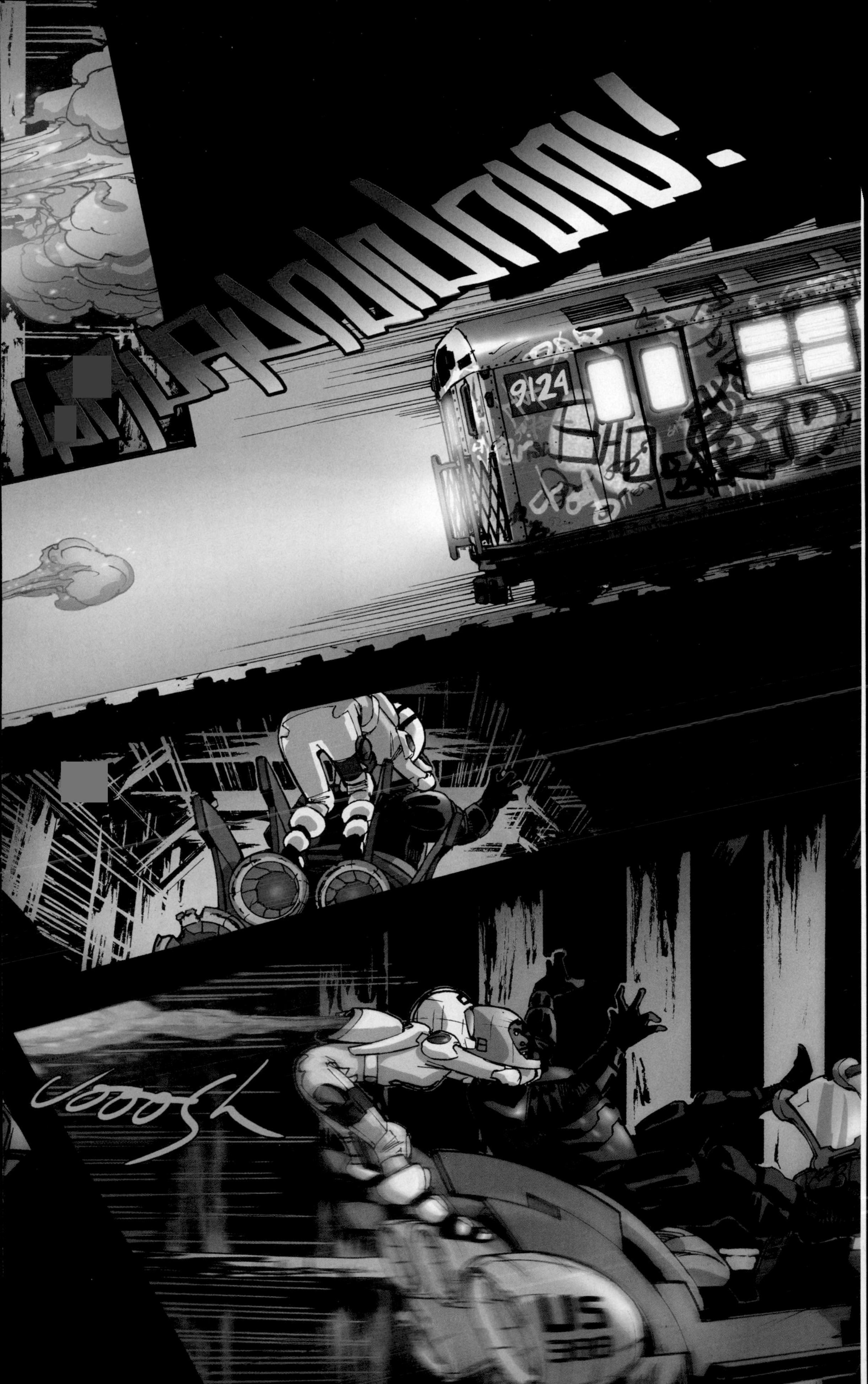
9124
vooosh
US

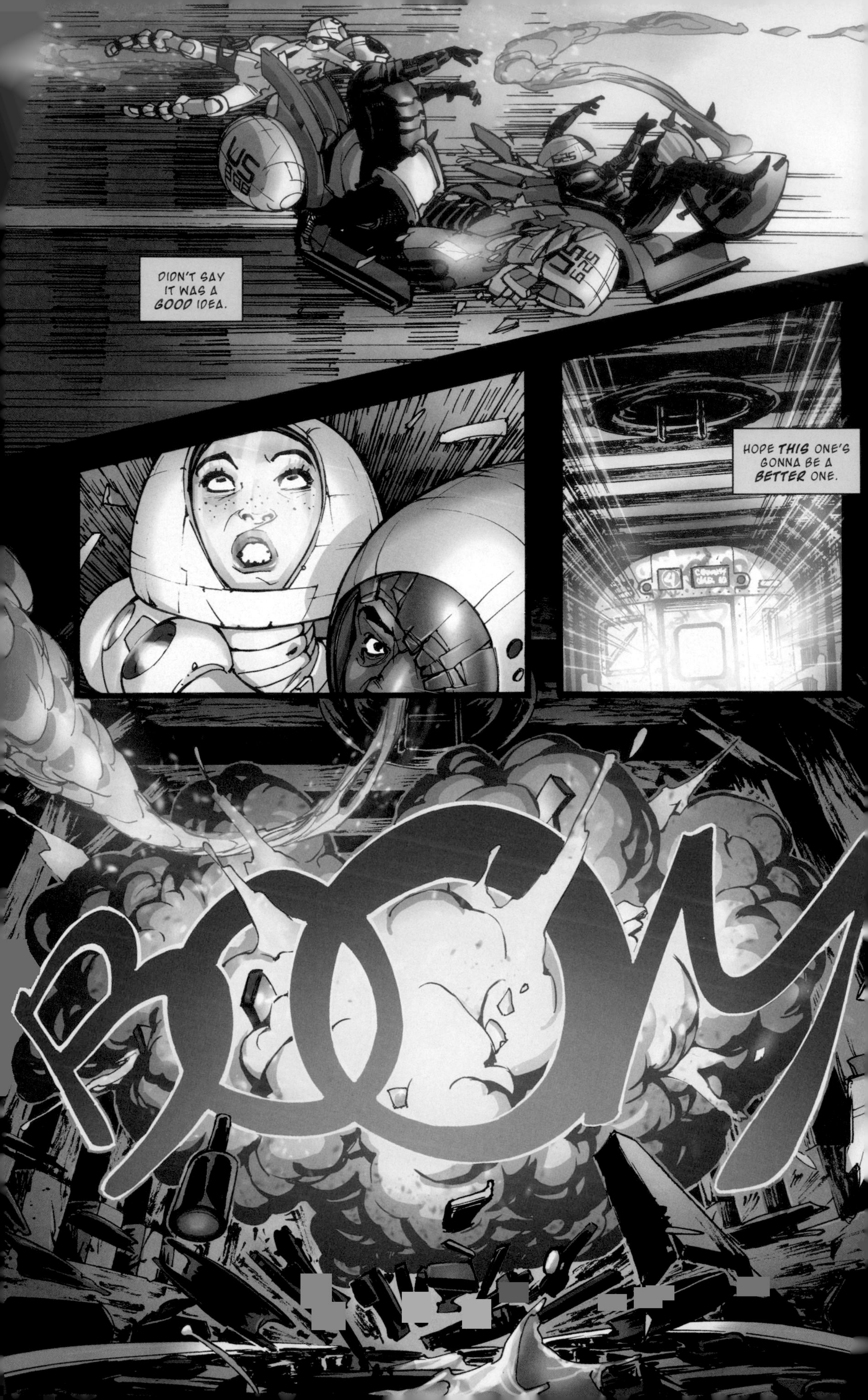
DIDN'T SAY IT WAS A GOOD IDEA.
HOPE THIS ONE'S GONNA BE A BETTER ONE.
BOOM

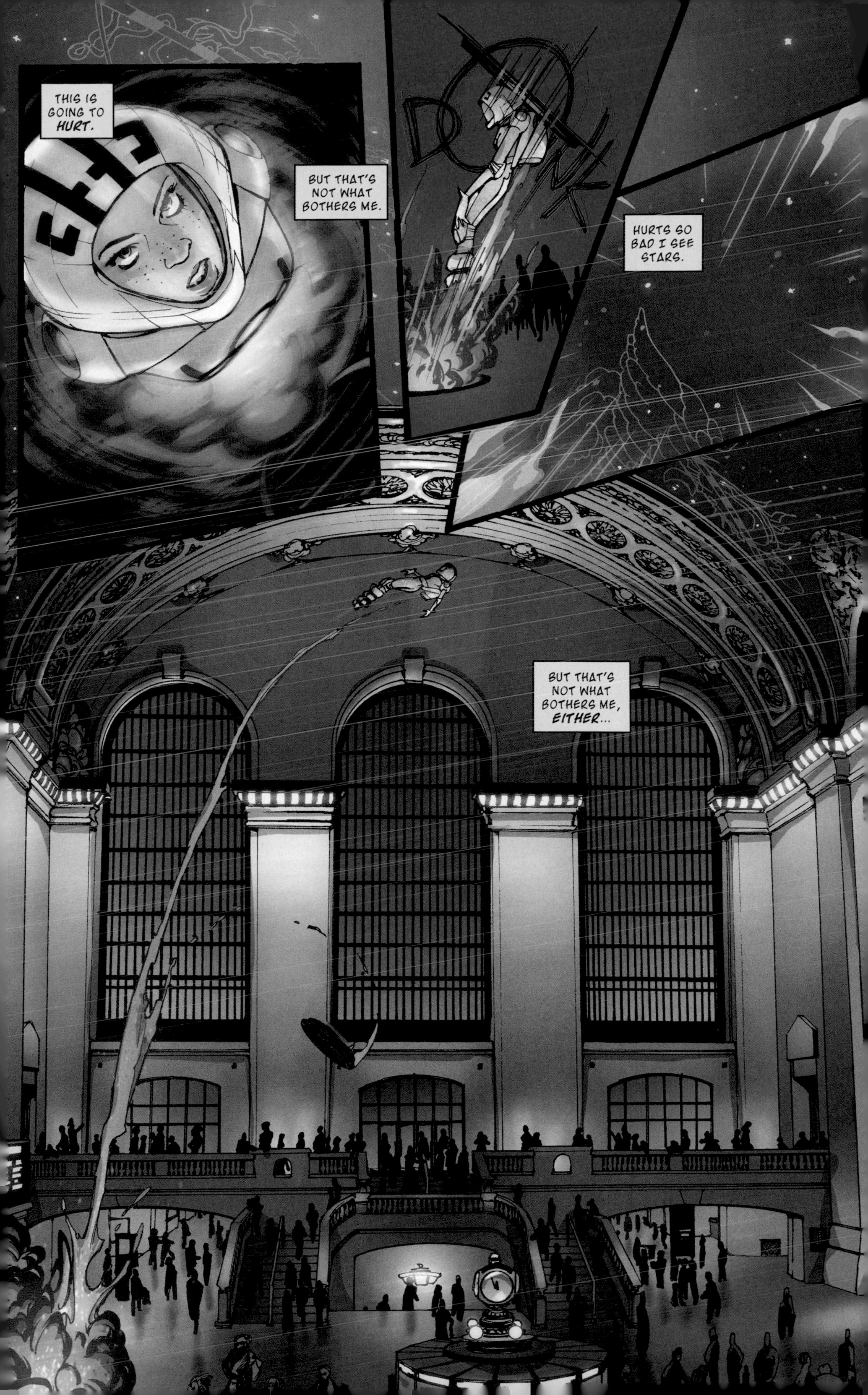
THIS IS GOING TO HURT.
BUT THAT'S NOT WHAT BOTHERS ME.
DONK
HURTS SO BAD I SEE STARS.
BUT THAT'S NOT WHAT BOTHERS ME, EITHER...

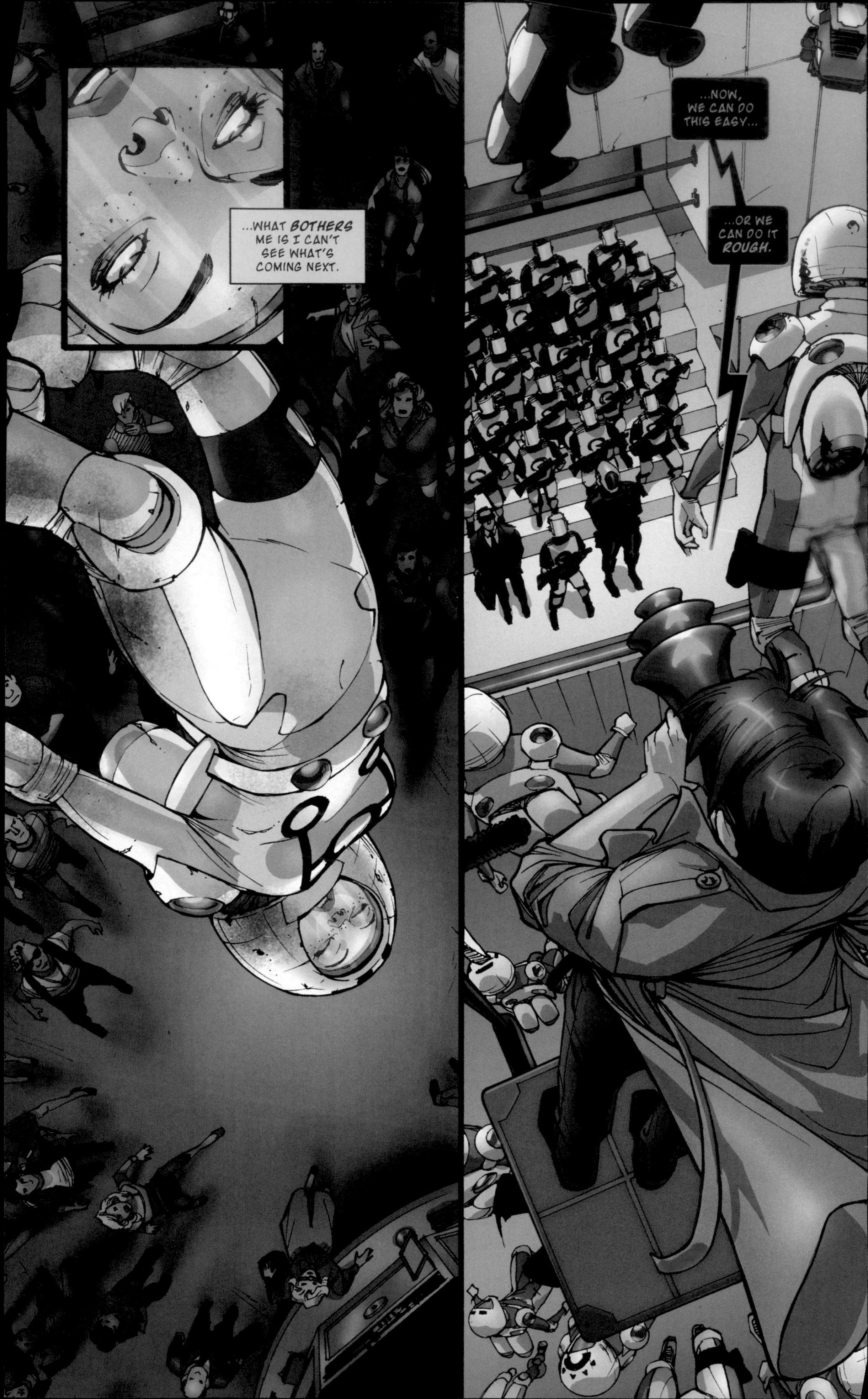
...WHAT BOTHERS ME IS I CAN'T SEE WHAT'S COMING NEXT.
...NOW, WE CAN DO THIS EASY...
...OR WE CAN DO IT ROUGH.

Chapter 5_Time Will Tell >>

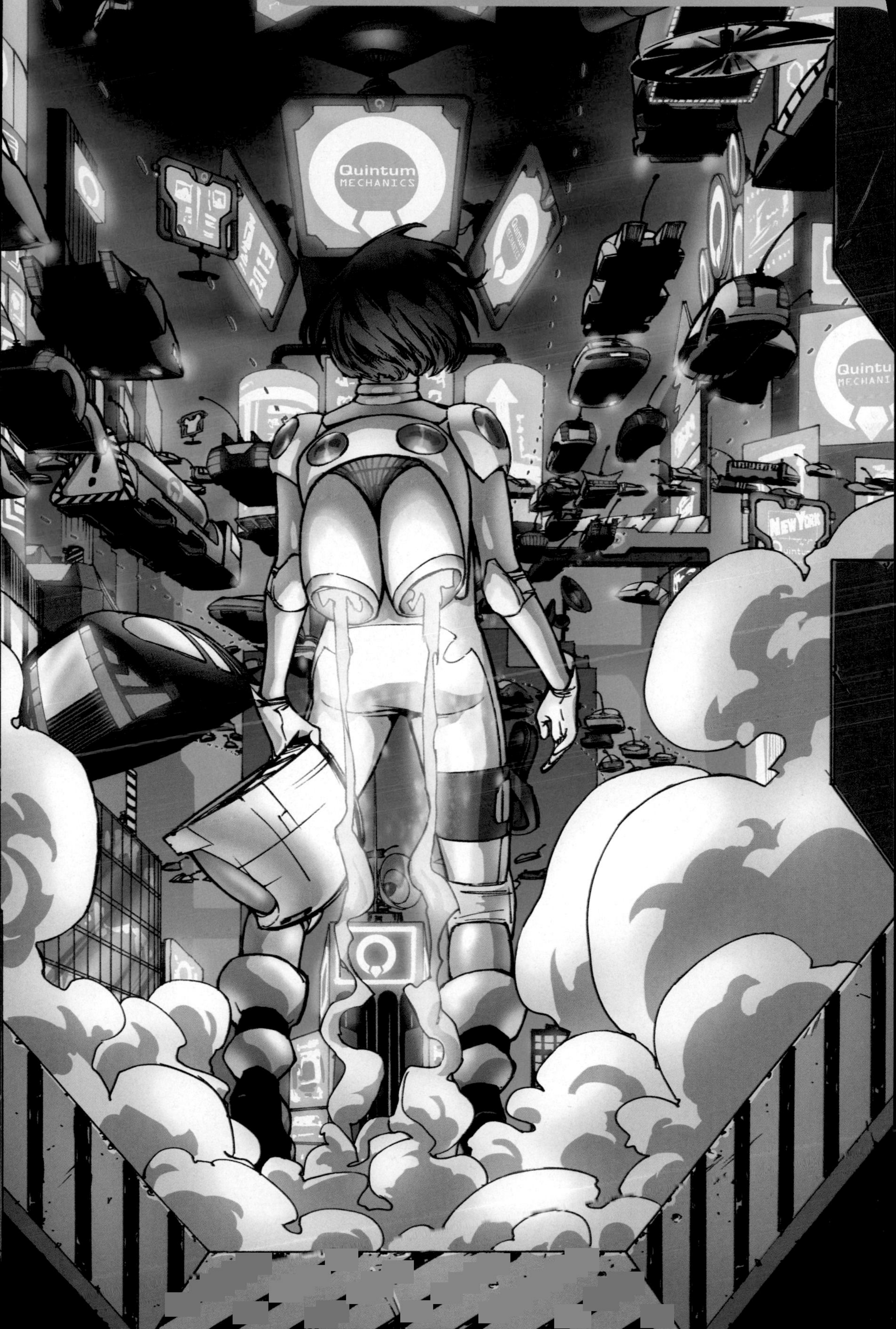
Quintum
MECHANICS
NEW YORK

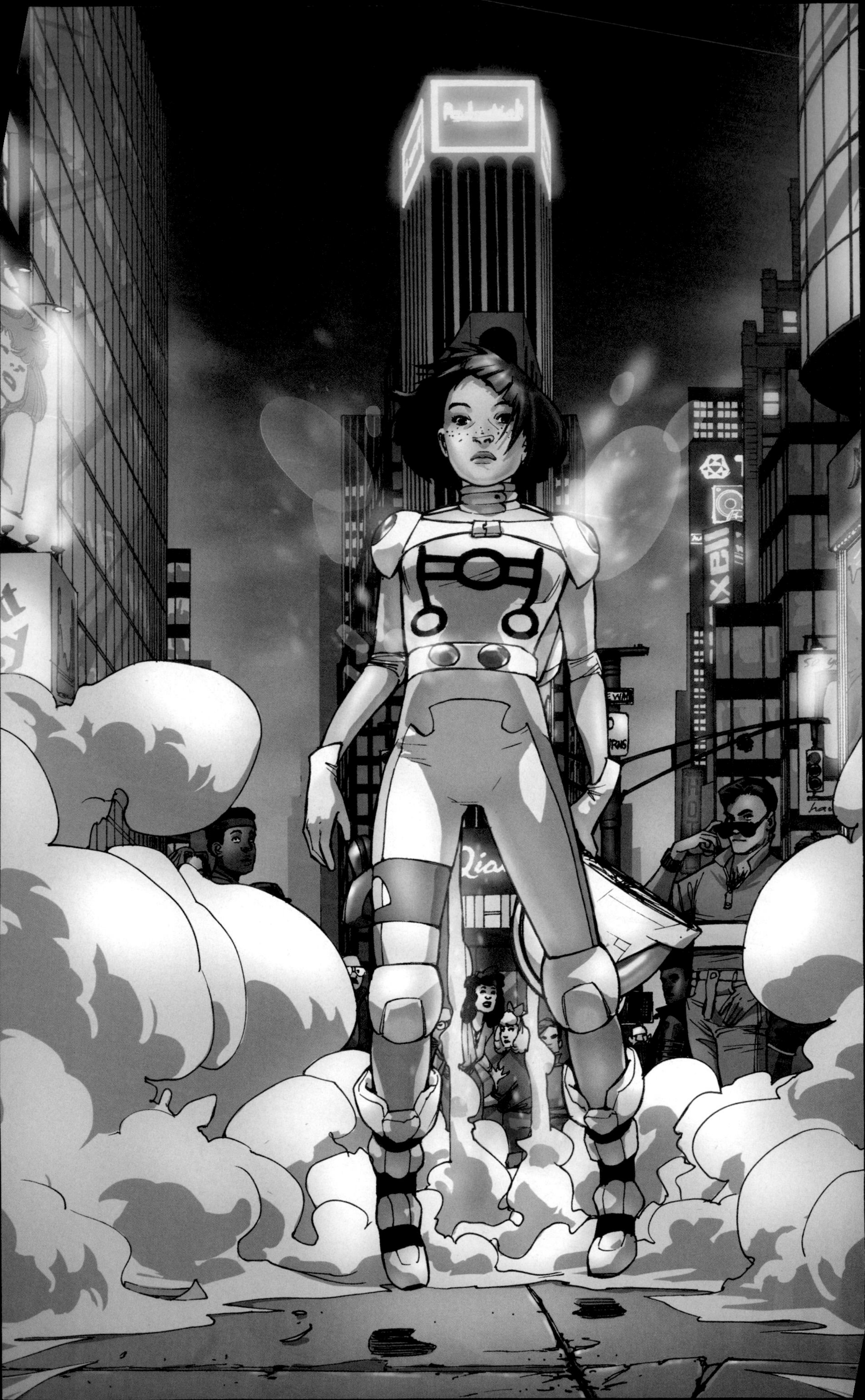

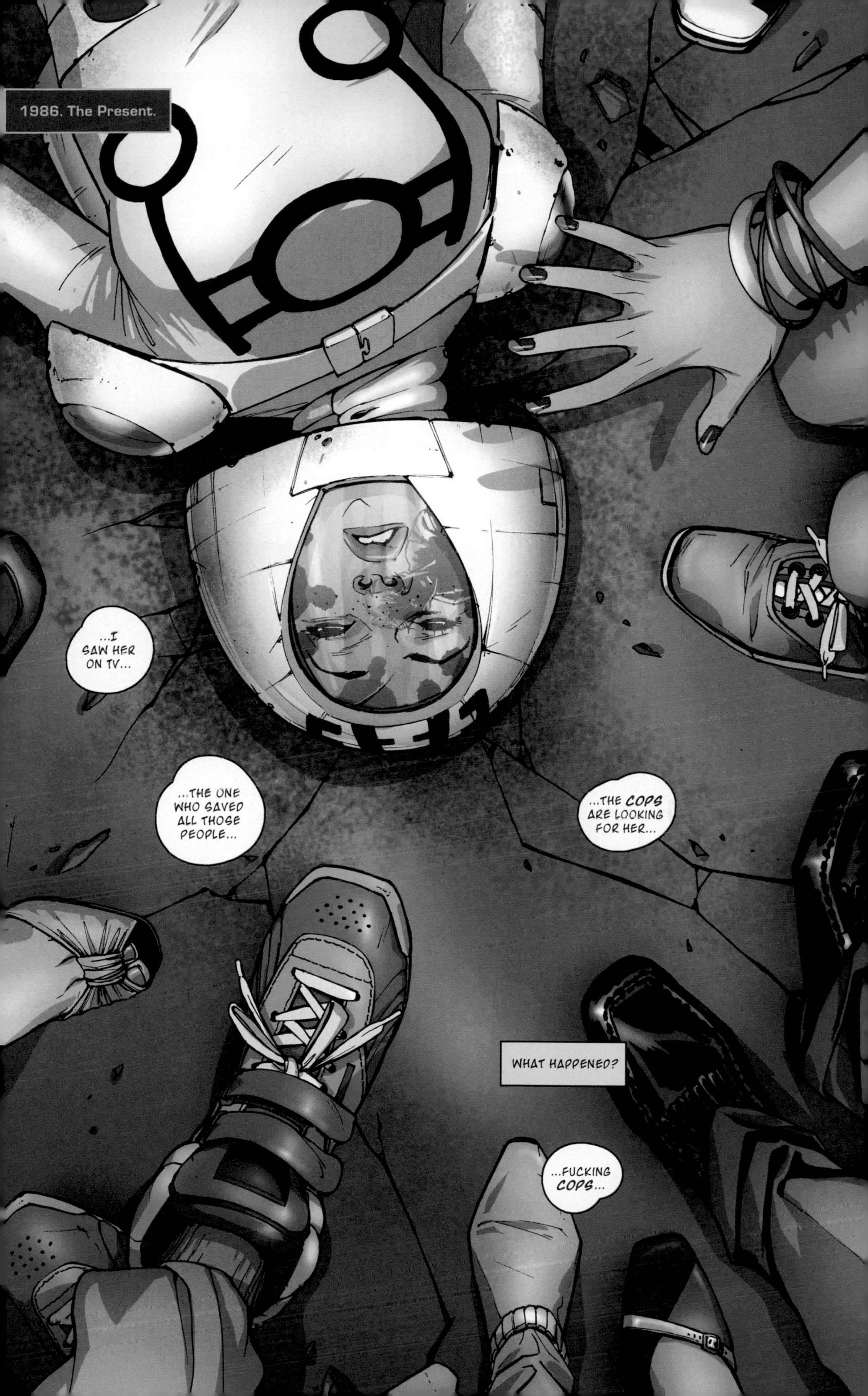
1986. The Present.
...I SAW HER ON TV...
...THE ONE WHO SAVED ALL THOSE PEOPLE...
...THE COPS ARE LOOKING FOR HER...
WHAT HAPPENED?
...FUCKING COPS...

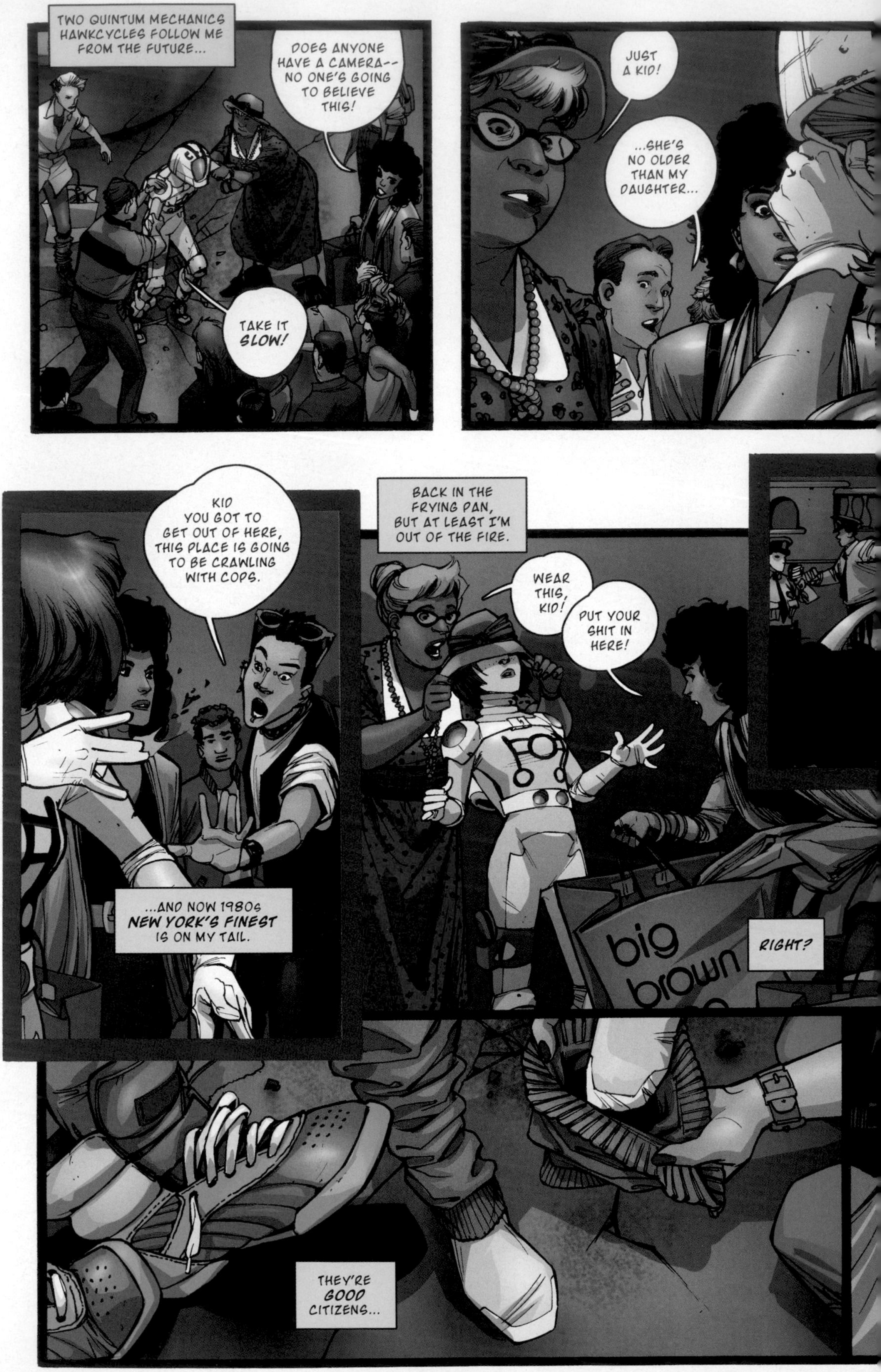

TWO QUINTUM MECHANICS HAWKCYCLES FOLLOW ME FROM THE FUTURE...
DOES ANYONE HAVE A CAMERA-- NO ONE'S GOING TO BELIEVE THIS!
TAKE IT SLOW!
JUST A KID!
...SHE'S NO OLDER THAN MY DAUGHTER...
KID YOU GOT TO GET OUT OF HERE, THIS PLACE IS GOING TO BE CRAWLING WITH COPS.
...AND NOW 1980s NEW YORK'S FINEST IS ON MY TAIL.
BACK IN THE FRYING PAN, BUT AT LEAST I'M OUT OF THE FIRE.
WEAR THIS, KID!
PUT YOUR SHIT IN HERE!
big brown
RIGHT?
THEY'RE GOOD CITIZENS...

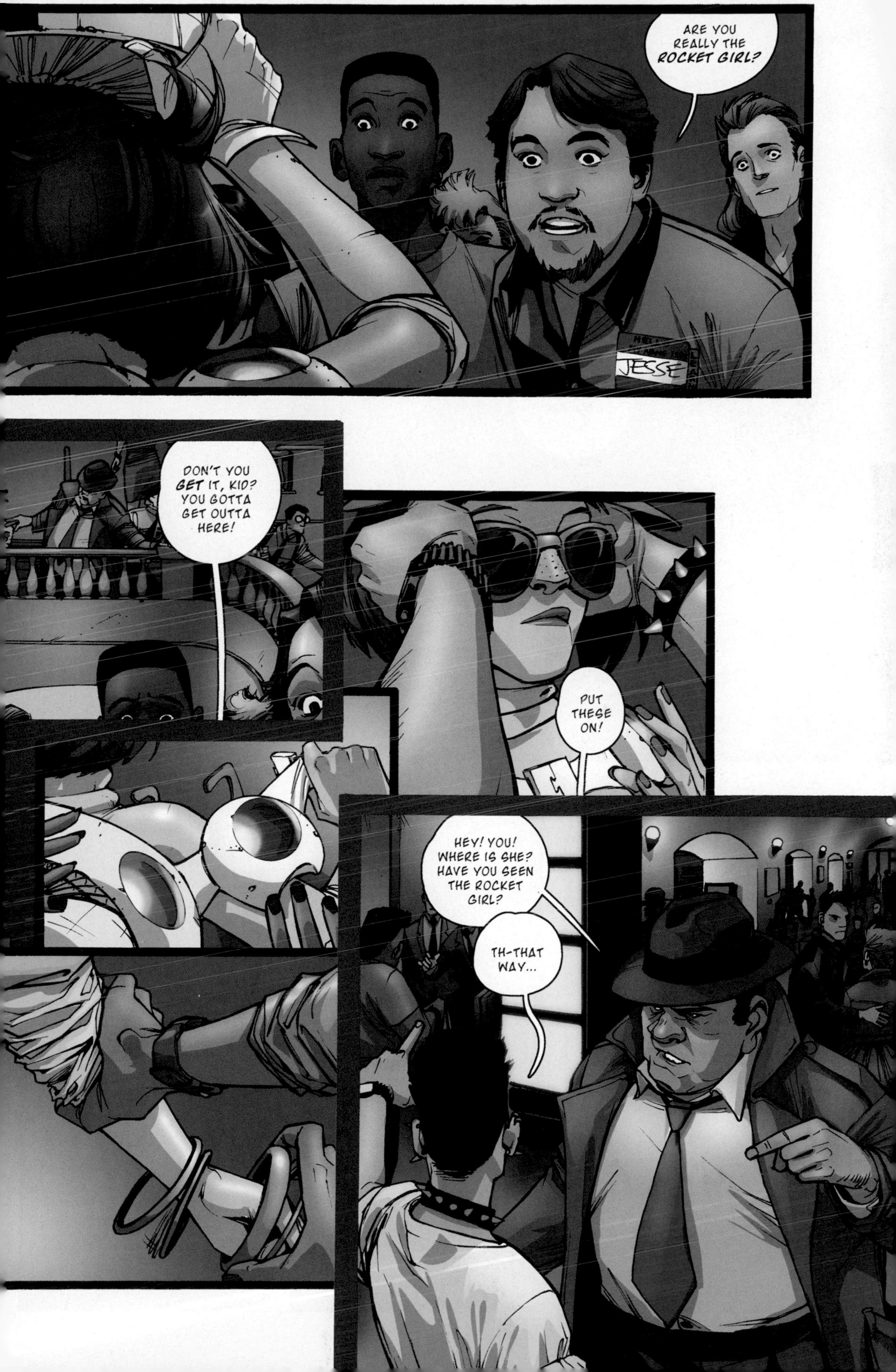

ARE YOU REALLY THE ROCKET GIRL?
JESSE
DON'T YOU GET IT, KID? YOU GOTTA GET OUTTA HERE!
PUT THESE ON!
HEY! YOU! WHERE IS SHE? HAVE YOU SEEN THE ROCKET GIRL?
TH-THAT WAY...

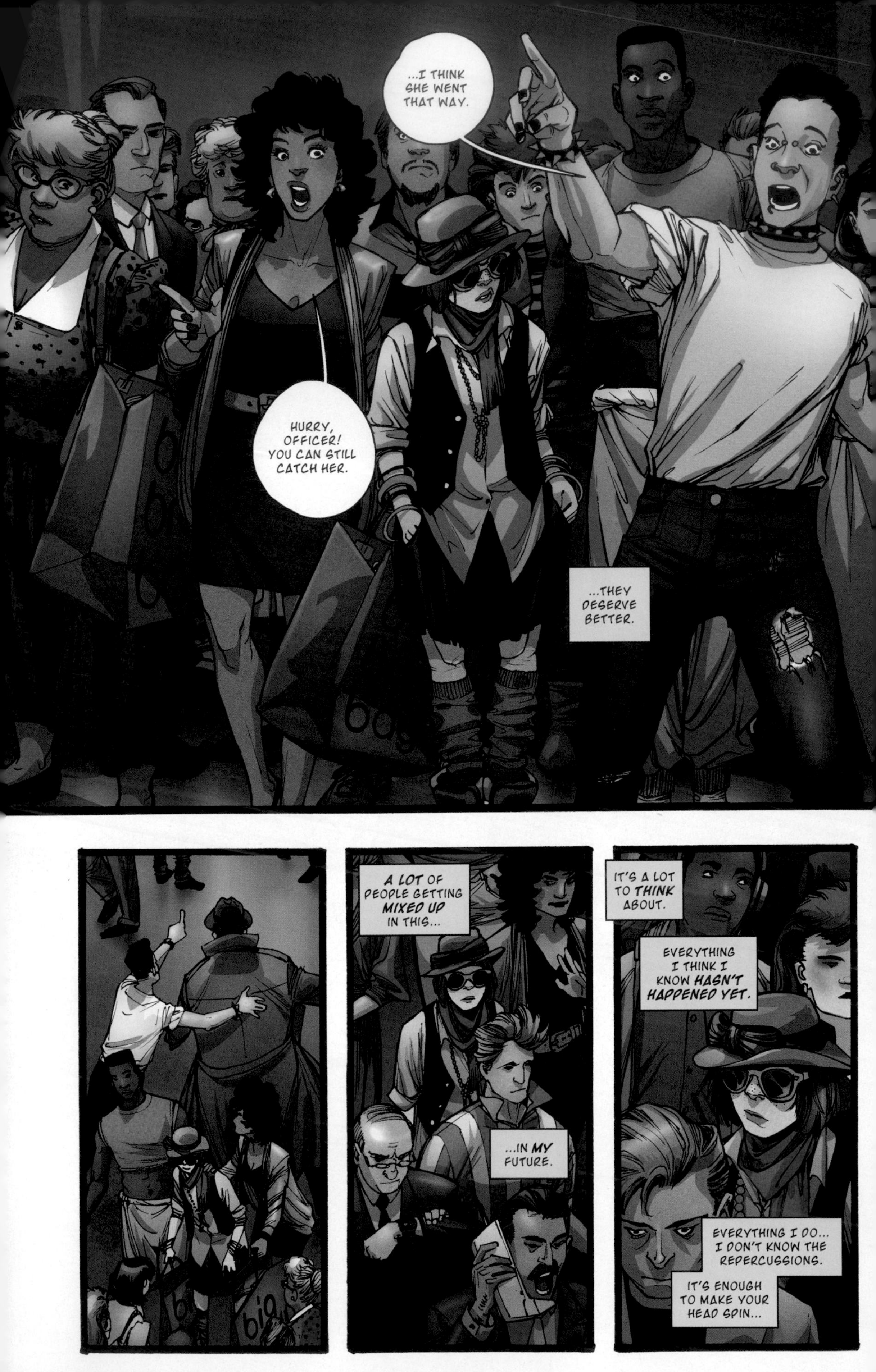

...I THINK SHE WENT THAT WAY.
HURRY, OFFICER! YOU CAN STILL CATCH HER.
...THEY DESERVE BETTER.
A LOT OF PEOPLE GETTING MIXED UP IN THIS...
...IN MY FUTURE.
IT'S A LOT TO THINK ABOUT.
EVERYTHING I THINK I KNOW HASN'T HAPPENED YET.
EVERYTHING I DO... I DON'T KNOW THE REPERCUSSIONS.
IT'S ENOUGH TO MAKE YOUR HEAD SPIN...

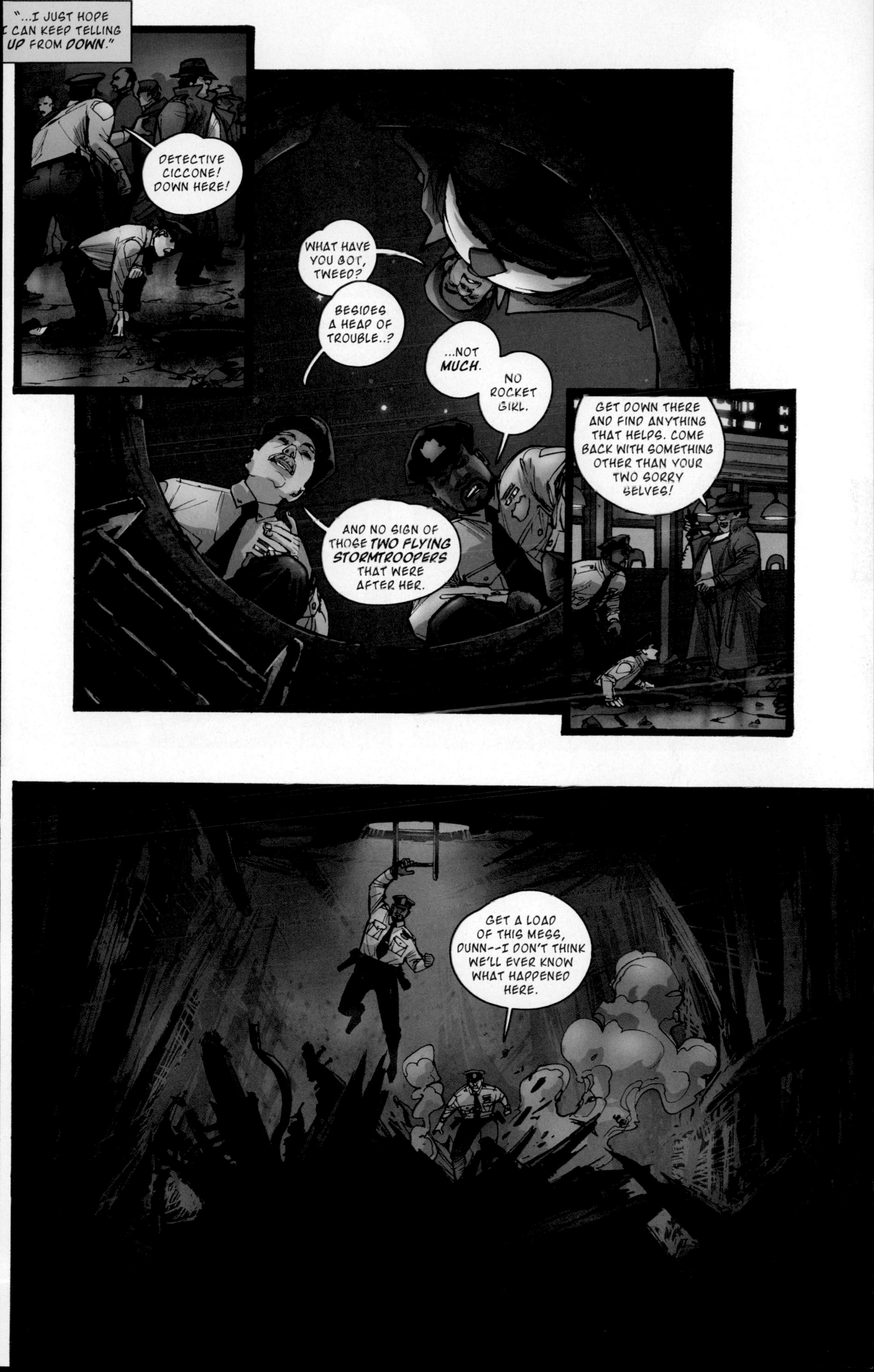
"...I JUST HOPE I CAN KEEP TELLING UP FROM DOWN."
DETECTIVE CICCONE! DOWN HERE!
WHAT HAVE YOU GOT, TWEED?
BESIDES A HEAP OF TROUBLE..?
...NOT MUCH.
NO ROCKET GIRL.
AND NO SIGN OF THOSE TWO FLYING STORMTROOPERS THAT WERE AFTER HER.
GET DOWN THERE AND FIND ANYTHING THAT HELPS. COME BACK WITH SOMETHING OTHER THAN YOUR TWO SORRY SELVES!
GET A LOAD OF THIS MESS, DUNN--I DON'T THINK WE'LL EVER KNOW WHAT HAPPENED HERE.

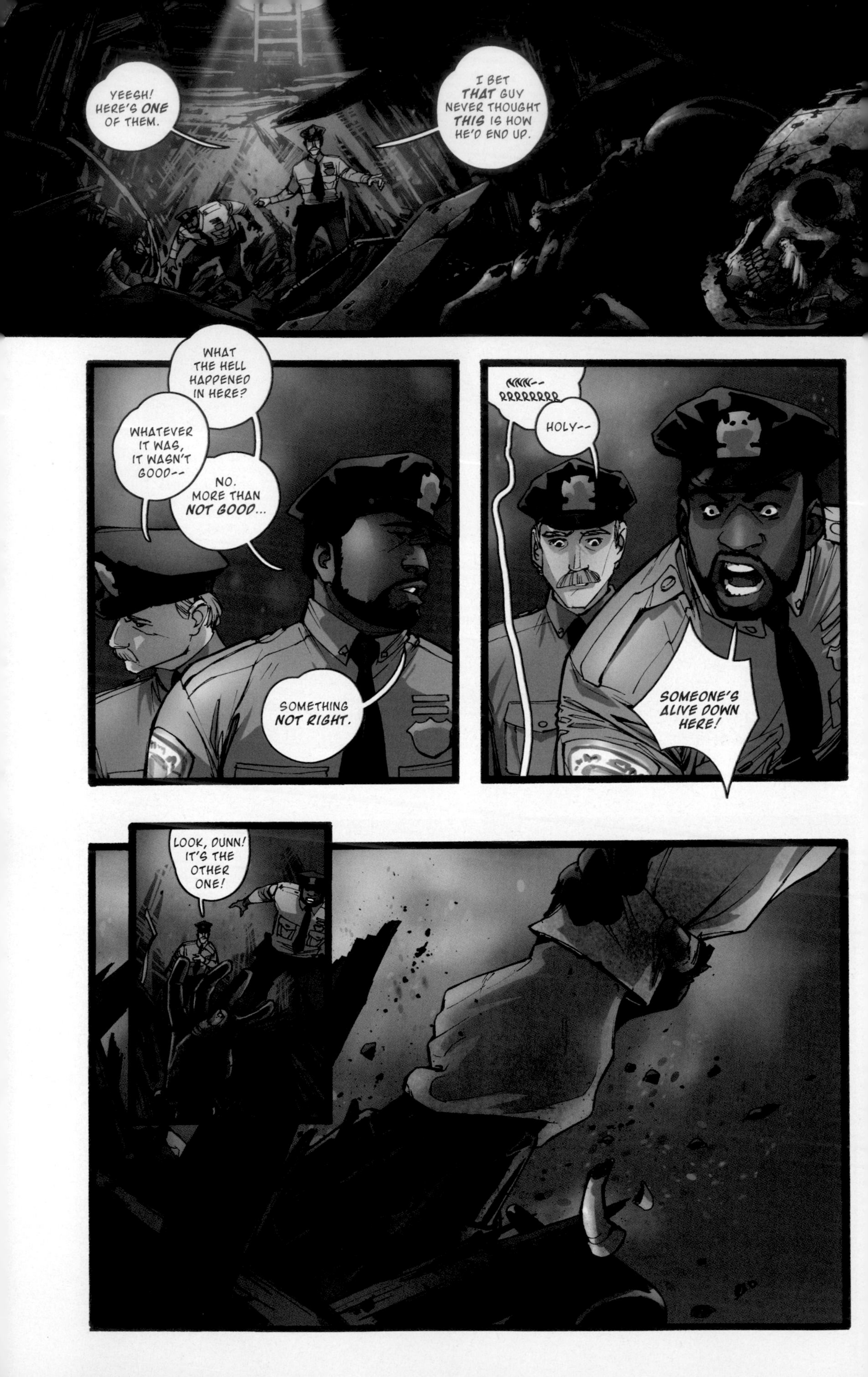
YEESH! HERE'S ONE OF THEM.
I BET THAT GUY NEVER THOUGHT THIS IS HOW HE'D END UP.
WHAT THE HELL HAPPENED IN HERE?
WHATEVER IT WAS, IT WASN'T GOOD--
NO. MORE THAN NOT GOOD...
SOMETHING NOT RIGHT.
NNN-- RRRRRRRR
HOLY--
SOMEONE'S ALIVE DOWN HERE!
LOOK, DUNN! IT'S THE OTHER ONE!

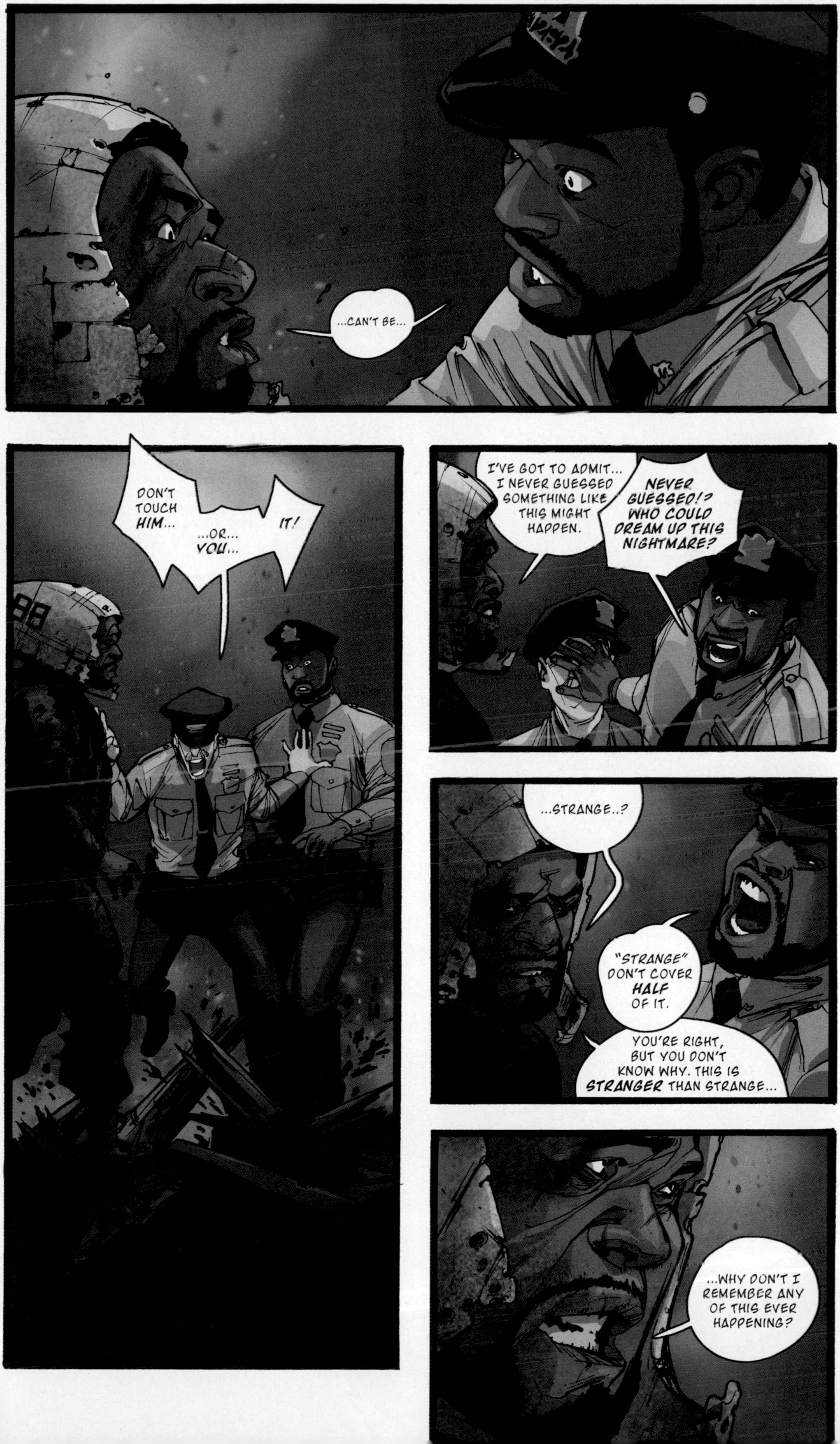
...CAN'T BE...
DON'T TOUCH HIM...
...OR... YOU...
IT!
I'VE GOT TO ADMIT... I NEVER GUESSED SOMETHING LIKE THIS MIGHT HAPPEN.
NEVER GUESSED!? WHO COULD DREAM UP THIS NIGHTMARE?
...STRANGE..?
"STRANGE" DON'T COVER HALF OF IT.
YOU'RE RIGHT, BUT YOU DON'T KNOW WHY. THIS IS STRANGER THAN STRANGE...
...WHY DON'T I REMEMBER ANY OF THIS EVER HAPPENING?

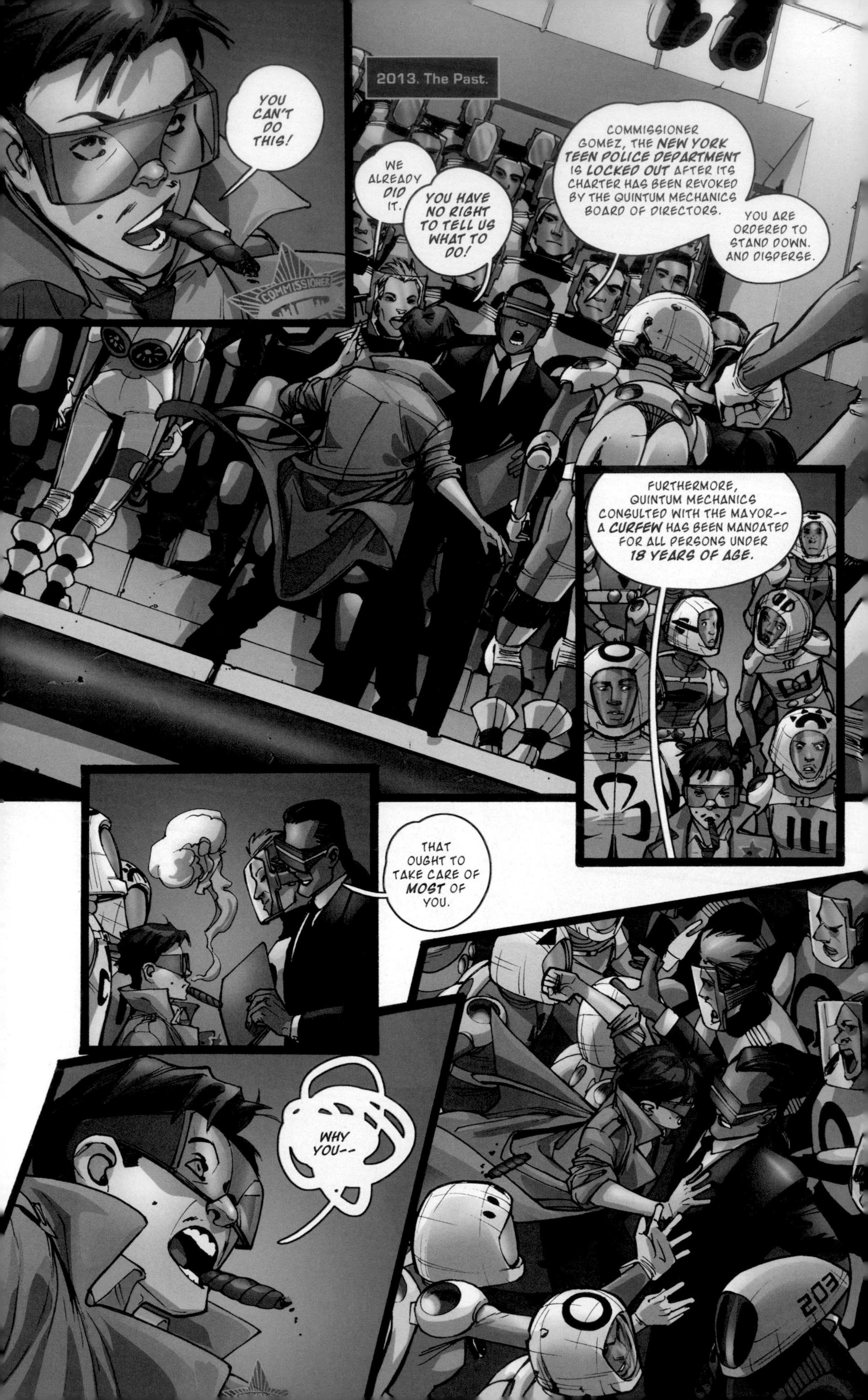
2013. The Past.
YOU CAN'T DO THIS!
WE ALREADY DID IT.
YOU HAVE NO RIGHT TO TELL US WHAT TO DO!
COMMISSIONER GOMEZ, THE NEW YORK TEEN POLICE DEPARTMENT IS LOCKED OUT AFTER ITS CHARTER HAS BEEN REVOKED BY THE QUINTUM MECHANICS BOARD OF DIRECTORS.
YOU ARE ORDERED TO STAND DOWN. AND DISPERSE.
COMMISSIONER
FURTHERMORE, QUINTUM MECHANICS CONSULTED WITH THE MAYOR-- A CURFEW HAS BEEN MANDATED FOR ALL PERSONS UNDER 18 YEARS OF AGE.
THAT OUGHT TO TAKE CARE OF MOST OF YOU.
WHY YOU--

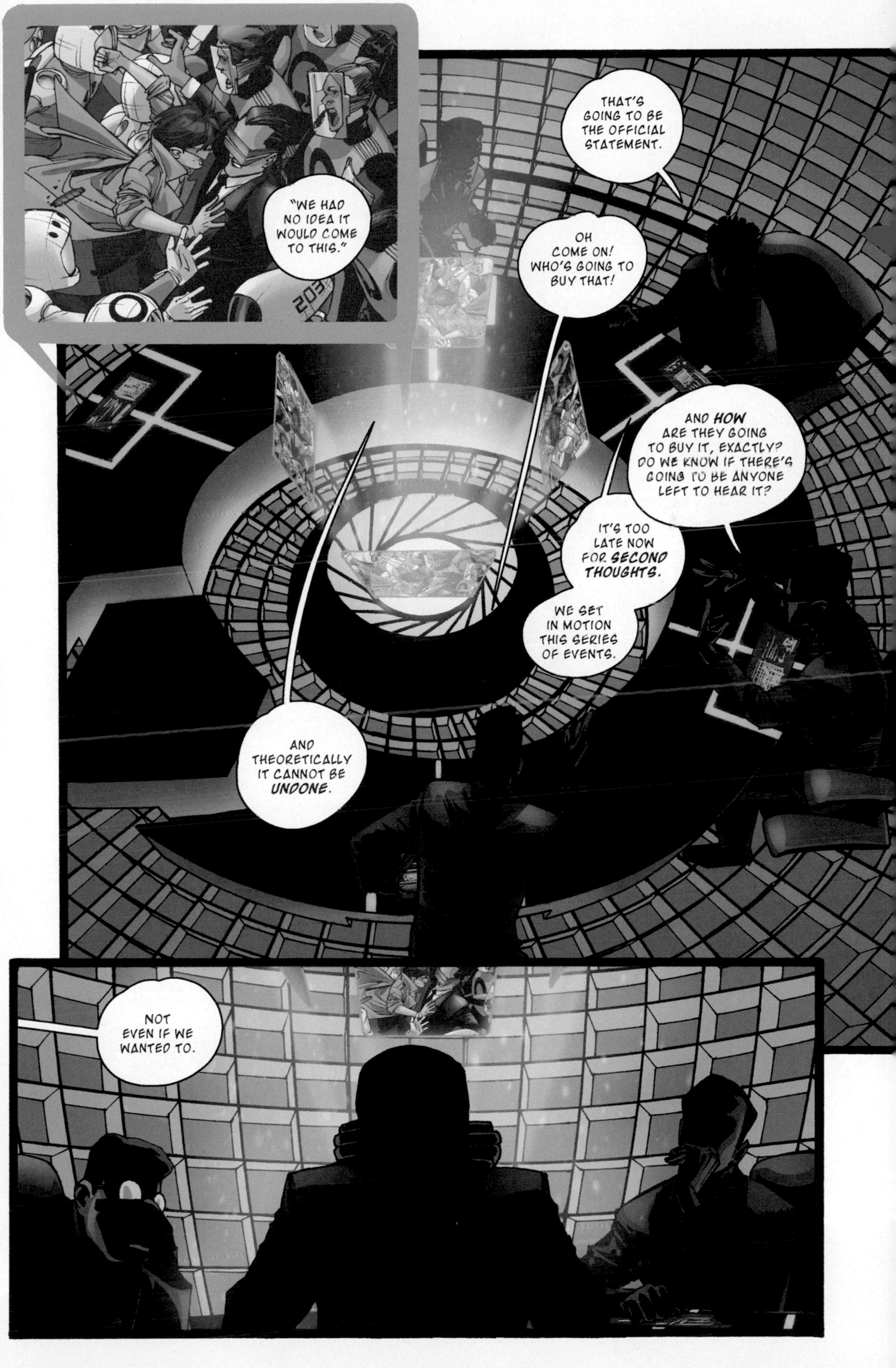
"WE HAD NO IDEA IT WOULD COME TO THIS."
THAT'S GOING TO BE THE OFFICIAL STATEMENT.
OH COME ON! WHO'S GOING TO BUY THAT!
AND HOW ARE THEY GOING TO BUY IT, EXACTLY? DO WE KNOW IF THERE'S GOING TO BE ANYONE LEFT TO HEAR IT?
IT'S TOO LATE NOW FOR SECOND THOUGHTS.
WE SET IN MOTION THIS SERIES OF EVENTS.
AND THEORETICALLY IT CANNOT BE UNDONE.
NOT EVEN IF WE WANTED TO.

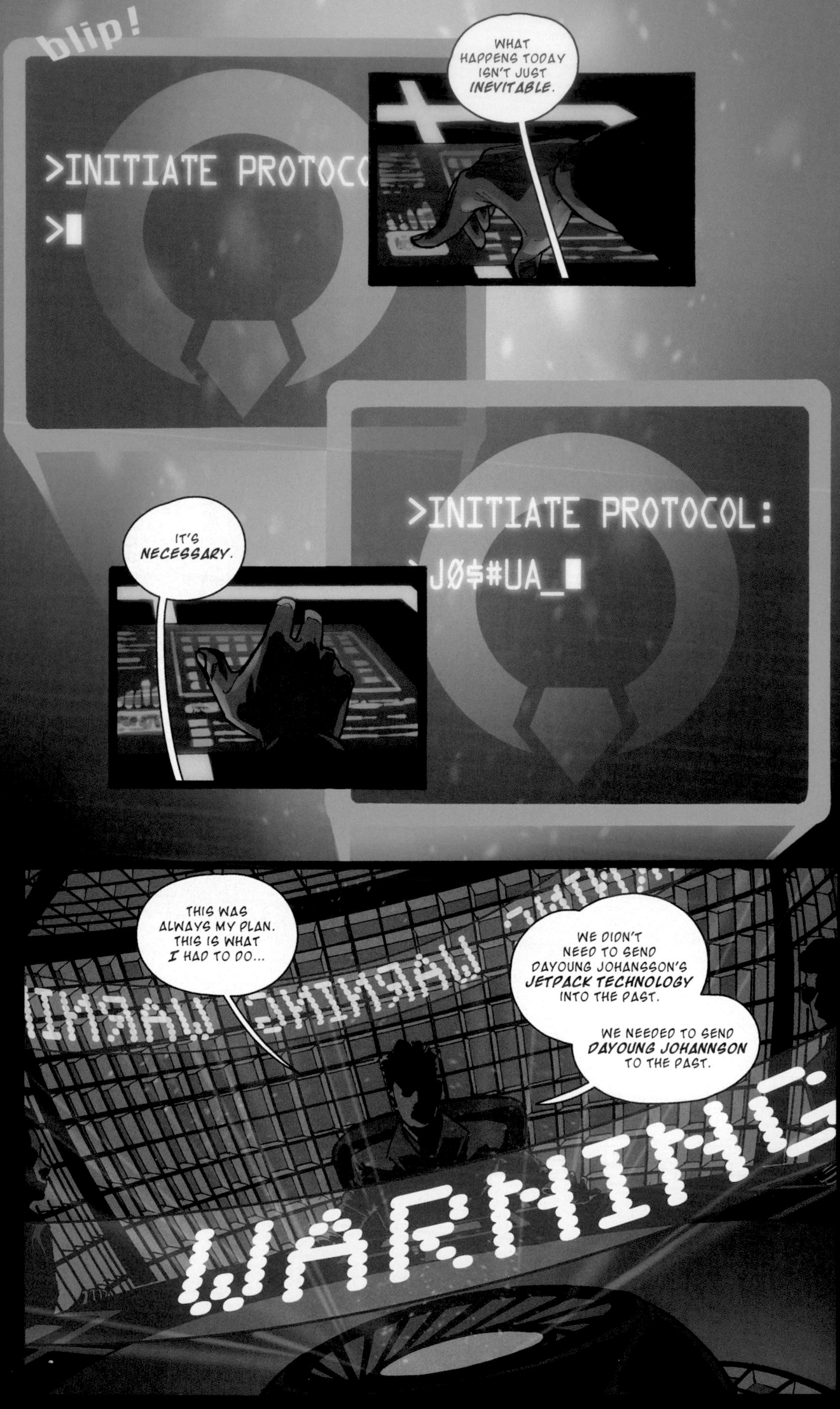
blip!
>INITIATE PROTOCO
WHAT HAPPENS TODAY ISN'T JUST INEVITABLE.
>INITIATE PROTOCOL:
>J∅$#UA_
IT'S NECESSARY.
THIS WAS ALWAYS MY PLAN. THIS IS WHAT I HAD TO DO...
WE DIDN'T NEED TO SEND DAYOUNG JOHANSSON'S JETPACK TECHNOLOGY INTO THE PAST.
WE NEEDED TO SEND DAYOUNG JOHANNSON TO THE PAST.
WARNING

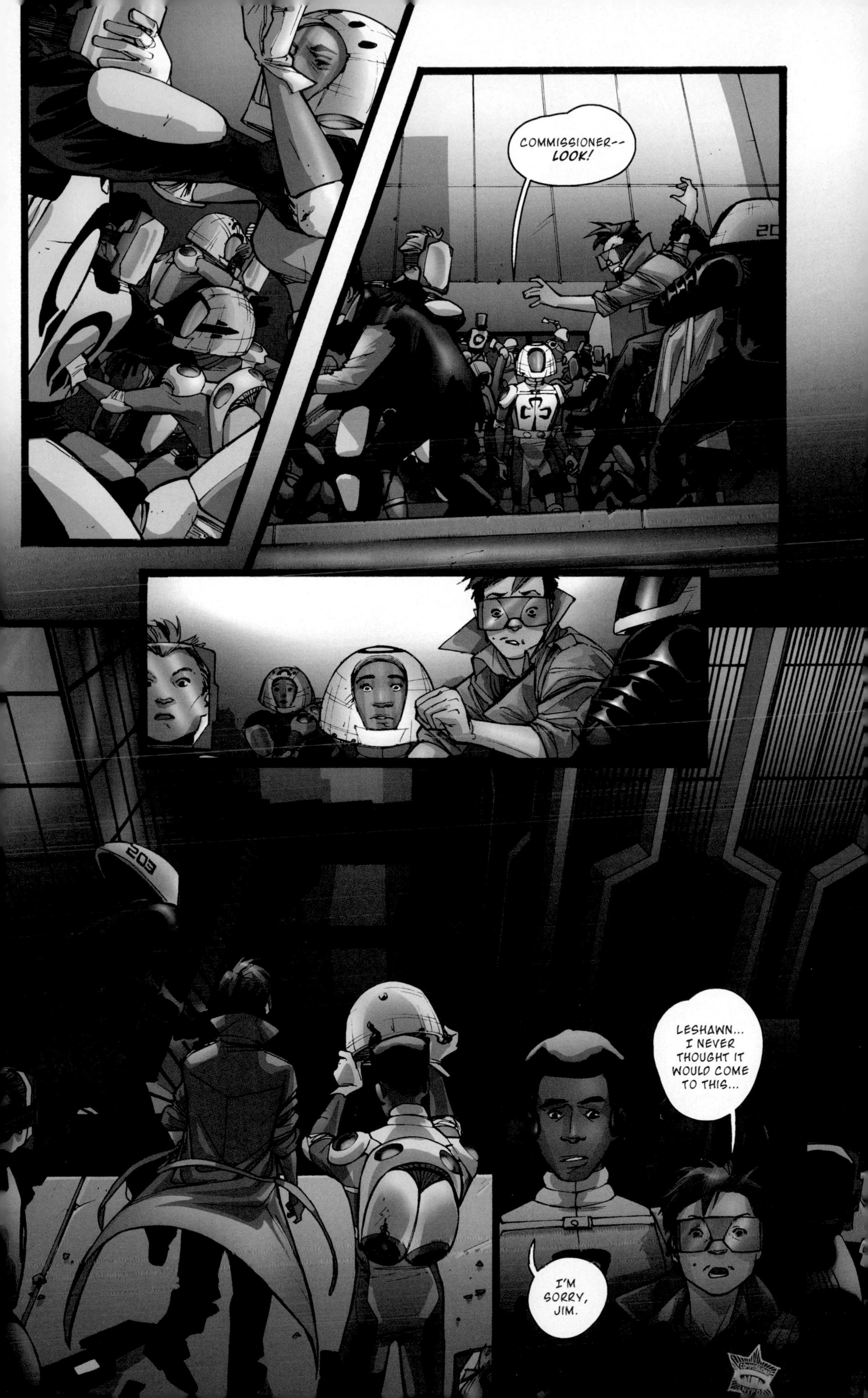
COMMISSIONER-- LOOK!
LESHAWN... I NEVER THOUGHT IT WOULD COME TO THIS...
I'M SORRY, JIM.

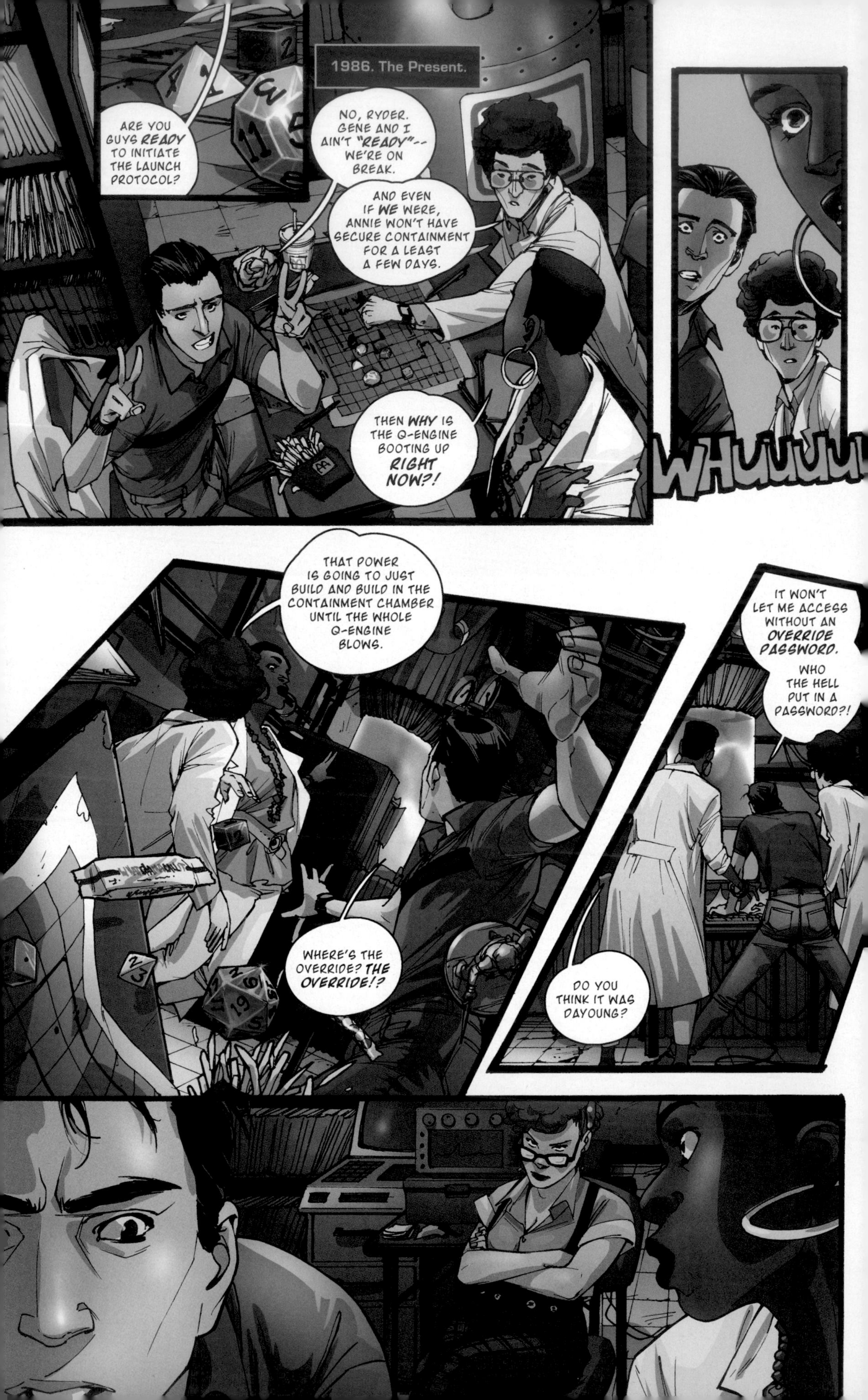
1986. The Present.
ARE YOU GUYS READY TO INITIATE THE LAUNCH PROTOCOL?
NO, RYDER. GENE AND I AIN'T "READY"-- WE'RE ON BREAK.
AND EVEN IF WE WERE, ANNIE WON'T HAVE SECURE CONTAINMENT FOR A LEAST A FEW DAYS.
THEN WHY IS THE Q-ENGINE BOOTING UP RIGHT NOW?!
WHUUUUU
THAT POWER IS GOING TO JUST BUILD AND BUILD IN THE CONTAINMENT CHAMBER UNTIL THE WHOLE Q-ENGINE BLOWS.
WHERE'S THE OVERRIDE? THE OVERRIDE!?
IT WON'T LET ME ACCESS WITHOUT AN OVERRIDE PASSWORD.
WHO THE HELL PUT IN A PASSWORD?!
DO YOU THINK IT WAS DAYOUNG?

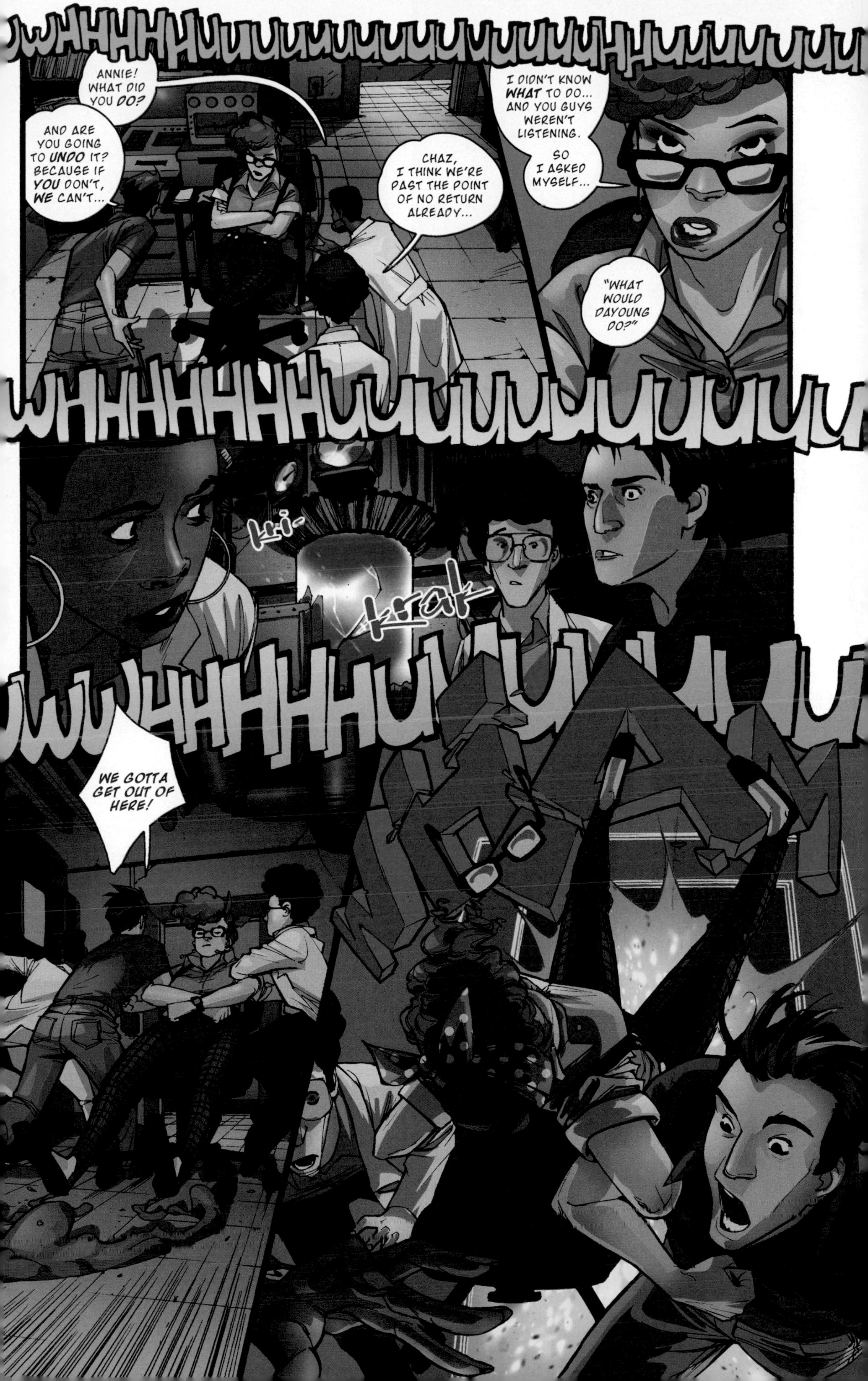
WHHHHuuuuuuuuuuuuuuuuHHuuuuuuuuu
ANNIE! WHAT DID YOU DO?
AND ARE YOU GOING TO UNDO IT? BECAUSE IF YOU DON'T, WE CAN'T...
CHAZ, I THINK WE'RE PAST THE POINT OF NO RETURN ALREADY...
I DIDN'T KNOW WHAT TO DO... AND YOU GUYS WEREN'T LISTENING.
SO I ASKED MYSELF...
"WHAT WOULD DAYOUNG DO?"
WHHHHHHHuuuuuuuuuuuuuuuuuu
kri-
krak
WHHHHHUUUUUU
WE GOTTA GET OUT OF HERE!

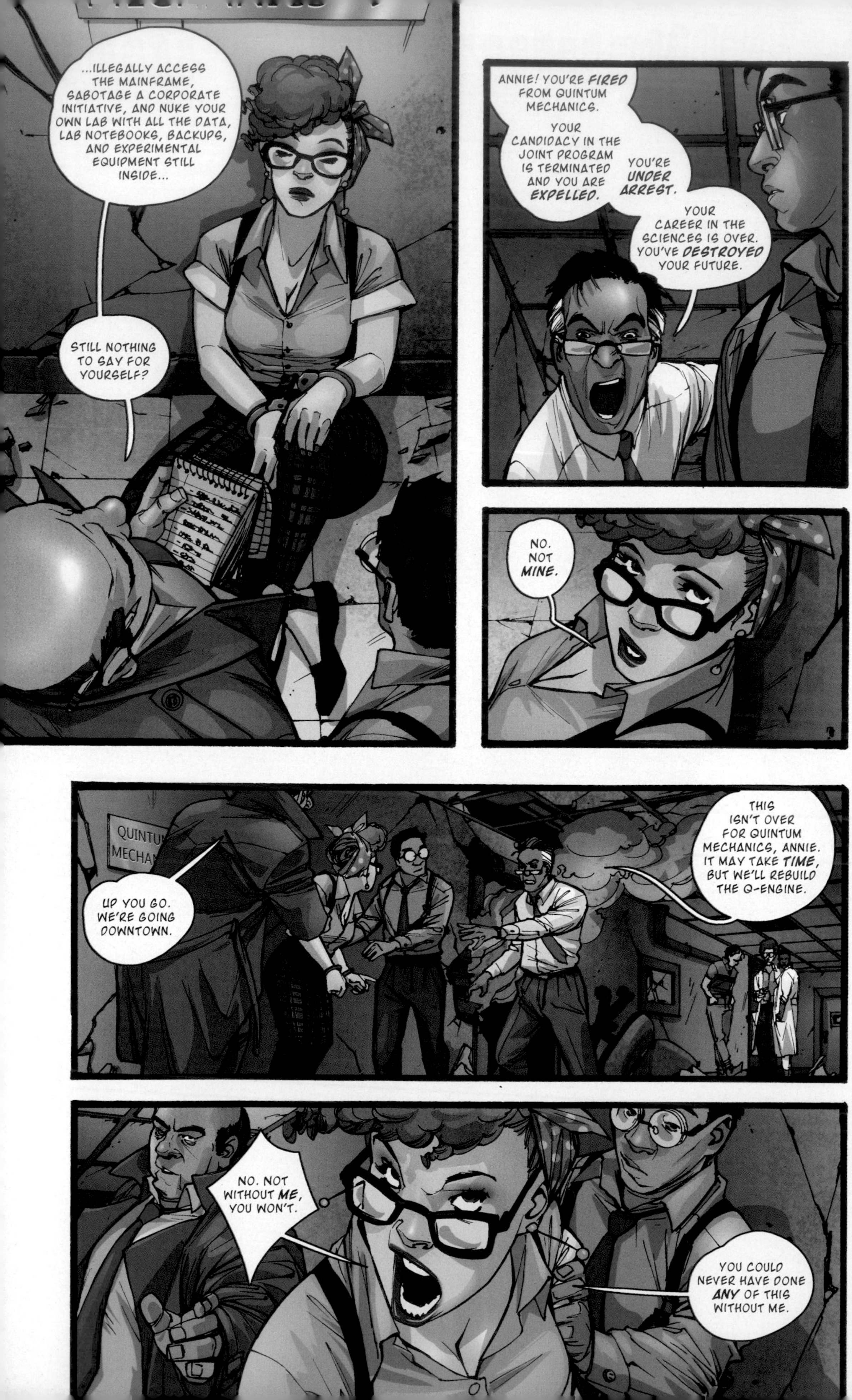
...ILLEGALLY ACCESS THE MAINFRAME, SABOTAGE A CORPORATE INITIATIVE, AND NUKE YOUR OWN LAB WITH ALL THE DATA, LAB NOTEBOOKS, BACKUPS, AND EXPERIMENTAL EQUIPMENT STILL INSIDE...
STILL NOTHING TO SAY FOR YOURSELF?
ANNIE! YOU'RE FIRED FROM QUINTUM MECHANICS.
YOUR CANDIDACY IN THE JOINT PROGRAM IS TERMINATED AND YOU ARE EXPELLED.
YOU'RE UNDER ARREST.
YOUR CAREER IN THE SCIENCES IS OVER. YOU'VE DESTROYED YOUR FUTURE.
NO. NOT MINE.
QUINTU
MECHAN
UP YOU GO. WE'RE GOING DOWNTOWN.
THIS ISN'T OVER FOR QUINTUM MECHANICS, ANNIE. IT MAY TAKE TIME, BUT WE'LL REBUILD THE Q-ENGINE.
NO. NOT WITHOUT ME, YOU WON'T.
YOU COULD NEVER HAVE DONE ANY OF THIS WITHOUT ME.

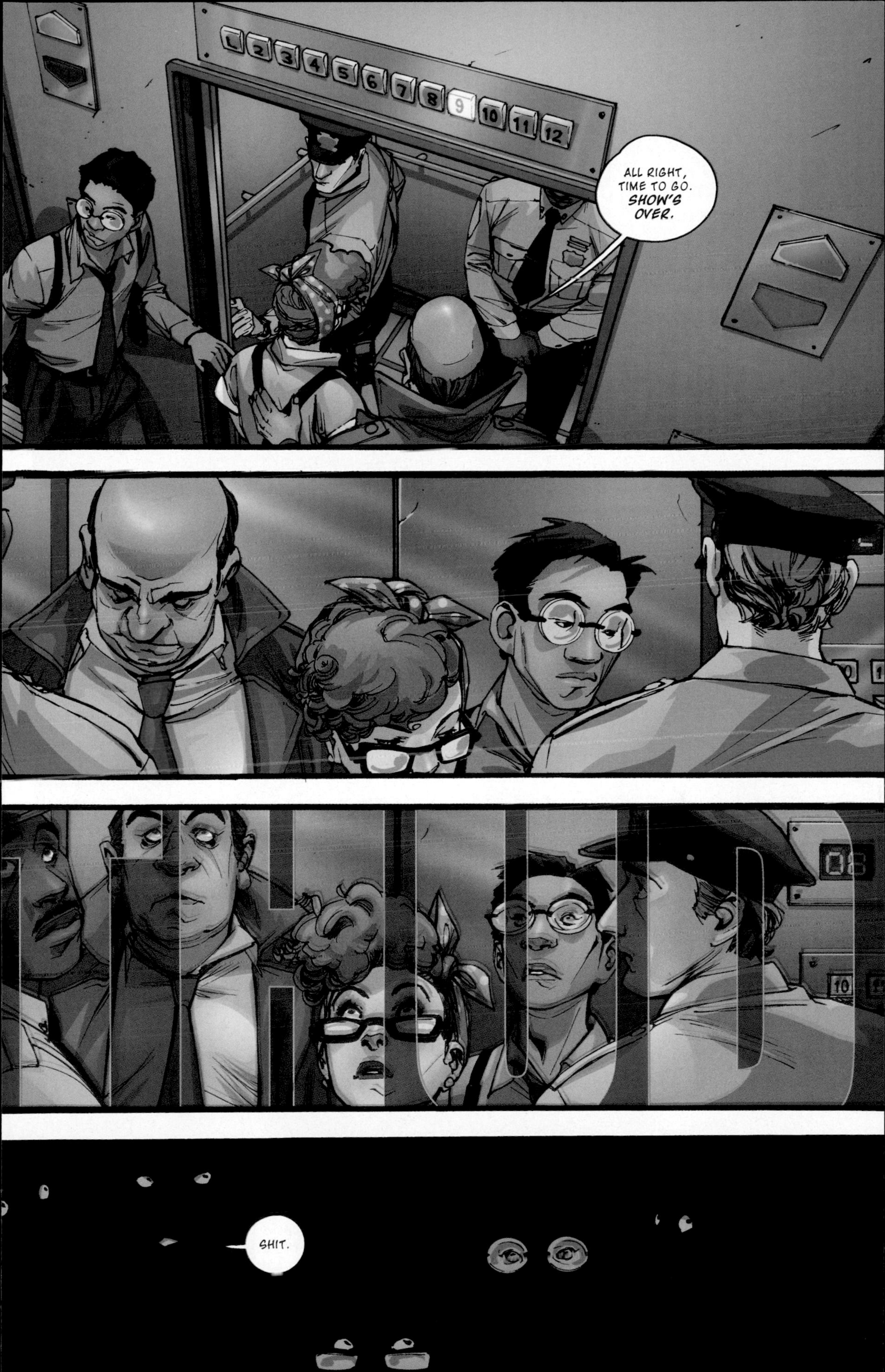
ALL RIGHT, TIME TO GO. SHOW'S OVER.
THUD
SHIT.

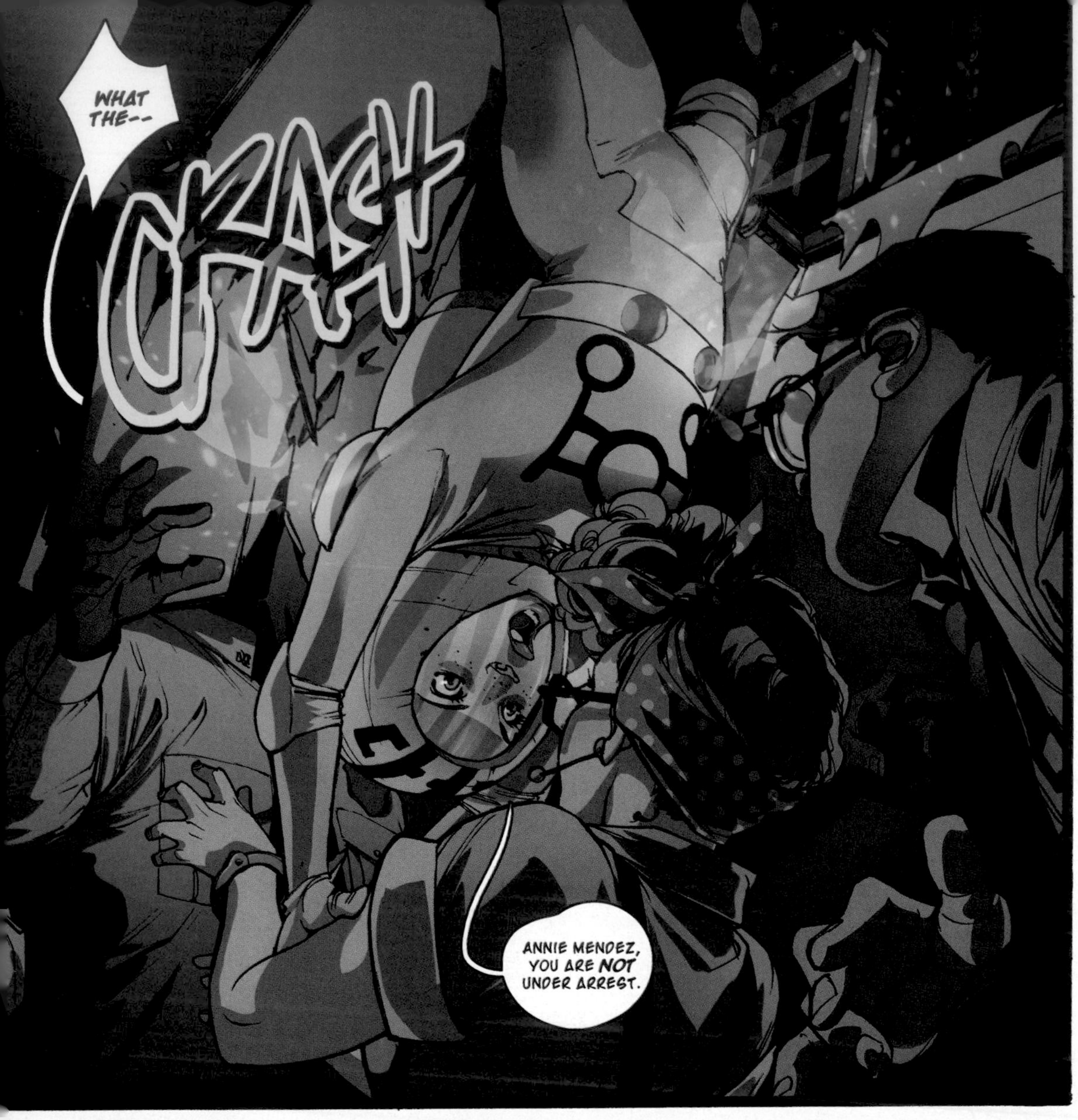
WHAT THE--
CRACK
ANNIE MENDEZ, YOU ARE NOT UNDER ARREST.

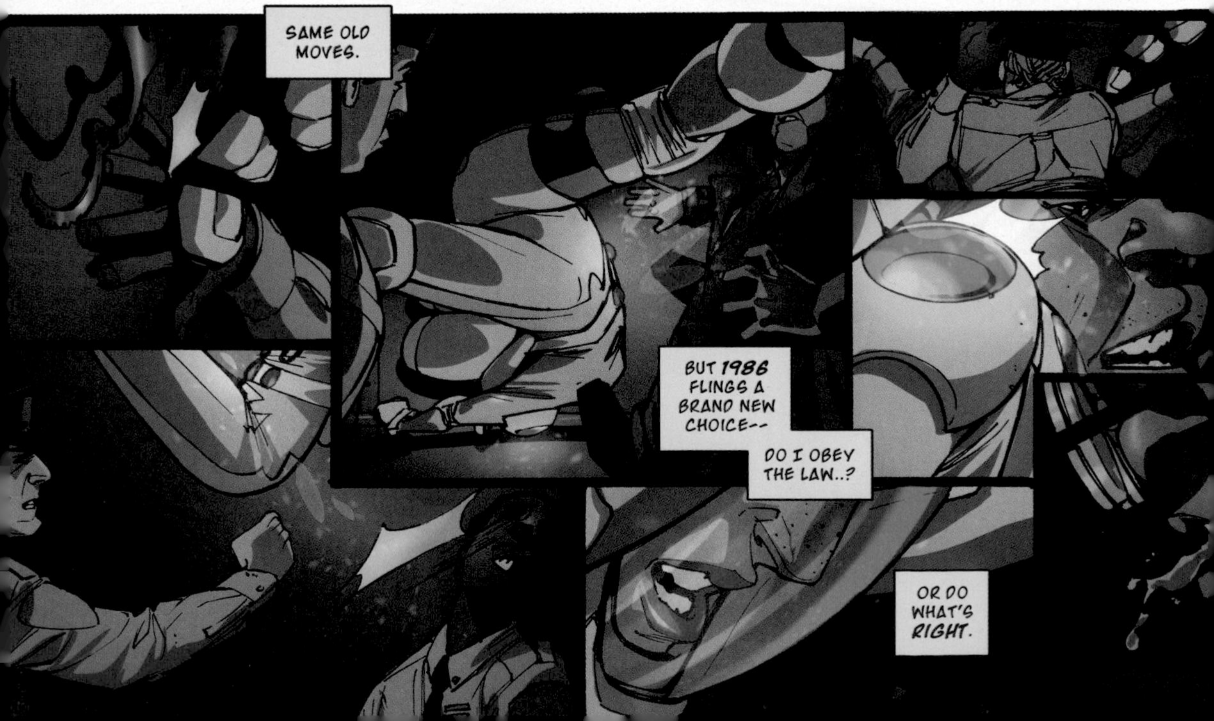
SAME OLD MOVES.
BUT 1986 FLINGS A BRAND NEW CHOICE--
DO I OBEY THE LAW..?
OR DO WHAT'S RIGHT.

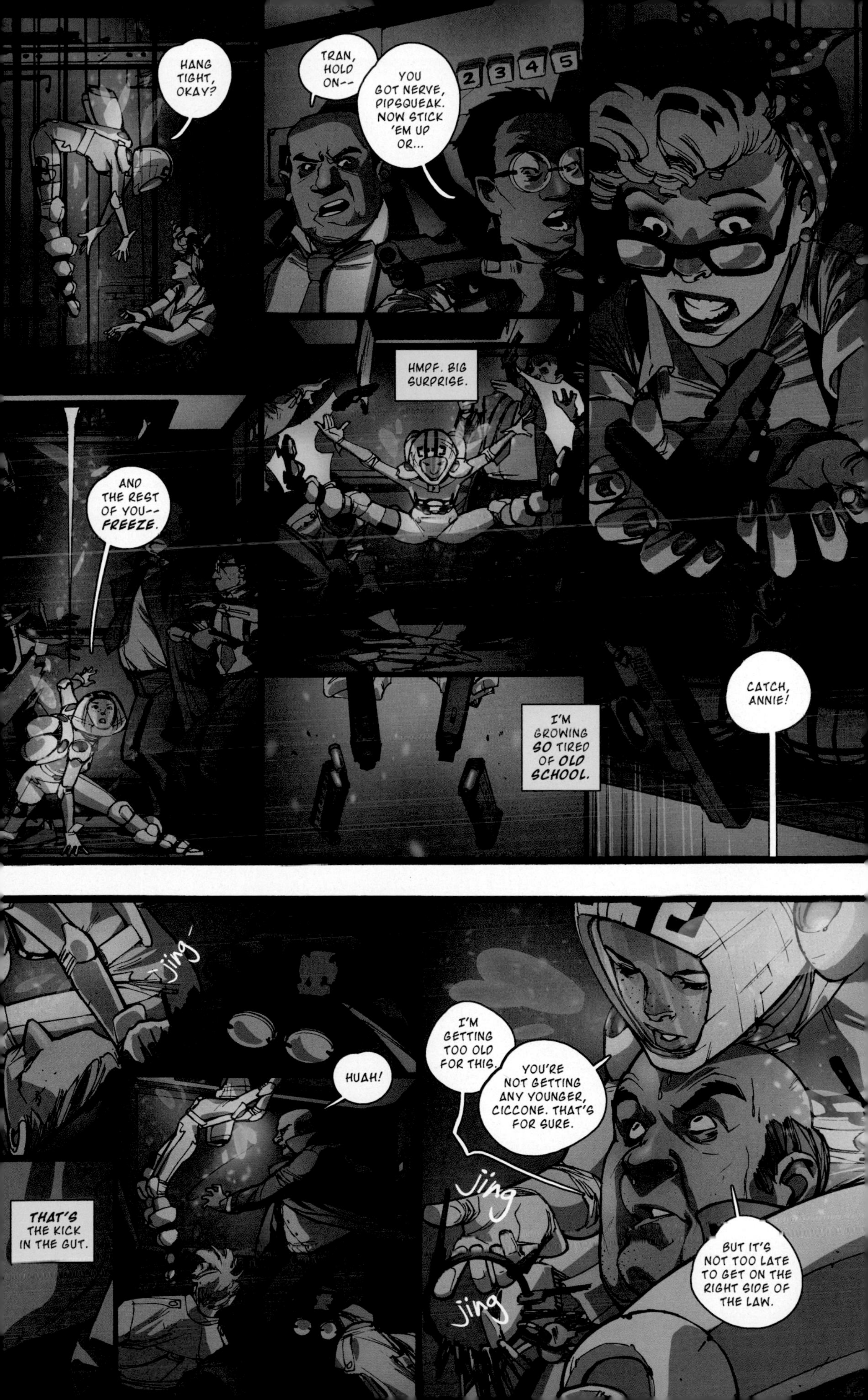
HANG TIGHT, OKAY?
TRAN, HOLD ON--
YOU GOT NERVE, PIPSQUEAK. NOW STICK 'EM UP OR...
2 3 4 5
HMPF. BIG SURPRISE.
AND THE REST OF YOU-- FREEZE.
I'M GROWING SO TIRED OF OLD SCHOOL.
CATCH, ANNIE!
jing
HUAH!
I'M GETTING TOO OLD FOR THIS.
YOU'RE NOT GETTING ANY YOUNGER, CICCONE. THAT'S FOR SURE.
THAT'S THE KICK IN THE GUT.
jing
jing
BUT IT'S NOT TOO LATE TO GET ON THE RIGHT SIDE OF THE LAW.

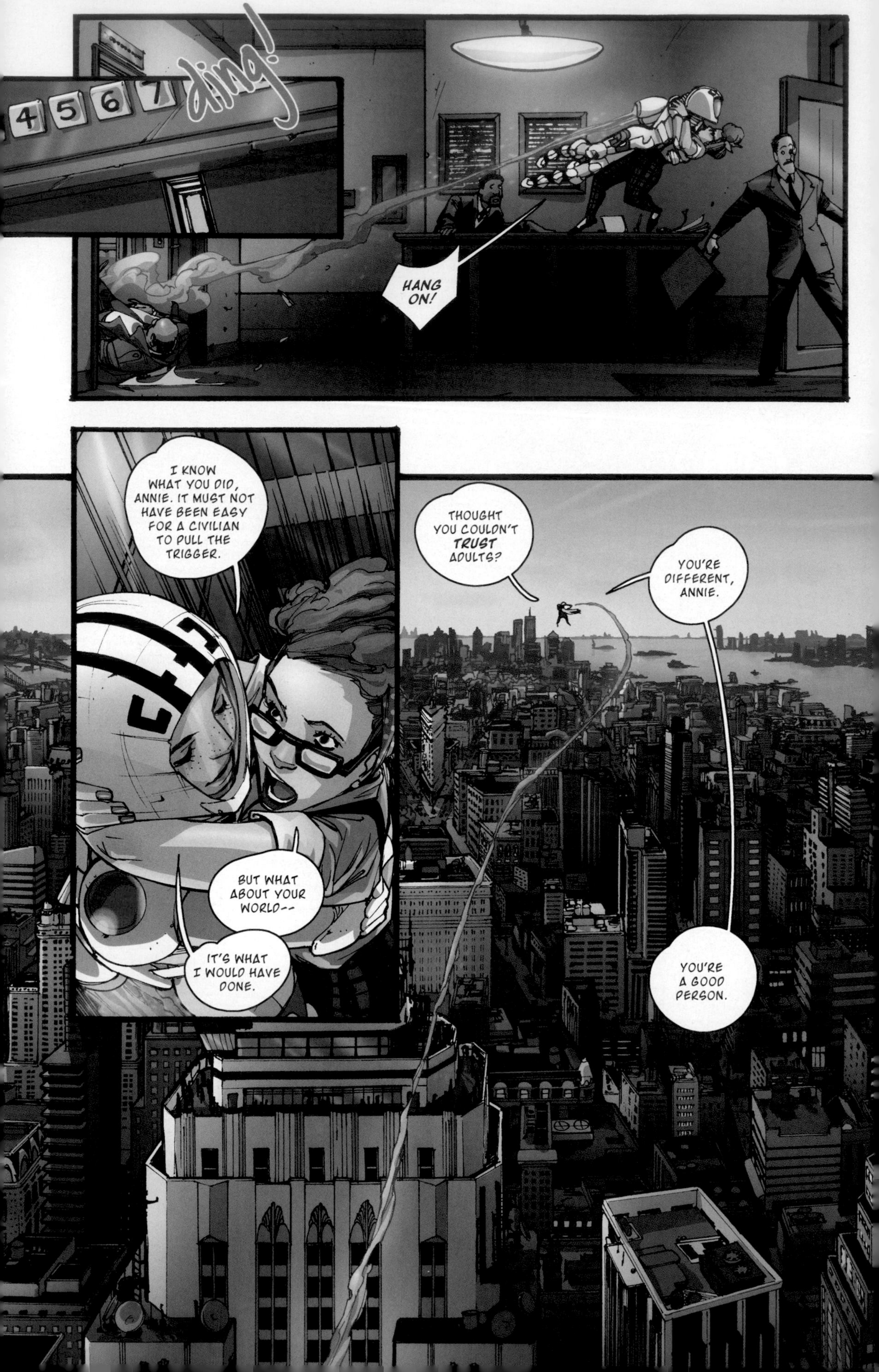
4567
ding!
HANG ON!
I KNOW WHAT YOU DID, ANNIE. IT MUST NOT HAVE BEEN EASY FOR A CIVILIAN TO PULL THE TRIGGER.
BUT WHAT ABOUT YOUR WORLD--
IT'S WHAT I WOULD HAVE DONE.
THOUGHT YOU COULDN'T TRUST ADULTS?
YOU'RE DIFFERENT, ANNIE.
YOU'RE A GOOD PERSON.

ARE YOU SURE ABOUT THIS, DAYOUNG? NO MORE *ROCKET GIRL*?

I CAME BACK TO FIX MY *2013*, NOT CHANGE YOUR *1986*.

I DON'T BELONG HERE. CAN'T CHANGE *THAT*.

BUT YOU CAN STILL DO SO MUCH GOOD.

MAYBE. A *BIG MAYBE*. BUT AT THE SAME TIME, THIS QUINTUM MECHANICS TECH CAN CAUSE A LOT OF TROUBLE IF IT EVER FELL INTO THE WRONG HANDS.

I KNEW *1986* WAS GOING TO BE A *ONE WAY TRIP*.

THE PAST IS THE PAST.

IT'S ALWAYS FUNNY TO HEAR YOU SAY IT THAT WAY. 2013--THAT'S THE *FUTURE* FOR EVERYONE ELSE.

WELL I GUESS NOW'S THE TIME I START ACTING LIKE EVERYONE ELSE.

DAYOUNG..?

WHAT ABOUT *YOUR 2013*?

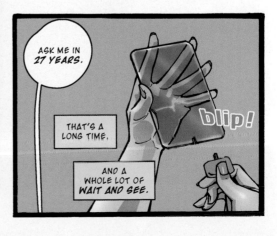

ASK ME IN *27 YEARS*.

THAT'S A LONG TIME,

AND A WHOLE LOT OF *WAIT AND SEE*.

blip!

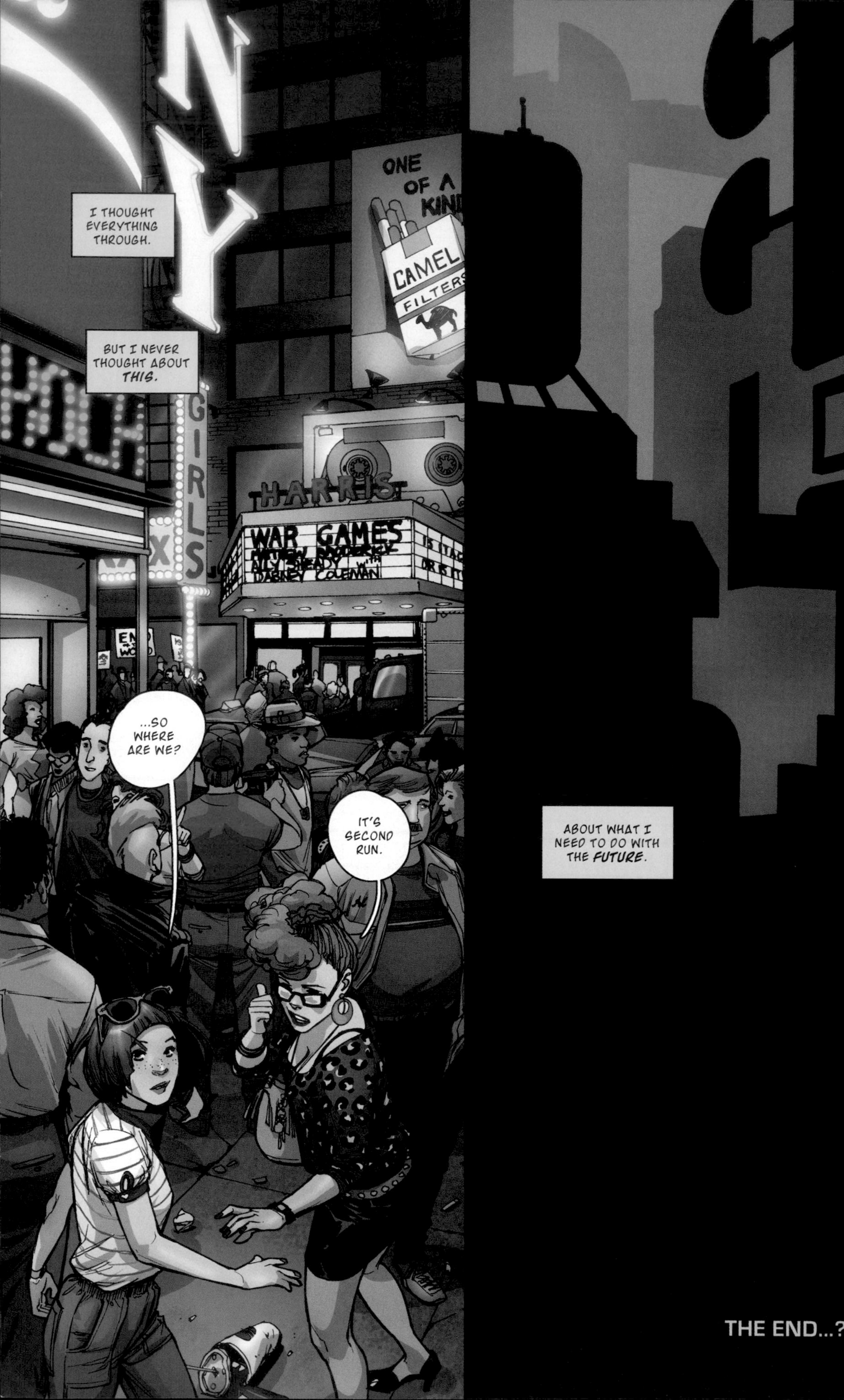
I THOUGHT EVERYTHING THROUGH.
BUT I NEVER THOUGHT ABOUT *THIS*.
ONE OF A
CAMEL
FILTERS
GIRLS
HARRIS
WAR GAMES
...SO WHERE ARE WE?
IT'S SECOND RUN.
ABOUT WHAT I NEED TO DO WITH THE *FUTURE*.
THE END...?

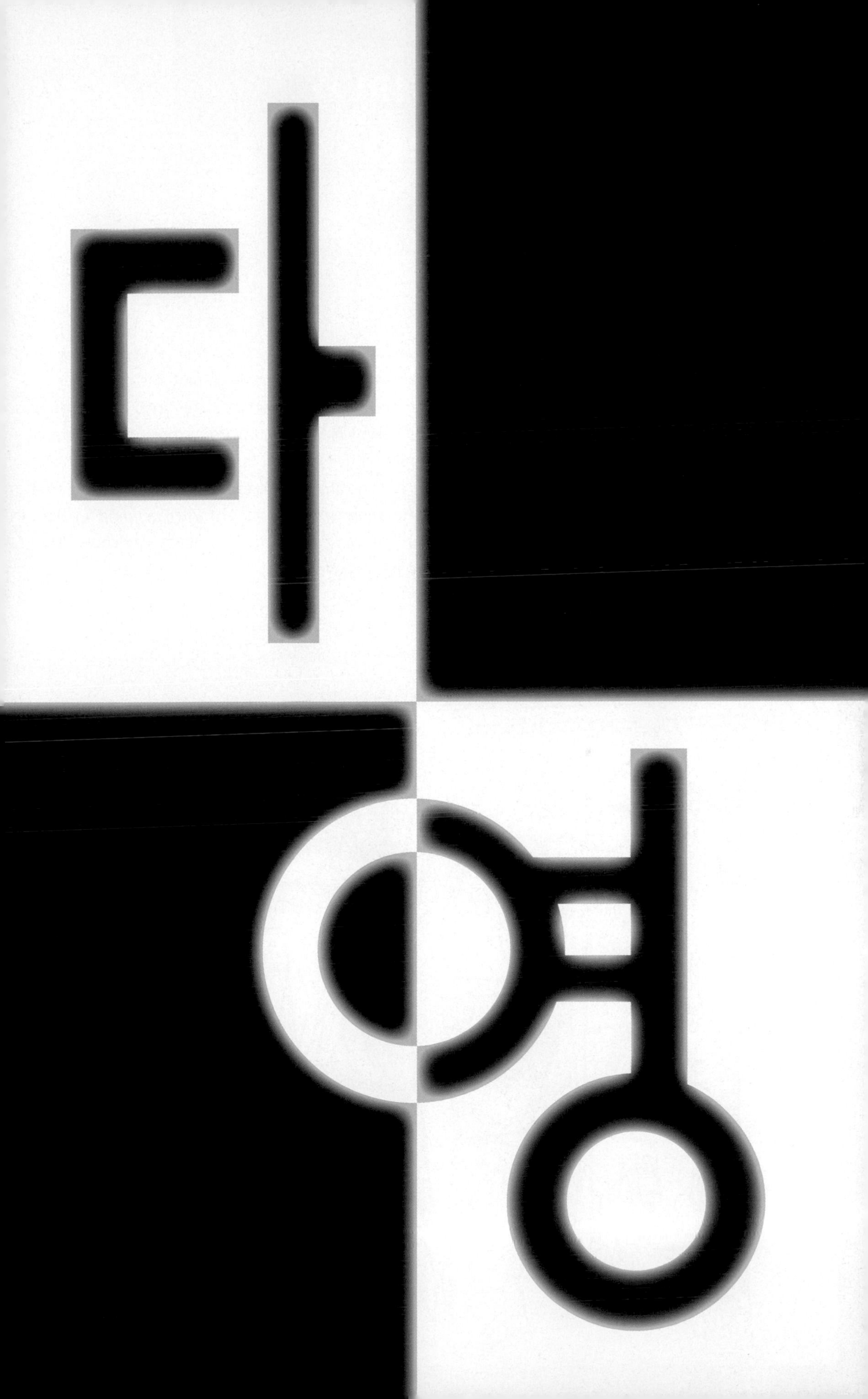
다양

ISSUE #2:

PAGE EIGHTEEN-NINETEEN:

18-19:1: DaYoung takes out the sticker-uppers. An action spread, so we'll go 'Marvel Style' like we had in the first issue handcuffs scene—I'll caption and dialogue it after it's drawn. Point A is right after where page 17 leaves off. Point Z is a tumbling DaYoung. At point A—Simon's gun fires, but DaYoung is already letting the miscreant Daniel spring free—while also kicking him toward his partner in crime, to add momentum. She dodges some more shots and rockets in—*fast*. By the end of the spread, she's neutralized the creeps—but in doing so has spun out of control and is skidding with all the rolling fruit. The theme of the interior monologue will ultimately be things spiraling out of control—going further than anticipated, and the disastrous results which can follow biting off more than you can chew. The layout should be something linear—so the set-up is Dayoung overshoots the mark. *INERTIA.*

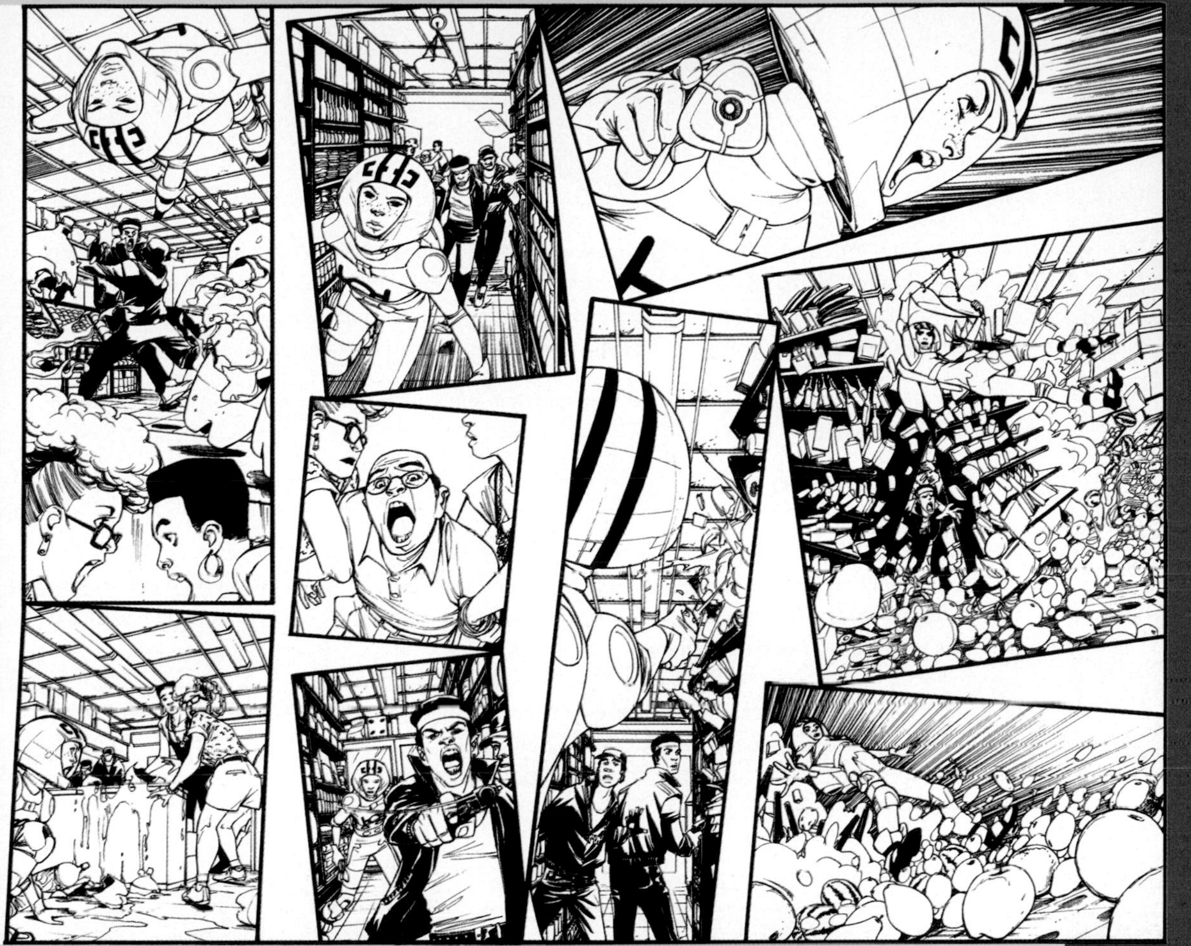

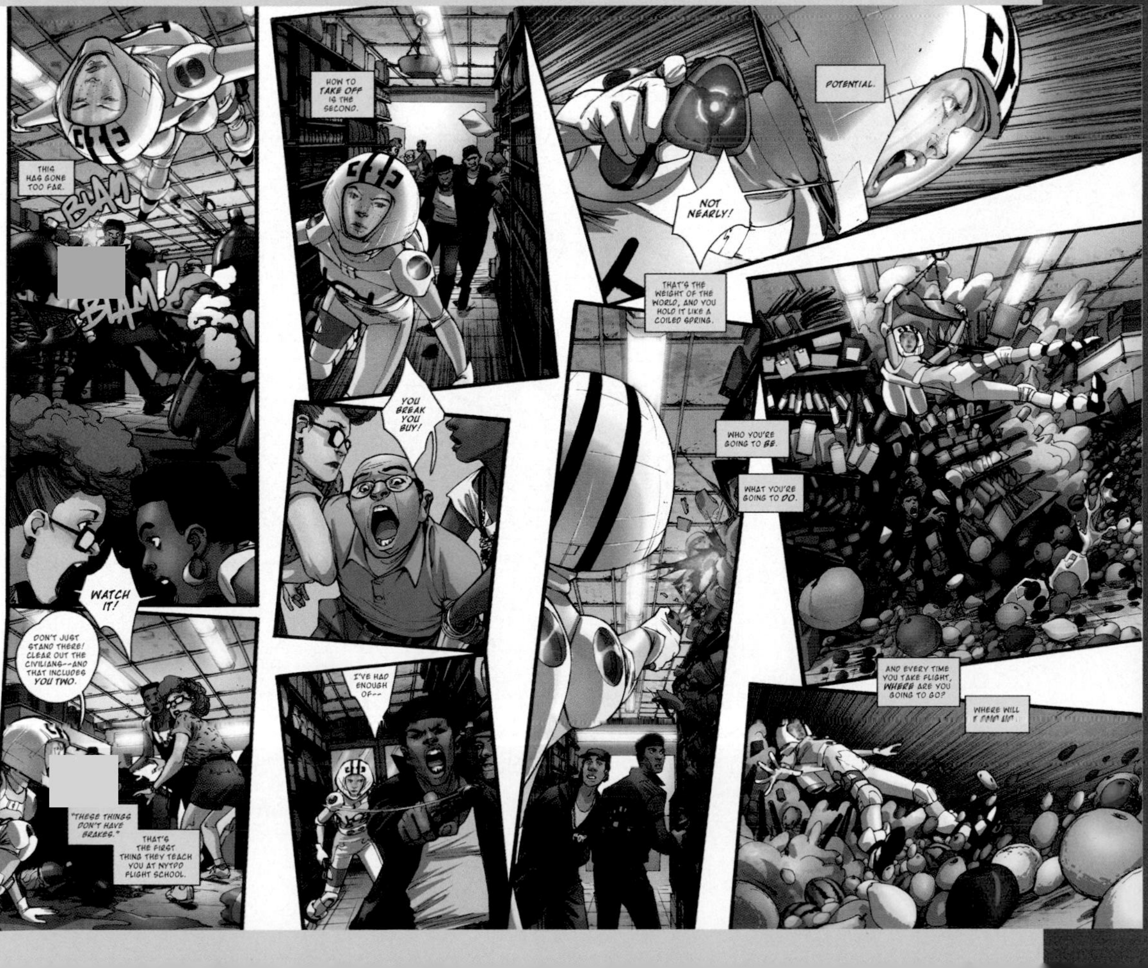

THIS HAS GONE TOO FAR.
BLAM
BLAM!!
WATCH IT!
DON'T JUST STAND THERE! CLEAR OUT THE CIVILIANS--AND THAT INCLUDES YOU TWO.
"THESE THINGS DON'T HAVE BRAKES."
THAT'S THE FIRST THING THEY TEACH YOU AT NYPD FLIGHT SCHOOL.
HOW TO TAKE OFF IS THE SECOND.
YOU BREAK YOU BUY!
I'VE HAD ENOUGH OF--
POTENTIAL.
NOT NEARLY!
THAT'S THE WEIGHT OF THE WORLD, AND YOU HOLD IT LIKE A COILED SPRING.
WHO YOU'RE GOING TO BE.
WHAT YOU'RE GOING TO DO.
AND EVERY TIME YOU TAKE FLIGHT, WHERE ARE YOU GOING TO GO?
WHERE WILL

PAGE FOUR-FIVE:

4-5:1: Double Page Spread. This issue's "Marvel style" action scene; I'll dialogue this after you've drawn it. DaYoung escapes from the interrogation room and avoids further capture. Two rooms in this spread. We start with a rat's eye view: DaYoung is spread eagle under the table; each appendage bracing against a table leg; her body pressed small against the underside of the table top. Also in this first panel, we see the legs of Ciccone and Tran running by.

As they both look out the window, DaYoung plants her feet; and then she's huffed the table back on them, knocking them over as she runs out the door.

1.Cap: **STRIKE THREE.**

Still inside a classic 80s NYPD office. File cabinets; typewriters for reports; stacks and stacks of paper. All kinds of cops. All kinds of crooks, cuffed. Phone cords. Big monitors where there are computers. Face-to-face desks that DaYoung gets up and over as she beats feet. She's nimble and surefooted—and awe-striking—everyone else in the room has trouble even just standing on the ground. Ask me for reference—there's a plenty.

Post art captions will talk about who she can (or more likely, can't) trust; her worries about Annie and the others. Most of all, how thinking and choices make for a big MESS. Some exposition, too.

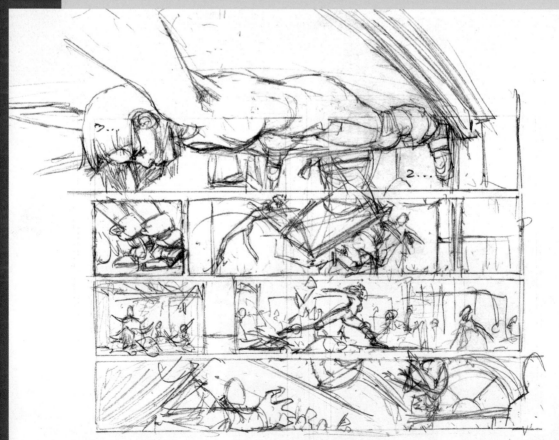

4

5

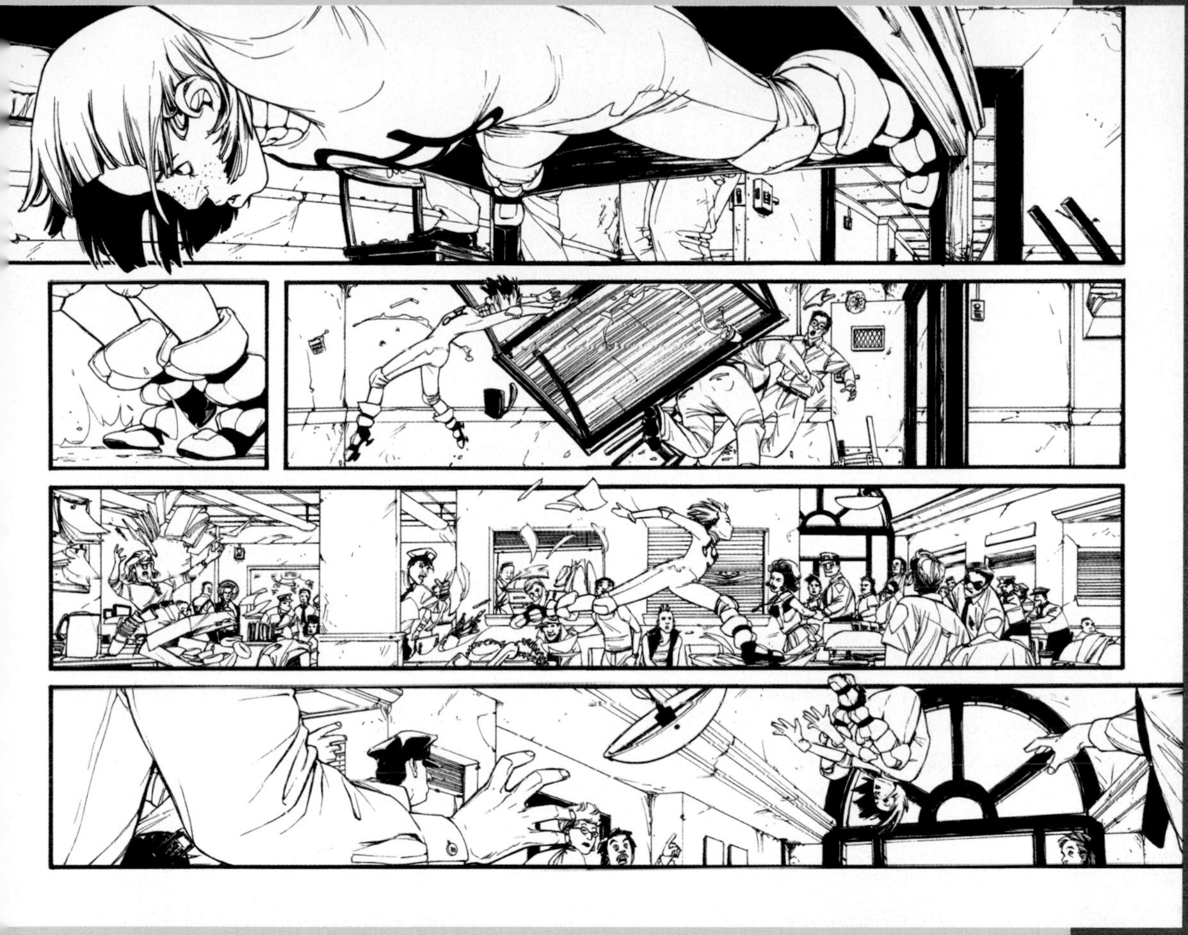

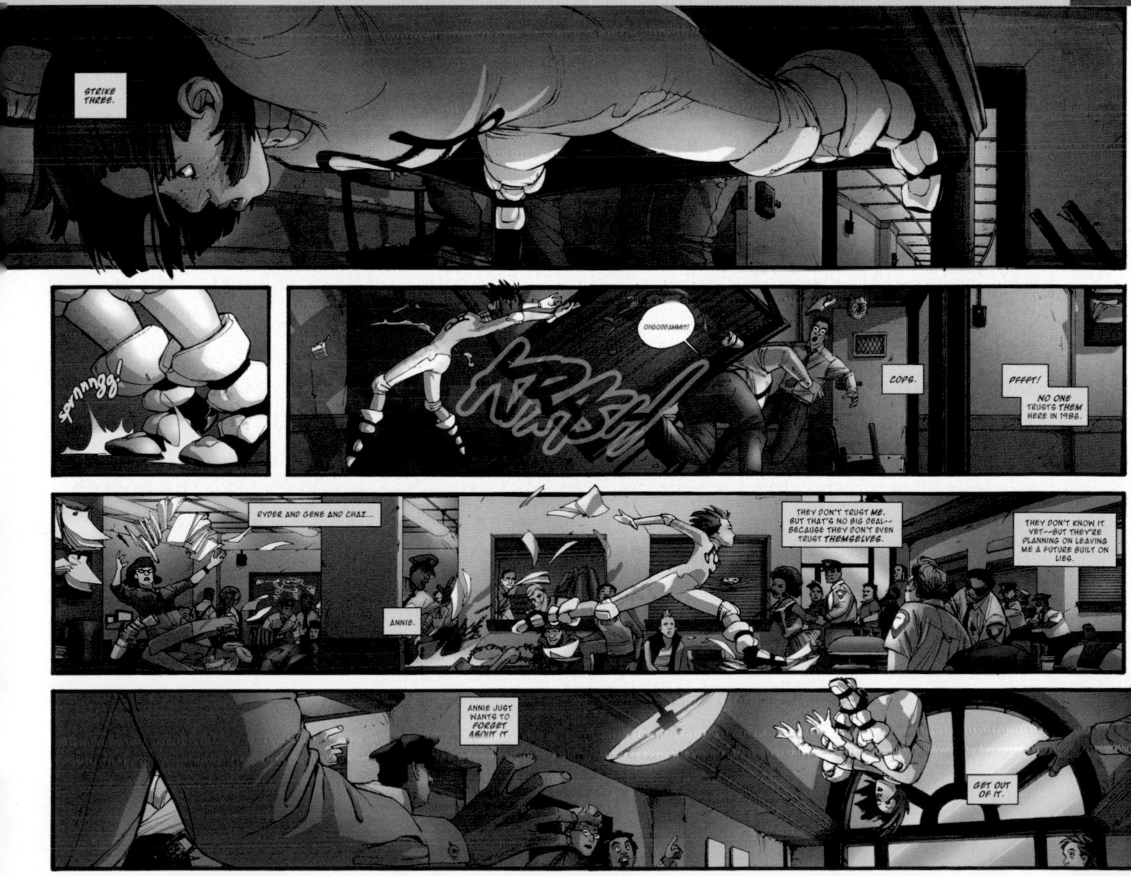
STRIKE THREE.
sprnnngg!
OHGODDAMMIT!
KRASH
COPS.
PFFFT!
NO ONE TRUSTS THEM HERE IN 1986.
RYDER AND GENE AND CHAZ...
ANNIE.
THEY DON'T TRUST ME. BUT THAT'S NO BIG DEAL-- BECAUSE THEY DON'T EVEN TRUST THEMSELVES.
THEY DON'T KNOW IT YET--BUT THEY'RE PLANNING ON LEAVING ME A FUTURE BUILT ON LIES.
ANNIE JUST WANTS TO FORGET ABOUT IT
GET OUT OF IT.

brandon MONTCLARE>> the original sample script

<u>PAGE EIGHT (4-page sample script):</u>

Page 8: Panel: 1: Inside NYC skyline at twilight, as some electric illumination coming out of square windows. While the sky still has some blue in it, it darkens. It's like we're in another office downtown—looking out the window. There's a pinpoint of arc flare—an odd, futuristic color that arrests the eye. It's DaYoung Johansson. Helmet off. Sitting Indian-style out on the ledge. She's working a mini blowtorch thingamabob on here busted jetpack. It needs a tune-up. And with the sparks flying it's not the type of thing you do indoors. As much as we can see here (it's ok if you save this for later panels), she's next to an open window; it's the offices of Quintum Mechanics. We definitely DON'T see her, but Annie is inside the window. Again as much as we can see: her helmet and gloves are on the ledge next to her. A half eaten hot dog from Papaya King and a paper cup with a bendy-straw weighs-down a few comics from 1986 like Love & Rockets and Grendel and Dark Knight Returns. It's casual. She would also have an "iPad"—these are of course, very '2013': so let's make them look like what we have today, only amped up enough to show that DaYoung's 2013 is very different from Amy's.

1.Cap (DaYoung): There's something wrong with the **forward thrust.**

2.Cap: It keeps getting stuck and I can't move right.

3.Cap: ...I shouldn't **complain.** I can fix it **myself**. It's just that back home any junior tech could have me ready-to-go lickety-split. But **here..?**

8:2: Reverse angle to inside the window. Interior of Quintum Mechanics. It can be scientific, but not a full blown laboratory. Annie (one of the Q-Engineers, and who will become DaYoung's closest friend in 1986. She'd be in her mid-twenties. A Ph.D student—smart, and not totally socialized—but she should be in fitting 80's paraphrenailia. And she's wearing a labcoat with Quintum Mechanic's corporate symbol on it) is on the phone. It's an analog phone with a curly cord. In the background we see DaYoung out the window, on the ledge. Her back is turned to us as her focus is in her lap. In the foreground Annie faces us, her back to DaYoung—she's cupping the receiver with her hand, bunching her shoulders...like she doesn't want DaYoung to overhear. She's a bit wild-eyed—leaning toward panic because only a few minutes before, years of work resulted in the Q-Engine blowing up, and when the smoke cleared there was a girl from the future standing there. We only hear her half of the conversation.

4.Cap: ...**here** they're **hopeless.**

5.Annie: ...I'm telling you—she just appeared out of nowhere...

6.Annie: ...we booted up the Q-Engine and the containment chamber **blew!** I spent a semester just **double-checking** the protocols. This wasn't supposed to happen...

7.Annie: ...I don't know **what** happened...

8:3: On DaYoung again. Her nimble fingers work a mini, high-tech blowtorch... maybe it's a component of a space-age Swiss Army knife. She's tweaking the circuit board of her jetpack. Whatever details you couldn't get into 1:1, you can maybe fill in here. We especially need the iPad.

8.Cap: In **1986** a bunch of scientists at Quintum Mechanics made history. Their discovery would change everything, forever.

9.Cap: But they didn't know **what** they were doing. It was **never meant to be**. So someone had to go back in time to stop it.

10.Cap: I volunteered.

11.iPad (radio font):   >sqwak<

8:4: On Annie.

12.Annie: ...I'm **not** crazy...

13.Annie: ...Professor Sharma is in the lab—with everyone else...

14.Annie: ...she's with me...

15.Annie: ...she's like 15!

PAGE NINE:

9:1: Back on DaYoung. She hears a radio report picked up on her iPad—cops calling for back-up. Even though she has specific mission in 1986, she's not going to ignore fellow officers in peril. She has already snapped off her blowtorch and closed up a compartment or whatever on her jetpack. She's alert—paying attention to the alarm. But she's also rough with her pack—maybe closing it up with a thumping fist—in contrast to the careful work she was performing in 1:3.

1.Cap: I **am** 15.

2.iPad: >sqwak< ...officers in need of assistance...>sqwak< OFFICER DOWN! OFFICER DOWN!

9:2: Annie rushes to the window, ignoring her call--worried as to what the curious future girl is about to do! We see DaYoung has stood up on the edge of the ledge. She's shouldering her jetpack on, like a kid might sling a back-pack.

3.iPad: >sqwak< ...all available units please respond...

4.Annie (bold):   **DaYoung! What are you doing?!**

5.DaYoung: My gear is picking up the old emergency bands. They need help down there.

6.Annie (bold):   **Come back in here! Let the police handle it.**

9:3: Close up on DaYoung, who has now pulled her helmet over her face. Grim determination.

7.DaYoung: I am the police.

9:4: On spring heeled sneakers as DaYoung doesn't so much jump as she merely steps off the ledge.

NO TEXT

9:5: DaYoung falls like a stone downward toward off-panel oblivion.

NO TEXT

9:6: Inside with Annie. She's rushed all the way to the window, which is now empty, DaYoung seemingly have plummeted. Annie is leaning out all that she can, looking down toward the street--the curly cord is stretched, the phone's base is suspended in air as the wall-connecting cord is also stretched to the max.

8.Annie (bold):   **DAYOUNG!**

PAGE TEN-ELEVEN (double-page spread)

10-11:1: It's a second later, and we see DaYoung rocketing up toward us. The trail of smoke and sparks originates 25 or so feet below the open window where Annie now looks up and out—wide-eyed at the flying Rocket Girl. DaYoung can wink or salute or both—but it's not campy. She's a serious teen—filled with confidence; moreover, a faux-maturity where she doesn't get too excited at things which SHOULD clearly excite her. Like a cop's attitude: 'move along, there's nothing to see here.' Maybe those comics get caught up in her tail wind and flap about like pigeons. As DaYoung blasts toward the scene of the police emergency (coming at the reader, of course), you can cap this page as a single panel. Or you can have her maneuver in flight for a few panels, swerving in the canyons of buildings and/or near the street level. If you don't start that maneuvering here, we need to start it on page 11. You could also, therefore, draw this as a spread (note, since this is the sample, these pages in the final draft would hopefully not be starting on an odd page number). Oodles of Noodles steaming on the top of Times Square. Mayor Koch. Her rocketing to-and-fro. I'll have DaYoung's interior monologue go over it a bit. But more important is to get her down to the street level: people looking up in awe as she zooms by. But more important still: getting it to be very 1986. Adidas without laces. Bigger Taxicabs. Walkman and boom boxes. More graphitti. Mets jackets in satin blue with orange script. Three-piece suits in brown. Feathered hair and Kajagoogoo kids.

1.DaYoung: Don't worry, Annie. I'm here to save **everyone.**

2.SFX (off jetpack):   PEEL!

3.Cap: I get to fly.

4.Cap: ...it's why I joined the **NYTPD.**

10-11:2: DaYoung soars. Climbing she almost hits her peak.

5.Cap: I used to lay in bed thinking all about it. Hoping when I fell asleep I'd be rocketing through my dreams.

6.Cap: **Force it.** Focus. Fantasize real hard and hope when your eyes shut you don't know the difference.

10-11:3: DaYoung crests. It feels like she's floating; suspended in air before the plunge.

7.Cap: Usually didn't work! My concentration would drift off...

10-11:4: She falls. Gravity pulling her downward—but she's poised perfectly in her descent. Like an Olympic diver.

8.Cap: No matter how I tried, when my head got up in the clouds I couldn't ever control what came next.

10-11:5: She zooms. DaYoung rockets through Times Square. People are shocked—literally some are nearly blown over. It's not so much fear as amazement. But she moves so fast, some of the civilians can't even trust what their eyes just saw.

9.Cap: But right now..?

10.Cap: Right now I'm **living** the dream.

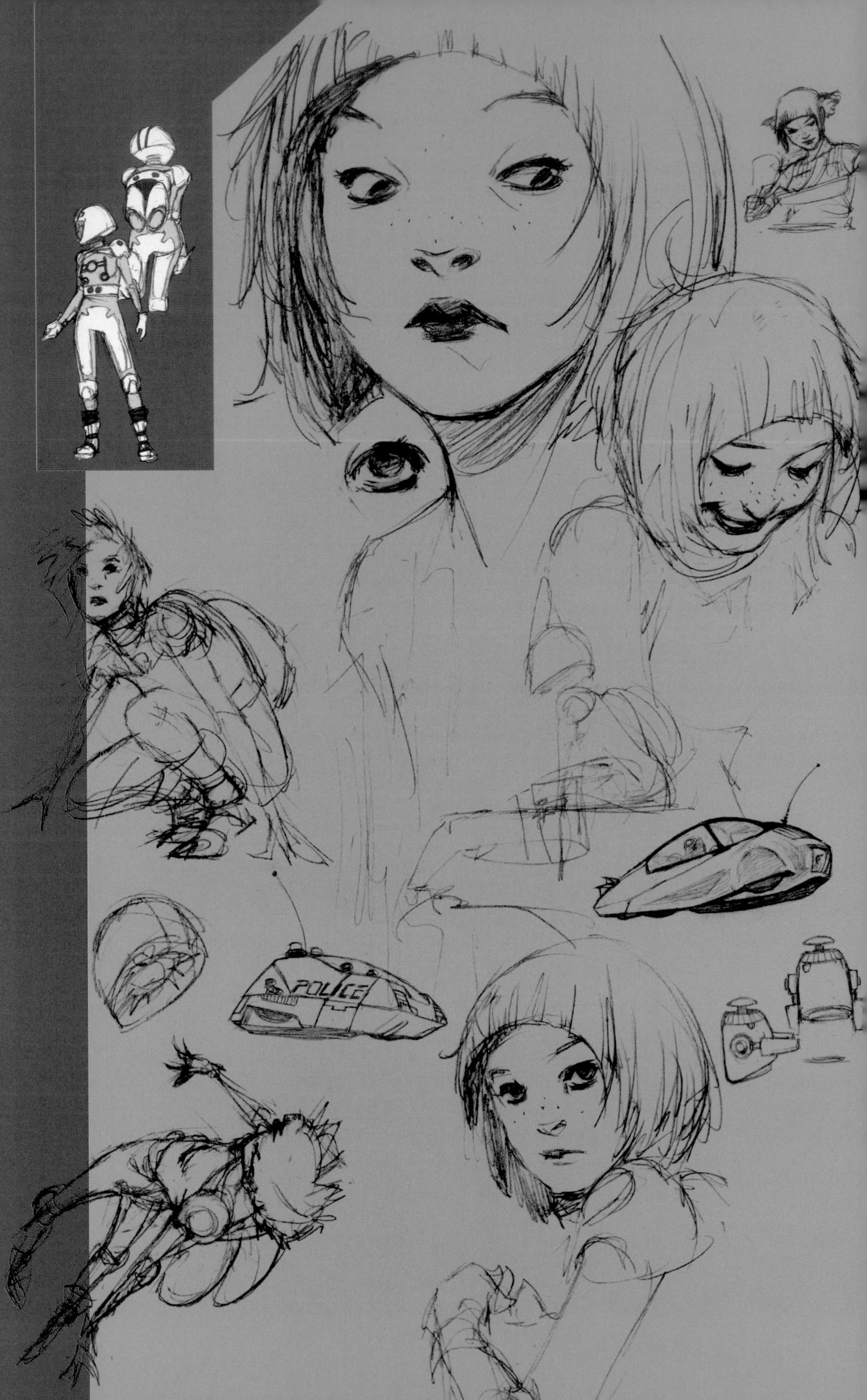
POLICE

sketches

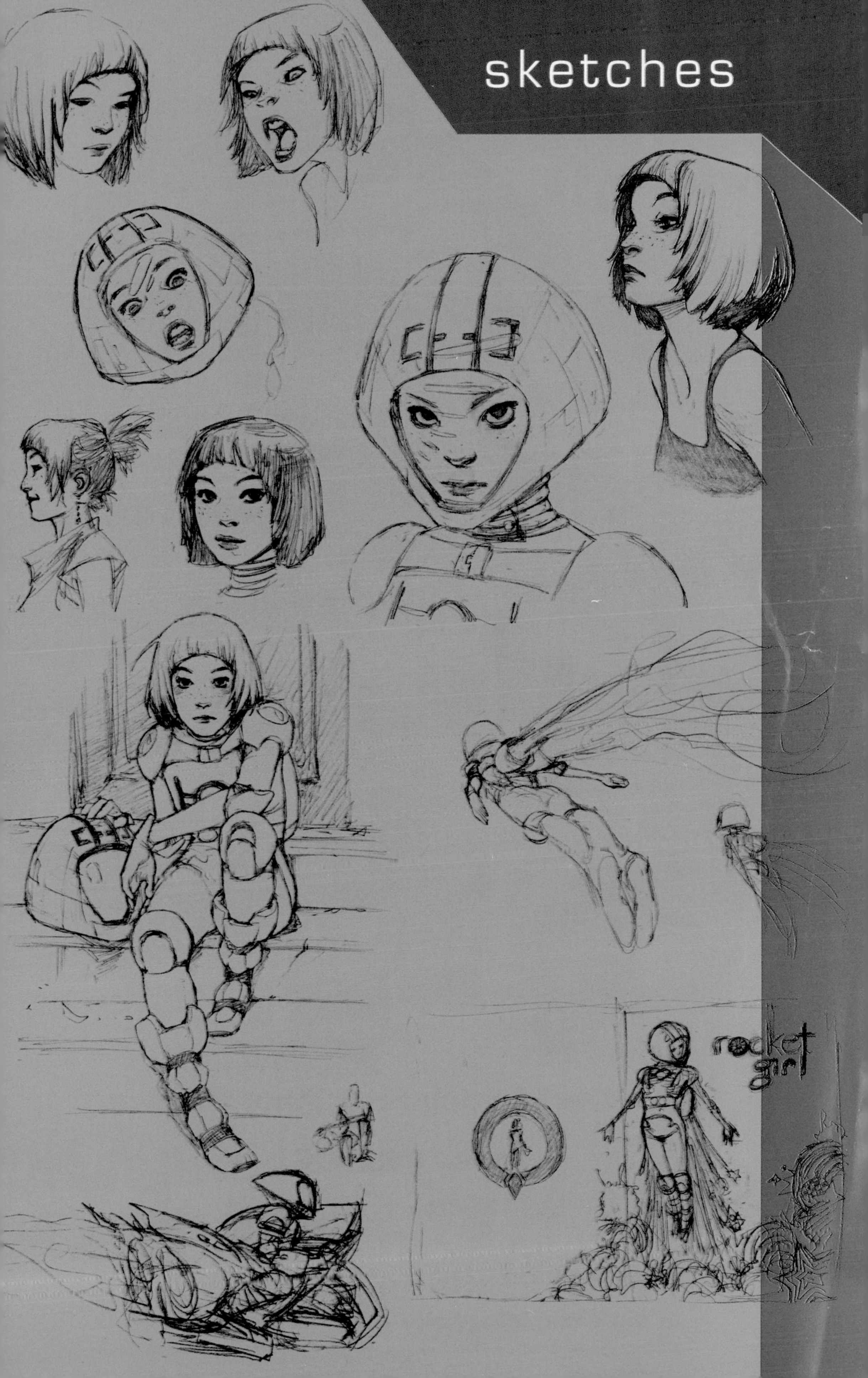
rocket
girl

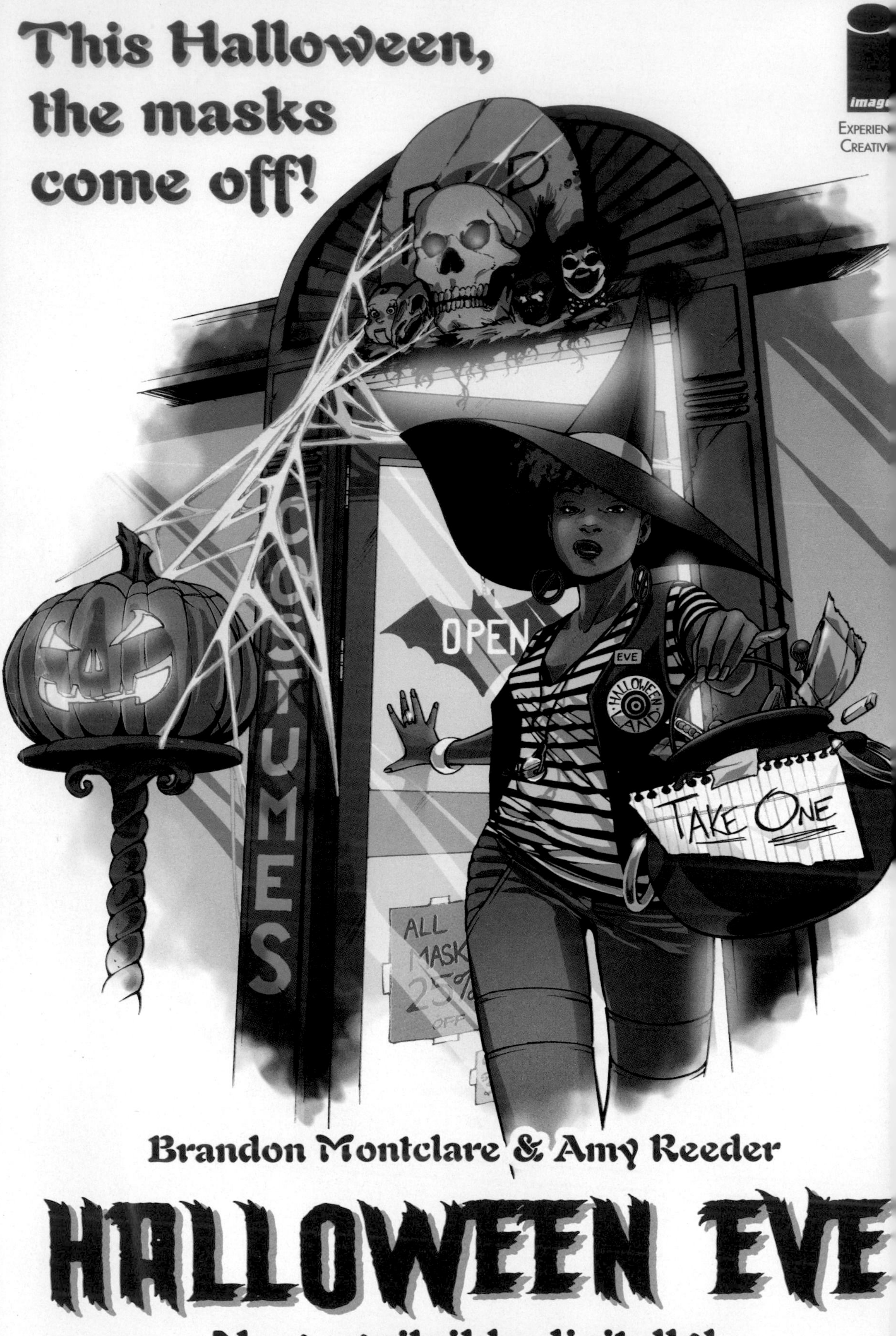
This Halloween, the masks come off!
COSTUMES
OPEN
EVE
HALLOWEEN LAND
TAKE ONE
ALL MASK 25% OFF
Brandon Montclare & Amy Reeder
HALLOWEEN EVE
Now availaible digitally!
via Comixology and Imagecomics.com

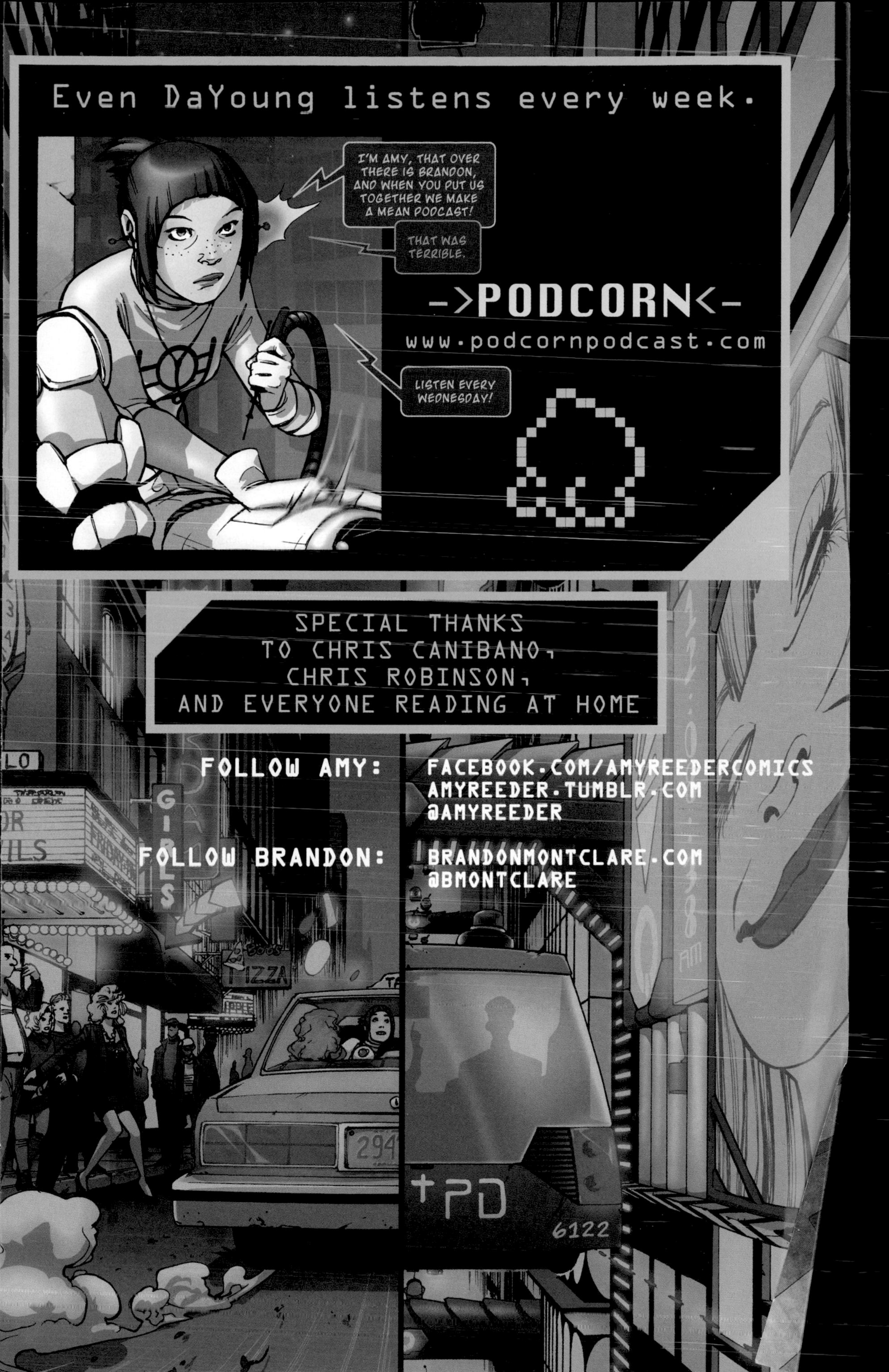
Even DaYoung listens every week.
I'M AMY, THAT OVER THERE IS BRANDON, AND WHEN YOU PUT US TOGETHER WE MAKE A MEAN PODCAST!
THAT WAS TERRIBLE.
->PODCORN<-
www.podcornpodcast.com
LISTEN EVERY WEDNESDAY!
SPECIAL THANKS
TO CHRIS CANIBANO,
CHRIS ROBINSON,
AND EVERYONE READING AT HOME
FOLLOW AMY: FACEBOOK.COM/AMYREEDERCOMICS
AMYREEDER.TUMBLR.COM
@AMYREEDER
FOLLOW BRANDON: BRANDONMONTCLARE.COM
@BMONTCLARE
GIRLS
PIZZA
TPD
6122

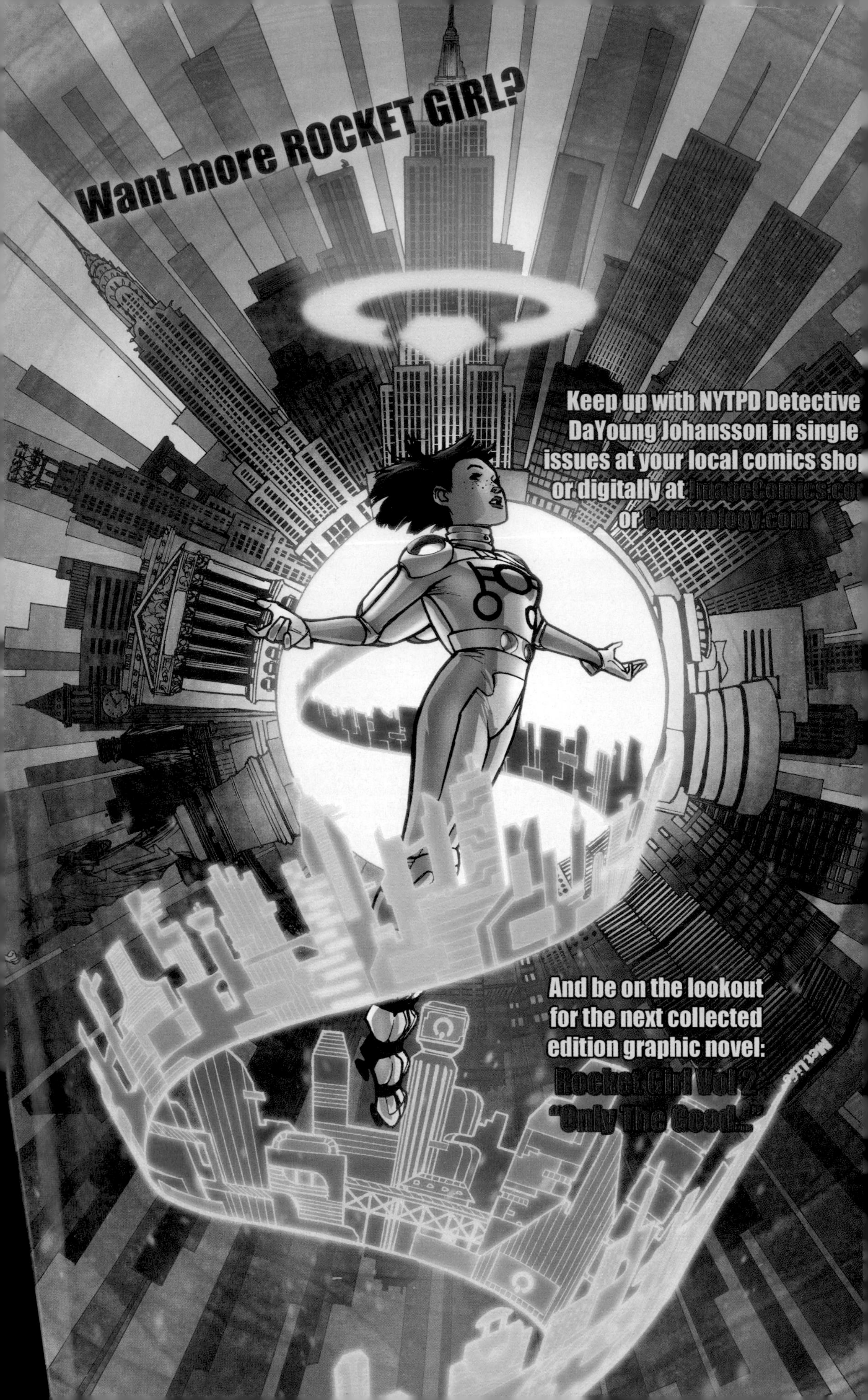
Want more ROCKET GIRL?
Keep up with NYTPD Detective
DaYoung Johansson in single
issues at your local comics sho
or digitally at ImageComics.co
or Comixology.com
And be on the lookout
for the next collected
edition graphic novel:
Rocket Girl Vol 2
"Only The Good..."